(01)

Wh... fools fall in love?

Why do fools fall in love?

LOUISE MARLEY

POOLBEG

Published 2003
Poolbeg Press Ltd.
123 Grange Hill, Baldoyle,
Dublin 13, Ireland
Email: poolbeg@poolbeg.com

1 3 5 7 9 10 8 6 4 2

A catalogue record for this book is available from the British Library.

ISBN 1-84223-030-1

Cover designed by Slatter-Anderson
Typeset by Patricia Hope in Palatino 10/14
Printed by Cox & Wyman,
Reading, Berkshire

www.poolbeg.com

About the Author

Louise Marley was born in Southampton and previously worked as a civilian administrator for the police. She got the idea for *Why Do Fools Fall In Love?* after living near Bath for eighteen months and watching an endless succession of costume dramas being filmed in the city.

While Louise would like to base her characters on interesting people she might meet, she spends most of her time in front of a computer, writing novels and short stories, and therefore doesn't get out much.

Smoke Gets In Your Eyes, her first novel, was published by Poolbeg in 2002. She currently lives in Hampshire with her husband and their two children.

For more information about Louise Marley visit her website
www.louisemarley.co.uk

Acknowledgements

Thanks to:

Bath Film Unit, for explaining the joys of location filming.

Barbara Large, for organising the Annual Writers' Conferences at King Alfred's College, Winchester – without which I would have given up writing a long time ago.

All at Poolbeg – especially Paula and Gaye.

And finally, Andy – yes, I do know I'm hell to live with.

This book is dedicated to
Pauline & Bryan Cozens
and
Mary & Richard Marley

Chapter One

WPC Shelby Roberts had never believed in ghosts. She had never believed in vampires, the Loch Ness monster or little green men from Mars. But at midnight on Hallowe'en, in a crumbling four-hundred-year-old house, it was incredibly easy to forget what one didn't believe in and suddenly think of a whole lot of things in which one did.

Yew Tree Hall would have given Wes Craven nightmares, decided Shelby, as she paced the master bedroom, cursing the elderly heating system which rattled like a smoker's cough behind the ubiquitous oak panelling. Every time a colleague downstairs clicked a light switch, the whole house dimmed. And, as an owl swooped amongst the chimneys, screaming like a banshee, the police dogs prowling the gardens began to howl in chorus.

1

In dire need of a large brandy and a whole packet of Prozac, Shelby would have felt a lot safer armed with a crucifix and holy water instead of her standard-issue police firearm. Particularly as, at that very moment, the bedroom door smashed open behind her, accompanied by a rush of frozen air.

Shelby spun round, swinging her gun up against her shoulder, aiming it into the dark chasm beyond. "Who the hell is that?"

Sergeant Rackham stepped out of the shadows and eyed her balefully. "The technical phrase is, 'Armed police, stop or I'll shoot'."

She quickly lowered her gun before he could see it was trembling. "Sorry, sir. This place has got me spooked."

"If you can't hack it, I'll get someone else."

"Yes, sir."

Sergeant Rackham suddenly and surprisingly grinned, floodlighting his Mount Rushmoor features. He was the sort of lean, almost emaciated man who would always look good in the dark overalls of the Tactical Firearms Team. Although Shelby sometimes felt he would be better suited to a black Stetson, a pale horse, and a fistful of silver dollars.

"Don't let the place get to you, Shelby. It's only a house, not the Bates Motel."

Only an old *haunted* house, she thought caustically. Where its Elizabethan owner had been sealed up, alive, inside this very room – and had been leaping out of the woodwork from spite ever since. But she waited for her sergeant to leave before she wiped the sweating handle of the gun on her black boiler suit, and attempted to pull herself together.

There was another blood-curdling scream. What the *hell* was that? Shelby bit on her lip to stop herself harmonising. She had no wish for Sergeant Rackham to come thundering back up the staircase, expecting at the very least to find her brutally murdered with her entrails draped all over the furniture.

She crept over to the window to investigate, pulling the dusty curtains apart an inch, praying that they wouldn't fall to bits in her hand. But the terrace below was silent, save for some furtive scurrying in the shrubbery. The scream must have been the owl after a mouse.

As the building settled down to an uneasy silence, Shelby sank wearily onto the four-poster bed and regarded her reflection in the cracked dusty mirror opposite. Minimum height, freckles and long carroty hair scraped back and beaten into submission with Kirbigrips. No one could accuse her of being a stereotyped WPC. *The Bill* wouldn't even have her as an extra.

After three years pounding the beat, why the *hell* had she picked Firearms for her first major posting – when she could have been having fun chasing sales reps along the motorway, digging ecowarriors out of burrows – even helping little old ladies across the road? Instead of guarding a corrupt film producer from his imaginary hitman.

As the clock struck midnight, and Shelby's head

began to nod from sheer boredom, a shadowy figure glided through the panelled wall opposite.

Shelby jumped to her feet. "Armed officer!" she bellowed – and then realised she no longer had the gun. It lay glinting conspicuously on the bed behind her, exactly where she had left it. She carried on speaking in an authoritative voice and hoped the intruder would not notice the gun. "Put your hands in the air where I can see them and move slowly into the light!"

A little chubby man obligingly padded towards her. He was certainly too well-fed to be a ghost. "Don't shoot. Don't shoot!" he grinned.

Shelby was not amused. "How the hell did you walk through that wall?"

"Walk through –" he suddenly broke into laughter. "Did you think I was a ghost?" More hysteria. She was sorely tempted to put a bullet through him just to shut him up. "It's the servants' staircase. I came in the back way – didn't want to bother any of those nice young fellows out front."

Shelby realised she was talking to the owner of Yew Tree Hall. "What are you doing here, Mr Wohlberg? You're supposed to be at the safe house."

"I left some paperwork behind. I explained the situation to some young lad called PC Wells and he escorted me here. Such a nice polite boy."

Bloody PC Wells! He'd never thought to radio her.

Oscar Wohlberg was looking her up and down in a rather familiar fashion. "Say, you're rather small for a police officer . . ."

Shelby frowned. This was a sore subject. Lately, the other officers on her shift had taken to calling her Pippi Longstocking.

"And where's your gun?" he continued relentlessly. "I thought you were one of the Firearms Squad?"

"Tactical Firearms Team," she snapped. "I am. And my gun is right –"

"Here?"he grinned, picking it up and squinting down the viewfinder.

Oh, *shit!* "Yes, that's my gun, Mr Wohlberg. Please let me have it back."

"It's big, isn't it?" He flicked the muzzle up towards the ceiling and inspected it. "It looks like a sub-machine gun. Have you shot anyone with it?"

No, but give me a couple of minutes. "Mr Wohlberg, I beg you, please hand me the gun. It's loaded; it's dangerous; I wouldn't want you to hurt yourself."

Her fingers tightened over her radio, to call for back-up, but she hesitated. One wrong word from her and he would think it a huge joke to pull the trigger and blast a hole through the wall behind her. All Americans were frustrated cowboys, no matter how thick the apparent veneer of sophistication.

"Put your hands in the air and gimme all your money," smirked Oscar.

Shelby began to edge towards him. "Mr Wohlberg . . ."

Oscar slid his finger through the trigger guard and attempted to rotate the gun. It might have worked for Doc Holliday but Oscar's fingers were far too pudgy. Shelby threw herself on the floor just as an explosion lacerated her ears. Oscar screamed and staggered backwards, sliding down the bed and crumpling onto the dusty wooden floor.

Cautiously Shelby lifted her head and saw Oscar lying flat out. *Oh my God, he's shot himself!* Her heart frantically beating a bass rhythm on her ribs, she levered herself on to her elbows and crawled slowly towards his motionless body. Scooping up the discarded gun, at once making it safe, she sprang back to her feet and leant over Oscar, resisting the temptation to prod him with her toe. It was her fault after all. If she hadn't left the Heckler & Koch on the bed, he would never have been able to play *Gunfight At The OK Corral* with it.

"Please don't be dead," she muttered, undoing his shirt, revealing a large expanse of hairy chest. He seemed to be breathing all right. And there was not the smallest drop of blood. It seemed Oscar had just fainted from the shock.

She stood up and tried to remember the firing line. The floorboards were OK, no bullet holes there. The ornate plaster ceiling, too, was unmarked. Shelby slowly followed the line across towards the mantelpiece, carefully stepping over Oscar's prostrate body. Running her fingers lightly across the pale stone surround, she couldn't see any new marks, although there were plenty of old ones. And it didn't look as though anyone had dusted the mantelpiece for a while either.

In the centre of the mantelpiece, lying on its side, was a gold statue. A little golden man, all hard and angular, standing on a plinth, leaning on a sword. Solid gold? Shelby picked it up, feeling the weight of the thing. Plate, she scoffed – and then realised the head was missing, as though someone had . . . blasted it clean away? Slowly, returning it to the mantelpiece, she looked again at the panelling over the fireplace.

Just behind where the statue had stood was a jagged hole. Shelby grinned. The only thing Oscar had shot had been . . . his Oscar.

* * *

NOVEMBER

The Assistant Chief Constable for CID & Operations had one of the most luxurious rooms in Police Headquarters. With lush carpeting and comfy sofas, it was awash with all the latest technology, and had large French windows giving access into the beautiful landscaped gardens – enabling a quick getaway if the Chief Constable turned up unexpectedly for coffee and a gossip.

The ACC sat behind a massive oak desk, flanked by Shelby's Chief Inspector and the wimpy female Personnel Officer. The Three Wise Monkeys, Shelby thought bitterly. Hear No Evil, See No Evil and Say Bloody Nothing.

Shelby had long ago ceased to listen to their politically correct waffle. By staring past the ACC's right ear she could gaze through the window to the terrace and still appear to be paying attention. The Chief Constable had cornered the Head of CID by a large terracotta urn. A group of probationers was sitting in a huddle around a little wrought-iron table, worriedly discussing their last lecture. She had sat there herself once, looking forward to the challenges ahead.

Beside Shelby, on a small, round coffee table, was a lemon geranium swarming with whitefly. Occasionally they would launch an offensive and dive-bomb her. On the opposite side was Sergeant Rackham, whom she had requested to sit in on the preliminary discipline interview, instead of the Federation Rep as was usual.

The Assistant Chief Constable shuffled his papers together, slipped them into a box file and leant back in his 'executive' leather chair, regarding her through narrowed eyes. He was short-sighted but too vain to wear his spectacles. He was only thirty-eight and had a determined wandering eye on the Chief Constable's job.

"Personnel will arrange your transfer from Calahurst to Norchester Police Station," he drawled. "It won't be too far for you to travel but unlikely you'll have the embarrassment of working with anyone you know."

Shelby started. That would teach her not to pay attention. "Why can't I stay at Calahurst?"

The ACC feigned surprise. "We thought you would prefer a new start. Calahurst Station has three officers from the Tactical Firearms Team, not including yourself. You have to admit it would be difficult for you working alongside them, seeing them called out on jobs. The only TFT member at Norchester is PC Wells and I'm sure he won't give you any trouble."

"Little runt wouldn't dare," snorted Shelby. Then cold reality set in. "Are you saying I've been kicked out of the TFT?"

The ACC looked meaningfully at the Personnel Officer, a civilian, who squirmed, fiddled with the hem of her short skirt and avoided looking at Shelby directly.

"We do not feel you are suited for the role of Tactical Firearms Officer, Miss Roberts," she said. "Poor Mr Wohlberg, he had no idea that the gun was loaded. He had a terrible shock."

"*He* had a terrible shock?" Shelby scowled. "The only thing that idiot shot was the head off his Academy Award – and that was a fluke. You know, he never did have a stalker. He set us up to get publicity for his rotten stinking movie."

The ACC regarded her coldly. "You do not appear to comprehend the seriousness of your situation."

"I appreciate that if I had not put down the gun, there would not have been a situation. Mr Wohlberg didn't mean the gun to go off. It was an accident. I won't let it happen again."

"You're damn right it won't happen again. I am proud that since the TFT was set up, only once has a bullet been fired during an incident. That was during a siege situation, which ended without bloodshed."

"But no one was hurt."

"That is not the point."

"Then what is?"

"Shelby," muttered Sergeant Rackham between clenched teeth, "shut up."

She glanced at him irritably. He was supposed to be on her side for Heaven's sake! Why didn't he stand up for her? Too busy protecting his own back to watch out for hers. Bloody police, they were all the same. When she had joined she had the idea she would be fighting criminals, not filling out paperwork and playing office politics. Was this the only way to rise up the ranks? Kiss butt?

"WPC Roberts," began her Chief Inspector wearily, "we have already been through this. You said yourself you did not realise who Mr Wohlberg was when he entered the bedroom. You should have challenged him and called for back-up. You should never have put down your weapon."

Shelby began to feel as though she was speaking Japanese. "I *did* challenge him." Why would no one listen to her story? Unless they had already made their decision . . .

"So how did he end up with a loaded police gun in his hand?"

Hadn't he even bothered to read her report? She'd spent most of last week slaving over it. What a waste of time! She should have gone clubbing.

"I was trying to get it *back* at the time."

"You're the Force Judo Champion. Why didn't you put him in a headlock or something?"

Shelby lost the grip on her patience. "Because I'd have ended up with more perforations than a Tetley's tea bag! He had the gun. I didn't!"

"You could have called for back-up though," goaded the ACC. "You had a radio, you had your voice. The lads were only downstairs."

Ha! That was a laugh! "The 'lads' were so bloody scared when they heard the gun go off, they were halfway to Norchester."

"Miss Roberts!" pleaded the Personnel Officer.

"Please! It does no good to blame others for your mistakes."

"I'm not trying to put the blame on anyone. I'm just telling the truth!" She made imaginary quote marks in the air. "You know, '*The truth is out there*'?"

PS Rackham had a sudden coughing fit.

The ACC merely regarded her with indifference. "Grow up or ship out, Roberts. Your flippant, facetious attitude is another reason why I feel you are no longer suitable for the Tactical Firearms Team."

Her eyes whipped back to his face. "You three sit there like judges in a witch hunt, don't listen to a word I say, and take me off a job I love, that I'm good at. Of course I'm going to have an attitude!"

"Shelby," muttered Sergeant Rackham, not unkindly, "remember who you're talking to."

Patronising bastard!

"Why did you let Wohlberg take the gun, Roberts?" barked the ACC.

"I don't see –"

"Why didn't you yell for back-up?"

"I –"

"*This* is why you're out of the TFT. *This* is why you are so close to getting the sack." He stood up, towering over her. "*This* is because you're *no fucking good*, WPC Roberts. I'm not having you endangering the rest of the Firearms Team. Got that? Now you can get over to Norchester or you can get out of the police force. I don't really give a shit."

She stared at him in shock, a nasty squirmy feeling

11

in the pit of her stomach threatening to make her sick. It was worse than when her parents admitted they were divorcing, after fifteen years of uncivil warring. It was even worse than when her boyfriend of three years upped and left her for the Pamela Anderson wannabe who worked at her father's pub. And he had taken his precious collection of *Big & Busty* magazines with him, so she knew he wouldn't be back.

"You . . ." Her throat was so dry she had to try again. "You can't talk to me like that!"

He regarded her with disinterest. "I can talk to you any way I choose."

The Personnel Officer trembled in her chair. The Chief Inspector stared unblinkingly out of the window. Sergeant Rackham appeared mutinous but had the good sense to leave his bottom firmly on his seat.

Shelby's gaze flickered from face to face. They don't care about me, she realised. They only care about their precious reputation. They just want to brush the whole thing under the carpet, hold onto their own jobs. Think what would happen if any of this got out? A two-bit movie producer disarms a crack firearms/martial arts expert. What a monumental cock-up! And what a glorious tabloid story it would make. She was beginning to understand their fear.

Shelby looked through the window at the probationers. She had had so many dreams. But now it seemed so long ago, as though the last five years had happened to someone else.

"OK," said Shelby. "I'll give you what you want.

My resignation. You can have my head on a silver platter too if you like." Her voice began to tremble. "And if you squash it right down, you can catalogue it in one of those cute little box files, along with your morals, your principles and what's left of your conscience. I quit!"

Chapter Two

"Why did this have to happen to me, Irving?" grumbled Shelby. "I loved working for the police. That's all I ever wanted to do." Frustratedly, she kicked out at the glass-topped table in front of her. "How *dare* they sack me?"

"You resigned,"her elder brother felt obliged to point out. He made a swift grab for his mug of coffee as the table wobbled precariously, threatening to spill it across Shelby's sitting-room carpet. "You weren't fired."

Shelby was about to say, 'Don't be so bloody pedantic,' but, as that was likely to send Irving scurrying off down the pub for a bit of comparative peace and quiet, she thumped the arm of the chair instead. "I was goaded into it," she muttered. "It was so unfair."

"Life's unfair," said Irving wearily. "What makes you think you have the monopoly?"

Shelby watched her brother's gaze flit around the

14

sitting-room, alighting on the thick layers of dust over every surface, particularly the lighter patch where the TV and video had been. She cringed, waiting for his interrogation, but it never came. After all, it would not take a genius to work out they'd been sold to meet the bills.

She should have made the effort to tidy up, she scolded herself. Depression was no excuse. She hoped Irving wouldn't get a pressing need to visit the kitchen where, in addition to two days' worth of washing-up in the sink, he'd find her underwear draped over all available surfaces (she had flogged the washer/drier too) amidst piles of application forms for every police force in the country. She was still plucking up the courage to send them off.

Shelby knocked back the remainder of her orange juice and wished she'd put vodka in it. Anything to jolt her out of this debilitating self-pity. Irving was about the only person left who was willing to listen to her ravings. Besides, she realised, as she hit the bottom of the glass and an ice cube bonked her on the nose, she was beginning to repeat herself.

"So what are you going to do for money?"Irving wanted to know.

Shelby avoided his direct gaze. "Dad gave me a job working behind the bar at The Parson's Collar."

He regarded her in despair. "You *must* be desperate."

Shelby said nothing. Even their father was beginning to lose patience, since she felled some poor youth – who had had the misfortune to brush up against her bum on

a particularly busy night – with a drop-kick Jean-Claude Van Damme would have been proud of.

"Do you have to dress as a Naughty Nun?" Irving added, with a commendable straight face.

"Don't be stupid!"

Irving glanced at his watch, without bothering to be subtle about it. "Why don't you just phone up police personnel and say 'Sorry'?"he suggested. "Perhaps they might take you back."

Shelby avoided meeting his eye. "Not after what I said to the Assistant Chief Constable."

"I can imagine."Irving ran short, stubby fingers through his blond, floppy hair while he seemed to have an inner debate about the correct thing to say. Diplomacy had never been a Roberts family quality. "Look, Shel, you're going to have to find another job. Once you have a job, you can afford the mortgage on this place, you can go on holiday, go out with your friends –"

Basically, the sympathy stops here, thought Shelby glumly. But she couldn't blame him for being honest. "Which, roughly translated, means 'Stop boring me with the finer points of your god-awful life'?" she asked. "I can take a hint, Irving – it's just not that simple. What work am I supposed to do? What police force is going to want me? And that's before we get onto the touchy subject of a discipline record."

"So do something else?"

"*What*? I can't type, I know bugger-all about computers –"

"After five years in the police?"Irving feigned disbelief.

"Incorporating Uniform, Traffic, CID, Firearms," he ticked her rather erratic career path off on his fingers. "Surely they must have trained you for something?"

"Yes." Shelby stared morosely at her feet. "Chasing sales reps up the motorway and shooting cardboard cut-outs."

"Ah . . ."

"You see my point? There are not that many jobs for ex-police officers. Particularly ones who left in a hurry. I didn't even qualify for the dole."

His freckled face softened. "It was an accident, Shelby. Everyone knew that. It wasn't your fault. It's not as though anybody died. You make the teeniest of mistakes –"

"Almost letting the person you're supposed to be protecting accidentally shoot himself is not really a teensy mistake," she said dryly. "Can't *you* get me a job?"

"And let you loose on a film set?" Irving looked horrified. "Do you think I'm crazy?"

"There must be something I can do. Make coffee, fetch sandwiches – what are those girls you're always complaining about called? The ones that run errands?"

"Runners? Forget it! You practically have to have a diploma from the National Film and Television School just to get a foot in the door. Don't you remember how I started out? Collecting the director's lunch, walking the star's pet pooch – and all for nothing? You need *paid* employment, Shelby. Besides, you don't have the temperament to be someone else's skivvy."

Shelby slumped down in her seat. "So I suppose it's

back to the Employment Office. The only vacancy they could come up with was as a store detective in Boots. Hmm, I wonder if I'd get free make-up?"

"Store detective?" Irving frowned.

"Uh huh – I suppose I'd better practise looking inconspicuous."

"And you'd really consider doing that?"

"I'm desperate," she admitted. "I know you're too polite to say but surely you've must have noticed that anything not nailed down has been sold to pay my mortgage?"

Irving glanced towards the empty bookcase. "Even your judo trophies?"

"They went first."Hating the pity on his face, she added brightly, "Silver is such hell to clean." She could see she had failed to convince him. "And before you say anything," she added firmly, "I don't want a loan."

"You can be *too* proud, Shelby."

"I refuse to bum off my brother. I'm a big girl now. I can take care of myself."

She watched as his eyes flicked towards the table where the TV had stood and knew that Irving, with his six televisions, cable TV and huge video library would not be able to contemplate life without one. But who cared? She didn't miss it. Not every household in Britain had a TV. It was totally unimportant.

And then she had a rather unpleasant glimpse of the future, a few months down the line when the three-piece suite and table had gone, when they might be sitting on deckchairs and eating off an upturned grocery box. And drinking those free samples of revolting tea bags that came through the letterbox every once in a while.

Irving had paused for thought too, as though turning something over in his mind, plucking up the courage to speak the words.

Shelby recognised the look. "Out with it, Irv!" she demanded. "Whatever you're thinking, I can take it."

"I've just had an idea. Firestorm Productions have runners coming out of their ears but the guy who supplies the security for us is always on the look-out for new people . . ."

"Security?" Shelby's face fell. "Like, making sure no one walks off with one of the cameras?"

"Yes. He particularly likes ex-army and ex-police. I reckon you'd be in with a good chance there, Shel."

"There is *no* way I'm going to be a security guard," said Shelby resolutely. "I've seen them poncing up and down in supermarkets. They can hardly see where they're going beneath their silly peaked caps, they have them pulled down so low over their Neanderthal foreheads. Real ego-trippers."

"It's not *just* security guards. The film company also hire minders – to keep the stars out of trouble, protect them from over-zealous fans, that sort of thing. Why don't you just give it a try?"

"So that I can launch a career as a glorified baby-sitter? Terrific! You know what minders and bodyguards are like – great brainless thugs. This security chief is going to love little old me. And I can just imagine what he's like. A despotic police reject who likes to think he has his own private army."

"You ought to know," said Irving. "He used to be your Chief Inspector."

* * *

John Ivar's Security Agency was located above Kayleigh's Hairdresser on Calahurst High Street, just around the corner from the police station – where John had once been Shelby's boss in CID. Shelby walked past it twice, before she could summon the courage to enter.

The reception was very squashed but someone had gone to a lot of trouble, decorating it in a bright, zingy yellow, presumably to cheer the place up, although the overall effect was claustrophobic. There was just enough room for a pale beech desk, a couple of chairs, a few wilting pot plants and a coffee table overflowing with magazines.

Behind the desk sat a very glamorous secretary, blonde hair piled high on her head and such a snooty expression she resembled a thoroughbred camel. She was wearing a smart lemon suit, as though she had been colour co-ordinated with the office. Shelby smiled before she could stop herself.

"Yes?" said the secretary haughtily. She ran cold blue eyes across Shelby's dark shiny suit, mentally clocking up the name of the High Street chain Shelby had bought it from and, most importantly, the cost.

Shelby summoned herself up to her full height of five foot five. "I'd like to see John Ivar, please."

"Do you have an appointment?"

"We're old friends," said Shelby quickly, if not terribly truthfully. "He asked me to pop by."

The secretary's practised eye slid over Shelby's short skirt and thick wool tights. Shelby hoped she could not see the darn above her left knee, where she had grappled with a mugger last autumn, and been dragged all the way down Calahurst Quay before she could get handcuffs on him. She winced at the memory. Ever since, she felt she knew every cobblestone intimately.

"He's very busy," said the secretary.

Shelby frowned. "Tell John that Detective Sergeant Roberts is here to see him."

"Detective Sergeant?" repeated the secretary in disbelief. "Do you have ID?"

Shelby leant on the desk and looked bored. "Don't be stupid, woman. I'm undercover."

The secretary flushed and, not taking her eyes off Shelby for a minute, presumably in case she vanished with a box of paper-clips, picked up the phone and dialled an extension number.

She murmured into the receiver for a few moments. "He's in the middle of something," she said frostily. "If you'd like to take a seat, he'll be with you shortly."

Shelby positioned herself next to the window, next to an over-familiar cheese plant. After tugging her skirt down over the darn in her tights, she half-heartedly picked up the magazine on top of the pile. *Country Life?* Yawn yawn. She supposed she could always look at the pictures.

The secretary returned to her computer, her fingers

flying over the keyboard like a classical pianist. She never once looked at her fingers. Shelby sank into a deep gloom. Was she ever going to get a job? Even Irving could type better than her.

John Ivar kept her waiting for over fifteen minutes, during which time she was convinced she had sweated off most of her new make-up, bought to disguise her freckles. She had refused two offers of coffee in case she needed to go to the loo at an inopportune moment.

Eventually the secretary ushered her into Ivar's office. It was considerably larger than reception, and looked across the mix-and-match rooftops of Calahurst towards the Quay. John had his desk in front of the window, where he liked to swivel round in his chair and admire the view, judging from the coffee rings adorning the windowsill. He had a computer on his desk, which surprised Shelby, as he had always cited computerisation as his reason for retirement.

John Ivar was a big man, in his early fifties, gunmetal hair in the same short back and sides he had sported for the past three decades. His half-moon spectacles were sliding down his bulbous nose, his shirt-sleeves had been rolled up past the elbows, his jacket was slung awkwardly on the chair behind him. He had a cheap biro clamped between his teeth, like a Great Dane with a favourite bone, as he rifled impatiently through his post tray, scattering paperwork like a miniature hurricane.

"Won't keep you a moment, lass," he muttered. "Take a seat."

There were two grubby lemon chairs directly in front

of his desk. Daft colour to decorate an office really. Both seats were piled high with paperwork. After helplessly glancing at the secretary, who stared stonily ahead, Shelby carefully removed one of the piles, stacked it neatly against the desk, and sat down.

The remainder of John's office was much the same, Pisa-like towers of magazines and paperwork mushrooming around the office with just the narrowest strip of dingy beige carpet leading from the desk to the door. Perhaps the secretary's duties did not run to filing.

John finally shoved his biro behind his ear and leant forward to shake Shelby's hand. He seemed genuinely pleased to see her. "Did you have a good Christmas? It's lovely to see you again." His rich Yorkshire accent poured out an endless succession of words, almost tripping over each other to get out first. "You should have told me you were coming. We could have gone down the pub. Pie and a pint like the old days."

She grimaced. "I think I've had enough of pubs."

"I remember now, your father runs The Parson's Collar? Do you help out when he's busy? I hope he doesn't make you wear a Naughty Nun get-up?" He laughed, a deep gurgling chuckle.

"Has your agency got any vacancies?" blurted out Shelby, before she could stop herself. *Tact, girl, tact,* she cursed herself. *Let's try to be a little more subtle . . .*

"Vacancies?" He looked at her in amazement. "Do you mean you want a job?"

She nodded, finding that the sudden lump in her throat would not allow her to speak. The utter misery she

23

had felt over the last couple of months began to catch up on her and demand emotion with menaces.

"What about your career with the police?"

"Me and police work were not suited."

He laughed. "An undisciplined scatterbrain with a terrible temper?"

She smiled wryly. "You wrote that on my first appraisal. I nearly resigned there and then. I wish I had. It would have saved a lot of heartache."

He regarded her speculatively. "So why *did* you resign?"

"I was working for the Tactical Firearms Team when I made a serious mistake," she replied, knowing it was pointless to be anything less than honest. Besides, for all she knew John Ivar still had contacts at Police HQ and knew the whole story already. He could be a devious bastard. "ACC Operations wanted to move me to a uniform shift at Headquarters. I declined."

"Was anyone hurt?"

"No. I relaxed my guard, put down my gun, the Principal picked it up and blasted the head off his own Academy Award." She dropped her gaze to stare at her feet, in case her eyes were too pleading. "If you can't trust your Principal, who can you trust? I won't make the same mistake again."

"In this job you don't get second chances."

Shelby twisted her fingers anxiously. "I understand if you feel you can't take a risk on me but I need work . . ." Again she tried not to sound too eager. "I'll do anything – filing, sweeping the floor –"

"I already have a cleaner," said John, smiling kindly.

"Although you wouldn't think it. And a secretary. I don't mean to sound sexist but you don't appear to be the sort who types."

Shelby hung her head. "I'm not."

"However, I provide security guards for factory premises, bouncers for night-clubs and private parties, drivers and minders for celebrities." He paused. "Anything appeal?"

Her eyes darted up to his face. Inscrutable as ever. "Are you . . ." *Mustn't sound too hopeful*, she told herself sharply. "So . . . er, are you offering me a job?"

He grinned broadly, his whole face creasing. "Yes, I'm offering you a job!"

It took all her self-control not to leap onto his desk, punch the air and yell, *YES!* "What would you like me to do?" she asked calmly.

"We'll start you off with something cushy," he replied. "Firestorm Productions are filming a new costume drama, based on a romantic novel by Marina Grey. It's being touted as 'Jane Austen with attitude'. They're at Shepperton now and in April they move to Bath for three weeks on location." He paused. "Have you heard of an actor called Luke McFadden?"

"Wasn't he the one who turned up to his own wedding wearing a dress? His best man had apparently abandoned him in Trafalgar Square for a joke? The bride was so furious she called the whole thing off. I suppose Firestorm want a minder to prevent any more indiscretions being captured on film?"

"You're ahead of me," said John ruefully. "Luke's a

handsome lad – there's always going to be some daffy woman sending him her knickers through the post – but this hounding by the media is something else. The press crucified him after the wedding fiasco – you'd have thought he was a child murderer, the vilification he suffered. So, instead of being stalked by mad fans, he's being stalked by journalists and the paparazzi, desperate for their next scoop. It would drive a lesser man over the edge."

"I can imagine," said Shelby. Personally she thought Luke McFadden's problems were all self-inflicted but she remained quiet. She didn't want to get the sack before she'd even started.

"Your job would be to look after Luke on location," continued John. "Charles Smith, another of my minders, will be protecting him in London and Shepperton but he currently has family commitments which are preventing him from taking on work too far from the capital. Are you interested?"

Three weeks in Bath keeping an eye on hunky Luke McFadden? Sounded a complete doddle. It was difficult stopping a huge grin from spreading across her face. "So I just have to protect him from the press and sex-mad fans?"

John winced. "I'm afraid the work's not very glamorous. The truly big names are few and far between. The Yanks, when they come over, have their own people. But I still manage to scratch a living. It's become very fashionable for otherwise non-celebrities to have 'minders'. Some so-called 'stars' would not even be recognised if they didn't step out with half-a-dozen bodyguards. Get your minder to punch a journalist, or a photographer, and there you are, headline news and oodles of free publicity."

"You always despised those thugs," she reflected, then coloured. "I mean –"

He grinned. "*My* 'thugs' are trained thugs. Anyone can be a bodyguard. But a *good* bodyguard is someone who uses his head for thinking, not for butting, keeps his hands by his sides and not in his pockets, or even in some poor journalist's face. If pop stars and actors want the best, they pay for the best. And that's me. It's not quite how I envisaged spending my retirement but my clients are impressed that I was once a copper."

"Like me," said Shelby and beamed.

He regarded her doubtfully. "Are you sure that this is what you want? It's not as exciting as it sounds. Most of the work involves standing around, waiting. Perhaps you'd be better off applying for a job with another police force?"

She grimaced. "You have got to be joking!"

"OK, I'll draw you up a draft contract. Read and sign it at your leisure. I'll arrange for you to take some training courses – evasive driving, first aid, nothing too taxing – I think we'll skip the self-defence. You can start as soon as you like. If you don't come up to scratch, you repay any costs I've incurred. If you agree to take the job, I'll book you into the same hotel as Luke McFadden. Location filming starts at the end of April."

"Hotel?" Shelby perked up. The last hotel she had stayed at had been a sleazy concrete hellhole in Benidorm when she was seventeen. It was all she had been able to afford. Even the cockroaches had checked out after one night.

He regarded her over the top of his spectacles. "Five stars."

This was too good to be true. "I suppose I'll be sleeping in the attic?"

"You'll have the adjoining room."

"So long as it's not the adjoining bed," she said mischievously, adding, "What's the current going rate for an exposé in the gutter press?"

"Would you rather wait until another job came up?" he asked. "There's a female pop singer due over from the States in May."

John Ivar, she remembered belatedly, had not had much of a sense of humour when it came to his work. "Oh no, this'll be fine," she said hurriedly. "Besides, how much trouble can an *actor* get into?"

Chapter Three

Monday – Bath

Irving Roberts had been named after the man who wrote 'White Christmas' and, apart from a lifetime of spelling it out to bank clerks, he thought he had escaped quite lightly – his brothers were called Cary and Harrison. As he was a puny 5'6", with thick specs, freckles and the pallid complexion of someone who watches TV in the dark, he felt he looked like an Irving too.

Three months of working with Luke McFadden had given Irving a nervous twitch and a growing fondness for Foster's Export. And now, as he walked reluctantly towards Luke's dressing-room trailer, he was sure he could feel his palms perspire, and his heart begin to palpitate.

He had just raised his hand to knock on the trailer door when it flew open and one of the extras barged past, sprinted across the pavement and threw up into the adjacent municipal rose bushes.

"Hi, Irv," he said, emerging at length from the bushes,

29

his face a fetching shade of green, his hair decorated with delicate pink petals. "I think the curry's off."

"Poor you," said Irving, already enveloped in the scent of freshly smoked grass emanating from the trailer. "Take the next three weeks off."

The extra saw his opportunity to be the next Ewan McGregor disappear into the sunset. "But I'm feeling better already."

"Too bad, you're fired. You know how Mr Whitney feels about drugs and alcohol on set."

Irving turned his back on the cringing actor and stepped into Hades. Barely visible through the thick fog of cigarette smoke, were grips, sparks and extras squashed tightly into every corner, laughing and shouting above the deafening rock music, the floor littered with discarded cans of beer and suspicious-looking fag-butts. And if that wasn't enough to give Irving a coronary, they were playing strip-poker onto the tummy of a brunette, naked save for her rather grey knickers, who stared vacantly at the ceiling, languorously smoking her way through a sweet-scented roll-up.

Luke, still in his costume of breeches, lawn shirt and boots, was stretched back on the bed, dangling a bottle of his favourite Chardonnay from his fingers. "Hi, Irv," he said cheerfully. "*Abandon hope all ye who enter here.*"

The crew tactfully melted away but the brunette on the floor merely began to snore. Irving yanked her to her feet, scattering playing cards across the trailer.

"What's going on?" she grumbled. "Who won? I was supposed to be first prize."

Not trusting himself to speak, Irving threw Luke's dressing-gown at the girl and shoved her out of the door.

As there was no one left to party with, Luke finished his bottle of Chardonnay and swung it lethargically in the direction of the bin. A direct hit. It smashed into a million pieces. "Party-pooper," he sighed. "You've been working with Ross too long."

Irving began opening the windows and wafting away the smoke.

Luke watched in amusement. "What a wonderful housewife you are," he said. "You'll have to marry me, Irving. No one else will."

"I'm not surprised. Oh fuck," added Irving, as he picked up a cigarette end and discovered it was still smouldering. "What if Ross had come in and found half his crew partying in here? You know alcohol – and the rest! – is banned from the set."

"And how *is* Vlad the Impaler?"

"Baying for your blood. You should have been on set twenty minutes ago."

"Yeah, to sit around and wait," mocked Luke. "Bastard does it on purpose to unnerve me. It's a complete waste of time."

"And working your way through the entire crop of Chardonnay isn't?" Irving, realising he was starting to sound like his father, began to gather up the empty bottles. He found two under the bed and one in the shower.

"For emergencies," said Luke.

Opening the wardrobe, Irving found a couple more – hidden inside a pair of 19th century riding-boots.

"Stops them sagging," said Luke blithely.

"I'll be sure to pass on your tip to the wardrobe master." As the wardrobe door swung back, crashing against a chest of drawers, Irving caught sight of a small snapshot of the actress Paige Lorraine tacked onto the inside. She was wearing jeans and T-shirt, her silver-blonde hair blowing in the wind. It was the first photograph Irving had seen where she was smiling naturally rather than pouting. It was also the first shot he'd ever seen of her wearing jeans. Then Luke was beside him and the door crashed shut.

For a moment Irving stared up at Luke, noticing, for the first time, the lines etched upon his handsome face, his eyes two dark hollows of misery. "Does it get any better?" he asked gently.

"No," replied Luke, dropping a pair of dark glasses onto his nose and gathering up his script. "I'm afraid it's terminal."

* * *

Shelby arrived in Bath later that evening, and found she was booked into a beautiful Palladian hotel at the end of a long one-track lane which meandered through meadows and woodlands – until it abruptly plunged down a cliff-face. Constructed of the inevitable honey-tinged stone, slowly turning amber with the last rays of the setting sun, the hotel clung precariously to the edge of the cliff, a short lawned garden dropping away before it, affording splendid views across the wooded valley.

Shelby checked in, showered, carefully made up her

face and changed into a smart black suit, consisting of bootcut trousers and a jacket with ornate silver buttons, before she went in search of the rest of the film crew.

The hotel receptionist, a neat blonde with incredibly clean fingernails, pointed her in the direction of Neptune's Bar. Shelby entered the gloom, expecting something along the style of Disney's *Little Mermaid*. The room, large and square, was painted an aquatic blue-green, with large gilt-framed mirrors between mock Corinthian columns. There was the odd fishing-net, strung lethargically from the ceiling, but Shelby could tell the designer's heart was not really in it. She neatly sidestepped a ship's figurehead of a mermaid looming from the wall, and stood, peering into the darkness, desperately hoping to see someone she recognised.

The bar was empty, save for a couple of old biddies by the bay window, drinking sherry extremely slowly and occasionally glaring at the disreputable crowd of students propping up the bar. She could not see Irving or John, or even the glamorous Luke. Shelby had just turned back towards the door, when someone raised a hand and shouted her name. There could not be two people in Bath called 'Shelby'.

"Hey, Shelby, over here!" the voice repeated urgently. It had a strong Yorkshire accent.

At length she noticed John Ivar, towering over the gang of scruffs she had taken for students, frantically waving to her. Turning herself sideways, she plunged through a sea of denim, leather and cigarette smoke, feeling her bottom determinedly pinched, but unable to detect which of the raucous mob was responsible. By the time she reached John she was fuming.

John was happily chatting up a vampish brunette in a bum-skimming lilac frock, his style cramped by a lanky, red-headed geek in spectacles. Luke McFadden? Definitely not. Shelby squinted through the cigarette smoke. The producer? Let the butt-kissing commence. She gave him a huge grin and enthusiastically shook his hand. He seemed rather taken back by her ebullience.

"Evening, Shelby," said John. "This is Ross Whitney, producer and director of *A Midsummer Kiss*."

Ah hah, 'God' himself. She widened her friendly grin.

"And this is Octavia Shannon."

Despite the copious amounts of black eyeliner, Shelby vaguely recognised Octavia from a murder and mayhem romp on TV a couple of months before and thrust her hand forward. It was left dangling in mid-air. Octavia did not even deign to glance in her direction, just breathed deeply on her cigarette, sending the smoke in an apathetic spiral to join the haze gathering above their heads. The pain of rejection. Shelby felt her smile droop. It was beginning to make her face ache anyway.

"Did you have a good journey?" asked Ross politely.

"Yes, thank you." Shelby looked up at him and saw her image reflected back to her in a pair of round, silver-rimmed glasses. Then the large grey eyes behind blinked, rather like a large, unfriendly barn owl, and she started. His pale face was topped by dark-red hair, slicked back like an estate agent. Suddenly he smiled, and it was as though someone had turned up the colour on a TV picture. Perhaps he wasn't such a geek after all.

"Bruno's about somewhere," said John vaguely. "Ex Royal Marine. Terrific lad. Very keen. He'll be looking after Courteney O'Connor, the little American girl. She's got some mad fan stalking her."

"I wish someone would look after me," complained Octavia. "I haven't been able to get near the bar since the sparks arrived. They're knocking it back like there's no tomorrow. Ross is footing the drinks bill tonight," she added, in Shelby's general direction. "It's a sort of 'Breaking The Ice' party. And I haven't been able to get any of that either," she muttered discontentedly. "Warm gin. Ugh!"

"Here, let me," sighed Ross, uncoiling himself from his stool, and waving to the girl behind the bar.

As he accidentally brushed against Shelby's shoulder, she caught the faintest whiff of citrus aftershave. She hadn't realised he was so tall. He was wearing tattered jeans and a red-checked shirt, like an unemployed lumberjack, but she could still see the outline of some serious muscle tone. Definitely worth further investigation.

She waited patiently for him to sit back down, so that she could stun him with some intelligent witticism, when suddenly a teenage blonde exploded into their circle, spilling Ross's drink and treading on his foot.

She glanced back through the clouds of cigarette smoke and shuddered. "Quick, talk to me. I need rescuing."

Shelby followed her gaze and could just make out a man, not much taller than herself, but squat and bulky, as though some giant had just banged his head between his shoulders. Whether it was fat or muscle, Shelby could not tell, as he was wearing an expensive-looking suit, emerald silk tie and matching handkerchief. He was staring after the girl with the typically lovelorn gaze of a repressed Englishman.

"Who is that creep?" the girl muttered to Ross. "Who let him in? You were supposed to be fixing me a bodyguard so I wouldn't have to talk to guys like that."

Ross sighed. "Shelby, may I introduce Courteney O'Connor? Courteney, meet Shelby Roberts – Luke's new bodyguard."

Courteney O'Connor! Shelby stared at the girl in shock. Why hadn't she recognised her? But then, would she recognise Drew Barrymore if she was standing at a bus stop?

Courteney looked much the same as she had done in her films, although in the last one she had been a brunette. Now her hair was spikily blonde, cropped a ragged two inches all over. She had a huge lipsticked grin, her round face lighting up with the mega-watt dimples which had made her such a hit at the cinema, and large shining eyes, the colour of aquamarines.

"You're a *bodyguard*?" Courteney's face dropped. "Wow! Have you got a gun? Can I have a look?"

Shelby winced and quickly changed the subject. "How long have you been filming in Bath?"

"Just today. We shot a lot of the interior stuff at Shepperton just before Easter, so everyone knows each other. We had great fun." And she launched into a detailed account of every shot, every set-up, every fluffed line.

Usually Shelby might have found all this insider gossip interesting. However, intrigued by the hunky/geeky Ross Whitney, she had one ear open for the conversation going on beside her.

"Where's Luke?" asked John, as soon as Octavia wandered drunkenly off to the loo, bouncing off a couple of star-struck tourists, before marching confidently into the Gents'.

"How the hell should I know?" snapped Ross. "This is why we're hiring him a keeper. Although this pocket-sized Venus isn't quite what I had in mind. We're supposed to be keeping Luke out of trouble, not giving it to him gift-wrapped."

Pocket-sized Venus! Shelby clenched her fists. No, she must not lose her temper. Count to ten . . . *One, two, three* . . .

"Since Luke's break-up with Paige," Ross was saying, "There have been so many women traipsing in and out of his trailer to help mend his broken heart, the set handyman is thinking of installing revolving doors."

Irving, arriving at the table with a tray of drinks, muttered, "I think you'll find his exact words were 'cat flap'."

Courteney startled them by laughing uproariously. "*Miaow!* And you guys reckon women are the bitches?"

Ross, not the slightest bit abashed, turned to her to ask grimly, "So, do *you* know where he is?"

Courteney shrugged. "Flirting with some babe? I wish I had his stamina. He's always out clubbing with the sparks and the grips," she added to Shelby. "Drowning his sorrows, poor guy. Paige's defection must have hit him hard. I mean, can't the girl take a joke?"

"Not when the joke is in poor taste." Ross's voice was cold. "Luke turned up at the church in a wedding dress; he obviously wasn't going to take his vows seriously. He humiliated Paige, in front of the world's media. It was unforgivable."

"Who rattled your cage?" grumbled Courteney. "If Luke had asked *me* to marry him I wouldn't have cared if he turned up to the church, butt-naked, with a rose stuck up his –"

"Ross has a point," said Irving quickly. "I switched on the TV last night to unwind and there was some comedian still making jokes about it. Four *months* later. I don't know how Luke can stand it. I'd go crazy."

"Luke deserves all he gets." Ross took a long drink of his whisky. "But why do none of you think of Paige, how she feels?"

John, Irving and Courteney exchanged the faintest of smiles but said nothing. In fact, the lull in conversation swiftly turned into an uneasy silence. And Shelby, rather taken aback by the candid words which had been just been exchanged, had no intention of breaking it. Let someone else put their foot in it for a change.

"Twelve hours on location and you've already run out of things to say to each other," said a new voice. "Sad, I call it."

Shelby, who had her back towards the speaker, slowly turned. Even if she hadn't recognised him from his films, she would have known that this was Luke

McFadden from the way everyone started guiltily and looked every which way rather than directly at him.

Luke was so handsome it hurt. As tall as Ross, yet broader in the shoulder, he sauntered over with lazy self-assurance. Black hair, curling into the collar of his leather jacket, together with his Mediterranean complexion, gave him the appearance of a marauding pirate. His eyes, instead of the expected brown, were an extraordinary violet-blue. His jaw was firm, his cheekbones high; in fact, he had all the qualities beloved of romantic novelists everywhere.

His face was his fortune and he knew it.

"Luke!" squealed Courteney, flinging her arms around him. "Where have you been? We were just talking about you."

For a moment Shelby caught a glimpse of cynicism in those beautiful, thickly lashed eyes, then Luke grinned, displaying a row of perfect white teeth. "Taking care of business," he replied, casually dropping his motorcycle helmet onto the table.

"Not the barmaid at The Saracen's Head?" said Courteney in awe. "You are naughty! The focus-puller's been stalking her since we got here."

"Then he'd better stick to pulling tape measures. He's crap at pulling women." He thumbed nonchalantly in Shelby's direction. "Aren't you going to introduce me to your little friend?"

Little! Shelby bristled. She realised his eyes were slightly glazed over. Perhaps it was just from sheer tiredness – if he was drunk he was hiding it remarkably well.

"This is Shelby," said Courteney. "She's going to be your bodyguard . . ."

Luke took Shelby's outstretched hand and raised it to his lips. "Yeah, and I'm Whitney Houston."

"One . . . two . . . three . . ." muttered Shelby under her breath.

"Enchanté," he murmured softly and kissed her hand.

Lay it on with a JCB, she thought, as his lips brushed lightly against her skin.

This must be his standard movie-star behaviour. He was probably so used to women dropping their knickers at the slightest encouragement he had forgotten how to act normally. She felt herself becoming hypnotised by those glorious cornflower eyes, and tried to imagine him wearing a lacy wedding gown to take her mind off his blistering sex appeal. Although perhaps white satin would suit him better. He certainly had the right sort of hips for a sheath dress.

Luke leant back against a Corinthian column and ran his eyes languidly over her body. "You're a sweet little thing," he murmured. "Who are you really? You look very smart. You must be the new receptionist."

Shelby had the distinct impression that, if the column hadn't been there, he'd have fallen over. "I'm *not* a receptionist and actually I'm five foot five. That's not little; that's the national average."

"Never mind. Eat up your greens and I'm sure you'll grow."

Shelby gritted her teeth. She could see Irving making zipping signs across his mouth. Even John was starting to look anxious. OK, so she had a temper. Did they seriously think she was going to lose her rag and jeopardise her first decent job?

"Shelby really is your bodyguard," said Courteney, mischief-making for the hell of it. "John hired her."

"My bodyguard? That's a good joke. Who's Ross got lined up for my stunt double? Britney Spears?" He ran his finger lightly across Shelby's reddened cheek. "If you're guarding my body, honey, who's going to be guarding yours?"

"Crass sexist pig!" Shelby exploded. "Who the hell do you think you are?"

All around the bar conversations abruptly ceased.

"An actor?" suggested Luke.

"Well, I'm a *bodyguard*, Mr McFadden, with a black belt in judo and karate, trained to protect you from assassins, kidnappers, and middle-aged housewives. And what are you? You're a fucking *actor*."

"A fucking good 'fucking actor'," he returned blithely. "So, you're a black belt in macramé, eh? Going to crochet those assassins to death?"

Shelby caught hold of the front of his shirt. There was a swift tug on his lapels, the room did a circuit without him and he crashlanded on the floor to see stars, and Shelby dusting off her hands.

"Get knotted," she said sweetly.

"Wow," said Courteney. "Can you teach me how to do that? There's a couple of guys I know who would really benefit from –"

"Shelby," said John coldly, "may I have a quiet word?"

41

Luke staggered to his feet. "It's all right," he grinned. "I can take a joke." He held out his hand to Shelby. "I'm sorry. Can we start again?"

Did he mean it? She regarded him warily. Her first instinct was to pack her bags and go straight home. To Calahurst and the Employment Office? Perhaps not.

"OK," she relented, "but pull any of that sexist crap on me again –"

"I won't, cross my heart. How about some champagne as a peace offering?"

"You can buy me a *beer*," she muttered grudgingly.

The conversation began to buzz around them.

Ross moved over to Courteney. "I see you've already met Bruno."

"Bruno?" Courteney stared across at the balding lump of lard still gazing forlornly across the room. *"He's* Bruno?"

"He'll be watching over you for the next couple of months. He'll take care of that chap who's been hassling you."

"He's my *bodyguard*? I thought he was some mad fan! I was just about to get Shelby to lay him out with one of her Jackie Chan impressions."

"Sorry, I should have introduced you sooner. Is something wrong?"

Courteney glowered. "Whitney Houston had Kevin Costner for *her* bodyguard and who do I get? *I* get Danny DeVito."

Chapter Four

Tuesday

Forty-five minutes after Luke's head hit his pillow, he was woken by a phone call from Baz, the second assistant director, to remind him he was due in make-up at six, on set by eight. He staggered into the bathroom and threw up. Hangover City. And, judging by the frenzied party still jangling inside his head, it was going to take more than a couple of aspirin and a glass of orange juice to evict this one.

Even a hot shower failed to revive him. Studiously avoiding the congealing fried breakfast laid out for him on the dining-table, he hauled his wreck of a body to the door to check if his copy of *The Sun* had arrived – and met a pair of sensible lace-ups standing right outside. And they had sensible legs sticking out of the top.

He dragged his eyes higher, feeling as though they were swimming naked through half a ton of shingle

43

and several large coral reefs, and focused on black bootcut trousers, a shiny jacket with threadbare cuffs and a dazzling array of filigree silver buttons. He stood up, pulling his bathrobe more firmly around him, and found he was looking at an impudent pixie face surrounded by a cloud of red hair.

Great – the bodyguard.

"Christ," he grumbled, "have you been camped out here all night?"

Her tentative smile vanished into a prim scarlet line and she pushed past him. "Of course not, I have a perfectly good room of my own."

Last night came back to haunt him. Now he remembered why he had a bruise on his backside the size of a small rain cloud.

"Oh, what beautiful flowers!" said Shelby, pausing by a huge vase of red roses. "Are they from one of your fans?"

"No," replied Luke shortly. "My agent. He says they're for good luck. I think he's taking the piss . . ."

Realising Shelby had just waltzed towards his bedroom, and unable to remember where he had deposited last night's sweaty, smoky clothes, he strode after her, blocking her way.

"Excuse me, I believe this is my –"

She ducked under his arm and, stepping blithely over a pair of discarded jeans with boxer shorts nesting on top, went to look out of the window. "I was told you had a five am call. You think I enjoy getting up this early?"

"No, else you wouldn't be so crabby."

"Crabby?" She turned to look at him in outrage. "Me?"

He felt his face smile despite himself. She looked so cute. Then his left buttock began to throb. There was going to be one helluva bruise . . .

"Crabby," he repeated firmly. The thing about women was that you had to show them who was boss. Allow them an inch and they'd be recommending colour schemes, leaving Garrard's catalogues all over the place and asking if Tarquin was a sensible name for a baby. "Give me twenty minutes and I'll meet you downstairs."

"I'll wait." She sat on the window seat, her arms folded defiantly across her chest.

He could have some fun with Miss Bodyguard, he thought. How much humiliation would it take for her pale freckly skin to turn the same shade as her hair?

His fingers slid through the knot in the belt of his bathrobe – and paused. In *Oxford Blues*, he had disrobed in front of a prospective six million BBC2 viewers, in a scene which included cavorting naked in the Cherwell – with several hundred students whooping from the riverbank which it had taken forever to edit out. Today there were no cameras, no script, no director to tell him how to play the scene. Miss Bodyguard was nervously chewing on her bottom lip. She was not nearly as tough as she pretended to be. God, he was a bastard. She was only doing her job after all.

Wearily, he re-knotted the belt and was about to turn caveman and kick Shelby out, when more of last night filtered back to him. "You'll wait downstairs," he said firmly.

"I'm your bodyguard. How the hell can I protect you if I'm downstairs?"

"As someone once said, I'm only an actor, not JFK. I want to get showered and dressed, without an audience. If there is an assassin in the shower I'll call room service."

He suddenly noticed her beautiful green-gold eyes, glittering dangerously. Her self-confidence had returned in spades.

"You're not taking me seriously," she complained.

He folded his arms. "OK, name me one person who was assassinated in the shower."

"Janet Leigh."

"That doesn't count. She was an actress."

"I rest my case."

He grinned. "Are you taking the piss?"

"Just checking to see if you have a sense of humour."

"I have; Ross doesn't. If I'm not in make-up by six o'clock I'm liable to be fired. *Please* may I get dressed?"

"OK, Bashful." She jumped off the window seat and cheekily twanged the belt of his bathrobe. "I'll meet you in the downstairs lounge in thirty minutes."

* * *

By five-thirty the minibus driver was impatiently revving up outside the front door. Luke, Shelby, Octavia, Courteney and a granite-faced Bruno all piled on, although it was only a short distance down the hill to the shoot – the landscaped gardens of Prior Park at Combe Down. Collapsing into the first seat on the bus, Shelby woke up ten minutes later with her head on Luke's shoulder.

"Just who is protecting who around here?" muttered Octavia waspishly.

Shelby was mortified at being caught napping. "God, Luke, I'm most terribly sorry –"

"That's what happens after five am calls." Luke smiled sleepily at her. "I once worked with an actress who used to nod off between takes, yet she never once forgot her lines."

"That would be me," smirked Courteney.

Luke playfully punched her shoulder. "No, you nod off *during* takes!"

"No one's wised to me yet!" Sticking out her tongue, Courteney jumped from the minibus and ran off towards Make-up, leaving Bruno panting in her wake.

Shelby caught Luke's arm as he was about to follow. "It won't happen again."

"Pity." He held out his hand to help her descend the minibus steps but she brushed him away in irritation. "I thought police officers were used to shift work?"

Which served her right for her over-familiarity earlier. Shelby stepped from the minibus to find it parked in a yard crammed with trailers and swarming with people, all pouring through the wooden gate into a huge meadow. It looked like Glastonbury Festival minus the mud. Luke disappeared into the make-up trailer and Shelby, deciding he was quite safe in there, joined

47

the queue at the caterers' van for some toast and coffee. In front of her was Bruno, his square head disappearing into his massive shoulders without the intervention of a neck.

She decided to introduce herself. "Hi, I'm Shelby Roberts and you must be Danny, Courteney's minder?"

"Bodyguard," he corrected pompously. "And my name is Bruno."

"It is? Then why did I call you Dan- Ah, yes . . ." She flushed with embarrassment but Bruno was too busy piling up his cardboard plate with toast, eggs, sausages, fried eggs and mushrooms. As the smell wafted across she began to feel sick.

"Is a film set always this chaotic?" she stumbled on, by way of covering her gaffe. "I never realised there would be so many people."

Bruno seemed to have an internal fight while he debated whether she was worth his condescension. "Sometimes it's worse," he shrugged, showering his meal with salt, pepper and a large dollop of brown sauce. As he folded the toast into a huge sandwich, the egg yolks started to drip down his thick, chunky fingers. He began to devour it in huge bites.

Courteney jumped down from the nearby make-up trailer, stuffing the last of a peanut-butter sandwich between her lips and licking her fingers. Ignoring Bruno, she bounced off towards Irving, scattering hairpins like fairy spears, fake ringlets bouncing beneath a shocking-pink hairnet.

Bruno crammed the remainder of his sandwich into

his mouth, scrunched up the paper plate and aimed it at the bin. Dead on target. He stomped after Courteney without another word.

Shelby didn't know whether to feel relieved or snubbed but drank her coffee and wandered over to the fence to look at the view. It certainly was stunning. Two man-made lakes, one transversed by a beautiful Palladian bridge, and a stunning sweep of meadow up to an imposing mansion on the hill. Prior Park, once the country house of Ralph Allen who, according to the history lesson she had received from Irving, had made one fortune from the Post Office and the second for supplying Bath with the distinctive honey-coloured stone from his quarries in Combe Down.

Hearing a commotion, Shelby turned back to the trailers in time to see Ross squeeze his smart red sports car into the yard, blithely parking it across the minibus, effectively blocking it in. After a cursory exchange with Irving – who was the first assistant director – he wandered off around the site on his own, pausing on the bridge in a complete trance, his hands deep in his pockets, the early morning sunlight turning his auburn hair gold.

The location manager, Jasper Gilbert-Ellis, a handsome young blade with a mop of Byronic black curls and bruised blue eyes who could certainly give Luke a smoulder for his money, had supervised the removal of a length of fencing and was now on his mobile phone to Bristol Airport, checking on the weather report. Shelby glanced up at the sky. Surely he could see there was not a cloud in sight?

She watched Irving, looking a lot like he was filming sheepdog trials, attempting to get the extras onto their horses and halfway up the hill, ready for the first shot. The extras had mostly been drafted in from a local riding school and were chatting nineteen to the dozen, thoroughly over-excited, their horses leaving great piles of manure which the crew were slipping and swearing about in.

Apparently Ross had envisaged a fox fleeing through the woods and down the hill, chased by the Hunt, a violent baying mob, rupturing the calm of the meadow and woodland.

The animal trainer burst out laughing as Irving earnestly relayed Ross's instructions. "Horses *can't* gallop down such steep hills – it's impossible! I'm surprised Mr Whitney doesn't give them parachutes and make them jump."

"Give him time," muttered Irving.

A middle-aged woman, in raincoat and green paisley headscarf, nervously tapped Shelby on the shoulder. She was clutching a little red autograph book and a chewed biro. "Excuse me," she said, "do you know Luke McFadden?"

Another woman, younger and brassier, shivering in a short, purple skirt and matching bare legs, hurried to stand beside her. "We've been here since five o'clock. Do you think you could get us his autograph?"

Shelby regarded them helplessly then, like the answer to a maiden's prayer, Luke chose that moment to step down from the wardrobe trailer, glorious in skin-tight breeches and tight-fitting coat, his gypsy curls gleaming, his white teeth shining. Shelby could almost hear angels sing 'The Hallelujah Chorus'.

"Good morning, ladies," he said cheerfully. "You're up very early."

A strange transformation came over the two women. They turned quite pale and began to shake. The older woman mouthed inaudibly and held out her notebook.

"No problem," said Luke. Indicating for Shelby to turn around, he leant the book against her back to inscribe his message.

Shelby fumed. She was being paid to watch his back not have him write all over hers.

"There you go," Luke said, returning the book to its owner.

"Thank you," breathed the woman. Then, gathering up her courage, gulped, "Are there any other famous actors in this film?"

"Courteney O'Connor?" suggested Luke, keeping a straight face. "She's playing the part of Lady Charlotte, the heroine."

All three women turned to look where he was pointing. Courteney was dreamily wandering up and down the path leading to the bridge for the benefit of the crew, muttering her lines, closely followed by the grips laying tracks, carpenters fitting wedges of wood to level out the tracks, and the visual-effects designer trying to work out where to put his smoke machines. She was still wearing her jeans and sneakers. Bruno was drooling at a discreet distance.

"Hmm," said the woman, the disappointment evident in her voice. "Anyone else?"

"Octavia Shannon? She's the one in the blue riding-habit, talking to the man with the horses."

Octavia, nervously stroking the nose of a beautiful black mare, was in the rather undignified position of having a sound man disappearing beneath her skirts with a microphone but was doing her imperious best to ignore him.

"What's she been in? Is she on the telly?"

"She's done a lot of theatre work."

"A nobody," said the woman to her companion. "Thanks, Lukey. Look forward to seeing you in the film." And the two women waddled off.

Luke laughed at Shelby's dumbfounded expression. "That is what stops me from getting big-headed."

"You're treated like a commodity."

"Polite word," he shrugged. "I've got to go and bond with my horse. Want to tag along?"

"That's what I'm paid for."

He grimaced. "I know, but can't you just pretend to be interested?"

Luke's horse was an elegant chestnut, all tacked up and waiting patiently beneath an oak tree. Luke introduced himself to the animal trainer, a wiry ex-jockey with a weatherbeaten face, who was quite chatty.

"Sherlock," the trainer said proudly, patting the horse's rump, "is a stunt horse, specifically trained to fall on cue."

"Let's hope he's read the script," said Luke.

Shelby loved horses. Her mother, long since divorced from her father, owned a riding stables named Moon River. For the two years between leaving school and taking the police entrance exam, Shelby had worked as a groom. Which basically meant she had spent two years mucking out and cleaning tack, with the occasional 'treat' of dragging a truculent six-year-old and his fat little pony through the King's Forest on a leading rein. She gravitated to Sherlock immediately.

He nudged at her pocket but she turned to him regretfully, "I'm sorry, darling. I don't have anything to give you."

Luke handed her a couple of sugar cubes. "Give him these. I intended them as a bribe."

Shelby promptly handed them back. "Perhaps you'd better hang on to them!"

Luke turned out his pockets to show handfuls of glittering sugar. "I tipped in a whole bowl from the catering van."

The animal trainer suddenly noticed Irving waving frantically from the bridge and took hold of the horse's bridle. "I'm going to take Sherlock up the hill now, Mr McFadden."

"OK," said Luke. He gave Sherlock's nose a last pat. "And remember who it is that gives you the sugar, boy."

"Why do you call him Sherlock?" Shelby asked the animal trainer. "Is it after Sherlock Holmes?"

The animal trainer smiled. "I think you misheard me. The horse's name is Shylock."

"Shakespeare's Shylock?" asked Luke faintly.

"That's right." The animal trainer winked at Shelby. "Because he always gets his pound of flesh . . ."

* * *

The camera had been set up to take a 'wide' shot, on the far side of the top lake, next to the bridge. Ross wanted the Hunt to swoop down the hill towards the bridge and at the last moment veer away. In the second scene, Luke's horse would run straight towards the lake, stop, and Luke – or rather the stunt double – would go straight over Shylock's head and into the water.

Shelby set herself up behind Ross who called, "Action!"

"Quiet on the set!" yelled Irving.

At first the meadow was glorious green tranquillity, then there was the pounding of hooves and the hounds exploded from behind the trees as though they had just charged down the hill, closely followed by a swarm of huntsmen. It was an incredible sight.

They re-shot the scene three times and then, "Cut!" said Ross. "And print."

"Sorry?" said Irving.

"Print," said Ross, irritably. "You know. A take."

"You mean, you don't want to do it again?"

"Even I cannot improve on perfection," said Ross and stalked off. "Set up the next shot."

"Bloody hell," said Irving, in an undertone to Shelby. "Last week he had poor Octavia repeating the same three words forty-two times."

"I *love* you," grinned George, the chubby camera operator, tearing open a bag of Liquorice Allsorts and handing them round. "*I* love you. I love *you!*"

Luke and Shylock gently trotted over. "What's going on?" he asked. "Where's Ross? Are we taking a break or doing a retake straight off?"

Irving attempted to look nonchalant. "Ross thinks that was perfect. We're setting up the next scene."

"Bloody hell," said Luke. He dismounted and handed the horse to his stunt double. "All yours, mate. And don't turn your back on him. He's already taken a chunk out of my arse."

"You ride well," said Shelby.

"I should hope so. I had intensive riding lessons before we started. I couldn't sit down for a month."

The stuntman was watching one rider, in a midnight blue habit, racing along the path at the top of the hill. "Where's Octavia going? Shouldn't someone tell her filming has finished?"

Irving turned to the animal trainer. "I thought you said your horses couldn't gallop uphill?"

"*Down*hill," said the animal trainer. "There's a difference. Besides, Mr Whitney didn't want Miss Shannon with the rest of the hunt as she can't ride. She was supposed to be watching from the top of the hill, as part of the background."

"Well, there's no way she's going to be appearing in the background at that speed," muttered Irving. "She's just a blue blur. Where *does* she think she's going? There's nothing in that direction except –"

"The road!" cried Shelby. "Her horse has bolted!" She grabbed Shylock from the bemused stunt double, lifted her foot into the stirrup and swung her leg over the horse's back.

Luke was almost knocked flying. "Shelby! What the hell are you doing?"

But Shelby dug in her heels and Shylock lurched away, indignant that he had been deprived of the sugar cubes the stuntman had been holding out for him.

"Steady, boy," she said, patting his neck, "you can have your sugar later."

It was a long time since Shelby had been on the back of a horse and it was not helped by the fact that the stirrups had been set up for Luke, who was nearly a foot taller. But Shelby hardly noticed, she was on auto-pilot. It was like being back in the police. There was no excitement, no fear. But she knew the surge of adrenaline would come later, when it was all over.

Shylock was surprisingly obedient and, after staggering up the hill, they cantered along the gravel path running in front of the mansion, then turned right, through the trees, after Octavia. It was dark and gloomy after the bright spring sunshine. All Shelby could see was green spots, so she just had to trust Shylock's judgement. As her leg smashed against a treetrunk she remembered the bit about the 'pound of flesh' and gripped tighter, lowering her head until her nose was almost pressed against Shylock's sweaty neck. She had no wish to be decapitated by a low-hanging branch. As her leg began to burn agonisingly, it was all she could do to hang on.

They were on the straight now, cantering past the National Trust Portaloos and the ticket office. Thankfully, the huge wrought-iron gates were shut and so Octavia's horse veered off down a woodland track, following the stone wall that bordered the road, heading in a circle back towards the lakes.

A young man in a red sweater, with a rifle slung casually over his shoulder, had to dive into the wild garlic as they raced past. "Sorry!" called Shelby but she doubted that he heard her.

As Shylock sensed he was free to do his own thing, Shelby realised she might have made a terrible mistake. Vaguely she remembered her mother telling her that, unlike the movies, the worse thing you can possibly do to a bolting horse is chase it – the horse just gallops faster. Shelby wound her arms around Shylock's neck and prayed.

Gradually, Shylock calmed down and began to catch up on the horse in front. From what Shelby could see of Octavia – which was mostly a blue velvet bottom – the actress had lost both her reins and stirrups and was clinging on for dear life around her horse's neck. At least this way she missed the overhanging branches which were scratching at Shelby's face and almost ripping her hair out like a Sioux Indian on the make.

The path suddenly plunged down a steep hill and Shelby, sensing it was now or never, urged Shylock level with Octavia. Of course, Octavia's horse, thinking this was a great game, inched ahead. Shelby risked a look forward and, through the burgeoning foliage, saw an open gate and the narrow ribbon of grey tarmac that was the road.

"Pull her up!" she shouted to Octavia. "For God's sake, pull her up!"

"I can't," screamed Octavia, between hysterical sobbing.

"If she gets out onto the road you'll both be killed!"

Octavia gave a whimper then, to Shelby's horror, she seemed to half-slither, half-fall from the back of her horse, crashing into the undergrowth and hitting her head on a tree. Her horse, confused, began to slow. This was the moment. Shelby spurred on Shylock and drawing level with the riderless horse, leant over and grabbed his reins. The horse tossed its head, yanking her arm, and she was pulled from Shylock's back and dragged along the gravel path, ripping her trousers to shreds.

Both horses suddenly stopped and stood still, their heads hanging guiltily, panting and snorting. Shylock nudged her shoulder.

"I'm all right," she laughed, half-crying, stroking his nose gratefully. But then she realised he was after the sugar in her pocket and irritably shoved him away.

The animal trainer appeared beside her, red-faced and sweating, hauling her up by her bad arm. He didn't appear overly appreciative that she had just risked life and limb to save his horses either.

"What the hell did you think you were doing!" he raged. "You should never chase after a bolting horse like that! You terrified the life out of them!"

Shelby sat back on the ground to save the trouble of

fainting onto it. "At least your horse is alive!" she snarled back. "And unhurt. Unlike poor Octavia!"

"Bloody actresses, they have two or three lessons and think they can ride."

Shelby shut her eyes and just let his fury wash over her. Suddenly she was lifted into a reassuring male embrace.

"I thought you were supposed to be *my* bodyguard?" grinned Luke, as he slapped a grubby-looking handkerchief over the blood pouring from her knee and then, heaving her into his arms, staggered down the hill to the First Aid tent.

Chapter Five

Filming had continued after Octavia's accident – the cost of making a movie was so high Ross could not afford sentimentality, although he did accompany Octavia in the ambulance to hospital, leaving Irving to shoot her scenes using a body double.

Shelby had also spent the rest of the morning in Casualty but was discharged after being told she had merely suffered cuts and bruising. When she emerged, blinking, into the bright afternoon sunlight, wondering if she could afford a taxi back to the hotel, she found Luke waiting in the car park. Back in his jeans and Clash T-shirt, he was leaning casually against a yellow Mini, signing autographs for a steady stream of hospital visitors and patients, some still in their pyjamas.

He grinned as he saw her approach. "I was coming to collect you but this was as far as I could get. Sorry!"

Shelby was touched that he'd made the effort. Maybe he wouldn't be so bad to work for after all.

Luke scrawled his name across a tatty appointment card, handed it to the teenage girl who had given it to him and then firmly put the lid back on the pen. "OK, folks, that's your lot."

His fans grumbled good-naturedly and returned to the hospital.

"It's very kind of you to come and collect me," said Shelby, as he unlocked the passenger door for her. "But shouldn't you be filming?"

"Yes."

Shelby regarded him helplessly. "Won't you get into trouble?"

"I'm sure Irving can do without me for one afternoon."

He squeezed into the car. Despite having the seat back as far as it would go, his knees were virtually jammed beneath his chin, his body bent double to avoid clunking his head on the roof.

Shelby recognised it as her brother's car by the Simpsons key-ring swinging from the ignition and the Corrs set up in the CD player. It took several attempts to start. Irving had owned the car since college, named it 'Alice' after his first (and last) serious girlfriend and was a bit vague about having it serviced. He was also a bit vague about cleaning it, realised Shelby, as a Coke can rolled against her ankle. She picked it up, absent-mindedly crunched it flat with one hand, and neatly tucked it into the glove compartment.

She was so relieved when the car finally spluttered into life that she missed the amused, sideways glance Luke gave her.

"Wave," he prompted, as they chugged past his fans.

With Luke lurching around corners, as though in second place at the Monte Carlo Grand Prix, it did not take them long to reach the hotel. Before Shelby could undo her seatbelt, he was standing beside her, holding the door open. As she hobbled painfully up the staircase to her suite, he disappeared off to the kitchens to cadge her some lunch.

This was all very nice, reflected Shelby, but she should really be doing this sort of thing for him. *Who's guarding who . . .* Octavia's scathing words echoed back to her. Or was this Luke's way of proving he didn't need a minder?

The faint chill of suspicion was well *in situ* as she clumped across the polished oak floor of her sitting-room and collapsed onto the squashy pink sofa. Damn, the remote control was just out of reach and she could really do with a drink. Her knee was killing her. 'Just cuts and bruises?' Ha! She'd never mambo again.

Luke arrived with her lunch on a tray. What a sweetie! She watched him lay it out on a little table. Wholemeal salad rolls, fruit and mineral water. How healthy could you get? That was the last time she'd ever send a vegetarian to buy her lunch.

"I had to kiss the assistant chef to get you this," he said, shaking out a pink napkin and dropping it onto her lap. "So I hope you think it's worth it."

Shelby visualised a temperamental Frenchman with garlic breath. "You didn't have to go that far."

He gave her another sideways glance. "She was very attractive actually." From the back pocket of his jeans he brandished a telephone number scrawled across a folded-up menu. "I've also promised to get her tickets to the premiere of *All That She Wants* next week."

Talk about a girl in every pub. Shelby pursed her lips with disapproval. Didn't he ever let up?

Catching her by surprise, Luke grabbed her ankles and swivelled her round so that her legs were resting on the cushions. "Now you just take it easy," he said, as the sofa virtually swallowed her whole. "Relax for the afternoon. You'll feel better in no time."

He was definitely up to something. Shelby struggled into a sitting position. "Are you going back to the set?"

"No, I thought I'd go for a ride on the bike. I need to get away, clear my head."

"You should have said." She swung her legs back onto the floor. "I'll come with you."

He laughed, not realising she was serious. "Are you crazy?"

"My knee's not that bad," she lied. "It's just a bit stiff, that's all."

He stopped smiling. "Sorry, but you'll be a liability."

Liability! "I've ridden pillion before. And besides, I'm your minder. I have to go everywhere with you."

His violet-blue eyes began to look seriously stormy. "I don't need a bodyguard when I'm not working."

Shelby gritted her teeth. Perhaps he wasn't very bright. "I'm supposed to be with you from when you wake up to when you go to bed. Within reason, of course," she added quickly. "I don't think I'm expected to go to the loo with you."

But his friendly, open manner had vanished. "I'm glad to hear it."

"I *am* coming with you." She met his gaze square on.

"The hell you are."

"Luke, I'm only trying to do my job."

"Let's get this straight. Ross hired you, Ross pays your wages but I call the shots. You can follow me all round Bath, like Mary's fucking lamb, but only when I'm working. The rest of the time I'm on my own. I've got to live, for Christ's sake."

Talk about Jekyll and Hyde, she thought sourly. Mr Sweetness & Light totally disappeared if he didn't get his own way.

"I only want to do my job," she repeated mechanically. If she'd known he was going to be this awkward, she would never have taken it on. And to think, she could have been wrestling with shoplifters at Boots. "Don't make this difficult for me."

"Then give me some time on my own. I've been filming non-stop since the end of February; weekends, evenings, I'm paying for this film in blood, beers and hangovers. If I don't take a break, without feeling someone is watching my every movement, I'm going to go crazy."

He smiled, a charming boyish smile which probably worked wonders on his girlfriends, but for Shelby, being brought up in a house full of men, it had no effect at all – apart from making her want to stake an early claim on the bathroom.

"I promise not to visit any houses of ill-repute, get into a brawl, or go partying with Chris Evans," he said. "Come on, give me a break."

Left or right femur? was the thought which popped involuntarily into her head.

For a long moment they stared at each other, attempting, through sheer willpower, to force the other to back down.

"Wherever you go, I go too," she reiterated quietly. "That's the job I'm paid to do."

Luke abruptly turned for the door. "Fine," he said. "Let's see how long you last running behind me."

* * *

Life was easy for Courteney O'Connor. Her daddy was rich, her mother stunning. They were even still married to each other – which was a bit of a record for the circle of high society in which they moved. Courteney never had to struggle for anything. Utterly gorgeous, extremely popular, naturally bright; she had been a straight 'A' student until she hit fourteen, then flunked all her exams and announced to her parents that she was, like, totally bored with Savannah and was off to Hollywood to be a movie star.

Her parents did not blink an eyelid. Her father had connections with a high-powered entertainment agency, Courteney went for an audition and by the end of the week was starring in her first Disney film. To everyone's surprise, not only could she act, she was actually rather good. Every film she starred in (and Courteney O'Connor always *starred*) made a fortune at the box office. And, thanks to her father's canny negotiations, Courteney was inevitably on a percentage of the profits.

In a career spanning just over four years, Courteney had never won an Oscar – but she didn't give a shit. In fact, Courteney was famous for never giving a shit about anything. Although she revealed all for a *Playboy* centrefold on her eighteenth birthday ("A present to myself before I get too old"), she had never taken illegal substances, never felt the urge to make a rap record and she never ever got hung-up on men. She happily slept with anyone who asked her and, if it didn't work out – well, hey, *c'est la vie*.

And then she met Ross Whitney.

They had met at a typical A-list Hollywood party. Courteney was the guest of honour; Ross, although a respected British director, was only in town to raise cash for his next film. Courteney, bowled over by his haughty, aristocratic good looks, found him hard going, particularly when she couldn't get him to utter more than one syllable all evening. The next day, however, he had invited her to lunch at his hotel and was positively gregarious. Apparently he had been a huge fan of hers for years. Just meeting her in person had been enough to make him totally clam up. He'd made a right idiot of himself. And now he wanted to make it up to her.

Courteney was touched. She was not quite sure how it had happened but, by late afternoon, they were lying in bed after hours of frantic sex – and she had signed a contract to appear in his next three films.

Ross took off for Europe the next morning, without bothering to say goodbye. Despite many transatlantic phone calls, faxes and e-mails, she did not meet him again until she started rehearsing *All That She Wants*, in some yucky school hall in South London. And found out she was only playing a supporting role in the film her father had financed and the main part had gone to (wait for it) *Ross's fiancée*!

Courteney's father, loyal to the last, had promptly withdrawn his support, confident the film would fold. This grand gesture made no difference – Ross's prospective in-laws were just as wealthy. Courteney, tied to an unbreakable contract, had been tricked into selling her soul to a devil.

Now it was payback time.

* * *

When Ross had taken off in the ambulance with Octavia, Courteney had bribed one of the sparks to drive her into town on a shopping expedition. She was unwilling to believe that Bath could offer anything that rivalled Rodeo Drive but she was desperate to avoid further contract with Bruno. This was the only way she could think to get away from him and simultaneously work on plan B: How To Get Ross Back And Make His Life Hell.

Ross still fancied her, she was certain of that, although he didn't love her. Courteney was unfazed; after all, Ross Whitney didn't love anyone.

In fact, Courteney had so much fun in Bath she had

to hire two taxis for the return journey – one for her and one for all her purchases. She was just negotiating with the hotel manager for another room to store them all in, when Luke suddenly swept down the wide curving staircase, very Rhett Butler-ish, with a face like an iceberg about to sink *The Titanic*.

He must have had a row with his bodyguard, she decided. As she watched him barge through a crowd of gawping tourists, she quickly handed the manager a wad of twenties in payment for her additional room and ran after Luke, as Plans C, D and E, exploded into her consciousness, all involving Making The Bastard Jealous.

"Where are you going?" she asked breathlessly, as he climbed onto a huge Harley Davidson parked outside, jamming his helmet over his head.

The answer was muffled but Courteney didn't care. She could see Ross coming up the drive in his Alfa Romeo sports car and the timing could not have been more perfect.

"Can I come?"

For a moment he did not appear to be listening, his gaze centred somewhere above her head, on one of the hotel's many windows. "OK," he said at length, "but you'll need to borrow Kit's helmet."

"Excellent," said Courteney, turning on her heel and running back into reception.

"Hurry!" hollered Luke. "If you're not back in two minutes I'm going without you."

He meant it too. He was already halfway down the

drive when Courteney got back. She yelled indignantly and he halted while she ran after him. She jumped up behind him and he shot off almost before she had got her arms around his waist. But it was worth it. Worth it for the look of horror on Ross's face as he watched his two most valuable stars roar off into the sunset. But she did feel a twinge of guilt as she caught the look of utter disbelief on the face of Luke's bodyguard as she was left standing forlornly on the doorstep.

Instead of driving into the country, as she had expected, Luke took the A4 to Bristol before veering off towards the Mendips. After thirty minutes of shooting down narrow country lanes, involving several, heart-stopping, near-misses with tractors and sheep, Luke rattled over a cattle grid and ended up in a large parking lot.

As he stopped in the shade of a huge chestnut tree, Courteney took off her helmet and looked around. "Where the hell are we? Ross is going to think we've eloped." *With any luck.*

Luke gave a wry smile. "And is breaking open the champagne right now."

Courteney swung her leg off the back of the bike and stretched, revealing two inches of tanned, goose-pimpled skin between her pink Capri pants and matching angora sweater. She caught Luke staring at the diamond through her navel. Men – they were so predictable.

"Do you like it?" She pulled up her sweater to give him a better look. "I had it done in London just before we started at Shepperton. Ross hates it. He makes Elliott stick a Band-aid over, in case it shows through the dress."

Luke shook his head in disbelief. "Why don't you just take it out?"

"The hole might grow over. It hurt like hell. Dean had his nipple pierced at the same time. It looks really cool. Why don't you have yours done?"

Luke blanched. "Dean is a twenty-one-year-old pop star. He can get away with that sort of thing."

Realising they were attracting attention from a group of picnickers, Courteney automatically ran her fingers through her silky blonde hair, spiking it all up. "So where are we?" She sauntered across the blistering hot tarmac, aware all eyes were on her, and peered through the rusty wire fence. "Is this a lake I see before me, or a false creation, proceeding from a helmet-oppressed brain?"

Luke watched her posturing with amusement, aware she was attempting to impress with her cock-eyed Shakespeare. "We're at Chew Valley Lake," he replied. "I dated a local girl while I was at Bristol University. We used to come here and talk for hours."

"Talk eh?" said Courteney dryly.

Luke did not reply, merely flipped out the stand on the motorbike and followed her onto the grass. He was instantly surrounded by a flock of squawking ducks, flapping around his feet, attempting to eat his jeans.

"Must be female ducks," grinned Courteney. "That will teach you to run off without your bodyguard."

Luke gently booted away the ducks and sat on an ornamental rock just as a little girl came running across the grass towards him. For a moment he tensed, then realised, as she was followed by her father carrying a bag of sandwich crusts, that they were actually there to feed the ducks.

Boy, was he twitchy, thought Courteney. She sat gingerly on the other rock, first checking for duck doo-doos.

"I don't need a bodyguard to protect me from the public," said Luke, staring out across the lake. "The only problem I have is with the press. Ross is over-reacting. This is a free country. If I'm in a public place my photo is going to be taken, either by some devoted fan or a freelance professional. There's nothing I can do about it. The best approach is to brazen it out until the press get bored. Wearing Mickey Mouse masks or bringing on the heavy mob just exacerbates the problem – and makes one look an idiot to boot."

"I totally agree," said Courteney fervently. "But we're still stuck with the bodyguards. Would you consider swapping Shelby for Bruno?"

"No way!"

A Japanese tour coach rumbled into the car park behind them. It had two storeys, tinted windows and dozens of excited holiday-makers pressing their noses against the glass, pointing and waving at Luke.

"Are you big in Japan?" teased Courteney.

Luke wasn't laughing. "Oh great," he murmured. "I declare it open season on movie stars. We'll have to go."

Courteney frowned. Plan C was starting to look shaky. "But we've only just got here," she protested, slipping her arm through his. "Are you sure they've recognised you?"

"Actually, the Japanese are always·mistaking me for Hugh Grant. If I get one more question about marrying Elizabeth Hurley, when I've never even met the woman –"

"I'll soon fix that." Courteney wrapped her arms around his neck, pulled him down to her level and kissed him soundly. After a few seconds Luke joined in. The Japanese, delighted at witnessing two such famous film stars necking in a Somerset car park, broke into a polite round of applause.

Luke pulled away first, frowning.

"Wow," said Courteney softly, pulling his head down for an encore.

Luke firmly took her hands from his neck and propelled her towards the motorbike.

"What's up with you?" grumbled Courteney.

"I've only just got out of one relationship," he replied slowly, and she could see he was carefully choosing his words. "I don't want to rush into another. Besides, I make it a rule never to get involved with my leading ladies. It can cause all sorts of problems."

"Like you and Paige," she said, and clapped her hand over her mouth. "Oops!" Worried about what else might come out of her mouth if she opened it, Courteney firmly clamped the end of her tongue between her teeth. The pain concentrated the mind wonderfully.

"Oops, indeed," said Luke dryly, pulling his leather gloves over his hands and picking up his helmet.

Courteney couldn't understand why he was so calm. Unless, "Don't you fancy me? You seem to fancy everyone else."

"You're extremely attractive, Courteney. You deserve better than a one-night stand. And that's all I'm capable of at the moment."

"Fine by me," said Courteney and reached out towards him, only to find her arms full of motorcycle helmet.

"Japanese at two o'clock," said Luke, as the electronic doors of the coach slid open and the tourists flooded across the car park. "Armed with Nikons."

Courteney sulkily pulled the helmet over her blonde curls and jumped up onto the bike. As they swept out of the car park onto the road, Luke almost collided with a BMW parked on the verge, its hazard lights blinking merrily. He swerved violently to avoid going straight over the bonnet, nearly depositing Courteney into the ditch.

"Bloody stupid place to park," he grumbled. "Are you OK?"

Courteney said nothing. Any excitement she had felt in kissing Luke had just disappeared through a hole in her stomach. There had been a logo printed on the side of the car. And underneath was written: *Firestorm Productions.*

Chapter Six

Wednesday

The resulting headlines were much worse than Shelby could have imagined. All the tabloids screamed 'exclusive' but ran pretty much the same story. With each paper she picked up, it just got worse. Oblivious to the interest she was causing to the reception staff, Shelby threw herself into one of the high-backed leather chairs around the fireplace and began to frantically leaf through the pages, her fingers turning black from the newsprint.

Stars In Their Eyes! Courteney O'Connor and Luke McFadden in love. It's official! proclaimed *The Mirror*.

All That He Wants! Skip Paige – I Love Courteney! declared *The Sun*.

"Oh my God!" she wailed, dropping the newspaper over her face. "Can it get any worse?"

It could and it did. Some of the other tabloids were not content just to publish photographs with witty comments. If they couldn't get in touch with Luke for a quote, they made up their own – and dragged up his wedding fiasco to boot. There were pages of the stuff. Reams and reams of drivel. All because of one little kiss. Shelby was amazed at the scale of it all. She had been employed to protect Luke from the press. He couldn't have received more media exposure if he had hired Tara P-T.

She had better apologise to Ross – and offer her resignation at the same time. It would be far more dignified than being fired. She smoothed down her skirt, tucked *The Sun* under her arm and went back upstairs to knock on the door to Ross's suite.

The door flew open and Ross was standing there, enveloped in one of the hotel's robes and a cloud of steam, looming over her like a bird of prey, unshaven and cantankerous. "Yes?" he growled. "What do you want?"

Somebody didn't get his beauty sleep last night.

Ross peered short-sightedly at her. He was not wearing his wire-rimmed spectacles and for the first time she could see his eyes without her own image reflected back. Somehow, it was worse. Like visiting a tiger's cage at the zoo – and finding all the bars had gone.

"Oh," he said at length. "It's you – the bodyguard. Come in." He stepped back to allow her to enter.

She had forgotten he was so attractive and endeavoured to keep her eyes firmly fixed on his face, rather than lingering on that triangle of golden skin at the base of his throat, where the blue towelling robe failed to wrap fully over. The sitting-room lights caught on the droplets of moisture trickling over his collar bone and, as he turned to face her, she found she was breathing the aroma of his expensive citrus shower gel.

"What's Luke done now?" asked Ross. "Has one of his girlfriends finally put a bullet through his brain?" He gave a twisted smile. "She'd have to be a damn good shot." Then, when she didn't reply, "What can I do for you?"

You're *gorgeous*, Shelby was horrified to find herself thinking. And had to move away in case he could read her mind. He had a nice suite. Larger than hers but smaller than Luke's. Pastel green walls. Pastel blue sofa. Very, er, pastel. She found herself staring at an Impressionist print, frantically counting waterlilies. *Get a grip, Shelby!*

Ross, perplexed, came to stand beside her. "Is something the matter?"

She thrust the paper at him.

He raised two black eyebrows. "You've been reading *The Sun*? Not quite my cup of tea admittedly but hardly a hangable offence."

Ha, Ha. She smiled politely. "Wait till you see page four." *Then you can fire me.*

"Page four," he repeated, carefully straightening out the crumpled newspaper and turning the pages. Then he stopped and gave a low whistle. "Luke and Courteney? Who would have thought it?" And he began to laugh, his eyes crinkling up at the corners; it totally transformed his face, making him look much more approachable. Almost friendly.

"I thought you would be furious . . ." she said slowly. "My job was to keep Luke out of trouble. I'm aware I've brought the name of your company into disrepute. I'll resign."

"Resign away but you haven't done anything to harm Firestorm Productions."

She stared at him. "But the bad publicity . . ."

"What bad publicity? The name of the film is mentioned – let's see, one, two, *three* times. Firestorm Productions twice. *I* even get a mention – *and* they spelt my name right." He smiled again; it lit up his harsh features. "I'd call that pretty good publicity."

"You would?" Perhaps it was because of the early hour but Shelby was having trouble getting her head around his logic. How could Luke and Courteney, snogging in a car park, get the British public into the cinema to watch a movie. *Because the film is called* A Midsummer Kiss, *dope!*

Ross, bored with the lack of stimulating conversation, had wandered into his bedroom and, rifling through his wardrobe, began to lay clothes neatly onto his bed. Briefly she wondered if he laid his women in a similar – *no*, she wasn't even going to go there.

She fidgeted while she waited for him to finish. Did this mean she was dismissed? Should she just mutter, 'See you', and leave, collecting her P45 en route?

"If you've had a fight with Luke I suggest you make it up," he said, his voice muffled as he ferreted around in the base of his wardrobe. "And if he wants to sack you that's fine. But it's between you and him. He's the one that's had his private life paraded through the press."

On pages 4, 5, 6 and 7, thought Shelby glumly.

He stuck his head back around the door. "Of course, if he hadn't gone tearing off on his motorbike, this would never have happened. So I think the best plan would be to stop him riding it until after filming."

"Oh no, please no!" Shelby stared at him in absolute horror. That would make her really popular. How would she and Luke ever forge any kind of working relationship now?

Ross was warming to his theme. "I'm sure there's something in his contract about insurance risks. After all, what's the point of hiring a stuntman to take a fall off a horse, while he's racing around the countryside as though he's remaking *Mission: Impossible 2*?"

Oh misery, Luke was really going to hate her now . . .

Ross strode back through the sitting-room, pausing with one hand on the bathroom door. "Now you've got this off your chest, may I have my shave?"

"Yes, yes, of course. Sorry to have bothered you." As she squeezed past him, she made the mistake of looking up and got the full force of those dark grey eyes, the high Slavic cheekbones, the slightly crooked nose. How could she have thought him a geek? There was more sensuality in those hawk-like features than in a room full of pretty-boy actors.

"Apology accepted," he said softly and opened the suite door.

* * *

By sprinting through reception and out into the car park, Shelby just managed to flag down the minibus before it began to lumber up the hill and, as all the seats were taken, ended up playing the gooseberry, sandwiched between Bruno and Courteney at the back.

Courteney, who had obviously not seen the unflattering pictures of herself, sticking her tongue down Luke's throat, splashed across every news-stand in Britain, was delighted to see her. And it wasn't long before she had launched into her usual running commentary on her life to date, pausing only to go into raptures at the views from the minibus as they drove down the hill, extolling the beauties of the English countryside and being overwhelmed about how green everything was.

That's because it rains all the time, thought Shelby, looking at the grey skies in trepidation. Bath seemed to have a weather zone all of its own. She let Courteney's little-girl voice drift over her, the Forrest Gump accent rising and dipping like the surrounding countryside, and stifled a yawn. Gush, gush, gush. Shelby hadn't heard so many adjectives since she had failed her English Lit.

In between bouts of tugging her skirt to a respectable length, Shelby watched Bruno from the corner of her eye. He was sitting in silence (not that he could get a word in edgeways), his face as impassive as a statue on Easter Island, immaculately dressed in a dark blue suit, highly polished shoes, silk tie and handkerchief. With his army haircut, he stood out from the hippie, scruffy film crowd like a Quaker at a *Star Trek* convention. Yet she had to admit he commanded respect. Or should that be awe? After all, he was built like a barn door. The stereotypical bodyguard.

Perhaps she should model herself on Bruno? Together they could run alongside the minibus, in their suits and dark glasses, squawking to each other through tiny hand-held microphones and ear-pieces, like the FBI agents surrounding the President of the United States. Shelby burst into laughter.

"What's the joke?" asked Bruno solemnly.

Shelby peered over the top of her sunglasses to check that he had actually spoken. Behind the rigid, almost military, facade there was something sad in Bruno's eyes. He had beautiful eyes, she realised suddenly. Brown and liquid, rather like a dog her mother had once owned. Shelby could quite imagine him as a dog. A rather melancholy Rottweiler.

"Oh nothing," she said airily. Instinctively she realised he knew she found his appearance amusing.

"I'm just thinking how ridiculous I must look," she improvised hastily. "Like a Girl Guide with a hangover. Maybe I should stick to the trouser suits. They're more practical."

"You look very smart," he said sincerely, keeping his melancholy gaze well away from her pale, freckled legs, as the minibus came to a standstill on the road outside Prior Park. "And you know, in our business, impressions really do count."

His sincerity made her feel worse.

After she stepped down from the bus, she walked over

to the bridge where the cameras were being set up but she couldn't find Luke anywhere. Which was an excellent start. A minder with no one to mind. She double-checked the wardrobe and make-up trailers but had no luck. So where was he? She was sure he was due on set today. It was written on the call-sheet Irving had given her.

She searched for Irving. He had disappeared too. This was getting ridiculous.

Her violet sandals, with their tiny heels and narrow straps (totally unsuitable for the rugged terrain) began to pinch. She eased them off and wriggled her toes in the cool grass. A couple of the crew wandered past and wolf-whistled. She smiled in resignation. They were too far away to thump.

Ross was discussing the day's scenes with Jeremy, the director of photography, a thin aesthetic man in brown cords, tweed jacket and flat cap. He looked as though he'd be more at home shooting game than Hollywood movies. Assistant directors two and three were hanging on their every word.

Ross smiled at her and raised his hand in a wave. He had managed to have his shave, she noticed, as she stooped to collect up her shoes. And he had slicked his auburn hair back into its usual style. It did suit him though, throwing into relief that marvellous aristocratic bone structure, only spoilt by the bump on his nose. She wandered over.

As those cool grey eyes settled thoughtfully on her, she realised he still wasn't wearing his wire-rimmed spectacles. Perhaps he had contact lenses?

"What are you shooting today?" she asked.

"Luke," said Ross, totally oblivious to any implied irony. "Today's the day he gets his soaking."

ADs two and three chuckled toadyingly.

Shelby flicked her eyes towards them and felt a wave of sympathy for the absent Luke. Bloody sycophants. "I thought the stuntman was to take the ducking?"

"He did," replied Ross. "Yesterday afternoon. Over the horse's head and into the river. Five takes, wasn't it, Baz?"

"Four," said Baz, the second AD, a short, pug-faced man with a receding hairline, a ponytail to make up for it and a Planet Hollywood baseball cap, worn the wrong way round. "Excellent man, that stunt double," he continued, in his carefully cultivated 'mockney' accent. He dragged his eyes up from Shelby's short skirt and smiled at her ingratiatingly. "That's the thing, you know. You can always get another actor but a good stuntman is worth his weight in gold."

"Hardly," snapped Shelby. "As my brother says, Luke's name above the credits guarantees 'bums on seats'."

"So does Mr Whitney's," scowled Baz.

"Talking of Luke," Ross hastily injected, "where is he?"

Shelby blushed. "I've . . . er, lost him."

"Perhaps you ought to consider another career?" suggested Baz.

Before she had the chance to retaliate, Ross slid his arm through hers and said, "Come with me – you used to work for the police – I've got something to show you."

Your etchings? thought Shelby hopefully, as he whisked her off down the hill.

But Ross was leading her to the bridge and Shelby realised that this was to be where they would be filming Luke's 'ducking'. The sparks had rigged up enormous arc lights, trailing thick black cables to the generators. The lighting technicians and their gaffer were re-arranging them, the grips laying the inevitable tracks and heaving the massive camera on top of them.

I wonder if it's got brakes, Shelby found herself thinking. The tracks seemed to go very close to the water.

The bridge, an attractive folly, was constructed from the inevitable Bath stone and transversed the man-made ponds at the bottom of the hill. Shelby could not see if there were any fish, but there were two swans weaving between the frilly green weeds, causing endless ripples, preventing the reflection of the bridge from becoming too chocolate-boxy. Courteney was feeding them the remains of her breakfast.

"You do realise," said Ross cuttingly, "that if any bread floats into shot you'll be the one fishing it out?"

Courteney just stuck her tongue out, defiantly tearing her baguette into larger chunks.

Ross led Shelby up the steps and paused, leaning over the balustrade and peering into the water beneath. "Beautiful, isn't it?" he said.

"Very romantic," agreed Shelby, arranging herself

romantically against one of the Ionic columns supporting the roof.

Ross gazed dreamily into the cool, green depths below. "Of course," he began, "go to any stately home, of around the same period, and you'll find an identical bridge and identical water gardens." He turned around. "Look, from here you can see the whole sweep of the landscape up to the house. They're setting up the camera over there, we'll have Courteney walking across the bridge with armfuls of wild flowers, we'll have the house in the background –"

Birds singing, violins playing, thought Shelby, stifling a giggle. The film sounded more Barbara Cartland than Jane Austen.

"And then the sight of the Hunt swarming down towards her," he continued rapturously. "Earthy, sweaty, bloody. Close-up of the fox, terrified, running for his life –"

"And then you'll have the RSPCA after you as well as the National Trust."

Which snapped Ross right out of his daydream. "We used a tame fox and the only person chasing him was the trainer's eight-year-old daughter. The shots are already in the can." He took her shoulders and turned her towards the balustrade. "Now, see this? Does that look like a bullet-hole to you?"

"A bullet-hole?" Who gave a monkey's about bullet-holes?

"You see here, this scar in the stone?" He ran his fingers across one of the columns.

Shelby forced herself to pay attention. "It looks like part of the graffiti. Is that what all the fuss was about yesterday?"

"It is a two-hundred-and-fifty-year-old bridge and a huge tourist attraction. Besides, they found the bullet." And he dropped it into her hand.

Shelby, going through the motions, turned the bullet over. So, she thought, because I was once in a police firearms unit, I'm now an expert in guns . . ." Well, I don't know how old this is," she said out loud, "but it certainly looks new. I would say it came from a hunting rifle."

He stared at her. "You can tell that from just looking at it? I'm impressed."

It would be a pity to shatter his illusions but she did anyway. "Don't be. I haven't the slightest idea what sort of bullet this is, but while chasing Octavia through the woods yesterday I almost knocked down a kid with a hunting rifle over his shoulder. I bet this bullet came from his gun." *Elementary, my dear Watson.*

"I told the National Trust we weren't using firearms yesterday," said Ross, "and they had someone watching the filming who backed me up. But they had checked the bridge before we began and checked it after we finished. So it looked as though we were to blame. Still, I'm surprised no one heard the gunshot."

"Someone did." Shelby handed him back the bullet. "Octavia's horse."

Chapter Seven

Luke finally turned up, just before lunch, wearing dark glasses and a hangdog expression, clutching a large bunch of red roses. He found Shelby sitting alone on Irving's picnic blanket, tucking into a round of bacon sandwiches and Cheesy Wotsits crisps.

"These are for you," he said.

Shelby licked the orange crumbs off her fingers and regarded him dubiously. He was hungover; every word he spoke caused him to wince with pain. And the flowers looked remarkably similar to the ones his agent had sent him for good luck.

"I'm sorry for being such a bastard." He held out the roses encouragingly.

"Thanks." Shelby took them and stuck them in Irving's coolbox until she could put them in water. (Well, she needed all the luck she could get.)

Luke, relieved his apology had been accepted, collapsed into a director's chair with Courteney's name emblazoned on the back. "I don't suppose you've got any codeine? Or paracetamol? Or a sledgehammer to put me out of my misery?"

"Nope," lied Shelby. Let him suffer a bit more. Bloody well serve him right for going on a pub crawl last night without her.

"I really am sorry," he said. "I know I overreacted."

"You did," Shelby took another bite of her lunch.

"If it makes you feel better, I didn't even enjoy my trip to the lake – I got propositioned by Courteney and mobbed by a coachload of Japanese tourists."

She nearly choked on a sandwich. If he thought that was bad, wait until he saw the holiday photos. "See what happens when you go out without me?"

"And did I mention the ducks?"

He really was making an effort to be nice. She smiled magnanimously. It was easy to be magnanimous when you were in the right.

"Where the fuck have you been, Luke?" grumbled Irving, who had turned up behind them without either of them noticing. "Ross is just about to put out a *fatwa* on you."

"I overslept," said Luke. "I'm terribly sorry. Get Baz to knock a bit louder next time."

"Hmm," said Irving disbelievingly. Then his eyes fell on the bunch of roses, dropping petals over his illicit cans of Foster's. "Ah ha, a peace offering!" And he swooped down on them. "Excellent idea. Give me ten minutes while I sweet-talk Ross and with any luck you *will* act in this town again."

Luke and Shelby exchanged amused glances.

"I'll buy you another bunch," whispered Luke.

As Irving walked away, he glanced back over his shoulder, "Although next time a bottle of whisky might prove more effective. I don't think Ross is a great one for flowers."

Shelby could see Ross pacing up and down the bridge, waving his arms about and yelling, "Lady Panthea is supposed to be a brunette! Don't think you're foisting an identikit Hollywood blonde onto me!"

"I suppose you know the bastard's banned me from riding my bike until the end of filming?" said Luke, following her gaze.

Shelby toyed with the idea of making a full confession – but thought better of it.

"We're all going for a drink in town tonight," he added. "Would you like to come too?"

Shelby gritted her teeth and was about to remind him that, as she was his minder, she was supposed to go everywhere with him but instead found herself asking, "Did you invite Ross?"

"What for?" Luke voice was terse.

"I get the impression he sometimes feels lonely."

"Somehow," said Luke dryly, "I can't see Ross socialising with the crew. He would think it beneath him."

"Have you ever asked him?"

Luke eyed her beadily. "It's his own fault. This is the second film I've done with him. We start at six am, finish at eight pm, sometimes later, and he spends the rest of the evening watching the rushes and writing me sarcastic notes on my performance. I'll ask him if you like but he won't come. All he cares about is the film."

Shelby looked across to where Ross, still yelling into his mobile phone, was waving his arms about, talking with his hands. The sleeves of his red lumberjack shirt were rolled back, showing tanned forearms. Perhaps it was because he spent so much time outdoors. Whenever Shelby went out in the sun, she just acquired more freckles.

She found herself murmuring to Luke, "How does his wife feel about him being away from home for such long periods? Does she ever visit the set?"

Luke regarded her with faint exasperation. "He's not married, he's not engaged and he doesn't even have a girlfriend."

She was surprised. "Is he gay?"

"Don't be fatuous. Haven't you seen the steady stream of women following him about the set, drooling? He's rich, he's famous, he's powerful – he owns his own film production company for heaven's sake. He's Mr Darcy with an Alfa Romeo and a mobile phone. Someone pass me a sick-bag, *please*."

"Do I detect a tiny note of jealousy here?"

"No."

"Then why don't you like him?"

"Because he's pretentious, has no sense of humour and thinks he's God."

"Yet you agreed to work with him?"

"Actors can't afford to be picky – ninety-five per cent of us are out of work at any one time. We're only as good as our last film or TV appearance. And besides, he's actually quite a clever bastard – he makes me look as though I can act."

She laughed. "Then you'd better not fall out with him."

Luke helped himself to one of Shelby's sandwiches, disdainfully removing the bacon first. "Now that would be very boring."

* * *

That evening they ended up at The Moon And Sixpence, a wine bar just off Milsom Street. Shelby was sitting next to Luke, along with Courteney, Bruno, Irving and Dulcie, who was the assistant make-up artist. Dulcie wore her hair in a severe orange bob, had a sullen dark-red pout and lots of black eyeliner.

It had not taken Shelby long to realise that Dulcie had a huge crush on Luke and that he was doing little to dispel it. In fact, at present he was actively encouraging her, sliding his hand in a leisurely fashion up her rather plump thigh, snagging her fishnet tights, while she gazed adoringly up at him.

As Dulcie did not look his type, Shelby decided he must be doing it from habit. Dulcie was dressed as a typical Goth, in dark nail-polish and a black leather dress with lots of zips and chains. Perhaps Luke was turned on by all the leather and chains. His type, decided Shelby, would be blonde and submissive, with a stunning figure, a private income and an ability to party all night. Much like Courteney really.

As Luke suddenly looked up, caught her staring and winked broadly, she was forced to hide her discomfiture by making polite conversation with her own brother.

"Have you heard how Octavia is?" she asked.

He nodded. "The poor girl's got concussion, a couple of bruised ribs and a broken ankle."

"Let's send her flowers," suggested Luke. "That'll cheer her up. Is she allowed visitors?"

Irving grimaced. "Ross has beaten you to it. I think he's feeling guilty after making her ride that horse. You know how terrified she was. He's already despatched half of Interflora to the hospital."

"Hypocritical bastard! At least when she comes back she'll be able to hide a plaster cast beneath her costume. The nude scenes could be a bit tricky though."

Irving seemed to be taking an unnatural amount of interest in his beer glass. "There's talk of a replacement actress . . ."

"Bastard," muttered Luke and stalked off to the bar for another bottle of Chardonnay.

As Irving valiantly attempted to keep the conversation going, Shelby found her attention wandering. John Ivar was right. Minding celebrities was very boring. Shelby noticed that Bruno made no effort to join in the discussion, just stared around at the rest of the clientele, making everyone feel nervous. He stuck to orange juice and so, after her first beer, did Shelby. I'm only the hired help after all, she told herself gloomily and looked around the bar trying to size up any possible assassins. It was a few moments before she realised Courteney was actually talking to her.

" . . . so how do you like Bath?"

"I haven't seen much of it yet," admitted Shelby. "What about you?"

"Oh, I had a day's enforced sightseeing with Ross and Luke when we first arrived." Courteney pulled a face. "Dullsville! Ross dragged us off to the Abbey and the Heritage Vaults and then told us off for fooling around and making too much noise. What I really like to do," she confided in a low voice, "is go shopping. Bath is great for shopping. Have you been in any of the boutiques?"

Not for the first time did Shelby wonder whether Courteney actually listened to anything she said. "No," she sighed, "I go where Luke goes and somehow I don't think he's going in any boutiques."

Courteney regarded her pityingly. "Don't you get any time off?"

"Only when he goes to sleep." Which, admittedly, he didn't seem to do very often.

"You poor thing! Hey, Luke!" Courteney yelled across the room. "What's this about you keeping Shelby up all night?"

"Do I?" he said blithely, returning to their table with his Chardonnay tucked beneath his arm and a tray of drinks for everyone else.

"Why don't you give her some time off?"

"I've only worked half a day since I got here,"

interrupted Shelby, unable to hide her irritation. Was Courteney trying to get her fired? "I'm not entitled to time off."

Luke seemed to find her discomfort funny. "You can have the weekend off if you want."

"I don't need any time off," she repeated firmly. "Thank you very much all the same."

"Actually, as I'm returning to London this weekend, you're free to do what you like."

Of course, Charles Smith was his minder in the capital. Shelby stared at him, wondering if he was antagonising her on purpose. "You didn't tell me you were going to London."

"You didn't ask," he returned evenly.

"Are you appearing on a chat show or something?"

"I'm not needed for the next couple of days so I'm going home for a break. I shall be spending most of the time asleep in bed. Of course," he added softly, "I'm sure I can always find room for you too . . ."

Shelby clamped her jaw shut before she said something she might regret.

He laughed. "Can't do much judo with a table between us, can you?"

Arrogant, sexist pig, she fumed silently. Just when she had decided that maybe he wasn't so bad after all. Bastard. He could stick his rotten flowers right up his –

"Well, that's settled," beamed Courteney, unaware of any undercurrents. "We can go shopping at the weekend. Have lunch. It'll be fun."

As Courteney had to stop talking to knock back a

glass of fruit wine, Shelby looked around the bar while pondering a get-out clause. Considering it was nearly ten o'clock it was not very busy. But with Bruno glowering at anyone that came within five foot of Courteney, it was not surprising. Someone ought to get him a muzzle. Luke had given up attempting man-to-man conversation with him long ago, after only achieving a series of surly 'yes, sirs' from him. Perhaps Bruno thought he was a rival for Courteney's affections.

Shelby's attention was caught by a gang of teenagers in one corner, laughing raucously, empty glasses lined up in rows as though they were having a drinking competition. The men were whistling and calling out to Courteney – who was giving as good as she got – with the exception of one youth, smaller and younger than the rest, who kept his head turned away and just drank his orange juice – until he could seemingly bear the behaviour of his friends no longer. Abruptly he stood up, shoved his way past the others, and marched out of the back door, through to the courtyard. Neither Courteney nor his friends noticed.

Some friends, thought Shelby.

Then one of the girls who had been seated with him suddenly called out, "Hey, William, you forgot your jumper!" and waved it in the air.

William did not return. The girl shrugged and threw the jersey back onto the seat. Shelby frowned. Now where had she seen a red sweater like that before? Her brain clanked through a couple more gears. Prior Park . . .

Shelby scrambled out of her seat, almost knocking

Luke's drink clear out of his hand. By the time she had squeezed past all the tables and sprinted across the courtyard, William was already a few blocks down. He turned his head, saw her and ducked into a narrow cobblestoned alley. Shelby thanked her guardian angel she had worn trainers but still the boy could run fast. By the time she had caught up, he was standing on the corner of Milsom Street, desperately trying to get across. Even at this time of night the traffic was constant.

She made a grab for his collar but he dodged away, over-balancing into the road. There was a fearful squeal of brakes and a big black taxi, crammed with boisterous young men, stopped just inches from where he had fallen. But even as the taxi-driver wound down the window to ask 'What the hell do you think you're doing?', the youth had picked himself up and was stumbling across the road, darting down another alley.

Shelby dived after him, weaving between the cars, jumping onto the opposite pavement. But he now had the advantage. She was never going to catch him. Damn, damn, damn!

Then, she couldn't believe it, the prat made the fatal mistake of slowing to look behind him. Shelby went into a last-ditch sprint and threw herself at his legs. He was floored by a rugby tackle her brothers would have been proud of. Rolling him roughly onto his back, she sat on him. Thank heavens the street was deserted and no good Samaritan could come to his rescue.

He struggled in vain. "Let me go. I haven't done anything!"

"Then why were you running?"

"Because you were chasing me!"

Which was reasonable enough. "I want to know why you were walking through Prior Park with a hunting rifle."

"It's a free country."

"The Park is owned by the National Trust. You have to pay to get in and I shouldn't think for one moment they allow people to go shooting on their property."

"I was only carrying the gun," he muttered sullenly. "I wasn't going to use it."

"Tell it to the magistrate."

Instantly the fear was back in his eyes.

"So we'll start again," said Shelby. "Whose gun was it?"

"My father's," he said slowly. "But please don't tell the police. He'll kill me."

"Just tell me what you were doing in Prior Park."

"I didn't mean to frighten the horse. It was an accident."

"Have you any idea of the pain that poor actress has gone through?" Shelby began to improvise. "She might never walk again."

"I thought it was just a broken ankle and bruised – *ouff!* That hurt! OK, OK, I was paid to do it."

"Someone paid you to let off a gun in Prior Park?" she said scornfully. "It's original, I'll give you that."

"I'm telling you the truth! Courteney O'Connor paid me to fire a bullet – so it missed her. For a joke she said."

Shelby stared at him in disbelief. "Courteney paid you to fire a gun at her – to *miss*?"

"That's what I just said! I'm an excellent shot. Why else would I miss? The bullet whistled straight past her head and sparked off one of those stone pillars on the bridge. No one even noticed. It was a complete waste of time."

"Why would she do that?" She shifted slightly so that she could see his expression. It looked truthful enough. "It doesn't make any sense."

"Nothing you women do ever makes sense," he complained and, catching her unaware, he wriggled free and before she could grab at him was on his feet, sprinting off towards Queen's Square.

Shelby thumped the pavement with her fist. "Damn!"

"What was that all about?" asked Luke.

Shelby started and looked up. "Where did you spring from?"

"I followed you." He helped her to her feet. "I thought something was the matter. Why were you chasing that kid?"

"I thought I saw him steal a woman's bag."

"And had he?"

Shelby hesitated. "No, I made a mistake."

"Jesus, Shelby! Anything could have happened!"

She looked at him blankly. "Like what?"

"Do I have to spell it out? It's dark, you're a woman on your own . . ."

"Oh, don't be ridiculous; the kid couldn't have been more than sixteen. Besides, I can take care of myself. I used to be a policewoman."

"A policewoman can call for back-up. What if

someone pulled a knife on you? If there was more than one person – a whole gang of youths? What then?"

Shelby stared at him in exasperation. After what she'd just been through, she really couldn't be doing with this macho crap. "What's your problem, Luke? I'm your bodyguard. I'm trained for this kind of thing. Karate, judo – if he'd have tried anything funny I could have made tikka masala out of him." She frowned. "You wouldn't talk to Bruno like this."

"No," his voice was raw, "because Bruno doesn't look like you."

"Am I missing something?" She looked down at her clothes. "I'm wearing jeans, a T-shirt, trainers. Not some party frock held together by its designer label."

"Oh Christ," he murmured and, sliding his fingers into her long auburn hair, he tilted her head back against his shoulder and kissed her.

For a moment she was so stunned she let him.

Luke did not notice her frozen body. He slid his arms around her waist and drew her closer until suddenly she grabbed his shoulders, twisted around and threw him onto the pavement, his skull cracking against the flagstones until all he could see were stars.

"Don't you *ever*," she hissed violently, "*ever* try that again!"

"I won't." Gingerly, he touched the ever-increasing lump on the back of his head. "Believe me, I won't!"

Chapter Eight

Luke tore open another packet of painkillers and gulped two down with a mug of scalding black coffee. He could feel the liquid warming his throat and all the way down into his empty stomach. Comforting – until he caught sight of his dead-eyed reflection in the illuminated mirror. How the hell had he let himself get into such a state? Any more codeine and caffeine and he wouldn't need to take the train back to London, he could fly all the way himself.

The make-up artist, an old friend of Luke's called Kit, glanced up from painstakingly curling the ringlets on Courteney's wig with the hot tongs. "That'll teach you to go drinking all night," he said.

"Thank you, Jiminy Cricket," muttered Luke. "If I want any more advice, I'll whistle."

He popped a couple more tablets from their plastic bubbles, wishing they could erase the events of last night as easily as a headache. Last night, when he had forced himself on his bodyguard, like a complete *asshole*. It was going to take more than flowers to win her around this time.

Irving stuck his head around the door. "Luke, HTV would like an interview."

Luke kept him waiting while he poured himself another black coffee from Kit's percolator. It was as thick and dark as treacle. "Tell them to sod off."

"Bums on seats," said Irving sternly. "We need all the publicity we can get."

"This bum is staying right here."

Irving regarded Kit darkly. "And what time did Prince Valiant get in last night?"

"He didn't," replied Kit. "We came straight here from the karaoke club. He was a huge success. You should have seen him doing his impression of STEPS. Not only did he know all the words to 'Tragedy' – he could do the actions too."

Irving smiled faintly. "Tell him it'll be a bloody tragedy for him if he doesn't get his arse into gear pronto." And he stomped back to the production office.

"Oh God," mumbled Luke and put his head in his hands. "STEPS? Tell me it isn't true!"

Kit regarded Luke unsympathetically. "Surely one little interview wouldn't hurt?"

"I'm an actor, not a bloody politician. I don't do interviews. Tell them to speak to my agent. Let him earn his ten per cent for a change." Luke picked up Kit's copy of *OK!* magazine and began to flick through the pages with shaking hands. It was all he could do to focus on the pictures. He must have got really rat-arsed last night. And Saint Shelby had drunk nothing but orange juice.

"It's your birthday next week, isn't it?" said Kit, putting two and two together and making the big three-o. "I remember when I hit thirty I didn't go out all week, just watched *Beaches* on video and devoured endless boxes of Ferrero Rocher. I put on eight pounds and had enough gold foil to plate St Paul's Cathedral."

"I shall be twenty-nine, actually," said Luke acidly. "And that's not why I'm depressed."

Kit looked at him thoughtfully. "That old McFadden magic not working on your new bodyguard?"

"My relationship with Shelby is purely professional."

"Sure it is."

"She's not even my type."

"You straight guys are all the same. Courteney offers herself to you on a plate but you want Shelby because you can't have her."

Luke glowered at him. "I can have her any time I want."

"Of course you can. How many days have we been filming? Three? And she's been following you around, day and night – and what have you got? Zip! You've lost your touch, sweetie. I'm sorry, but there it is. Happens to us all in the end."

Luke flung the magazine into the bin with such force it spun across the trailer. "Crap!"

"OK, smart-ass, two hundred pounds you can't get

Shelby the Shadow into bed – before the end of filming."

"Two hundred quid?" derided Luke. "I thought you were broke?"

Kit smirked. "I know I'm going to win."

* * *

Shelby watched Luke stagger down the steps of Make-up, wearing dark glasses and holding his head, and disappear into the wardrobe trailer. He could be ages yet, so she wandered over to the catering van for a coffee and drank it very slowly. Once she had drained the last dregs from the polystyrene cup she knew Irving would make her fetch Luke for his TV interview. Then she'd have to make conversation with the creep.

She couldn't believe how he'd come on to her last night. Maybe he was so used to women throwing themselves at him, he thought all he had to do was get ready to catch. Give her the casual sophistication of Ross any day. Give her Ross, period, she thought dreamily, scanning the crew for that familiar auburn hair.

He was being interviewed by a reporter for the local news, waving his arms enthusiastically as he talked, the sleeves of his Cambridge-blue shirt neatly buttoned at the cuffs. Instead of faded combat trousers he wore immaculate jeans; his favourite Timberland boots had been swapped for black leather shoes. Since she had seen him last, someone had cut his hair and tamed it with liberal amounts of gel, darkening the bright chestnut hue until it was the colour of an After Eight Mint. Despite all this, he was still eminently edible.

Shelby allowed a slight smile of contentment to curl her lips. She didn't realise Ross could look so smart. Fiona, his bossy PR, must have given him the once-over before shoving him in front of the camera. That was another thing which endeared her to Ross. He didn't seem to care how he looked – unlike someone else she could mention, who spent all *his* time preening in front of Kit's mirror.

As though her thoughts had summoned him, Kit came to stand beside her and ordered sandwiches and a cup of tea. Although Shelby had seen him around the film set, and of course last night on Luke's pub crawl, she had not yet had the opportunity to speak with him. She observed him covertly. So this was Luke's great friend, who had abandoned him, the night before his marriage to Paige Lorraine, in Trafalgar Square – wearing a wedding dress. She was amazed they were still on speaking terms. Weird too that Luke, so patently heterosexual, should have as his confidant a man who was unmistakably gay.

Kit's light brown hair was streaked blond and auburn and rippled down his back as though he ought to be playing bass for Status Quo. His leather trousers were jacked in over his bony hips with a large buckled belt; his eyebrows were suspiciously neat; he wore black eyeliner and what appeared to be clear lipgloss. Perhaps it was merely chapstick, thought Shelby, unwilling to believe that any man would be caught dead wearing lipstick in public.

He turned suddenly and caught Shelby staring. Not

in the least bit perturbed, he winked and said in a surprisingly gravelly voice, a bit like Rod Stewart, "You must be Shelby the Shadow?"

Shelby the Shadow? Shelby spluttered into her coffee. So that's what Luke called her behind her back!

"And you must be the guy who was responsible for putting his best mate in a wedding dress and dumping him in Trafalgar Square?" she replied sweetly.

"Ouch!" said Kit. "When was the last time *you* got laid?"

"When was the last time you ate a cobblestone?"

"OK, OK, I apologise!"

"Smart move." With a sideways glance, she added curiously, "So tell me, why *did* you dump Luke in Trafalgar Square dressed up like Edna Everage?"

"What's it to you?" shrugged Kit, taking a large gulp of tea before helping himself to a handful of chocolate Hobnobs. "He's not queer, if that's what you're implying."

"I want to be sure you're not going to do it again," she said evenly.

"I will if the need arises." Kit slowly dunked a biscuit into his tea, causing the chocolate to gradually melt and drip off. "Have you ever been drunk?" he said, "Completely intoxicated? In fact, so utterly stoned that some issues become of burning importance and others just fade into insignificance?"

"No," she said unsympathetically. "My father runs a wine bar. No matter how much I drink I only ever become tipsy."

"Why does that not surprise me?" muttered Kit. "Well,

at Luke's stag party we all got smashed and he stayed over at my flat. It became increasingly clear to me that I had to stop the wedding. Paige wasn't right for him. I knew she didn't love him. She just wanted to be famous."

Having seen off several prospective stepmothers over the years, using rather less elaborate schemes, Shelby could feel some empathy with Kit. "Couldn't you have thought of some other way to prevent the wedding? Some more *subtle* way?"

"I *could* have dumped Luke on some remote Scottish Island. But I didn't! Besides, if Paige had really loved Luke, don't you think she would have forgiven him?"

Kit might be gay but it appeared he had a typically male view of the marriage ceremony – all froth and no substance. Did he think women put themselves through the pre-wedding hell of crash diets, disastrous experiments with hairstyles and fights with the prospective in-laws just so that they could get to wear a pretty white dress? And that was without having the worry that the bridegroom might turn up in one which was sexier than theirs.

"Well, *I* wouldn't!" she retorted. "Just think of all the time, expense and organisation that goes into arranging a wedding – the most important day of a woman's life."

"It's only a crummy certificate. Surely the man she is marrying is more important than a piece of paper? If Paige had really *loved* Luke she would have forgiven him."

"I suppose you're right." She grinned. "Of course, if it were me, he'd have to grovel a lot first."

But Kit's attention had become enthralled by the sight of Irving battling with a gang of students, fresh out of the nearby Roman Spa. He had already sprinted past twice, looking harassed, having stopped worrying about Luke's interview with HTV ages ago. Irving's main problem seemed to be the crowd of onlookers pouring down the narrow alleys which led out from Abbey Green like a giant spider's web. John Ivar's security guards, with the help of a couple of hired police officers, had blocked off the area where the trailers were parked. Abbey Green, which security had rather casually roped off with bits of coloured tape, was starting to look as though it was under siege.

"Your brother's not a bit like you, is he?" said Kit.

Shelby followed Kit's gaze and sighed. The students, gabbling excitedly in French when they saw Courteney emerge from wardrobe, practically went into orbit when Luke jumped down the steps. Shelby had never seen anything like it. It was only *Luke*, for heaven's sake. Pathetic, drunken, philandering Luke. What was all the fuss about?

"It's the breeches," said Kit, apparently reading her mind. "Does it every time."

"Luc!" cried the gang of French students, distinguishable by their elegant bright clothes and rucksacks. They surged forwards as one. *"Luc! Je t'aime!"*

"Oh bugger," said Irving. "Help, someone! Don't just stand there sniggering!"

This was to the camera crew, who were practically killing themselves laughing.

Shelby handed Kit her coffee cup and waded to her brother's rescue, holding the girls back in order that Luke could duck past.

"What's French for 'Piss off'?" asked Irving, as the girl he was wrestling with raked his face with her long blue nails. "Ow, you bitch!"

For an encore, the girl kneed him in the groin, leaving him bent double in agony, as she threw herself into Luke's arms.

"It's all right," snapped Luke, as Shelby made a grab for her. "Don't overreact. She's a fan. She only wants my autograph."

"I want your body," breathed the French girl. "We can make love all night."

Luke pushed her away, horrified.

"Where are you staying, Luc?" the girl called, as Shelby briskly hustled her away. "I will come and see you."

Luke realised she had even wrenched a button from his waistcoat as a souvenir. "Bloody hell," he grumbled, "she can't have been more than fourteen!"

"Jailbait," agreed one of the grips. "You lucky bastard."

As Luke watched Shelby berate the security guards for failing to maintain the crowd barriers (nice to see someone else getting it in the neck for a change), he became aware of a bogus blonde standing beside him.

"Hello," she said, smiling at him in a rather predatory fashion. Her smoky almond eyes were absorbing every detail of his costume, particularly his breeches which clung to every goose-pimple.

He regarded her warily, then relaxed as he recognised her as being a well-known journalist with one of the Nationals. She might be a bit tatty around the edges but she at least she was over the age of consent.

"Hello," he said, forcing a friendliness he did not feel. He had never trusted the press and, since his 'This Is Your Life' special in yesterday's paper, he was starting to experience a positive aversion for the whole profession. "Did you want an interview?"

"That would be kind," she purred. "I've just been having a nice long talk with Ross. He's very proud of you."

Unlikely, thought Luke.

"I understand that filming is going well. Bath is a beautiful city and it must be very encouraging to have so many of your fans turn up to watch?"

Hell, actually. Playing to a live audience made him feel nervous and twitchy. Unlike his contemporaries, he had no desire to 'prove' himself with Shakespeare at Stratford. Give him the multi-take world of celluloid any day.

Realising she was expecting a quotable response, he said blandly, "I think some of them are Courteney's."

She smiled, revealing the slightly yellow teeth of a chain smoker. "Your minder is a bit of a battleaxe, isn't she? It's ironic really – a woman protecting *you*."

Before Luke could find himself in the unlikely position of espousing equal opportunities for women, a photographer sidled from the shadows. "May I take your picture, Mr McFadden?"

It was on the tip of Luke's tongue to tell him to piss off but the guy had to make a living after all. However, Ross could become bloody-minded if too many photographs were taken during filming – it spoilt the suspense for the prospective audience. So Luke searched the crowd for Fiona, the PR girl, who was totally in love with Ross and spent all her time dishing out copies of his press-cuttings. She was easy to spot, with her shortest of skirts, mobile phone permanently clamped to her ear and Psion organiser tucked under her arm. But she was deep in a 'Yah, yah, you're so right, yah,' conversation with a crew from HTV.

"Yeah, sure," he said.

It was simpler to agree.

* * *

"You really hate me, don't you?" said Courteney.

As Ross stood with his back to her, his hands behind his back, absent-mindedly twisting his signet ring like Prince Charles, it was hard to gauge his reaction. He was staring through the yellowed net curtains of the production office trailer at the film set beyond, though what he found so interesting was beyond her comprehension. After all, it was a scene he saw every day of his life.

"Hell, you're not even listening to me," wailed Courteney, anxious to provoke a reaction. It was that or strip off all her clothes and while she had no problem in principle, the production office was a little on the chilly side.

"What?" Ross turned irritably. "Yes, yes, of course I'm listening to you. What were you saying?"

Through the net curtains Courteney could just see the top of Shelby's carroty head. She seemed to be arguing with a bunch of security guys twice her size. Amazingly they were hanging their heads and taking it.

"Do you fancy her?" she asked suddenly.

Ross regarded her blankly. It was one of his specialities. He had the blank, disinterested aristocrat down pat. She could imagine him at the court of Louis XVI: 'Revolution? What Revolution? Tell them to get back to work and not to be so silly.'

Actually, he seemed genuinely bemused by her question. "Who?"

"Shelby," she said, watching him closely for any reaction. The answer was not what she was expecting.

"What's it got to do with you?"

Bastard. Courteney felt a sharp pain in her ribcage. Maybe it was just the corset Elliott had bullied her into, complaining she had put on weight since her costume-fitting. Or maybe, as she preferred to think, it was her heart, finally breaking. She squeezed a tear drop from her curiously dry eyes and allowed it to hover prettily on the end of her lashes. She hoped Kit used waterproof make-up.

Ross's fine patrician features assumed a pained expression and he handed her a box of tissues. It wasn't quite the reaction Courteney had been hoping for. It was also faintly disturbing to find he had tissues so easily to hand. Did he make a habit of making girls cry?

"Don't I mean anything to you? What about that night at the Four Seasons? I guess you just wanted to sweet-talk me into making your rotten little movies. Boy, was I stupid!" She threw the box back at him. It glanced off his shoulder, taking him by surprise.

"You know that's not true." He picked the box off the floor and returned it to his desk.

"Seems pretty much like it to me. If you couldn't bear to spend more than one night with me, why bother to hire me at all?"

Ross settled himself comfortably on the edge of the desk. He had a certain glint in his steely grey eyes which she didn't much like. "Sometimes I ask myself that very same question."

Courteney fixed him with her own aquamarine glare, which had made lesser directors quake. "And what's that supposed to mean?"

"You show up late for filming, you forget your lines, your English accent would embarrass Dick Van Dyck. You're bursting out of your costumes, you flirt with anything in trousers, you disappeared for a whole afternoon yesterday, leaving Irving in the lurch. The production staff can't keep up with your ever-increasing demands: personal make-up artist, personal hairdresser, personal assistant, personal trainer, personal chef. Do you know how much it costs to have Hershey Kisses flown in from the States? And when I call you in here for a little talk about improving your attitude, you invent a non-existent love-affair and throw histrionics – and tissue boxes. I can't take any more, Courteney. You want out of your contract? That's fine by me. Start walking."

She stared at him, speechless. Well, perhaps not quite speechless. "*You* can't take any more. What about me? What I have to put up with? To think, I could have been filming in Mexico with George Clooney. I only signed up to make these movies with you as a favour – because I thought you loved me."

"Well, *that's* a good reason."

She stared at him. He didn't even bother to hide his contempt any more. Didn't she mean anything to him? She decided to call his bluff. "OK, I guess we can't work together any more. Let me out of my contract."

"Fine," he said wearily. "I've already had to replace Octavia with Paige Lorraine. I'll call up Cate Blanchett to replace you."

Irony was lost on Courteney.

"Paige!" she screeched. "You've hired *Paige* to star in this film? After everything that happened on *All That She Wants*? And what about poor Luke? How's he going to feel? He was engaged to the bitch! Christ, you are unbelievable, totally insensitive. You know, I think I'm gonna stay – if only to spite you!" And she picked up her skirts, swooshed past him and out the door (which she slammed for added effect).

Ross sank into his chair and lit another cigarette. "Actresses," he sighed. "Can't work with them, can't kill them."

* * *

While the photographer got Luke in focus, Evie slipped a mini tape recorder out of her handbag, holding it in the palm of her hand, perhaps hoping Luke wouldn't see it. His opinion of journalists skidded down another notch.

"So, what's the name of your bodyguard?" asked Evie casually.

With his hackles on standby, Luke was rather taken back by her seemingly harmless question. "Shelby," he muttered, from the corner of his mouth, as the photographer clicked frenziedly, "Shelby Roberts." After all, he told his conscience, it wasn't as though the girl was undercover.

"Has she worked for you long?"

"Only a week." Even though it seemed like forever.

"A bit more to your left, Mr McFadden," called the photographer.

Luke automatically turned his head to profile. It took him right back to his days as a male model.

"That's perfect!" called the photographer. "Hold it right there! Don't even *breathe*."

"So, Luke," continued Evie, "what did Shelby Roberts do before she was your minder?"

"Eh? Oh, she was a policewoman."

"A policewoman?" Evie sounded impressed. "Special Branch?"

"Dunno. Firearms, I think. Why don't you ask her? Then you can interview her instead of me." Luke turned, searching the crowd behind the barrier for that distinctive flame of red hair.

Evie was now standing very close to him, almost leaning against his arm. Luke looked down in surprise, then glanced suspiciously at the photographer. He had been caught like that before – with 'a mystery blonde' on his arm. But the photographer, oblivious, was fiddling with his lens, polishing the surface with a corner of his black T-shirt.

"Luke?" she said softly. "Did you know Firestorm have hired your ex to take over the role played by Octavia Shannon?"

"Paige Lorraine?" For a moment he was completely thrown. Was she winding him up? In the four months since Paige had jilted him, no one (apart from Courteney) had dared mention her name.

He decided to play it cool, call her bluff. "Firestorm have hired Paige? That's news to me. How come you're so well informed?"

She avoided answering directly. "I wonder why Ross didn't tell you?"

"Do you really?" said Luke sarcastically. "I think not."

So, Ross, with half of Hollywood to choose from, had hired Paige? What was he playing at? Was this a deliberate ploy to provoke him or was Ross genuinely desperate? Luke doubted those faceless LA money-men were involved. He knew of old that no one had ever been able to force Ross to do anything he didn't want to do.

"Ross has always got on well with Paige, hasn't he?" said Evie. "And of course he owns Firestorm. And he is the director . . . The choice of actress is up to him, isn't it?" She was desperate to get a definite quote on the subject but Luke said nothing. He wasn't stupid.

"Ross and Paige were engaged once – before you came along and broke it up. Perhaps now that Paige is free, they'll get back together . . . What do you think?"

His lips pressed firmly together. *I don't think you really want to know what I think.*

"What do *you* think, Luke?" Evie's voice was as persistent as a wasp after a jam sandwich.

"What?"

"Do you think Ross blames you for his break-up with Paige?"

Luke forced himself to concentrate. "What are you getting at? We're supposed to be discussing the film, not my director's love life."

"Perhaps they'll get back together again?"

"I don't think so," said Luke blithely. "But then, I'm hardly in a position to know. Why don't you ask him?"

"Paige is a free agent, and Ross is a very handsome, and wealthy, man . . ."

Luke feigned disinterest. This must be the first interview he'd ever given where no one wanted to talk about *him*. Maybe later he'd see the funny side. But not now. He was still struggling with his emotions. *Paige. Paige was coming here. He was going to see her again.*

Suddenly their attention was caught by the sight of Courteney, in full period costume, hurdling the crash barriers like Kriss Akabussi, charging across the cobblestones, her blonde wig askew, tears pouring down her face.

"Luke," she wailed, shortly before throwing herself into his arms, burying her face in his chest, weeping copiously.

That should finish off his waistcoat nicely, thought Luke in weary resignation. "What's the matter?"

"Ross, he's a total bastard!" came the muffled reply.

"What's new?" Then Luke remembered they had an attentive, note-taking, audience. "Er, Courteney," he muttered softly, "these people are journalists."

Courteney looked up at him. "Darling, Ross has refused to let us get married until after the film."

"He *what*?" For a split second, it was as though Courteney was speaking Greek. Then the full horror of what she'd said hit him like a ton of bricks. "Courteney –"

Courteney quickly turned to Evie, her beautiful aquamarine eyes shining with unshed tears. "Isn't that the cruellest thing you ever heard?"

"Absolutely," agreed Evie, turning up the volume on her tape recorder. "The man's a total shit. Tell me more."

The photographer, who had taken two steps back to get both Courteney and Luke in the same shot, began clicking wildly.

Luke placed his hand firmly over the lens of the camera. "Come on, mate, give us some privacy." *So I can throttle my co-star without any witnesses.*

"You've got to be kidding!" The photographer blatantly laughed in his face. "This stuff pays for my kid to get through college. Besides, it's a free country."

Luke smiled evilly. "No, it's a film set. And everything you see, costumes, props, the lot, are copyrighted to Firestorm Productions. Give me the camera."

"Piss off."

"Ah well, you can't say I didn't ask nicely."

Courteney and Evie watched open-mouthed as Luke seized the camera. The flash popped a couple of times before he worked out how to open the back.

The photographer screamed with rage. "What the fuck are you doing?"

Luke unravelled the film, exposing it to the light, before effortlessly picking up the photographer by his lapels. "Now, let me show you the way to go home."

"He's only doing his job," protested Evie, tugging frantically on his arm. "Please don't hurt him."

Luke obediently dropped the photographer onto the cobblestones, where he scrambled around on his hands and knees, his bottom up in the air, as he collected up the film and bits of his camera.

Unable to resist the temptation, Luke took careful aim with his smartly polished 19th century riding-boot and delivered a hefty kick.

Chapter Nine

Luke read the morning papers over breakfast in the hotel restaurant and put his head in his hands. "Have you seen these headlines?" he muttered. "I think I'm going to shoot myself."

"It'll save Ross doing it," said Shelby, dropping two sugars into her coffee and stirring vigorously.

Every clink of the spoon against the cup went right through his head. Intensive filming always had this effect on him, making him feel jet-lagged and headachy. After spending so much time pretending to be another person, it was hard to make that adjustment, that change of gear, back into the real world.

"I feel a bit like a rat deserting the sinking ship," he said at last, tossing the newspapers aside. He watched Shelby raise the cup to her mouth and tried not to think about those beautiful heart-shaped lips pressing against the thick, white china. "You know, going back to

London today?" He paused, waiting for a response. Wouldn't she even miss him? "Are you sure you won't come with me?"

"Why?" she asked bluntly, cupping the coffee in her hands and staring directly at him with those green and gold filigree eyes.

He wasn't entirely sure himself and dropped his gaze first, looking down at his untouched breakfast – greasy fried eggs, bacon, sausages, *et al* – congealing on the plate. The waitress, thinking he looked pale, had piled his plate high. Where was Bruno – 'the Human Garbage Disposal' as Courteney had christened him, amongst other things (and she could talk) – when you needed him? Bruno could have wolfed down this lot in five seconds flat.

Paige, I'm in love with Paige, he tried to convince himself crossly. But the words, "Well, I might enjoy a bit of company . . ." slipped out before he could stop them.

"I'm sure you would," she teased, raising her coffee to her mouth again.

Oh that beautiful, beautiful mouth, thought Luke, as she took a long drink.

"Are you feeling OK?" she asked, regarding him curiously over the top of the cup.

"What?" Luke realised he'd been staring. "Oh yes –" Clumsily knocking his cutlery onto the carpet created a welcome diversion. What the hell's the matter with me? he asked himself irritably, as he and the waitress almost banged heads diving for the fork.

"I'll get you another one," said the waitress, and whisked it off towards the kitchen.

Oh God, thought Luke despairingly, I'll have to eat now.

"I'm going to spend the day relaxing in the hotel," Shelby was saying.

He forced himself to concentrate on the words.

She continued. "I thought I would have a work-out in the gym, a swim in the pool, lie on the sunbeds –"

With her fair skin?

She grinned impishly, reading his mind. "One day, all my freckles are going to join up and I'll have the most beautiful tan . . ."

"And wrinkles, and skin cancer . . ."

"Killjoy," she returned and actually poked out her tongue.

It was small and pink and Luke began to feel restless. The only woman on the set worth screwing and she wasn't even remotely interested in him. He could wave goodbye to that £200. But, somehow, the bet didn't matter.

Shelby seemed quite happy this morning, he reflected. He hoped it wasn't because she was having three days away from him. "Will you be visiting the film set?" he asked, breaking up his bread roll into thousands of tiny crumbs.

"Not if I can at all possibly help it. Irving always told me filming was boring – now I believe him. How can you stand it, day in, day out, being fussed over by Kit, bossed about by Ross and Irving, goaded by journalists?"

"Beats working for a living," said Luke automatically. It was his standard reply.

The waitress returned with the fork, her lips pursing when she saw the mess he had made with his bread roll – for a moment Luke felt he was back at school – but she said nothing, just cleared away Shelby's plate and returned to the kitchen.

"Do you want a lift to the train station, Luke?" asked Shelby. "I can borrow Irv's car."

"No, thanks." It came out more brutally than he had intended. "The receptionist has ordered me a taxi and I'm meeting Charles at the station." He watched her face tighten. Charles Smith was his other minder. However, it was comforting to realise she felt jealous – even if it was over a man! Luke hesitated. "Are you sure you won't come too?"

"So me and Charles can fight over you?"

"I'll give him the weekend off."

"Where would I stay?"

"I have a spare room, you could sleep there. It'll be strictly platonic –"

"Platonic?" she mocked.

"Platonic," he repeated firmly. "We could catch a movie, go to the theatre . . ." He trailed off. He was wasting his time. She wasn't remotely interested.

"That's very kind of you, Luke, but you did say you were going home to rest."

Yes, and he'd been kicking himself ever since.

They looked at each other. There were so many things he wanted to say but he knew however hard he tried, the words would come out wrong and she would have an even worse opinion of him than she had already.

"Hi y'all," cried Courteney gaily, bustling up and giving Luke a hug as he stood up for her, almost knocking him off balance. "Aren't you going home today, Luke?" Kiss, kiss. He started as she pinched his bottom. "Has anyone ever told you what a cute English butt you have?"

"Erm . . ." said Luke.

Courteney flopped into the spare chair between them, helped herself to a slice of cold toast and thickly spread it with marmalade. "Yum," she said, taking a huge bite. "We can't get English marmalade like this in the States."

Luke slid one of the newspapers across the table. "Courteney, we need to talk."

"I know," agreed Courteney. "It's a terrible photograph. With my wig askew you can see a good clear inch of black roots. Do you think if I asked Kit nicely he might do a touch-up for me?"

Refusing to become distracted from the point, Luke jabbed the headline with his index finger. "'*Luke and Courteney to Wed*'," he read out loud. "Admittedly getting blind drunk every night can play havoc with one's memory but I'm sure even I would remember proposing to you."

"But it's excellent publicity." Courteney regarded him with genuine surprise. "Aren't you pleased?"

Luke could feel his teeth grinding in impotent fury and forced himself to calm down, lest he knocked one of his expensive porcelain crowns out of synch with the others. "It might be a bloody good joke to you but when we put out a statement telling everyone the truth, I'll be crucified as some kind of Jeremy Beadle prankster. The world already has me down as a fruitcake for turning up at my last wedding ceremony wearing a dress –"

"Then don't tell them the truth," replied Courteney simply. "At least now no one is gonna think you're a transvestite – not that I've got anything against transvestites. I mean, if that's your scene then, hey, that's cool."

"Transvestite!" Luke could hardly trust himself to speak.

"And if Paige thinks she has competition, maybe she'll come back to you in double quick time. Really, Luke, I've done you a huge favour. You should be thanking me."

Strangling her seemed the more likely option, thought Luke furiously. "Paige and I are history," he said firmly. "And I'll thank you not to meddle in my sex life, Courteney. How am I going to take a girl out to dinner if she thinks I'm about to marry someone else?"

"Never stopped any of the guys I know," replied Courteney, reaching out for another piece of toast.

Luke moved the rack out of her reach. "You're going to call up these papers and get them to print a retraction. Tell them you're very sorry, it was a silly joke and that you never thought anyone would take you seriously."

"Do it yourself," grumbled Courteney. Standing abruptly, she picked up her bag, slung it over her shoulder and almost took out the waiter's eye. "I've got stuff to do."

Luke caught her wrist, forcing her to sit back down. "*Courteney?*"

He didn't have to say any more. One look at his nasty, totally humourless expression and the actress quickly acquiesced.

"OK, OK, don't bug me." She shook his hand off. "I only wanted to – Oh Jeez, you're so tetchy! You know, I'm glad I'm not marrying you. I'd probably kill you a week after the ceremony. And then where would I be? Death row, that's where I'd be."

Luke had to smile. "A whole week? What amazing control." He glanced slyly at Shelby. "Some folks I know wouldn't even last that long."

But Courteney was still muttering fretfully, "And then they'd get Shannen Docherty to play me in the true-life movie – I feel depressed already."

Luke pushed his plate towards her. "Have some more toast, take your mind off it. What's the important 'stuff' that you've got to do today? *After* you've rung round the tabloids of course . . ."

Courteney gave him a black look. "Me and Shelby are going to go shopping, have our lunch out, visit the Roman Baths –"

Luke could tell that it was the mention of the Baths that swayed Shelby.

"I'm sorry, Courteney," she interrupted firmly, "but I can't go shopping."

Courteney looked hurt. "Don't you like me?"

"I don't have any money! I was unemployed for three months before starting this job and my wages from Firestorm aren't paid into my bank until the end of the month."

"But I'm paying – it'll be my treat."

Shelby was aghast. "But I couldn't possibly accept –"

"You English!" Courteney linked her arm through Shelby's. "Stop trying to spoil my fun. Look, here's Bruno, we mustn't keep him waiting. Come on, Luke! Don't look so miserable! At least you're getting three whole days off. A regular vacation."

Purgatory, more like.

As he walked out through reception and climbed into the taxi, Luke reflected that he was not the only one. Shelby looked as though she was about to have her teeth pulled with a pair of rusty pliers. Shopping with Courteney and Bruno was not something he'd relish either. Pure torture.

But at least it would keep her away from Ross.

* * *

Saturday

Shelby woke up the following morning with a headache. She turned and looked at the clock. Seven-thirty. Thank heavens for Saturday, the Patron Saint of the Lie-in. And then she remembered her shopping trip with Courteney and groaned. They had spent the whole day in a orgy of spending, culminating in dinner at an expensive Indian restaurant, Shelby frantically keeping a running tally, so that she could arrange to repay Courteney later. They had not, however, had time to visit the Roman Baths, *thank God*, but unfortunately Courteney had suggested they meet again this morning. What was it with Americans and culture? Courteney had hated the

Abbey – so why was she so determined to visit the Baths?

Spending Saturday morning walking around a hot and sticky city centre, crammed with shoppers and tourists, sounded like hell on earth. Shelby was determined to be out when Courteney called. She had to escape – but where to? Deciding she could work that out later, she hastily showered and dressed in new bootcut trousers and geometric print shirt, paid for by Courteney, despite her protests. She stuffed everything she thought she might need into a black rucksack and hurried off downstairs.

She bumped into Ross, cramming the last pieces of a croissant into his mouth as he strode out of the restaurant, scattering golden pastry flakes across the polished floor of reception. Perhaps in too much of a rush to bother with his gel this morning, his dark chestnut hair was curling in all directions and he was back in old-fashioned khaki combats and Timberland boots. And a *Star Wars* T-shirt which didn't look 'him' at all.

"Sorry," he mumbled, "I didn't see you."

"You have a bit of um . . ." She trailed off in embarrassment.

"Breakfast around my mouth?" he grinned. "Thanks. I was in a hurry but I couldn't resist stopping for one of their delicious croissants. There, is it gone?"

She nodded, cursing herself for being unable to think of anything to say which might keep him talking. It was the weirdest thing but there was something about him that made intelligent conversation turn to a string of gibberish as it came out of her mouth.

"You're up early. Making the great escape from Courteney?"

"How did you –" she began, then broke off before she incriminated herself.

He looked at her rucksack. "Can I give you a lift? Where are you headed? I'm off into Bath if that's any help?"

Shelby cast a swift look over her shoulder, as though half-expecting Courteney to come skipping down the staircase with a gleeful 'Hi y' all!'. "That would be great."

"OK, come with me. My car is parked around the side."

She reverently climbed into his red convertible and fastened the seat belt. Fast cars and fast men. This job just got better and better. Ross slid the car into gear, reversed out of the car park and shot down the hill into the city centre. It was a pity it took less than five minutes; perhaps Ross wasn't the sort of person who walked. Never mind, there was always the return journey to look forward to.

"I'm off to the Roman Baths," said Ross, as he parked in the car park beneath Waitrose. "Before the tourists get there. Want to tag along?"

For a moment she thought she had heard him wrongly. Or maybe he was just being polite. "Oh, you don't have –"

Those grey eyes seemed strangely warm. "Please?"

Provided I don't talk too much, thought Shelby, remembering her conversation with Courteney. "Oh well, thanks. I'd like to." She smiled at the irony. The

Roman Baths were the last place she had wanted to spend the morning.

They arrived at the Baths a little after nine o'clock, just as it opened. There was already of steady stream of people walking through the doors. Ross bought a couple of glossy guidebooks and, as they went through the entrance, a young man handed them each what looked like an extra-long mobile phone. Shelby regarded hers distrustfully.

"It's an audio guide," explained Ross. "If you key in the number displayed next to the exhibits, you'll hear recorded information about what you're seeing."

She followed Ross down some steps and into the museum. "Is everything underground?"

"Only the museum," grinned Ross. "You're beneath the Pump Room. The Georgians didn't care much for archaeology and even though they discovered a Roman temple when digging the foundations for the Pump Room, they still went ahead and built it."

After that, Shelby didn't bother much with her audio guide, just pretended to hold it to her ear as she trailed around the museum after Ross, admiring his long legs striding up and down the steps to the different levels, listening to his soft melodious voice, and hoping he wouldn't be asking technical questions later. He spent a lot of time muttering into a miniature tape recorder. Perhaps he was planning a documentary?

As they moved from the museum to the baths themselves, even Shelby had to be impressed. It was such a contrast, moving from the gloomy beige-browns of the museum back out into the sunlight, watching it glitter on the jade-green waters of the Great Bath.

Having zipped around the museum in record time, they were ahead of everyone else. Standing alone beneath the Victorian colonnade, it was easy to imagine herself back almost two thousand years, to visualise men and women resting on the steps of the baths, talking, laughing, immersing themselves in the healing waters. Then she tripped over a piece of Roman plumbing and landed back in the 21st century.

Ross helped up her from the ancient flagstones. "Watch your step," he said, examining her palms for grazes. "The floor is uneven and the water makes it slippery."

She glanced back across the steaming bath but now the tourists were crowding around, taking photographs, flipping through their guidebooks, unable to resist trailing their hands in the opaque water, even though there were signs telling them not to. They were chattering in languages she did not understand. Were she and Ross the only English people here?

She glanced up at the statues, gazing down from the top of the colonnade. "What stories they could tell," she sighed, "if only they could speak."

"Yes," agreed Ross, "but they're actually Victorian."

She had not realised she had spoken aloud. He must think her a complete idiot. Realising he still held her hands, she tried to pull them away but he held her too tightly. Those long, artistic fingers . . . she imagined them running lightly across her skin . . .

"Hot in here, isn't it?" said Ross, watching the colour rise in her cheeks. He suddenly released her. "You realise that these Roman baths were the forerunner to our modern-day saunas and Jacuzzis?"

She grimaced. Another history lesson . . . just when she thought her day was getting interesting.

As Ross continued to recount the background of the place, they moved back under cover to view the Circular Bath. Large, round and very cold. Shelby, seeing the shimmer of coins just below the surface, scrabbled in her pocket and threw in a handful of change, hopefully before Ross noticed. Damn, there went a couple of pound coins. She watched them sink rapidly to the bottom. She deserved at least two wishes for that.

"Please, God," she breathed, "or Goddess, give me Ross. And, if possible, get rid of my freckles at the same time."

"What *are* you doing?" muttered a voice by her ear.

She uttered a squawk and almost fell over the barrier. Nothing missed the eyes of a predator.

"Oh um, it's for charity, isn't it?"

"I suppose so." Ross regarded her curiously. "So what did you wish for?"

"Oh you know, usual stuff, world peace, etc, etc."

A smile lifted one corner of his mouth. "Liar," he whispered softly. He hooked a stray lock of hair back over her ear. "Why do redheads blush so much?"

"You said yourself, it's hot in here." Shelby jerked away, running up the steps of a wooden terrace behind, peering through the arched stone window to view the medieval King's Bath. She had to stand on the step because she wasn't tall enough to see through the semicircular gap. The light breeze wafted the steam towards her face and she breathed deeply, hoping to inhale some of those miraculous minerals which had helped what's-his-name, Bladud, the swine-herding Prince with the skin condition. Instead, all she could smell was the cooking wafting across from the Pump Room Restaurant.

"You're supposed to bathe in the water, not breathe it in," said Ross from behind her.

"I know," she said crossly, turning her head and finding his eyes on a level with hers. "But I think I'd get kicked out if I jumped in."

He laughed. "Especially as you're supposed to take off your clothes first."

"And then what?" she asked, feigning interest purely to hear the seductive drawl of his voice.

"First you would go into the sweat room, known as the *tepidarium*," He led her down the steps, "and have oil massaged into your body, which was then scraped off with a blunt razor, called a *strigil*, removing the oil, sweat, dirt and hair from the skin."

"Ugh," said Shelby, leaning over the barrier and staring at the piles of terracotta tiles stretching out before her. It looked just like John's office – but neater. "How revolting!"

Ross frowned. "All you can see now, of course, are the *hypocausts*. Did you know the Romans invented central heating? Furnaces heated the air below the rooms, warming these brick pillars. Then you would jump into the Circular Bath, to cool off."

He really was a walking encyclopaedia. She hoped he didn't reel off a similar list of facts and figures when he was making love. Not that she was likely to find out, she told herself soberly. She should just quit all this fantasising. This guy could have his pick of glamorous actresses. Why would he be interested in a tomboy scruff like her? He was only being courteous. As far as he was concerned she was just 'staff'.

"How do you know so much about the place?" she asked politely.

"I lived in Bath as a child. In fact, our school came here for swimming lessons, until they discovered something nasty in the water."

"I saw you taking notes earlier," she said. "Are you planning to make a documentary?"

"Maybe . . . it's one of many projects I have lined up. I certainly don't want to spend my life filming bodice-rippers." He led her up the stairs to the exit. "Would you like to visit the Pump Room? Have a cup of coffee? We'll be filming there in a couple of weeks but the place will have been cleared and won't look the same."

"That would be very nice," said Shelby carefully. Stay calm, she told herself. He's only being nice. Friendly. Sociable. He's not the slightest bit interested in getting into your knickers. You're not even his type. He probably goes for big-busted blondes like Courteney. What on earth would he see in a skinny, freckly, carrot-top like you?

There were times when her conscience could be too cruel.

"Cheer up." Ross picked up her hand and squeezed it. "Sometimes," he said wickedly, "wishes do come true."

Chapter Ten

It was weird, after whinging about the tourists all week, to finally become one. Shelby bought some postcards in the gift shop to send to her family, balked at the prices of the souvenirs, and hurried after Ross as he strode away to the Pump Room Restaurant.

He had such long legs she could never manage to keep abreast of him, and began to feel like Prince Philip, permanently trailing three paces behind the Queen. Of course Ross never waited for her to catch up, or glanced back to check she was still there. He just assumed she was.

They sat at a little round table at the front, dead centre, so that they were virtually nose to nose with the three musicians on stage, who were playing some classical number, which Shelby only recognised as being the current soundtrack to a car advert on TV.

A waiter offered them menus but Ross waved them away, muttering, "Two coffees."

"Would you like to try the spa water?" Ross asked her, indicating a small stone fountain in a bay window behind her. "I warn you, it tastes disgusting."

"Then why are so many people queuing up to drink it?"

"Because you come to the Pump Room and that's what you do. And it's a lot cheaper than the cream teas."

So she wandered across to the fountain to look. Water constantly poured from a stone urn into the mouths of four copper fishes. The waiter unceremoniously held a cup beneath one of the taps and handed it to her. She sniffed the water. It looked much the same as the stuff which came out of her sink back at the hotel.

"Well?" Ross asked, as she returned to their table. "What did you think?"

"Lovely," she fibbed, having not even tried it. "Better than the stuff you get in bottles at the supermarket."

"You have no taste," he said. And handed her a chocolate-chip cookie.

There was no reply to that so, her glass of water untouched, Shelby bit into her cookie, scattering crumbs across the table. Ross didn't notice, he was gazing unseeingly at something two inches to the left of her head. Shelby, fed up with the confused signals she was receiving from him, picked up the leaflet in the centre of the table for something to do and found she was reading the history of Bath's spa water. Never had she been so educated.

Ross's eyes returned to her and frowned. "Are you bored?"

Ten out of ten for observation, she thought. It was no wonder he didn't have a girlfriend if this was the way he treated his dates. Still, she ought to give him a chance to improve on his social skills . . .

"I'm sorry, I didn't realise you wanted to talk. I was just interested in the history of the Pump Room." Any moment now her nose was going to be two feet long.

"I wish I knew what was going on inside your head," he said at last. "I don't think I've ever met a bodyguard like you before."

She smiled. "They're normally more like Bruno?"

"Er, yes."

"Even the women?" She was teasing him now.

"No, the women are usually older, more self-confident – they don't blush so much. And they certainly don't pray to the Goddess Minerva to remove their freckles."

Oh hell, what else had he overheard? Feeling her cheeks begin to colour, she took a hasty swig of spa water and nearly choked.

"I told you it was disgusting," said Ross smoothly and signalled to the waitress for some more coffee.

I'm out of touch, thought Shelby sadly. How does one go about chatting up men? She could always flutter her eyelashes and ask him just exactly what it was that a director did. But she had no wish for him to think her more stupid than she already was. And besides, she had been watching him behind the camera all week, as he snarled instructions at Irving, for him to relay to everyone else.

"So what made you decide to become a bodyguard?" asked Ross suddenly.

"Minder," she corrected automatically. "Necessity. I needed to eat."

"I thought you were an ex-policewoman."

"An unemployed ex-policewoman."

"Were you sacked?"

"No, I was not!" she said hotly. "I resigned."

"Why?"

It was such a direct question there was no way of fudging an answer. But she tried anyway. "Because I was a pretty crap police officer, basically."

He took her hand and closed his fingers around it. "I'm sorry, I shouldn't have asked. You intrigue me. Did you know that? You're so full of contradictions."

That makes two of us. Shelby hid a smile. Perhaps he just wasn't very good with women. These intellectual types never were.

"Tell you what," he said, signalling for the bill, "let's just skip these dreary preliminaries and spend the afternoon in bed." He paused for his words to sink in, before adding, totally deadpan, "Unless, of course, you'd rather go shopping?"

* * *

The afternoon in bed. The words burnt into her mind as they walked back to the car, hand in hand. In fact, by the time they reached the hotel, she had more or less convinced herself that the word 'easy' was tattooed right across her forehead.

Rception was deserted as they walked through and up to Ross's suite. He strode in first, locking the door behind them. Pouring himself a drink from the mini-bar, he asked her what she would like.

Shelby, who had had it beaten into her by Irving to not, under any circumstances, use the mini-bar because it was a complete rip-off, was momentarily thrown.

"Baileys?" suggested Ross.

Shelby nodded her head dumbly, even though she hated the stuff, and hoped it wasn't what he gave all the other women that came up to his hotel room. What the hell was she doing? Ross wasn't the woman-shy intellectual. In fact, she was beginning to think he was an even bigger wolf than Luke.

Ross's room was much the same as Luke's, but smaller, and there was no Jacuzzi. She knew that because while Ross was pouring the drinks she dashed into the bathroom to dab make-up over her freckles.

"Would you like to see the rushes?" asked Ross, as she returned from the bathroom, pretty much as red-faced and flustered as when she went in.

Green grow the rushes-o, thought Shelby and wondered what on earth he was talking about. Did he have a fixation with ponds and baths – or just water generally?

"The film is developed in a lab overnight, then transferred to videotape for me to watch," said Ross, while he ripped open a Jiffy bag and pulled out a tape. He shoved it into the video machine. "Sometimes we film on video simultaneously, to get a rough guide that the scene works, but these tapes are the real thing."

Rushes . . . he was talking about the film. The bloody film . . . Come up and see my etchings, thought Shelby gloomily. Perhaps his idea of 'an afternoon in bed' was to spend it watching one of his own movies?

As she sat on one of the armchairs, Ross crouched in front of the video, adjusting the tracking, before flopping back onto the sofa. The screen flickered and then Luke, leading Shylock, and Courteney were walking around the gloom of Abbey Green, supposedly talking about the weather but with lots of passionate undercurrents crackling between them. After not many minutes Shelby found herself leaning forwards, practically on the edge of her seat.

Courteney was virtually playing an 19th century version of herself, and occasionally the English accent went all round the British Isles, spending a lot of time in Yorkshire and on the Welsh borders, before bombing back to Sloane Square and an excellent impersonation of the Queen. But Luke – Luke was amazing. Shelby had dismissed him as just a pretty face, a mannequin, but where were the strings? He *was* Lord Ravenscroft. The spoilt, arrogant Regency rake, desperately in love, desperately trying to conceal it. She almost fell in love with him on the spot. Until she remembered how he came onto her that night in Queen's Square.

"It's brilliant," she whispered.

"Thank you," said Ross. "It won't win an Oscar – the Americans have been flooded with this sort of thing over the last few years – especially since *Shakespeare In*

Love – but I'm hoping for a BAFTA. Provided, of course, that Luke doesn't cock it all up by playing the fool."

She had meant Luke's performance but didn't correct him. As the tape flickered and went blank she stared at Ross, hypnotised by the passion in his eyes. At last she had found the key to his character. He was in love with his work. It was almost as though he was turned on by it.

"Your glass is empty," he said.

She looked down at the glass, confused. She hadn't even remembered drinking it. He poured her another. Surely he wasn't trying to get her drunk? It was no good; she simply didn't understand him. Did he want to make love to her or not? Was he expecting her to make the first move? He'd be waiting a long time. She might be upfront but she wasn't forward.

She got up and wandered over to the window. The view was the same as hers. The garden, the wooded valley, the glimpse of Westbury far away in the distance.

"It is beautiful here," she said. And waited for a compliment to follow.

He said nothing. Damn him. She felt the hairs on the back of her neck rise as he stood up. Without even looking at him she could sense his every movement. It was as though they were tied by a ribbon of electricity. Yet *nothing* was *happening*. Unable to understand it, she began to feel piqued. Didn't he fancy her?

"Perhaps I should be going now," she said, turning, unable to hide the disappointment in her voice, "and let you get back to work?"

"Why don't you come over here?" said Ross softly.

Her heart did a triple backward somersault. But still she hesitated.

"Now," he added firmly.

It wasn't multiple choice. He stepped towards her, took hold of her hands and slowly pulled her towards him. Unwilling to look up, she gazed instead at the 'v' of his green shirt, his lightly tanned skin, the hollows of his neck, anywhere rather than those beautiful charcoal eyes. She could feel them, burning into her. She could smell the scent of his citrus aftershave. She could smell the scent of him . . .

"I know I'm moving fast," he murmured, as he bent his head to lightly kiss her forehead with unbearably cool lips. "But I don't want anyone else beating me to it."

Like who?

"You're so beautiful . . ." He moved his hands, still holding her own, behind her back, beneath her shirt and digging his thumbs into the back of her trousers.

At least my chest will look bigger, she thought, and she felt his skin warm against hers as he lowered his head, seeking her lips with his, kissing her relentlessly.

He backed her against the wall and she was trapped, her arms still behind her as his mouth devoured her, his tongue pressing urgently into her mouth, his body moving against hers. "Shelby . . ." he groaned.

"Mmm?"

"I don't want to spoil the moment but I have to know . . ."

"It's OK. I'm on the pill."

He broke away, laughing. "Actually, I was going to ask you about Luke?"

"Luke?" she repeated, thinking for one ghastly moment he was suggesting a threesome. "Why on earth do you want to talk about Luke?"

"So you're not sleeping together?"

She stared at him dumbfounded. "You have *got* to be *joking*!"

He laughed, "Sorry! I obviously misread the signs." And he ran his finger down her throat, pausing on the top button of her shirt. "Are you sure? Would you rather wait?"

Undo it, undo it, her heart screamed. Her mouth was too bourgeois to utter a word. Impatiently she wound her arms around his neck and pulled him down towards her, kissing him hungrily. Their teeth clashed. He joined in, bearing her back against the wall, but took her arms from around his neck and began to undo the buttons of her shirt, eventually losing patience and ripping it apart, the buttons pinging all across the room.

The shirt slithered to the floor. The wall was cold against her back but she was only aware of his fingers, sliding beneath the straps of her black lace bra, roughly dragging them to her elbows, his mouth suddenly hot against her skin.

Shelby gave up trying to keep up. She rested her hands on his shoulders and let him remove the rest of her clothes, and as he began to kiss his way up from her feet, all she could do was think how wonderful it was, and exactly like you saw in the films. And there was no need to say, 'Up a bit' or 'Left a bit', because Ross knew exactly where everything was, and where everything was going. And in no time at all, she was pulling his clothing off him and curling one leg around his back, and the universe was exploding somewhere inside her and she knew precisely why Ross had locked the door and was grateful he had.

There was no way she was going to let go of him long enough to sprint after any invading photographers.

* * *

It was a shame Ross did not have a Jacuzzi but there was a very large bath. And there was always the sofa and, after it got dark, the window seat with the marvellous view across the valley, although she had her eyes shut in ecstasy for most of the time.

And then, finally, they tumbled into bed – too tired to do anything other than sleep.

* * *

Sunday
They were woken the next morning by Jasper, the location manager, hammering on the outside door.

"Piss off," growled Ross. "It's Sunday!"

"This is an emergency," came Jasper's muffled voice.

Ross planted a kiss on Shelby's nose, kicked back the covers and strode out of the bedroom without bothering to put on any clothes. Shelby admired his lightly tanned, perfectly toned body and sighed. The only way she would ever look that wonderful was if she spent her entire life in a gym.

"This had better be good," she heard him say, as the door to the suite creaked open.

"You've got to sign this contract," said Jasper, "or the National Trust won't let us film in the Assembly Rooms on Monday."

"Contract?"

"Yeah, you signed one when we filmed at Prior Park, don't you remember?"

"Vaguely. Can't I do it tomorrow? I don't like signing things without reading them first."

"I've read it," replied Jasper anxiously. "It's kosher."

"Hmm."

"You can't sign it tomorrow. If the National Trust don't have this today they won't let us in tonight to rig up the lights."

"Oh, for Christ's sake, give it here and stop wittering. Have you got a pen?"

"Er, no. I thought you'd have – but, I can see that you, er, haven't."

Ross gave a sound of exasperation and walked over to the desk opposite the bedroom door, where he kept his briefcase. Irritably he snapped it open and ferreted around for a pen.

Jasper followed, acutely embarrassed by Ross's nakedness, and managed to stare all round the suite in an effort to avoid looking directly at him, only to have his gaze fall through the bedroom door and land upon

Shelby, sitting up in bed, wearing nothing but a rapidly fading smile.

Jasper went maroon with embarrassment. "Er, hi, Shelby," he muttered, quite unable to tear his eyes away.

"Hell!" said Shelby disappearing beneath the bedsheets. And knowing that Jasper was gay did not make her feel any better.

"When you've quite finished staring at my woman?" said Ross coldly. He held out the contract.

"What? Oh, terribly sorry." Jasper snatched it out of his hands. "Um, thanks for signing this. Erm . . . well. . . I suppose I'd better be going?"

"Yes, I think you better had."

"OK for our meeting this afternoon?"

"Yes."

"And you hadn't forgotten Floyd Mulligan is due tonight? And, er, the actress taking over from Octavia tomorrow?"

"No. Goodbye, Jasper."

"Bye, Ross." He raised his voice. "Bye, Shelby!"

"Bye, Jasper." It was like living with The Waltons.

There was silence and then the bedcovers were abruptly torn from her fingers and thrown onto the floor, and Ross was slowly trailing his tongue across her stomach and up the soft white hill of her breast.

"What's up?" he said at last, when he got no response.

"He saw me," whispered Shelby.

"So?" Ross moved away, covering her up again with the sheet. He threw one of the hotel's fluffy blue bathrobes around his shoulders. "This is a film shoot, darling. You can't keep anything secret." He paused. "Did you want to?"

"No . . ."

"Good," he said curtly. "I'm off to take a shower, I've got a meeting with the production team later. Why don't you order yourself some breakfast?"

Slowly Shelby pulled the bedsheet up until it was tucked beneath her chin. Somehow the magic had gone.

Chapter Eleven

That evening, Shelby waited in Neptune's Bar, hope flaring every time the door swung open, in case it was Ross. She had been there over an hour already and was beginning to feel like a spinster stood up by a blind date.

She had spent the afternoon in the gym and swimming endlessly up and down the pool in her new black string bikini. Extraordinarily tacky but Courteney, buying something equally ostentatious in metallic green, had put her up to it. Shelby had fantasised about waiting for Ross in his suite, still in her string bikini. But as he was currently closeted in the hotel function room with the entire production team, a dry-wipe board, a fistful of marker pens and a video recorder, she realised she could end up waiting all day.

She picked up her beer and wandered over to the French windows for something to do. There was an elderly pianist hunched over the piano, working through a repertoire that consisted of hits from the fifties and sixties. It was not to Shelby's taste but she leant against the grand piano, idly tapping her foot, staring at her unhappy reflection in the polished wood. Although an inadequate looking-glass, she could still see the dark hollows beneath her eyes. Too much sex and not enough sleep. No wonder Ross was not beating a path to her bedroom door.

"He who has never loved and lost has never loved at all," she told herself sadly, and hurriedly wiped away the tear threatening to trickle unromantically along her nose.

There was a chuckle from the other side of the piano.

Through the shadows and cigarette smoke Shelby could just make out a short, elderly man, sitting on the piano stool, cigarette-holder clamped between his teeth. He had pleated, rumpled skin, as though someone had recently slept in it, and shaggy white hair falling into his eyes. A cross between Noel Coward and the mad professor from *Back To The Future*.

"What's your problem?" she snapped, picking up her beer for a swift exit through the French windows.

The man lifted his left hand from the keyboard to remove the cigarette from his mouth, still playing the melody with his right. "My dear girl, surely you don't expect me to stay silent while you misquote Tennyson? Although you do it beautifully." The cigarette was again clamped between the teeth.

Shelby was taken aback. One didn't expect pianists to swap insults. "Tennis what?"

The cigarette came out again, creating delicate wispy patterns of smoke in the air. "Tennyson."

She frowned. "Is that a person or a place?"

"What do they teach you at school nowadays? Irvine Welsh, I suppose. Shudder, shudder."

"Sorry?" said Shelby, wondering if he was perhaps not all there.

"Allow me." He breathed deeply and closed his eyes. "'*Tis better to have loved and lost, than never to have loved at all.*'"

She finally twigged. "You're an actor."

"My dear, you flatter me." This time he did not bother to remove the cigarette-holder, as his fingers slid up and down the keyboard, softly playing a very familiar melody.

She wondered where she had seen him before. "Have you been on TV?"

"Hundred of times. Once," he sighed, "a very long time ago, I was as famous as Luke McFadden. The youth of Britain idolised me – they even named a hairstyle after me." He grinned suddenly. "Not this one though."

"Really?" Shelby didn't believe a word of it. Why did she always attract the weirdos? She wanted to edge away but knew it would appear rude.

"Girls would scream when I walked on stage, women would abandon their husbands for just one night of love . . ." His bloodshot eyes began to twinkle self-deprecatingly. "Now . . . now they misquote Tennyson at me."

Despite herself, Shelby had to smile – and then recognised the Chris de Burgh song he was playing. Her smile faded. "I'm not wearing red," she said shortly. Surely he wasn't coming on to her? He was old enough to be her grandfather. To hide her embarrassment, she took a swig of her drink but found she had already polished it off.

"Now what are you going to do with your hands?" he mocked.

Shelby scowled. "Can't you play something with a bit more go?"

He switched from 'Lady In Red' to 'Rock Around The Clock'. She pulled a face.

"A bit before your time?" he asked politely.

"A bit before my mother's time. Do you know any Travis, Stereophonics?"

"No, thank God. Here, do you recognise this?"

She grinned. "Even I can play 'Chopsticks'."

He stubbed out his cigarette. "Come on, then," he said and slid up to the other end of the seat, patting the space beside him. "Duet?"

For a moment she hesitated and glanced round the bar. 'Chopsticks' in a five-star hotel? It was tantamount to playing the Sex Pistols at Glyndebourne. Then the devil got into her. She was tired of being on her best behaviour. She wanted to have fun – and she was hardly going to be fired for crashing out a few wrong keys on a bar-room piano.

The man smiled approvingly as she squeezed next to him on the piano stool and offered her a drink from a small silver flask. "Dutch courage?"

What the hell. She took a large swig, found she was drinking neat whisky and almost choked. She handed it back, her eyes watering. "I'm surprised you can find the piano, let alone the right keys."

"Practice, my dear girl. Years of practice."

Music or alcohol? But he was already counting out the beat and soon she was too busy attempting to keep up, to hold her own against his artistic little flourishes, to think of anything else.

By the time they had finished they were giggling hysterically and the manager was walking very purposely in their direction.

Shelby's new friend elbowed her off the piano seat. "Time to be sensible." Assuming a serene expression, he began to play something soft and anonymous.

"Mr Mulligan," began the manager, "I'm most terribly sorry but, well, I'm afraid we've had complaints."

"I'm not surprised," came the reply. "When was the last time you had this piano tuned? I ask you, does this sound like an 'A'?"

The manager was taken aback. "Well . . . I'm afraid I couldn't say . . ."

"My point exactly. Even 'Chopsticks' sounds perfectly dreadful, and as I'm sure you are aware, you can play 'Chopsticks' on any old thing."

"Causing trouble again, Floyd?" said a voice above Shelby's head. A hand slipped easily around her shoulder and she felt a familiar prickle of electricity shoot through her veins.

The manager melted away.

"Ross!" Shelby's new friend stood up and kissed both his cheeks. "How lovely to see you again, and so like your dear mother."

"You think so?" returned Ross frigidly. "She always accuses me of taking after my father."

"Floyd Mulligan?" gasped Shelby, staring at her new friend incredulously. "But I know you! My mother has all your records."

Floyd gave a rueful smile. "I'm grateful it's not your grandmother."

"But you're *famous*," she stammered. "You did all those films, about that detective concert pianist and his whisky-drinking cat. They were so funny."

"I hate to shatter your ideals, my dear, but I did it for the money. Four ex-wives to support. Or is it five?"

"Six," retorted Ross. "You left out my mother – although I seem to remember she paid *you* alimony."

Floyd failed to bite. "She was always number one in my heart, dear boy."

Shelby gaped. "Your *father*?"

"We assume so," said Ross coldly. "At least, his name's on my birth certificate."

Floyd was concentrating on inserting yet another cigarette into his holder. "I was always disappointed that you decided not to use my surname professionally."

"Ross Mulligan sounds like a potato farmer."

"You're right," sighed Floyd. "But I'm sure I christened you 'Russell'."

"I think it was the Vicar who christened me. According to my mother, you weren't even there."

"I was in spirit."

Ross looked pointedly at Floyd's little silver flask, which had left several sticky rings across the top of the piano. "The less said about spirits the better. As your director I suggest you sober up. You have a five am call. Excuse me, I wish to show my girlfriend the moonlight."

Floyd laughed. And as Ross took Shelby's hand and led her through the French windows, he began to play, very softly, 'Blue Moon'.

The night was warm but there was a faint cool breeze and, more as an excuse to get near to him, Shelby leant back against Ross's shoulder and soon forgot the peculiar exchange she had just witnessed, between supposed father and son.

Ross pulled her back against his chest, wrapping his arms around her, resting his chin on the top of her head. She could feel his warmth radiating through his faded denim shirt, the scent of his citrus aftershave, and closed her eyes to savour the moment.

"I'm sorry I've been neglecting you," he said, in his deep, oh so seductive voice. "Have you been horribly bored?"

"No," lied Shelby. "I've been swimming."

"The pool here is a good size."

Shelby had no wish to talk about swimming-pools. She wanted to talk about romantic things like the moon and stars. Love and life. Their Future. She wanted him to sling her over his shoulder and carry her off to his cave – or perhaps a four-poster water bed would be more comfortable – and ravish her. She wanted to drink champagne and eat strawberries dipped in chocolate. Off his delectable body.

Instead she asked, "Is Floyd really your father?"

Ross moved away and lit up a cigarette. "Yes," he said shortly, tossing the used match into a flowerbed. "More's the pity."

The breeze, free-wheeling along the valley, caused goosebumps over her exposed skin. "Is your mother famous too?" she asked, hastily changing the subject.

"Julianne Whitney."

The star of all those MGM musicals – it was like saying she had never heard of Elizabeth Taylor. Shelby gulped. "Do you have any brothers or sisters?"

"No. My parents divorced before I was two. I was brought up by my aunts."

Shelby's heart broke at the thought of that lonely little boy, abandoned by his parents, shunted from home to home. Although aware she was possibly digging a bottomless pit for herself, she gabbled on, "I've got three brothers."

Ross paused, cigarette glowing a deep dark red as the smoke twisted in a thin silvery column towards the stars. "Three?"

At last, a safe subject. "Irving, Cary and Harrison."

Ross flicked the ash from his cigarette. It showered onto the flagstones like pixie-dust. "And who saddled you with those ridiculous names?"

It was almost as though he had slapped her. "My mother adored going to the movies," she said slowly. "She especially loved the glamour of old Hollywood –

Marilyn Monroe, Fred and Ginger, Cary Grant. I suppose she thought their allure would rub off on us. But only Irving inherited her dreams. And, instead of dreaming, he did something about it." She spoke cheerfully but inside she felt hurt. Surely there was nothing worse than your parents calling you Jill or John, purely because they couldn't be bothered to think of anything more original?

Ross took another drag on his cigarette. He appeared to be having trouble concentrating on their conversation. As the silence began to linger on, to hang ominously in the still night air, he finally dragged his gaze from the distant gleam of Westbury and smiled at her.

"Lucky you didn't end up being called Dumbo or Goofy really."

He was teasing her now but she was stung into retorting, "Or Russell."

More uncomfortable silence, broken only by the squeak of the French windows as another couple joined them on the terrace.

"*Touché,*" he said eventually, just as she thought she had really lost him. He stroked her hair back from her forehead. "Sorry. I have something else on my mind."

The bloody film no doubt. She stared up at him, hypnotised by those grey forbidding eyes. Did he realise how much he could wound her with just a few casual words?

He broke the stare first and stubbed out his cigarette, grinding it viciously into the flagstones with his heel.

"I didn't know you smoked," she said, watching the sparks flicker then die.

"I don't. I'm feeling stressed. It was a cigarette or a double whisky – and I've a five am call tomorrow. It's the ballroom scene at the Assembly Rooms. I just know Luke is going to play me up." He sighed. "It's going to be hell."

"So I suppose you'll be wanting an early night?" It was difficult not to let the grudging note creep into her voice.

He tilted her face up and kissed her. "Is that an offer?"

She smiled. "I'm supposed to be waiting up for Luke. He's due back tonight. I think his train must have been delayed."

"To hell with Luke," he whispered, taking her into his arms, pressing her back against the wall.

"If anything happens to Luke, I lose my job."

"Only during working hours. Besides, Luke is Charles's responsibility at the moment. Forget about him. He's probably forgotten all about you and is quite happily propping up some barmaid."

Shelby closed her eyes as he slowly kissed her. His lips were cold and his mouth tasted of cigarettes and, despite his protestations, very faintly of whisky. As he increased the pressure, his hands sliding down the inside of her jeans, she could feel the hard rough stone against her back, grazing her skin. Remembering the last time they had kissed against a wall she shivered in anticipation.

"Are you cold?" Ross suddenly released her. "Do you want to go indoors?"

I want to go to bed. I want you to make mad passionate love to me all night, and bugger *your five am call.* She regarded him wistfully, eyes dark with longing, unaware her emotions were plastered all over her face like the headlines in a tabloid newspaper.

He smiled, surprisingly tenderly, and taking her hand he squeezed it reassuringly and led her back along the flagstoned terrace. As they stepped through the French windows they passed the couple who had come out earlier. Instead of being entwined in a passionate embrace, they were leaning silently back against the wall, a good two foot of stone and wisteria between them. They must have had a row, thought Shelby, and tried not to be caught staring curiously. It was too late. The woman glanced up and regarded Shelby with antagonism.

The man, his face in shadow, was obliviously shredding the blossoms from the wisteria behind him, scattering them like mauve grapes all around his feet. As Ross steered her through the door, Shelby suddenly realised the woman was Dulcie. Perhaps Dulcie had got lucky – or rather unlucky – with one of the crew? He was certainly too tall to be Irving. But why was she giving Shelby such filthy looks?

"Hello, Dulcie, you're looking well," said Ross cheerfully.

Dulcie gave him a tight smile but she looked at Shelby with positive daggers.

Shelby moved away, unwilling to be drawn into conversation. She wanted to keep Ross to herself, not become waylaid by pointless polite small talk with a woman who didn't even like her. But Ross had suddenly become Mr Sociable.

"Hello, Luke," said Ross, crushing the delicate wisteria blossoms beneath his Timberland boots. "Glad you made it back."

Luke smiled, although technically it was more a baring of teeth.

Ross did not appear to notice. "You don't mind if I borrow your bodyguard for the night, do you?"

* * *

Shelby followed Ross up the stairs to his suite, the usual three paces behind, and wondered why she felt uneasy. Just what was it between Ross and Luke that they felt they had to continuously score points off each other?

"Drink?" said Ross, pausing by the mini-bar.

She avoided looking at him, fiddling with the strap of her rucksack. "Perhaps I'll just leave you to sleep – you have an early call tomorrow –"

"What makes you think I'll be able to sleep with you lying beside me?"

"Oh but I wasn't –"

"Well, you're certainly not sleeping anywhere else," he said, lazily running his fingers through her hair. "I want you here, with me." And he kissed her, a sweet tender kiss, causing her such a flood of desire and love, she succumbed without another murmur, her rucksack

157

slipping from her fingers, hitting the carpet with a dull thud.

Ross slid his hands beneath her T-shirt, tugging it roughly from the waistband of her jeans, dropping to his knees to plant hot wet kisses across her freckled tummy. Shelby attempted to squirm away, giggling hysterically, until they both fell, laughing, onto the floor. And then suddenly, they were not laughing.

"You drive me crazy," he whispered, tugging off her T-shirt and bra in one swift, practised movement.

"Good." Shelby fumbled for the buckle on his belt, before the cold metal could press uncomfortably against her torso. But he pulled her hands away, holding them above her head, and removed the belt himself with one hand, then coiled it around her wrists and pulled it almost painfully tight before she could realise what was happening and stop him.

"Get out of that one, Houdini."

Kinky, thought Shelby, and attempted to wriggle free, first playfully then, as the belt failed to loosen, more frantically, not liking the unaccustomed feeling of helplessness. But she was pinned by the weight of his body.

"Let me go!"

"So bondage isn't one of your fantasies?"

Fantasy is one thing, cold reality quite another, she thought, as the leather began to bite into her wrists. "Why do you always have to be in control?"

"The same reason you do," he grinned wickedly. "And only one of us can win." His mouth closed over hers, his tongue flicking over her lips and into her mouth, just as she snapped her teeth shut. "Naughty," he chided, tapping her on the nose. "I can see I'm going to have to spank you."

At the look of absolute horror on her face, he began to laugh. "I was only joking!"

"This isn't funny any more." She glared at him. "I feel stupid."

"Try to relax," he said, sliding his fingers across her ribcage, stroking her tummy with small rhythmic strokes. "You're tense."

"Tense! Of course I'm bloody tense! I'm trussed up like Christmas turkey and —"

He kissed her again. "I do wish you'd be quiet. You'd enjoy it more." And his warm hand continued to massage her cool goose-pimply flesh. "Your stomach muscles are all knotted up."

"That is not my stomach."

"Mmm, I know." He licked his finger and ran it across the top of her nipple, causing her stomach muscles to knot up again, teasing the nipple round and round until it rose up like a raspberry soufflé. "That doesn't feel so bad, does it?"

"I am not responsible for the behaviour of my nipples," said Shelby, closing her eyes.

Ross laughed. She was vaguely aware of him tugging off her jeans, then nothing, just a cold blast of air. Where had he gone? A sudden fear that he might have abandoned her, in such a compromising position, caused her eyes to flick open in time to see two globules of red-brown liquid drop onto her breasts, hovering for just a second before trickling into rivulets across her tummy.

"Cherry brandy?" she muttered in disgust, recognising the sickly sweet smell. "Don't I deserve champagne?"

"Stop complaining," he said, leisurely licking it off. "It was the first bottle that came to hand. At least you're not the one drinking the revolting stuff."

She closed her eyes and sighed. "It's making my nipples tingle."

"It's making *me* sticky," and he and suddenly scooped her up into his arms. The belt fell from her wrists as he covered the distance to the bathroom in four long strides. He dropped her into the shower, stepping in beside her.

"You're still wearing your jeans," she said. "You'll get wet."

"Then take them off."

She had just managed to slide down the zip when suddenly the shower exploded somewhere above them, drenching them both in freezing water. She shrieked and reached for the hot tap.

"*Simonetta,*" he smiled as he picked up the soap and began to slowly lather her body in familiar citrus-scented bubbles.

Which had better be a literary allusion, she thought, and *not* the name of his ex-girlfriend . . .

* * *

And later, much later, Shelby woke up feeling cold and

realised the bedsheets had been thrown back and Ross was sitting hunched up on the window seat, wearing an old pair of jeans, staring bleakly at the lights dancing in the distance, smoking yet another cigarette.

Poor Ross, she thought fondly. Still worrying about tomorrow's filming . . .

Shelby pulled the duvet up to her nose, rolled over and went back to sleep.

Chapter Twelve

Courteney was depressed. This was a whole new experience so it took a while before she recognised the emotion. She had spent the day doing her favourite things; shopping, eating and being pampered at the hotel's beauty salon. She even had pink streaks put into her blonde hair to wind Ross up – but, as she stared at her reflection in the mirror above the hotel bar, she had to ask herself if she really cared any more. There was only so much rejection a person could take.

She had wandered into Neptune's Bar an hour ago and ordered a bottle of their finest champagne. Their only champagne actually; it was that kind of place. Five different brands of sherry but only one champagne. Courteney, feeling too flat to even make a scene, handed over one of her credit cards and the barman popped the cork, nearly taking out one of the overhead lights, and poured her a glass. Dispiritedly, she watched the bubbles bounce off the bottom of the glass, then race to the surface and explode.

Vaguely she wondered where everyone else was. It was no fun sitting in a bar getting drunk on your own. Having successfully lost Bruno in town several hours ago, she was surprised to find she would be pleased to see even him walk through that door. Mostly, however, she would be pleased to see Ross. Although after the last few days, she doubted whether it would be reciprocated.

Ross had made it obvious that he didn't want her; he seemed to positively detest her. How could he switch his emotions on and off so easily? How could he appear to be madly in love one moment, then hate her the next? What had she done to make him dislike her so? Or maybe he had never liked her at all and his protestations of love had been just a clever performance. Which would make him a better actor than Olivier – or alternatively, psychologically disturbed.

"Are you going to drink that champagne?" asked Irving, regarding her glass covetously.

Courteney nearly tipped the glass into his lap. "Don't creep up on a person like that!"

Irving sat on the stool beside her, ordering a Foster's from the barman. "What were you doing?" He smiled. "Having bubble races?"

Courteney shot him what she hoped was a disdainful look. Admittedly a bit tricky when you had pink streaks and plastic yellow daisies in your hair. "I was not."

"Sure looked like it." Irving picked up his pint, drank it in one go and promptly ordered another. "I needed that," he sighed, wiping the moustache of foam from his upper lip. "I've spent the whole day locked up with Ross and a sweaty film crew, watching rushes. Ah well, one week down, two to go and then *freedom*." And he punched the air in a fair imitation of Mel Gibson.

Courteney tried not to dwell on how much she'd enjoy being locked up with Ross – although she'd pass on the sweaty film crew. Instead she asked, "So, how were the rushes? Any good?"

"Bits. Luke is great. Dean can't make up his mind whether to play himself or pretend he's Robbie Williams. Octavia hams it up and talks too loudly, as though she's projecting to Wembley Arena but, as she was playing the villain, I don't think anyone's going to notice. Hollywood likes its villains over the top and English. She's going to be a huge success."

Courteney waited patiently but, as he was showing no signs of extolling the brilliance of her own performance, she was forced to meekly enquire, "And me?"

"You're OK," shrugged Irving, draining his second pint and waving a tenner in the direction of the barman.

"Thanks! I can see me at the Oscars right now – 'And now, for 'The Most OK Actress In A Movie' – Courteney O'Connor in *A Midsummer Kiss*'."

Irving blushed. "I didn't mean it like that. It just came out wrong. You're fine, honestly. Nothing to worry about. Really."

"Quit while you're ahead, Irving. I appreciate I'm not Oscar-winning material."

"I didn't think you were interested in awards? This

is the wrong sort of film if you want to line your bathroom with statuettes. *Midsummer Kiss* is just commercial pap. Join-the-dots costume drama, made easy for the unwashed masses to understand. Why else do you think Ross would hire a pop star to play one of the leads?"

"And why else would he hire me for the love interest?" derided Courteney.

"Oh heck, I've done it again, haven't I?" Irving slid off his bar stool and clumsily put his arm around her shoulders. "You're a great actress, Courteney. Funny, talented; the crew are all madly in love with you. I'm just trying to say, that if you wanted to win an Oscar you should have picked some gritty, low-budget film about heroin addiction, or AIDS, or young Americans dying horribly in some foreign war directed by Oliver Stone or Steven Spielberg. Not one of Ross Whitney's corny romantic comedies." Irving paused. "Why did you agree to do this film anyway?"

Because I had just had the most fabulous sex ever with the director and it seemed like a good idea at the time, thought Courteney. But of course there was no way she was going to tell Irving that. She could imagine his pale freckly face glowing pink with embarrassment.

He was already having trouble meeting her eyes; his gaze centred somewhere above her right ear. This was not a new experience for Courteney. Except men usually directed their conversation at her chest.

"I don't know if it's the light," he said, "but your hair looks pink."

"It is pink."

"Is that the fashion?"

"I haven't a clue. I only did it to freak Ross out." She grinned. "I kinda excelled myself this time, didn't I? The colour being permanent and all."

Irving smiled sympathetically. "I don't think Ross is going to notice. He's not very observant at the best of times and you do spend the whole film wearing a wig."

"Talk of the devil," muttered Courteney. She watched Ross duck through the French windows and stride imperiously through the bar, pulling Shelby in his wake. He did not even glance in her direction.

"Womanising pig," she muttered, and knocked back the rest of her drink.

Beside her, Irving had gone into shock. "What's that bastard doing with my sister?"

She shot him an old-fashioned look. "Didn't they have the birds and the bees talk at your high school?"

But Irving was watching Ross and Shelby disappear through reception and up the stairs, still hand in hand. "There must be at least twenty eligible women working on this film and the bastard has to pick my sister. And, more to the point, what the hell does she see in *him*?"

"If you can't work it out by yourself, I'm not going to tell you."

Her bottle of champagne was now empty and the barman had no more chilling in his fridge. Bored, Courteney began drumming her fingers on the bar, unconsciously in time with the elderly pianist, currently playing 'Your Cheatin' Heart'. The guy must be a mind-reader.

Catching Courteney watching him, he gave her a huge wink and launched into 'Mambo Italiano'. Courteney smiled ruefully. How did he guess she needed something bright and cheesy to cheer herself up.

"Do you think he knows any Corrs?" grumbled Irving, who was not keen on anything he termed 'fifties crap'."

Courteney, tired of his carping, bored of evenings closeted away with a bunch of unknown, eccentric, English actors, desperate for some fun, some love, hell, some *adventure* in her life, climbed onto the bar and began to dance, high-kicking any drinks out of her way.

Irving put his hand over his eyes and wondered if he was responsible for ensuring she didn't make a fool of herself but couldn't really work out how he was going to stop her. Although if he didn't, who would? Certainly not the group of inebriated businessmen cheering from one corner of the room or the rest of the clientele who were frostily ignoring the performance.

"Courteney," he said timidly, "I really think you ought to get down."

"No chance."

"You'll regret it in the morning."

"I only live for today."

"What if you slip and hurt yourself?"

"I'll be on the first plane out of here. Yippee!"

Which had not been the reaction he had been hoping for. "Think of Ross," he hissed. (After all, Ross frightened the life out of him). "What's he going to say?"

167

"I am thinking of Ross." She kicked Irving's pint of Foster's clear across the room. *"Bastard!"*

Irving climbed gingerly onto his stool, then up onto the bar beside her. The wooden counter top was awash with the beer Courteney had kicked over and was extremely slippery. Having finally got his balance, he checked on Courteney's progress and found her sashaying in his direction.

"Way to go, Irving!" she shimmied against him. "I didn't know you had it in you."

Irving didn't realise he had it in him either. Before he realised what was happening, he was part of the cabaret, as Courteney danced with him, up and down the bar, hopping over the pumps, skidding on the beer. The gang of cheering, inebriated businessmen sounded as though they might very well join in at any moment.

The barman, a thunderous look upon his face, was making cutting motions across his jugular vein.

"Come on if you think you're hard enough," mocked Courteney.

He wasn't – but he knew a man who was and picked up the telephone to call security.

Irving caught hold of Courteney's hands. "This has got to stop," he urged her. "Come on. Get down. I'll take you back to your room."

Courteney grinned and playfully slapped away his hands. "Fresh!"

"Be serious! Don't you understand the trouble you're going to be in? Hotel security will be here any moment, maybe even the police. Do you really want to spend the night in the cells, have your picture splashed all over the papers tomorrow, perhaps even get a conviction for drunk and disorderly?"

As Courteney suddenly stopped dancing and clutched hold of his arm, he thought maybe he'd finally got through to her.

Actually, she had more pressing things on her mind. "Oh my God," she muttered, her face turning a sickly grey-green, "I think I'm going to be sick. Now!"

Irving handed her the ice bucket and removed himself from the fall-out zone.

* * *

After that little exhibition, it didn't take much persuasion to hurry Courteney away from the bar, up the stairs to her suite – to the tune of 'Who's Sorry Now?'.

"Put some music on," muttered Courteney, as she dashed into the bathroom. "It'll hide the sound of me barfing."

Irving obediently wandered over to the expensive music centre, nervousness churning his insides. What did she want to be taking a bath for, with him still here?

He flipped through her extensive record collection and to his delight found an old Corrs album. He stuck it into the CD player and pressed 'shuffle'.

Despite turning the volume as loud as he dared (Ross's room was next door), he could still hear Courteney throwing up, then a long pause, followed by the sound of running water as she cleaned her teeth. He busied himself flipping through the pile of glossy magazines casually dumped on the coffee table. Disconcertingly, they all seemed to feature Courteney.

The girl herself emerged from her bathroom looking pale, but sporting fresh turquoise-and-gold eyeliner slicked around her aquamarine eyes. He could also see the remains of silver body-glitter dusting her cheeks and found himself wondering if it would come off when he kissed her. Not that he was going to, he told himself grimly.

"What do you look like without your glasses?" asked Courteney and promptly whipped them off.

"Blind," replied Irving dryly. "So give them back."

But Courteney had popped them onto her own snub nose. "Everything's gone out of focus," she complained. "How can you see in these things?"

"Perfectly," replied Irving, wearily. "Because I'm short-sighted. You, however, have perfect twenty-twenty vision. That's why everything looks distorted."

Courteney giggled. "Oh yeah." She took the glasses off and, ignoring Irving's outstretched hand, gently replaced them on his nose. "You have the most incredible eyes. A sort of emerald green with chunks of gold. I used to have some nail lacquer exactly the same colour."

Irving, who had never had his eyes compared to nail varnish but recognised a come-on when he heard one, quickly took two steps backwards but Courteney had already wound her arms around his neck.

"Dance with me, Irving," she pleaded. "I never get

to dance. Bruno won't let me go to any of the clubs with Luke in case I get mobbed."

Irving had hoped that, with all the throwing up, she would now be stone-cold sober. After all, there was no way she would feel attracted to him unless she was drunk. Was there?

As they began to dance around the sitting-room, slower this time, he felt genuinely sorry for her. In some ways she was still a child, he decided, her development having frozen at fifteen, when she first hit the big time. While her friends were going to sleepovers and proms, she was attending glitzy Hollywood parties and premieres with people twice her age. Like him.

"Can't you go out in disguise?" he asked, as they jived around the room to 'Breathless'. "You don't have any trouble shopping."

"When I'm shopping I dress down, hide my hair with a baseball cap and dark glasses. If I don't draw attention to myself then no one notices me. Nightclubbing is all about drawing attention to yourself. Besides, I don't want to get into a cat-fight with some woman jealous that her man is hitting on me. Or have beer thrown at me. That's another favourite. On one memorable occasion I even had my head stuck down the john and, well, I leave the rest to your imagination. Mind you, that time I had kinda asked for it."

"God, how awful," said Irving. At school, he had been a magnet for bullies. He had more in common with Courteney than he realised.

"I know," she agreed. "Sometimes it's hell to be me."

Irving realised she was taking the piss.

She took hold of his hands and pulled him against her. "Talk to me some more, Irving. You've got such a cute accent. Do you know any Shakespeare?"

Irving tried to ignore the way her body brushed against his and tentatively rested his hands on her waist. Was he really here, dancing around a luxury hotel suite with film star Courteney O'Connor? It was as though he'd walked into a Richard Curtis film.

"Talk to me!" Courteney dug her finger into his collar bone.

"Er, yes, of course." Although it was becoming increasingly difficult to concentrate, the way the tips of her fingers were stroking the back of his neck, her body pressed against his, her hip bones grazing his – well, perhaps it was better not to think about her hips. He tried to place a respectful distance between them but Courteney only wound herself tighter about his neck. "Erm, what would you like to talk about?"

"Tell me about your unhappy childhood."

Irving was taken aback. "I didn't have an unhappy childhood. Did you have an unhappy childhood?"

"Nope. I always had everything I ever wanted. And I want *you*, Irving Roberts. I think you're lovely."

Irving was glad the room was only lit by a small sidelight; he could feel his face light up like Blackpool Illuminations. He found his mouth forming the words, "That's nice," and clamped it quickly shut. Sometimes, the inanities he habitually came out with during moments of stress had a horrible habit of sounding like sarcasm. At least with his mouth shut he couldn't get his foot into it.

Or anything else, he realised, as Courteney suddenly pressed her mouth firmly on his. For several embarrassing moments they were stuck, mouth to mouth, nose to nose, looking each other straight in the eyes, confused.

Courteney broke away first. "Don't you fancy me, either?" She sounded close to tears.

"Of course I do! I mean –" So much for playing cool. "It's just, it's just, oh hell!" Irving quickly took her back into his arms and kissed her thoroughly, if not expertly. It was not as though he got much practice, he thought ruefully. But at least she couldn't doubt his enthusiasm.

"Whey hey," giggled Courteney and pushed him back onto the sofa. (One of the disadvantages of being 5'6" was that women could easily push you around.) "Give it to me, baby!"

Irving scowled. "If you're going to take the piss –"

"No, I'm just going to take off all your clothes." And she began undoing his shirt buttons.

Irving tried to sit up only to be pushed back down again. "Now, Courteney, I don't think –"

"Good idea," said Courteney, kissing her way down from his collar bone. "It's best not to think."

"Courteney!"

She sat astride his waist, her hands on her hips, and glared at him. "Now what's the matter? Honestly, you British do nothing but complain."

"I'm a lot older than you," he said gently, "and I

think you've had a bit too much to drink. I don't want to take advantage."

Courteney threw her head back and laughed raucously. "Silly boy," she said, ripping off his belt. "I'm taking advantage of *you*!"

* * *

Irving woke up on the dot of five-thirty, thank God, so he could get up and dressed and back to his own rather insignificant hotel room before Baz turned up to do his usual 'overture and beginners' routine, banging on Courteney's door.

But as he was about to get out of bed, he made the mistake of glancing across at Courteney, still asleep, her feathery lashes sweeping her cheeks. Sleeping Beauty's prettier (cheekier) little sister. How on earth had he managed to bed that? Although, to be honest, last night had been mostly her idea. He would never have dared to have, presumed to have – which was probably his trouble, he realised crossly. *A life lived in fear is a life half- lived*, as the heroine had said to the hero in *Strictly Ballroom*.

So from now on he was going to live life to the full. And he rolled over to snuggle up to her.

Something sharp dug into his cheek and he almost cursed out loud. Groping around on the pillow, he came up with a shiny square of white plastic, printed with a darker square in the middle. He squinted at it. It was no good, he'd have to put his glasses on. Trouble was, Courteney had flung them across the room in a fit of passion last night and they could be anywhere . . .

Carefully, Irving slid out of bed, expecting at any moment to hear a crunch underfoot. But no, miracle upon miracle, they had landed the right way up on the dressing-table, nestled between Courteney's collection of expensive moisturising creams and a large, gold-framed photo of her parents. Next time, Irving grimaced, he'd ensure their proud, beaming faces were turned to the wall.

He slid his glasses over his nose and padded back towards the bed. Christ, it was cold. In the sitting-room, the French windows onto the balcony had blown open, the voile curtains rippling in the breeze sweeping up the valley. Irving fastened the doors, then remembered the square of plastic he still held in his hand and held it up to the light.

With shock, he realised he was looking at a Polaroid photograph of himself.

And Courteney.

Together.

Making love.

* * *

Luke had always had Irving down as the easily bullied, timid type and could never quite work out how he had managed to land the job of first assistant director, except perhaps Irving was the only person Ross could get to put up with him. Luke was rather surprised, therefore, to open his door that morning to Irving, wearing just a hand-towel around his skinny hips. He was shivering but red-faced with fury, forcing Luke against the wall and holding him there with a surprisingly strong grip.

"Sorry," said Luke blankly. "Could you run that by me again? I'm not a morning person."

"Don't you get fucking flippant with me, you fucking fucking pervert!"

At least the guy was becoming more coherent, thought Luke, although unfortunately he still couldn't understand what Irving was going on about. He was also starting to get a crick in his neck.

"Irving," he said politely, "may I suggest you loosen you grip on my windpipe before I break off every one of your fingers and shove them up your arse?"

"Just because you're bigger than me –"

"Exactly," said Luke and, removing Irving's hand from around his neck, leant over to close the door to the corridor. The last thing he wanted was photographic evidence of the argument. He handed Irving a robe. "Put this on, before you catch your death. Calm down, and tell me what I'm supposed to have done – or not done. Would you like a cup of tea?"

"No," said Irving, but he threw the robe around his shoulders and stalked into the sitting-room.

Luke followed in bemusement. "Have I upset Shelby?"

"Shelby?" For a moment it was Irving's turn to look baffled. "This has nothing to do with Shelby and you know it. This time you've gone too far. You and your practical jokes – this time I'm going to make sure Ross fires you."

Luke attempted to remember the events of the last twenty-four hours. As far as he could remember, he had returned from London at ten, drank a couple of pints, half-heartedly chatted up Dulcie and then gone to bed. On his own. And to his great disappointment, not dreamt about Shelby. Practical jokes had not featured.

"Come again?" he said.

"This!" Irving waved a Polaroid beneath his nose.

Luke whistled. "Christ! Is that you and – well, yes, I can see it is but –" He checked himself. "That's really clever, very artistic – but how did you manage to take the photo yourself?"

Irving regarded him incredulously. "I didn't. *You* did."

Luke shook his head. "Group sex is not really my thing. Spreads the happiness a little too thinly."

"Are you saying you didn't take this photograph?"

"That's what I'm saying, Irving."

"So who did?"

"Some 'fucking fucking pervert' I guess."

"Someone sneaked into Courteney's bedroom last night, and took this photograph – and we didn't even notice? It's not possible."

"Must have been good sex."

Irving glanced sharply at him. "This isn't funny, Luke."

The time for joking around was past. "You're right," he agreed. "It's not. So, who do you think took the picture? Apart from me, of course."

Irving looked at his feet. They were freckly too. "I don't know," he said at length. "I was so sure it was you."

Irving certainly had a high opinion of him. "Perhaps it was one of the crew?" suggested Luke. "For a joke. How would they have got access to the bedroom?"

"The balcony window. Anyone could have climbed up there if they'd put their mind to it."

"It could have been a journalist," reflected Luke. "Although, on second thoughts, they'd have taken the photograph with them."

"Or a stalker," said Irving flatly. "Remember all that trouble we had at Shepperton, when Courteney started getting all that hate mail and the funeral wreaths? That's why Ross hired the bodyguards."

"Shit." Luke reached for the phone.

"We can't tell anyone," said Irving quickly.

"Why not? Courteney's got a right to know that there's some nutter stalking her."

Irving shivered. "It give me the creeps just thinking that there was someone there, all the time. Watching."

"We could tell the police," suggested Luke. "They could fingerprint the photo. I'm sure they'd soon find out who did it and bang them in jail."

"Yeah, right. And think of the huge fuss that would cause. The press would find out, Courteney would find out, the finance guys in LA would find out. They're just looking for an excuse to cancel the film, claim on insurance."

Slowly Luke replaced the phone. "OK, let's not tell the police. But we have to tell someone. We can't let it happen again."

Irving suddenly looked more cheerful, as though a huge weight had been lifted off his mind. "I know what we'll do. It's so obvious I don't know why we didn't think of it before. We'll tell Bruno."

Chapter Thirteen

Monday

Shortly after nine o'clock, Ross climbed the steps to Luke's trailer and thumped on the door. Shelby opened it. Ross felt a twinge of guilt at the pleasure on her face and bent to let her plant a kiss on his unshaven cheek.

"Hi," he grunted, glancing over her shoulder to check out potential witnesses.

There was Courteney, stuffing her face with peanut butter and Jell-O sandwiches and Luke drawing a moustache and goatee beard on a magazine photograph of Tom Cruise. Ross frowned. It was a pity that it was now far too late to fire the time-wasting bastard.

As Shelby moved away to make him a coffee as well, Ross glared at the two actors. "You should have been on set ten minutes ago."

"Sorry," mumbled Courteney, cramming the last piece of sandwich into her mouth and jumping to her feet. "The clock must be slow. Don't fret. I'm already history."

Ross said nothing. A look was enough.

Courteney, refusing to be intimidated, just patted his cheek as she passed. "Don't you guys go falling out now."

Ross caught sight of Luke's reflection in the mirror. His expression could have shattered the glass.

"How's my Star?" Ross asked, unable to stop the note of sarcasm creeping into his voice.

"Twinkle, twinkle," returned Luke.

Ross glanced uneasily towards Shelby, patiently pouring percolated coffee into three elegant china mugs. "Shelby, darling," he said slowly, "could you let Luke and myself have a quiet word alone?"

Shelby paused, biting her lip. "Sure," she said, throwing the coffee into the sink. "I'll just go and polish my Uzi." Without looking at either of them, she pushed past Ross and the door slammed behind her.

Ross glanced back to Luke. "What have you done to upset Shelby?"

"Me?" drawled Luke. Picking up a copy of *The Sun* he deliberately turned his back on Ross, putting his boots up on the dressing-table and turning to Page 3. "I'm not the one fucking her as part of some crap revenge scenario."

Ross plucked the paper away. "Nice tits," he murmured sarcastically, before tossing the paper into the bin. "Now, could I have your last little gem in English?"

"You're only sleeping with Shelby to piss me off."

Ross laughed. "And does it rattle you that much?"

Luke adjusted his cravat in the mirror before

collecting his script and standing up. For a moment the two men glowered at each other. "Just don't drop her the instant Paige turns up," Luke said softly. "It's not fair to take your quarrel with me out on someone else."

Ross had to step back to allow Luke to pass. "Is that what you think?"

"I know the way your mind works. Shelby doesn't deserve to be hurt by your Machiavellian power games."

"You do have a poor opinion of me."

Luke paused, one hand on the trailer door handle. "I've seen you in action."

"Ah yes," said Ross, lightly touching his broken nose. "I remember . . ."

* * *

The Assembly Rooms were where the rich and fashionable Georgians had played cards, drunk tea and socialised – with the occasional dance, concert and riot to liven things up. Today's filming was in the ballroom, which was long and narrow and painted pale green, the only windows high up near the ceiling. Already the crew were grumbling about lighting and that, with all the equipment, 'there wasn't enough room to swing a grip'.

The National Trust were watching everything, extremely beadily. There had been a few nasty moments when scaffolding for the lights – now disguised as flower strewn pillars – had wavered very close to one of the two-hundred-year-old cut-glass chandeliers. Ross, with his usual charm, had also managed to persuade the National

Trust to let his special effects team conceal the electric fittings with pretend candles – painted metal tubes with a stub of a candle stuck in the top.

The morning did not get off to a good start, as Luke consistently caused havoc on the dance floor. Shelby wondered if he was doing it to wind Ross up. As Ross called for a break, and Shelby disappeared for coffee, Floyd was genially patting Luke on the back, with all the sympathy of someone who was spending the entire scene on the sidelines.

"Never mind," Floyd said cheerfully, "Schwarzenegger couldn't dance either. They shot the tango scene in *True Lies* from the waist up."

"Tangos I can do," said Luke, wearily flopping into the director's chair. "Remember the bio-pic of Valentino we did together?"

Floyd shuddered. "Not if I can at all possibly help it. I had nightmares for months afterwards. Euro-puddings can be so indigestible."

Irving sidled up, looking embarrassed. "Mr McFadden . . ."

"Spit it out, Irv."

"Mr Whitney would like to know why you have not thoroughly researched your role as Lord Ravenscroft."

Luke took a long drink of mineral water. Floyd, seeing his eyes darken, tactfully melted away. "Irving," said Luke at length, "I spent three weeks at a dancing academy, fighting off the amorous advances of the male principal, learning triple minors, dupal minors and bloody Morris Minors. What more does Ross want? *Riverdance?*"

Irving's walkie-talkie squawked. He shuffled from foot to foot. "Erm, Mr Whitney says it doesn't show."

"Tell *Mr Whitney* that if he wanted a dancer he should have hired John Travolta." Then, seeing Irving pale, "No, hang on, I'll tell him myself. I don't need a stuntman to deliver a punchline."

Irving watched in dismay as Luke walked towards Ross, deceptively calmly, until he wrenched the walkie-talkie from Ross's hand and threw it across the room, narrowly missing the lighting gaffer.

"Is there a problem, Luke?" asked Ross.

"If you think I'm so terrible, you could have the guts to tell me yourself."

"Irving is the first assistant director," said Ross calmly. "That's what first assistant directors do."

"And actors act, although it helps if we have the teeniest smidgen of encouragement. Now what do directors do? Direct? Why don't we swap? You do the scene and I'll sit in that poncy chair and tell everyone you're crap."

Ross regarded Luke with eyes of flint. "OK, Mr McFadden, you've made your point. I haven't the time or the inclination to suffer another of your pathetic tantrums."

"Then why deliberately wind me up? Can't you see it's wrecking my concentration?"

"You're paranoid." Ross turned to smile at Shelby as she approached with two plastic cups of coffee. "Thanks, sweetheart."

Shelby held the other one out for Luke but he abruptly

turned away. "What's the matter?" she asked worriedly.

"Artistic temperament," shrugged Ross, sliding his free hand up the back of her leg. "You know what actors are like."

* * *

Matthew O'Bryan, the gangly, deadly serious, floppy-haired focus-puller, finally got up from his hands and knees on the floor of the Assembly Rooms and irritably brandished a cardboard roll at Luke.

"We've used a whole reel of tape, and a great lump of chalk, marking arrows right across this fucking dance floor. Fred Astaire you ain't."

Luke stared straight ahead. It served him right for stealing the man's girlfriend last week. "Just ensure the camera has me in focus," he said, "and I'll do the rest."

"Oh, you'll be in focus! Every spot, blackhead, stray nasal hair –"

Luke, at the end of his patience, turned but Matt scuttled behind George, the camera operator, who was currently engrossed in foraying into a bag of liquorice to dig out the pink sparkly ones.

"OK, Luke," said Irving, pausing nervously in front of him. "Just remember, you're travelling to your left. OK? Follow the arrows. Left, left, left."

"Right," said Luke.

Irving, unable to appreciate the joke, stalked back to his position beside Ross.

Courteney, stunning in a delicate muslin Empire dress so pale a pink it was almost white, with a narrow white ribbon and tiny rosebuds threaded into her ringleted wig, squeezed Luke's hand sympathetically.

"Isn't Irv cute?" she sighed, watching his retreating back with undisguised affection. "So polite, so *English*? He never shouts like the American ADs."

"Irving would never shout at anyone," muttered Luke, conveniently erasing this morning's pantomime from his mind. "He'd be too frightened that they might shout back."

Courteney heaved at the bodice of her dress, her large tanned breasts spilling out over the top. "God, this gown is tight! I reckon Elliott unpicks the seams every night to make it smaller. Damn sadist."

Luke diplomatically refrained from reminding her of the two chocolate ice creams she had consumed before the last take.

Dulcie sprinted over and attacked her considerable cleavage with a powder puff, in a frantic attempt to turn it white. "Haven't you ever heard of sunblock?" she growled. "In the Regency only farmworkers had suntans."

Courteney winked at Luke. "I suppose they were the only guys who could afford a vacation."

"Action," said Ross.

Dulcie dived back behind the camera line. George quickly handed his bag of liquorice to Matt. Flustered, Matt thrust it behind to the grip, who tipped the contents into his mouth before crumpling up the bag and tossing it over his shoulder. Irving wearily picked it up and dropped it into a black bin-liner.

"Left," muttered Courteney under her breath as the music started up.

"I *know*!" snapped Luke and promptly went right.

"Cut!" screamed Ross. "Cut, cut, cut, cut, *cut*!"

"Sorry, Ross," said Luke, genuinely contrite. "I'm just finding it bloody impossible to dance and act at the same time."

"You don't have to *act*," Ross's voice took on a vicious note. "The public is not interested in seeing you *act*. They only want to see you looking sexy in a pair of sopping wet breeches. That's all anybody ever wants from Luke McFadden – because you *can't* fucking act. You never fucking could."

"Fine!" Luke tore off his cravat and hurled it onto the floor. "See how well this 'fucking' film does without me – because I 'fucking' quit!"

Shelby watched in consternation as he stormed out, wondering whether she should run after him, or whether that would just make things worse. She looked across to Ross, who was laconically calling for another break and lighting another cigarette with shaking hands. She marched over, snatched it from his fingers and tossed it over her shoulder where it landed, sparking, on the polished floorboards, burning a little black hole.

"You shouldn't let your work get to you," she scolded. "It's only a film. It's not worth losing your health over."

Deprived of his cigarette Ross chewed on his thumbnail. "This is my livelihood that bastard's fucking with. My career. If this film goes down the tube it affects us all – the crew, the actors – even him. Why can't he see that? Why does he have to be so fucking *juvenile*? He's thirty years old, for Christ's sake. Why doesn't he grow up?"

"I think it's just nerves," said Shelby slowly. "I know it's hard to believe but I think Luke lacks self-confidence – well, in his acting abilities anyway. Like you and your cigarettes, the more stressed he feels, the more he plays the fool. It's as though, by making people laugh, he thinks they will overlook any deficiencies."

Ross raised one eyebrow. "What do you suggest? That I should hire a Unit Shrink? We're all under stress. We don't all act like Freddie Starr on acid."

"Perhaps if you praised him a bit more –"

"If he did something right I would praise him. But he just fucks up." Ross ran his hand through his hair, unwittingly spiking it all up. "Time after time he just fucks up. He's costing me a fortune."

Shelby realised his hand was shaking and was surprised. This was Ross, supposedly cooler than an Eskimo's deep-freeze. She thought he would be the last person to crack up. Forgetting they had an audience, she wrapped her arms around his waist and pulled him into what she hoped was a reassuring hug.

He leant against her. "Why are you so good to me when I treat you so badly?"

"You don't. You're just trying to do your job, under pressure. I understand that you have to neglect me from time to time . . ."

He sighed. "You don't know the half of it, Shelby."

187

He stepped back and stared at her, searchingly, taking her face in his hands and gently kissing her.

"I love you," she said, her voice trembling.

He hugged her tightly. "I know you do, darling. I know you do."

"What will you do now?" she asked. "You can't shoot a film without a leading man."

"Do you think you could go after him for me? Try to calm him down. Give him a couple of paracetamol and some strong black coffee. I would do it myself but the actress taking over from Octavia arrives in about half an hour."

"Sure," said Shelby, attempting to sound enthusiastic. "No problem."

* * *

She found Luke outside, fighting off several over-enthusiastic autograph hunters.

"Piss off!" he was yelling at them. "Stop hounding me and get a life!"

The women backed away, sour-faced.

"He's not as nice as he is on TV," one sniffed.

"*And* he's wearing eyeliner."

"'Scuse me, ladies," murmured Shelby, hurrying after him.

She caught up just as he flung himself into the driver's seat of the minibus and apologetically opened the door. "I'm afraid Baz still has the key. And, as he's in the BMW en route to the station to collect Octavia's replacement, I guess that means you'll have to walk back to Base."

"Walk?"

She hadn't seen his face look so black since he'd played Heathcliff. "You know, put one foot in front of the other?"

He suddenly smiled. "Left foot first or right foot?"

She held the door open for him. "Come on. I'm your escort. You'll be safe with me."

"But will you be safe –" he broke off. "OK, we've been through that before – and I've got the bruises to prove it. Let's go; we're drawing a crowd." He swung his long legs from the minibus. Shelby had to admit he looked stunning in his cream breeches and dark, high-collared coat – although she wasn't so sure about the thick white stockings and buckled shoes.

He certainly attracted a lot of attention as they walked quickly back to Base. They were able to avoid the streets crammed with shoppers, but became entangled with a crocodile of Japanese schoolgirls as they sprinted around The Circus. Shelby had to take two quick strides to Luke's one, and while she barely broke into perspiration, his 'street' make-up was soon streaming down his face and turning his snow-white collar orange.

"I suppose I'm really out of condition," he sighed. "But I spend most of my working life sitting around on my bum, waiting for some cretin to yell 'Action'."

"Don't you belong to a gym?"

He gave her a sideways glance. "I have to keep in shape, that's what directors hire me for – Ross was right about that. No one wants me for my acting abilities. But my work takes me all over the country and into

Europe too, and not every film company is willing to pay for five-star hotels with gyms and Jacuzzis."

Shelby wondered on Luke's criteria for slumming it. Double en suite at Trust House Forte? They were now walking down the gravel path to where the trailers were parked along one side of Royal Avenue.

"Where to?" she asked, pausing by the catering van. "Do you want lunch?"

"I'm going to Make-up," he replied. "To get all this muck off my face."

"Oh but –" she began, before quickly shutting up.

He studied her thoughtfully. "Don't tell me. Ross asked you to sweet-talk me into coming back later and finishing the scene? I suppose it shows he cares." Luke took one large stride to clear the two steps up to the make-up caravan and, throwing open the door, caught Kit watching the lunch-time edition of *Neighbours*.

"What are you doing here?" grumbled Kit. "Dulcie's supposed to be doing the touch-ups. You're not due back 'til four."

"I've fallen out with Ross."

"You're getting predictable in your old age. How many times have you quit?"

"Three," said Luke. "But the old dear just keeps taking me back."

"More than I would ever do. Christ, look at the state of that collar. Wardrobe are going to kill me. Only last night Elliott was insinuating I used watery foundation. The duplicate costumes never arrived and I don't think he's got the last lot of shirts dry yet. The weather's been foul."

"What's wrong with the tumble-driers?"

Kit rolled his eyes at Shelby. "There speaks a man who never has to iron his own shirts. Come in, my dear, can I get you a cup of tea? Dulcie's nicked all the hot chocolate, but I can certainly offer you better char than the catering van."

Shelby sat in a leather swivel-chair in front of a large mirror surrounded by light bulbs. Luke took the seat next to her. "So," she ventured to Luke, while Kit busied himself with the kettle. "You quitting is a regular feature of this film?"

Luke looked sheepish. "Er, yeah. How many times did I quit on *All That She Wants*, Kit?"

"Six," called back Kit. "But that's your absolute record."

"Ross offered to quit that one too. Perhaps I should try a bit harder."

Kit switched on the lights around Luke's mirror and swung his chair around. They both winced at the damage. "Well, sweetie," sighed Kit, "are we going for broke or just a touch-up?"

"Touch-up," said Luke. "I do have a life outside this make-up trailer."

Kit began to arrange his make-up brushes on the counter. "Thank heavens it's an indoor shoot. The gloom in the Assembly Rooms should hide a multitude of sins. What time are you due back on set?"

Luke glanced at Shelby.

Shelby, who had been watching in fascination, stirred. "Five-thirty," she replied without thinking. "Erm, I mean . . ."

Kit smirked. "Ross is so predictable. Always gets someone else to do his dirty work."

Luke shot him a warning glance but Shelby was now picking up the pots of foundation and pressed and loose powder, turning them over in her hands. "Do you have anything to cover freckles?" she asked idly.

"And why would you want to do that? Trust me, sweetie, all you need is translucent powder. I know a dozen hags who would kill for your skin."

"Bollocks!"

Kit sighed. "Try this," he said, tossing over a well-known and hideously expensive brand of concealer. But you'd be better off leaving well alone." He paused as he caught sight of Ross through the trailer windows, helping a tall slim blonde from a BMW. Kit parted the net curtains with one of his brushes to get a better view. "Talking of old hags . . . is that who I think it is?"

Luke followed his gaze. "Uh huh."

They both grew silent and looked at Shelby speculatively.

"What?" muttered Shelby irritably, feeling as though she'd just grown an extra nose or something. "Who is it? Why are you looking at me like that?"

The trailer door suddenly opened and in walked Ross, closely followed by the most beautiful woman Shelby had ever seen. She was tall but fragile, as though the slightest breeze might blow her away. Pale gold hair was piled casually on top of her head, revealing a slender neck and the creamy white skin that men dream about kissing. Not a freckle or mole in sight. Her dark smoky eyes, in contrast to the rest of her, burned as she leant against Ross's shoulder, just as Shelby had done so recently, and regarded Luke speculatively.

Shelby began to feel uneasy.

"Hi, Luke," said Ross, as though that morning had happened in an alternate universe, "I've brought our newest recruit, Paige Lorraine, along to meet you. As you know, she's taking over from Octavia and shoots her first scenes later this afternoon."

Luke raised one eyebrow. "Actually, Ross, we've already met." He stood politely to shake Paige's hand. "It's good to see you again, Paige. You're looking well."

"You too," she returned coolly.

"I know this is going to be difficult," said Ross, "but I think you are both professional enough not to let personal and private grievances spoil the filming." He guided Paige into the chair that Luke had just vacated. "You're due on set at four, Paige," he said, bending to gaze over her shoulder at her immaculate reflection. "Baz will drive you up to the Assembly Rooms."

"Lovely," returned Paige. Turning her head, she lightly kissed him. "See you later, darling. Don't work too hard. I'm looking forward to our drink this evening."

As Ross left the trailer without uttering another word, or even glancing in her direction, Shelby felt her heart plummet into her sandals. Paige is an actress, she told herself firmly. That's what actresses do. Courteney kisses Luke all the time. It didn't mean anything. It didn't mean anything at all.

Chapter Fourteen

Tuesday

Shelby woke up and found the bed empty. "Ross?" she said tentatively. "Are you there?"

There was no reply except that of the empty silence. Not only was his side of the mattress cold but the sheet was unrumpled, the pillow undented. Sliding out of bed, she was startled by a thump and found she had knocked one of Ross's film magazines onto the floor. Picking it up, Shelby remembered she had been flicking through it last night while she waited for Ross to return. She must have fallen asleep while still reading. Which meant Ross hadn't come back after his production meeting with the crew, following the viewing of the rushes.

She stepped into the sitting-room, where she knew he worked late into the night, hunched over the tiny desk in the corner, or endlessly replaying the rushes on video. The early morning sunlight streamed through the open curtains but the place was deserted. There was a large, unopened Jiffy bag still on the coffee table. Irving must have left it there after she had gone to bed. She felt a sudden chill. Ross hadn't even seen it. Which meant there had been no production meeting. So where the hell was he?

Shelby glanced at the clock. Five am. She padded into the bathroom. That too was deserted. This was getting ridiculous. As though she'd woken up in one of those silly made-for-TV movies, where the entire population had been kidnapped and replaced by screeching aliens.

On auto-pilot, she peeled off the oversized T-shirt she used instead of a nightdress, switched on the shower and climbed in. Perhaps Ross couldn't sleep? She knew he was worried about the ever-spiralling budget and those hard-hearted studio executives in LA who were financing the film. Maybe he had nipped out for a walk around the garden?

She took her time washing her hair, using up all the complimentary bottles of shampoo and conditioner. She shaved her legs, even though she'd done it yesterday. Anything to delay the moment when she had to return to the empty bedroom.

She dragged back the shower curtain. The bathroom was thick with steam. She wrapped herself in one of the hotel's thick fluffy towels, wound another tightly about her head, and padded back to the bedroom to dry herself and cover her body with talc, body lotion, expensive perfume. Her eyes strayed to Ross's citrus cologne on the dressing-table. What was the point when the man was not here to appreciate it?

She had to shake herself out of this mood. She had only been dating – correction, *sleeping* with Ross for three days – and already she was planning the wedding. Let the poor guy take a break if he wanted to. Surely a man could take a walk without her calling out a search party. She switched on the dryer and dried her hair. By the time she finished she was red-faced, hot and cross. She hoped Ross had not spent the night locked in the function room with the production team. He would have a breakdown at this rate.

She carefully made up her face, dressed in her black suit and sat down, wondering what to do next. Perhaps she should call Jasper, or Irving? They would know where he was. But Ross would be furious. It would look as though she was checking up on him. She glanced across at the clock for about the hundredth time. 5.45 am . . .

The outside door clicked. She resisted the impulse to run out of the bedroom and fling her arms around him – after all, it might be the waiter with breakfast! Instead she slid quickly onto the dressing-table stool and pretended to be applying her lipstick.

Ross entered the bedroom. Casually she glanced up from her reflection. Boy, did he look rough! His chin was coated in ginger stubble, his slicked-back hair had become unslicked and was now sticking up at the front like Tin-Tin, and his frosty eyes had such dark circles underneath he would make Keith Richards look healthy.

"You look as though you had a good night's sleep," Shelby said waspishly.

"I don't really want a scene," sighed Ross, stripping last night's clothes off and dropping them into the linen basket. "I've got forty-five minutes to get showered, changed and up to the Assembly Rooms."

"Where have you been?"

"Out."

"Why?"

"Oh for Christ's sake, stop nagging!" Naked, he strode off to the bathroom. The bolt slid back on the door and she soon heard the water hammering from the shower.

Nagging! And here she was, worrying he'd been mugged, or murdered, and was lying in a ditch somewhere on the A36. Pig, she thought sourly, slapping the lipstick onto the table, breaking off the top. Ignorant git. She was glad she had pinched all the shampoo. She didn't really want to be around when he found out though and, picking up her bag, she slowly slipped past the bathroom and out into the corridor.

As Shelby walked past Octavia's old room on her way to meet Luke, the door opened and Paige Lorraine, wearing nothing but a minute white towel, opened the door to pick up her newspaper.

"Hello," said Shelby, making an effort to be friendly.

Paige glanced up and frowned. Not so attractive first thing in the morning, thought Shelby smugly. Without make-up to shade in her brows and lashes she looked positively albino. Her skin was blotchy, her sleek blonde mane frizzy, she had a spot coming up on her chin; in fact, Shelby was pleased to realise, she even looked rougher than Ross.

"Hello," drawled Paige in her Boston accent, scathingly looking her up and down. "You must be Shelley."

"Shelby."

"Ah yes." Paige smiled, revealing perfect white teeth. "Luke's . . . er, bodyguard . . ."

"Minder," replied Shelby, wondering if Paige was doing this deliberately.

"Whatever." Paige shrugged carelessly and her towel began to slip towards the floor.

Shelby became hypnotised by a drop of water slowly teetering down the curve of one perfect voluptuous breast and had an overwhelming desire to drag Paige's towel up around her neck. And strangle her with it.

Paige smiled. "You're up early. Did you have trouble sleeping?"

"Luke has an early call," said Shelby shortly.

"Don't we all, honey," Paige yawned, "but I thought your bedroom was in the opposite direction?"

Shelby could not be bothered to argue. "See you around," she said, sidling past, deciding she had seen quite enough of Miss Paige Lorraine.

"At a more civilised hour, I hope." Paige moved to close the door, then hesitated, another pussycat smile passing over her perfectly regular features. "Are you going up to the Assembly Rooms this morning?"

"Yes."

"Hold on a sec." Paige suddenly disappeared into

her room and returned with a little black case. She held it out to Shelby. "You'll be seeing Ross before me. Can you return his mobile phone? The silly boy's just left without it."

* * *

Luke woke up and felt fine. No headaches, no hangover, no tongue wearing a puffa jacket; he even had a smile on his face – and it had been at least two weeks since he'd got laid. No more country dancing. No more horse-riding. Just a bit of card-playing, a couple of sex scenes and he could go home. Finito. And then he remembered. Today was his birthday.

He groaned. Twenty-nine years old. Another twelve months and he'd be thirty. Practically middle-aged. Pipe and carpet-slippers start here.

He had just turned back for bed when there was a thunderous knocking on his door. He looked at his watch. He wasn't due on set for ages. Unless there was a fire? He threw on his dressing-gown and opened the door. No sooner had it swung back than he found his arms fully of a wildly sobbing Shelby.

He had to steady himself against the wall. "Darling, what on earth's the matter?"

"I hate her! *The bitch*! I hate her!"

Luke kicked the door shut with his foot and helped her into the sitting-room. He was rather at a loss. He had always had Shelby down as the iron fist, iron glove type, like Ross. Useful in a crisis but not the sort to cry during *ET*. It was a shock to see her completely lose the plot.

"Can I get you a drink?" he suggested, as she curled up on his sofa, hugging one of the scatter-cushions close against her chest and staring blankly at the carpet.

"Anything," she muttered tearfully, "provided it has alcohol in it. I'll even drink Baileys."

He had meant coffee or tea, even water. Luke diplomatically refrained from reminding her it was only six o'clock in the morning and quickly sloshed out a measure of brandy into a glass. His grandmother had always sworn there was nothing better for treating shocks. And she had lived to be ninety-three.

"Here you are," he said, sitting beside her, still in his navy-blue dressing-gown. When she made no effort to take it from him, he slid it back on the sideboard and cautiously lifted up a section of long red hair, peering at the pink blotchy face beneath. Searching his pockets he found a crumpled but clean piece of loo roll that he'd used to clean his spectacles. He handed it to her. "Has somebody died?"

She lifted her head, pushing her hair away from her face. Her beautiful green eyes were now all piggy, her nose was red – and running – and he still wanted to take her into his arms and kiss the life back into her. "No . . . no one's died . . ." she choked.

"Then what is it?"

"Oh God, it's just so awful! I should have seen it coming. I am so stupid. So *pathetically* stupid." She blinked determinedly to keep the tears from rolling down her cheeks. "And I don't know why I'm crying.

I never cry – I'm a tough old nut, me!" At which point she dissolved into tears again.

Luke cautiously put his arm around her shaking shoulders. The bruise on his bum had all but vanished but he still had a tender spot on the back of his head. Although as she showed no inclination to lay him out with some karate chop, he gently removed the cushion and, placing his other arm around her, pulled her against his chest. He could feel her whole body trembling. Was she sick?

"I loved him!" she sobbed.

"Sorry?"

"Ross. I loved him so much."

It was like a knife going through to his heart. In, out, in, out, shake it all about.

Shelby dabbed her eyes with the sodden mass of pink tissue. "I really loved him – and I thought he cared for me. Just a little bit – but I thought it would grow into love . . ."

Luke found he was unable to form any words of comfort and stared helplessly at the top of her head, smoothing her hair back from her face as she buried it into his towelling dressing-gown, trying not to think of that erotic scent she was wearing, the way her breasts were pressing against his chest.

He was wearing only his dressing-gown and she hadn't even noticed. She had forgotten that he was a man – perhaps he was now an honorary woman. I'm 'safe', he thought sadly. Because I haven't tried it on for a few days she now thinks I'm harmless. He continued to mindlessly stroke her hair, keeping an iron grip on his control, when all he wanted to do was kiss the hurt away from those tragic eyes, that exquisite rosebud mouth. You're an actor, he told himself firmly. Fucking well act!

Shelby raised her head and blew her nose. "I'm sorry."

He managed a casual shrug. "There's nothing to be sorry about."

"I'm going to make you late on set and you'll get into trouble with that bastard Ross."

'That bastard', eh? Things were beginning to look up. "What's he done?" Luke was unable to stop his voice from sounding harsh. "If he's hurt you in any way –"

"He slept with Paige last night. The bastard. The utter utter bastard."

"That was fast work," Luke said, before he could stop himself. "She only arrived last night. Are you sure?"

Shelby showed him the mobile phone. "He left this in her room."

"Yesterday evening?" Hell, he couldn't believe he was defending the creep.

"No, I slept in his suite last night. And he didn't. He only turned up fifteen minutes ago. And then I met Paige in the corridor and she, as cool as anything, asks me to give him this because, 'You'll be seeing him before me'. The bitch. She knew I had a relationship with him."

Three days made a relationship? "I doubt it," said

Luke. "Paige has never been particularly interested in other people's relationships. Only her own."

Shelby regarded him curiously. "You were once engaged to her. Aren't you upset that she's now with Ross?"

Luke considered the question. And was surprised to find himself answering, "They're welcome to each other."

"But you were going to be married. And then . . . er, it was all called off."

Luke sighed. "Yes, I was caught by a photographer in Trafalgar Square. Yes, I was wearing a wedding dress. It was Kit's idea of a joke. I almost killed him when I found out. Yet I have a sneaking suspicion he would have done anything to jeopardise my relationship with her. He was determined that I wouldn't make a mistake that could affect my whole life."

"It's a pity no one warned me about Ross," Shelby said sadly. "You know, I think I was just something to while away the boring bits between filming."

Luke, who had his own suspicions, kept his mouth tightly shut.

Shelby moved away from him, taking a sip of her brandy, then pulling a face and pushing it back onto the sideboard. "Perhaps I'd better just stick to coffee."

She had knocked his dressing-gown askew. He made no move to adjust it, seeing her eyes follow the line of his throat. He was waiting for a reaction, any reaction. Anything that told him he was still in with a chance.

He found his mouth forming words he knew he would later regret. "I don't suppose I can interest you in an exciting affair with a very attractive reboundee? No strings?"

She looked away, studying the mobile phone she still held clutched in her hand. "No," she said slowly. "I think that would be a mistake."

"You can't blame a guy for asking," he said, and almost managed to make it sound like a joke. "What are you going to do with Ross's phone?"

Shelby glanced down at it. "I don't know." She gave a half-hearted smile. "I'd *like* to chuck it into your Jacuzzi and let it sink."

"Then why don't you?"

"I'm not that mean! Ross would be lost without it."

There was a bang on the door. It was Baz. "Luke, the minibus will be leaving in thirty minutes."

"Forget it! I'll get a taxi!"

"Rothschild," muttered Baz and stomped off down the hall.

"Thanks for listening, Luke" said Shelby. She attempted humour, "Usually I dump on Irving but he's another flight up."

"No problem. Stay in here in the sitting-room if you like. Order breakfast, read the paper – I'm not in it today!"

"I'm sorry I misjudged you, that we didn't hit it off at the start."

"You thought I was only interested in getting into your knickers?"

"It just shows how wrong you can be about people – *and* it was horribly big-headed of me. After all, I'm not even your type." She glanced up at him, pleadingly. "But we can be friends now, can't we?"

Friends? Or as Byron would have it, 'Love without his wings'. He regarded her in despair. Didn't she fancy him at all?

"Sure," he said slowly. "We can be friends."

It was a start . . .

Chapter Fifteen

"*Happy birthday to you*," sang the crew, "*Happy birthday to you, Happy birthday, dear Lukey, Happy birthday to you.*"

Luke looked around at the production team, the camera crew, the grips and the sparks, all cheering him and was touched. Then Courteney presented him with a large cake with three sparklers jammed into the top.

"Happy birthday, sugar," she smiled, kissing him full on the lips.

It was a while before he could get his breath back.

"Speech!" yelled the crew. "Speech!"

"I'd just like to say . . ." Luke glanced down at the cake and laughed. Iced across the top was a naked woman brandishing a clapperboard, with a big three zero iced onto it. *Thirty*? "I'm only twenty-nine!"

The crew cheered. That was the shortest speech they had ever heard.

As Luke handed over the cake to one of the caterers, Shelby thrust a little parcel into his hands. It was wrapped in blue shiny paper and hermetically sealed in Sellotape.

"I didn't know it was your birthday 'til today," she said. "I'm afraid it's not very much . . ."

He had to fight to get into the parcel but underneath all the wrapping was a little flat box. He lifted the flap at the side – and eased out a pair of socks. *Socks*? His *mother* bought him socks.

"Look," she said, sensing his chagrin and unfurling them for him.

Socks are socks, thought Luke, whichever way you looked at them. But these socks had squiggling blue and red writing all over them. *I'm Too Sexy For My Socks.*

"Do you like them?"

Well, they were certainly different. He frowned. So that was how she saw him: some joke sex-symbol.

He realised she was watching him, still awaiting a reaction. "They're really great," he said and, without thinking, kissed her cheek. Velvet skin. He could smell her tantalising scent, roses and jasmine. He paused, staring deep into her green-gold eyes. "Shelby . . ."

"I'm pleased you like them," she said and turned away.

* * *

Shelby sat on the floor and tucked into a slice of birthday cake. Mmm, not bad, she thought – despite the alcoholic flavouring not usually synonymous with sponge cakes. The caterers must have added it as a joke. At least it was too small for a naked girl to burst out of the top.

"Hi, Shelby!" Courteney flopped next to her, scattering seed pearls and silk flowers. "Did you know Ross has arranged a surprise party for Luke tonight? Everyone's invited. It's to be held at Ross's place and he's arranged a rock group, disco, fireworks . . . It's very suspect, don't you think? Considering they hate each other!"

Shelby was unable to reply as Courteney launched straight into her next sentence.

"I've always wondered what Ross's house looks like. Elizabethan, Floyd says – like Shakespeare? It's been in his family for hundreds of years. Do you think it's got one of those cute straw roofs?"

"Straw? Oh, *thatch*!"

"I'm going to wear my new white shift dress, the one with the silver embroidery? I found these really cute Greek sandals in a little boutique yesterday and I thought, if I chatted up Kit, he might do my hair Grecian fashion and I can show off those diamond earrings with the matching choker that I got from that antique shop in New Bond Street. How about you? What are you going to wear?"

Shelby tried not to laugh. "This, I suppose."

"You can't! Lots of important people will be there, producers, directors, everybody! You've gotta wear something really fabulous. It's the kind of party that gets a girl noticed. Maybe you'll be discovered!"

"I didn't bring a party dress," Shelby admitted, struggling to keep a straight face. Discovered? Like she was an uncharted planet? "Besides, I shall be on duty."

Courteney was perplexed. "But it's a *party*!"

"And I'm employed as Luke's *minder*. A party is just another evening's work."

Courteney frowned – and then suddenly smiled. Shelby regarded her apprehensively. She could almost see the light bulb switching on above Courteney's head.

"Wait there," commanded Courteney, suddenly scrambling up. "Don't move a muscle."

I'm not going anywhere, thought Shelby sadly. Cinderella had it cushy compared to me. Better go find me a pumpkin. It worked wonders for Cinders.

She watched in horror as Courteney barged her way into a conversation Ross was having with Irving and Jasper, playfully dragging him towards Shelby. How *could* Courteney be so *tactless*? Shelby cringed, wishing a passing alien might beam her up and abduct her, as Ross's Timberland boots paused six inches away.

"Go on," Courteney was urging him. "Tell her."

Shelby felt an overwhelming desire to strangle her.

"Courteney," said Ross coolly, reading Shelby's mind, "I think Dulcie wants to powder your nose."

"More likely my breasts," said Courteney. "She seems to have a fixation with them. Maybe I should give her the number of my surgeon." And hitching up her muslin gown she sauntered off for another large wedge of birthday cake.

Ross sat on the dusty floor beside Shelby and said, his voice hard, "Have I done something to upset you?"

"You need to ask?"

"Everything was fine last night. And then when I returned this morning –"

"It's taken you *that* long to work it out, huh?" She watched the special effects assistant clambering up ladders, methodically replacing all the candle-stubs in the huge cut-glass chandeliers. They burnt out so quickly. Like love affairs.

"I understand Paige gave you my mobile phone for safe-keeping –"

Shelby mutely handed it over.

"I think there's been a misunderstanding?"

"I *don't* think so." Shelby scuffed at the floor with the heel of her sandal. Why didn't he just leave her alone? She realised her sandals had made a mark on the polished wooden floor so she wet the paper napkin the cake had been wrapped in and rubbed at the smear. She only succeeded in adding butter-cream icing to the shoe polish.

"I respect you –"

"I don't respect you!" She crumpled up the napkin and hurled it towards the bin. It missed. "You led me on. You let me believe – well, who cares what you let me believe. But if you were going to dump me so publicly for Paige you could have had the guts to tell me first."

"It's complicated –"

"It seems perfectly straightforward to me."

Ross waited for a couple of electricians to walk past before he hissed, "Listen, this isn't the right time to discuss –"

Shelby did not bother to lower her voice. "There isn't going to be a right time. You've got your job to do. I've got mine. Just leave me alone."

Ross paused. "You're coming to the party tonight?"

As though she had a choice! "I wouldn't miss it for the world," she said sarcastically.

"You'll be a guest – just like the rest of the crew. It's a private party, in a private house. I've been in touch with John Ivar; he's supplying doormen and security guards for the grounds. Have a night off."

"I will," said Shelby. "Perhaps I'll catch a movie. Not one of yours."

"Cheap jibe," said Ross and at last his voice held that familiar note of steel. He got to his feet. "You will be there, Shelby. I want you to be there."

She watched him stride out of the ballroom, in the direction of the main entrance. Off for another bloody cigarette, she thought disgustedly. For a non-smoker he certainly got through a lot of tobacco. *I want you to be there*. Ha! He could bloody well whistle. Oh damn, here was Little Miss Sunshine, bouncing back for an update.

"Well?" said Courteney excitedly. "I fixed it for you?"

"Have you fixed it for Bruno too?" Shelby said scathingly. "I bet he likes parties."

Courteney looked at her as though she were crazy. "But Bruno's my bodyguard," she explained patiently. "He's here to protect me. He doesn't have nights off."

"And I'm here to protect Luke." Shelby stood up, dusting the pink and yellow crumbs from her ankle-length black skirt. "I don't have nights off either."

Courteney bit her lower lip. "OK, if that's how you feel. But what are you going to wear? It's a party, you want to be able to blend in. You won't in a suit – you'll look like a waitress."

"Thank you!"

"I could lend you something? I've got lots of gowns. You can borrow anything you like. Please Shelby? You're the only girlfriend I have in this country. That Paige is so –" She broke off and looked sheepish.

Shelby began to feel guilty. Courteney was only trying to be friendly. "Do you have any sackcloth and ashes?" she joked, by way of apology.

Courteney wrinkled her little turned-up nose. "I haven't heard of those guys. Are they British designers?"

Shelby began to feel as though *she* needed a cigarette.

Luke suddenly materialised in front of her. "What did Ross want?" he asked brusquely. "Was he hassling you? Do you want me to have a word with him?"

"Prince Charming has just invited me to the ball. Would you mind if I skipped it?"

"Yes," he said shortly. "If I have to go I'm buggered if I'm letting you off the hook."

* * *

To Shelby, Ross's house came as a bit of a shock. She knew he was wealthy but as the car swung through the high stone gateway and down a winding gravel drive, past acres of neat, striped lawns, and she finally saw the massive house in front of her all she could do was stare, open-mouthed.

Luke placed one finger on her chin and closed it for her.

"Ross lives here?" she asked.

He gave her a sideways glance. "It's all right, I suppose."

"Does he have servants?"

"Oh no, Ross likes to do the dusting himself. Quite the little demon in his pinny and pink Marigolds."

Shelby laughed. There was *no* way she could imagine Ross wearing an apron and rubber gloves.

When Courteney had mentioned Ross's house was Elizabethan, Shelby had vaguely imagined a red-bricked house with tiny windows, thatched roof and roses around the door. Instead it was a sprawling mansion of honeyed stone, with a great gabled front, lots of little turrets and spires and a massive oak door, which looked as though it had already withstood several sieges. That'll keep the press out, thought Shelby. I wonder if he's got boiling oil too?

The chauffeur stopped the car outside the front door. Every light in the house was on, creating an amber mosaic across the drive. Shelby hardly waited for the chauffeur to apply the brakes. She just sprung out and automatically ran round to open the passenger door for Luke.

He looked up at her in amusement. "I thought we'd agreed you weren't working tonight?"

"Sorry," smiled Shelby. "Habit."

Another car drew up beside them and, in a more leisurely fashion, out climbed Dulcie and Kit. Kit was wearing his usual black, his hair streaming down his back as though he was auditioning for a shampoo

213

commercial. Shelby was used to seeing him wearing kohl, but surely that wasn't blusher and lip gloss too? Must be the light.

He and Dulcie cut a peculiar couple. She was smoothing down a backless gold outfit (more intricate lace than substantial dress) and almost an entire bottle of eyeliner, making her look like Cleopatra on a bad hair day.

Kit had been stopped at the door by one of John Ivar's heavies, twice the size of Bruno. "Sorry, mate," the bouncer said. "You can't bring that camera in here."

Kit was taken aback. "Why ever not?"

"*Hello!* have exclusive rights to all photographs."

"Are you telling me Ross has invited a magazine to take pictures of the guests?" asked Luke.

"That's right, Mr McFadden," said the bouncer with decidedly more respect. "We have been instructed to keep all cameras here in the hall." He turned back to Kit and added, in a slightly warmer tone, "We'll give you a receipt. You can collect it on the way out."

Kit, for once utterly speechless, meekly held out his camera.

"I don't believe it," muttered Luke, as he strode up the stone steps into the hall and out of earshot. "Ross has sold the rights to the pictures of *my* party to a *magazine*? After all the trouble we've had with the press? How could he do it?"

"It's a form of control," shrugged Shelby. "Instead of ten photographers hounding you, you just get the one." She slid her arm through his. "Just think of it as good publicity for the film. 'Bums on seats'. At least this way you get to vet the shots."

Luke smiled at her naiveté. "I wouldn't count on it."

A positive army of staff were on hand to take their coats, show them the gold and marble guest bathroom, point them in the direction of a little anteroom where the photographer had set up a 'studio'. He asked so politely if he might take Luke's picture that it would have seemed churlish to disagree. Luke was determined that Shelby should be in the shot too – he clowned about, pretending to lean on her shoulder so that soon she was laughing and totally relaxed.

As they followed the crowd to where the refreshments had been laid out, Shelby dived back for the photographer's card. It would be nice to send off for a print, to remind her of the times she had mixed with 'the stars', particularly after Courteney had lent her this beautiful burgundy jacquard dress.

Ross's house was a series of almost identical neat square rooms, all leading into each other. The ballroom was at the far end and was decorated in white, with the most incredible plaster wall-mouldings of flowers, fruit, and little fat cupids, all liberally coated in gold paint. Shelby craned her neck to look at the ceiling. It looked like the Sistine Chapel.

"Tasteful," said Luke, wrinkling his nose.

"Does Ross open it to the public?" asked Shelby

"No," Luke helped himself to a couple of flutes of champagne from a passing waitress. "Ross doesn't like to share his toys."

Shelby suddenly clutched at his arm and he almost spilt the lot. "Oh my God," she muttered. "Isn't that Emma Thompson? In the blue dress?"

Luke squinted through the cigarette smoke. It was already making his contact lenses sting. "Looks like her," he agreed. "Shall I introduce you?"

"Hell, no!" Shelby was horrified. "What would I say?"

"That you adore her films, what is she working on now and where does she keep her Oscars?" He handed her one of the glasses.

Shelby glared at him. The dark blue eyes were twinkling. "Idiot," she said, realising she was being teased. "I bet you don't even know her."

Kit came to stand beside them. "That's Richard E Grant over there," he said in awe. "I did make-up for him a couple of years back. He was *so* sweet."

"I shall be sure to tell him," said Luke and downed his champagne in one gulp.

"And one of the McGann brothers," added Dulcie. "Although I'm not sure which one. And that bloke with the crew cut, isn't he in 'EastEnders'? I didn't realise you knew so many famous people, Luke?"

"I don't," said Luke dryly, disposing of his glass on the mantelpiece of an ornate fireplace, creating a huge ring. "They were all invited by Ross." He turned to check his reflection in what he thought was a gilt-framed mirror and found he was looking at a large, ugly painting instead.

Kit leant closer to examine it. "Crikey, a Holbein,"

he said reverently. "And I can't see any alarms connected to it. It's just hanging there!"

"Don't get any ideas. I should imagine Ross has mantraps set up all over the garden," said Luke, taking back Shelby's champagne as she appeared to be too over-awed to do anything with it. "He's always liked a good dollop of blood and gore, has our Ross. I'm only surprised he hasn't worked a duel scene into the film. It would be his perfect opportunity to get rid of me and conjure up the most delicious publicity all in one go."

"That is sick," Dulcie said with disapproval. She seemed to be the only one listening to him. Shelby was restlessly searching the room – presumably for more celebrities – and Kit was still muttering to himself.

"I could just pluck it from the wall," he was saying, caressing the gilt frame of the painting, "and no one would even notice. And here's a Reynolds, a Van Dyck –"

"Where?" asked Shelby idly. "I ought to get his autograph. My mother was always dragging me and Irving to see *Chitty Chitty Bang Bang*."

"May I take your photograph please, Mr McFadden?" A pretty little brunette, wearing an official press pass around her neck, had sidled her way into their group.

Shelby barred her access to Luke like a shot. "No more photos," she said firmly. "Please respect Mr McFadden's privacy."

Luke felt like being awkward. Anything to provoke Shelby and get some reaction. "Sure," he said. "No problem."

"Perhaps over by the fireplace?" suggested the photographer. "There is more light. And if you could just rest your hand lightly on the mantelpiece? Perfect!"

Luke winked at Shelby but she was scowling at him, irritated that she had been made to look an idiot. To make her disapproval even more clear, she turned her back on him to politely converse with Dulcie.

But Dulcie's eyes had glazed over after spotting a tall, dark handsome man standing alone in one corner. She thrust her half-drunk glass of buck's fizz at Shelby. "Pierce Brosnan," she breathed. "My absolute hero!" And promptly sprinted across the ballroom.

Shelby looked hopefully at Kit but he had wandered away, squinting at the signatures on the paintings. Shelby sighed. So this was a show-biz party? It was about as thrilling as Quiz Night down the Police Sports and Social Club.

She tapped her feet to music emanating from the funky young band set up at the far end of the ballroom. It was early so no one was dancing, in fact most people had got no further than the second ante-chamber, where the champagne cocktails were being served. Without bothering to glance back at Luke, she walked over to the window. It was too dark to see anything much of the famous gardens, just the occasional flash of headlights, as yet more cars proceeded slowly down the drive in convoy.

She suddenly felt someone grip her upper arm. For a moment she thought it was Luke but as she caught a glimpse of dark auburn hair she realised she was being held by Ross.

"Let go of me," she growled.

"No," he said and began to firmly lead her along the side of the ballroom to an insignificant little door, almost invisible in the ornately carved wall. "I want to talk to you. And before you try any kick boxing, do you really want to make a scene in front of all these people?"

He swiftly opened the door, thrust her through, and then they were standing in a narrow little corridor, tiled in grubby monotone lino, with yellow walls. In places the paint was peeling. Some kind of servants' corridor, she realised. Gold paint and cupids were obviously too good for them.

As the door to the ballroom swung shut, abruptly cutting off the music and shouted conversations, she pulled her arm free and glared at him. "Do you get off on being the dominant male?"

He glared at her, the thick black eyebrows furrowing. "What the hell is your problem?"

"*My* problem!" Shelby coolly met his intense gaze. "On Sunday night we went to bed, we made love, we went to sleep. On Monday night *you* went off to sleep with Paige in the room next door and you think *I* have a problem?"

"We talked about work," he said wearily, massaging his forehead. "That was all. She's having trouble with the nude scenes next week. Understandable when you take into consideration her former relationship with Luke."

"Really?" Shelby didn't believe a word. "Has she tried acting?"

219

"God, Shelby, why are you giving me such a hard time? I've only known you a matter of days, why do you have to get so heavy? I hate all this emotional stuff."

"Because I thought –" She paused. "I *told* you I loved you. You *knew* how I felt. Why didn't you warn me that you didn't feel the same way?"

"I didn't know you *meant* it!"

"I wouldn't say it if I didn't mean it!" she howled. "Christ, men!"

He considered her warily. "Can't we start again? Keep it light-hearted?"

"I'm not sure I want to. I don't want to get hurt."

"I wouldn't hurt you." He trailed one finger along her cheek, it came to rest against the corner of her mouth. Before she realised what she was doing, she had kissed it. Damn, she shouldn't have given in so easily.

Ross lifted her face to be kissed. And she let him. She wanted to taste that sensuous mouth on hers, to feel those fingers move lightly across her skin. She just couldn't help herself. She knew she was about to make all those same mistakes, all over again.

She loved him.

Chapter Sixteen

Luke had amassed quite a respectable collection of champagne glasses along the top of the mantelpiece; the muted light from the chandeliers catching the crystal, projecting a kaleidoscope of colour across the wall. He leant back against the marble fireplace, flanked by fat, gilt-painted cherubs, and regarded the noisy crowd around him with disdain.

The official *Hello!* photographer had approached him for another exclusive shot – this time with the other Brit-packers on the terrace, where Ross had arranged great flaming candles to light the outside in a positively Gothic fashion. Luke had merely ignored her. Instead, his eyes now moved restlessly across the ballroom, the despair only lightening whenever a redheaded woman moved into his vicinity.

Luke's glower certainly didn't put off any of the female guests, and one by one they sidled up to offer a drink, or a smart remark, or some without any excuse at all – just to ask him to dance or merely to be seen with him. Kit cringed at how offhand Luke was but worst of all, the women didn't seem to mind, or even notice, just took it as par for the course.

"Where's Shelby?" Luke grumbled, swiping yet another glass from a passing waitress. "I'm bored."

You don't say, thought Kit, regarding the ever-increasing number of glasses with irritation. Thank God the only Press were those that had been invited. Any more frightful headlines and Luke's career would take a spectacular nosedive. There were plenty more pretty actors desperate to take his place.

"I have no idea," lied Kit.

"Dulcie?"

But Dulcie was having such a splendid eyeing-up session with some intense, darkly handsome, macho man, that Luke had to repeat himself twice. "How the hell should I know?" she shrugged, her pale face pink and flushed with heady excitement as she winked again at the man she had mistaken for a McGann brother. "*I've* been dancing with Pierce Brosnan. He's gorgeous. A true gentleman," she added pointedly, in case her meaning still hadn't sunk in.

Luke took a large swig of champagne and took his wrath out on Dulcie. "Do you have something in your eye?" he enquired icily, or are you trying to attract the attention of Mack Stone, the stunt co-ordinator? He's married, you know."

Dulcie glared at him. "I thought tonight was Shelby's night off?"

"It is."

"Maybe she got off with someone?"

"Shelby is not the sort of girl to 'get off' with people."

"She got off with you," Dulcie muttered under her breath, "and she got off with Ross."

Kit kicked her sharply on the ankle.

If Luke and Ross had such a weakness for redheads, Dulcie thought bitterly, why did they keep picking that awful freckled tomboy over her? *And* Shelby was flat-chested. Practically minus AA cup. Weren't men supposed to like girls with big tits?

"Strange really," added Dulcie out loud. "I mean, Shelby's supposed to be *your* bodyguard, Luke, but she doesn't spend much time with you, does she? She spends more time with Ross." She smiled nastily. "Perhaps she wants to be *his* bodyguard."

"Leave it, Dulcie," growled Kit.

"You're out-of-date." Luke added the crystal flute to his collection. "They're finished."

"Really?" Dulcie smiled spitefully and moved out of Kit's kicking range. "So why has Kit just seen them snogging outside the kitchens?"

* * *

Ross raised his head and said thickly, "I've got to go and mingle. I am supposed to be the host."

"The host with the most." Shelby slid her fingers through his thick chestnut hair and attempted to pull his head back towards her. "Can't you stay here and mingle with me?"

223

He pulled up the zip of her dress. "If we don't go back, someone will come looking for me." He paused. "And Luke must be wondering what happened to you."

Bugger Luke, thought Shelby and then was ashamed of herself. He had been very kind to her this morning. She wriggled back into Ross's embrace, relishing the obvious effect she was having upon him, and laid her head on his chest.

"It's my night off," she said, sliding her hand between the buttons of his black Ralph Lauren shirt. "And I want to spend it with you."

For a moment she thought she had won. As her hand moved over his warm skin she paused over his heart. His hand suddenly closed upon her wrist. She glanced up. The dark eyes were burning.

"Me too, darling," he said, keeping his voice light, "but I've got to network. There are some influential people out there."

She allowed him to remove her hand but could not help the hostile note in her voice, spitting out her words like splinters of glass. "So long as one of them isn't Paige."

Instantly she regretted it. She didn't want him to think her a possessive bitch. But he said nothing, just smiled ruefully, ruffled her hair, and was then gone, his long legs striding along the corridor. She wondered where it led. The kitchens? Well, he wasn't going to find many influential people in there.

Locating a tiny handle on the door, she opened it a

few inches and slid her body through, trying not to look too conspicuous. The ballroom was now heaving with a sweaty mass of bodies, moving as one to the music. The live band had been replaced by a DJ, pounding out repetitive drum 'n' bass. Shelby decided against fighting her way between them and instead, her back against the wall, began to shuffle around the edge, intending to find the door which led back through to the entrance and fetch herself another buck's fizz.

Halfway around she decided she needed the loo more. But where the hell was it? Somewhere up that grand staircase they had passed on the way through to the ballroom. But which way was that? Catching a glimpse of Courteney, in a heavily embroidered, silver mini-dress, dancing with Irving, she squeezed through the crowds to join them. Irving, who was wearing his *Full Monty* promotional T-shirt, purely to antagonise Ross, did not look pleased to see her.

"Where's the loo?" hollered Shelby, as Irving briefly swung Courteney in her direction.

"I think he's in the garden with Dulcie!" hollered back Courteney.

"No – *toilet!*"

A tiny frown appeared on Courteney's unblemished brow. "Who's she?"

Shelby gave up and tried ducking through the nearest door, finding herself in yet another anteroom, although this one was slightly more splendid than the others, with blood-red walls and lots of velvet curtains. Apart from the wardrobe mistress necking with one of the grips, his large hairy hand ferreting around inside her metallic gold bustier, the room was empty. They sprang apart, crimson with embarrassment, as Shelby tiptoed past, and chorused 'Hello, Shelby'.

The anteroom led through to a drawing-room, threadbare chairs and sofas in pastel chintz grouped around yet another magnificent fireplace, elegant little tables awash with *Vogue* and *Country Life* jostling for position with well-thumbed copies of the *American Variety* and *The Stage*. Ross's mother lived here too, Shelby remembered, wondering where that lady was. Although the house was so big, Julianne Whitney could be closeted in one wing and be totally unaware that this raucous party was taking place.

As Shelby wandered around, admiring the knickknacks and ornaments she presumed were valuable antiques, stepping over the comatose body of Jeremy, the director of photography, curled up asleep on the Persian rug, pipe still smouldering in his hand, she tried to reconcile the image she had of a suave sophisticated Ross with the man who owned this incredibly imposing, but decidedly old-fashioned house.

Pausing only to extinguish Jeremy's pipe and drape a tablecloth over him, Shelby examined the family photographs grouped on the polished lid of a grand piano. They were mostly black and white, in mix and match frames, of Ross as a child, then later, receiving film awards and meeting the Queen, and his mother Julianne at the height of her glamorous Hollywood career.

The drawing-room led through to a small family dining-room, with a larger, far grander one glimpsed through an open door further along. The house was like the inside of a snail's shell. She felt as though she was just walking around in circles, not making progress. A bit like her relationship with Ross really. And this mausoleum – compare it to the council house she had been born in, the apartment over her father's pub that she'd grown up in. Ross existed in another world.

Feeling despondent, Shelby returned to the drawing-room, pausing by the window, pressing her nose against one aged, warped pane. As the moon played tag between the thick silver clouds, she caught glimpses of a beautiful garden, an extensive lawn stretching into infinity, as neat as an Axminster carpet, bordered by beds crammed with the last of the spring bulbs and perennial shrubs about to burst with the first of the summer flowers. How inviting it looked. How calm and peaceful.

Further along the wall of the drawing-room, other sash windows had been forced open to their limit, trying to disperse some of the overpowering heat. Shelby had a furtive look round before hitching up her dress and scrambling over the nearest sill and through the open window.

She crashlanded on a dusty flowerbed, several feet below, and trampled down the bowed tulips and the thick yellowed leaves of what had once been a glorious display of daffodils, before she finally staggered onto the lawn. A distinct improvement. She took a deep breath. It was like a long drink of iced water. The air cleared her head, cooled her hot, perspiring skin. The garden was glorious.

She strolled through a gap in the hedge, through an elegant formal garden, then past serried ranks of box hedging and herby things, hopping over silver-leafed lavender bushes to take a short-cut. Instead of the front of the house, as she had hoped, she found herself in a beautifully scented flower garden and was about to turn back when she caught a glimpse of the gravel drive through the arches of a little romantic gazebo.

How pretty, she thought, stepping through one of the doorways, practically hidden by some wildly out of control purple clematis. She pulled back the curtain of flowers and had moved halfway into the gloom before she realised she was not alone. She squinted worriedly into the darkness. Lord, she hoped she hadn't interrupted a furtive fuck.

A willowy blonde in an emerald satin sheath dress – very old-fashioned – was winding herself around a tall broad-shouldered man, much like the rampant clematis outside. Shelby couldn't see the man's face because it was buried in the woman's shoulder, but he had dark red hair, just like Ross. But not as handsome, decided Shelby, as she silently backed away, groping behind her for an exit.

Suddenly the man raised his head and looked straight at her. "Shelby," he said, his voice strangled in his throat.

"Ross," she said, pleased that her own voice came out quite steady. For a moment she had thought it wouldn't be able to come out at all and that she would just crumple into a sodden heap. Then he would have won.

"Boy," she continued, her voice level and calm, "are *you* a fast operator." She steeled herself to look at Paige. "If he tastes of orange juice and champagne that would be the buck's fizz I had earlier."

Paige looked at her blankly. "You're delusional," she drawled. "Go away."

"I'm not just 'delusional', I'm fucking insane," said Shelby. "Excuse my French," she added to Ross. "I'll just go and wash my mouth out with Domestos. Kills all known germs you know. Including yours."

* * *

"What would you like to drink *now*?" asked the barman apprehensively eyeing the fiery little redhead leaning unsteadily against his counter. He had been sitting behind his bar all evening, set up right next to the ornamental fountain, and his very first customer had to be a lush. He hoped she wouldn't strip off all her clothes and dive in with the koi carp. His hotel and catering course hadn't covered giving drunks the kiss of life.

"Oh, I don't know," she sighed. "What's left?"

"Not much," he admitted, reluctant to serve her anything else. The girl was already decidedly tipsy. It was easy to chuck someone out of a pub, but how could you chuck someone out of a twelve-acre formal garden, particularly as they were likely to turn out to be an

Italian princess or a French movie star. This was the first time he had worked for the wealthy Ross Whitney. He had no wish for it to be his last.

"How about that pretty blue bottle in the corner?" she asked. "What's that?"

"Blue curaçao?"

"Sounds cute." She pushed her empty glass back towards him. "I'll have some. Ta very much."

The customer was always right. But still –"It's really a mixer, ma'am. What would you like with it?"

"God, I don't know. Use your imagination."

"Yes, ma'am." He reached for yet another glass.

"I'm not drunk, you know," she snapped. "I never get drunk. My father runs a wine bar. I can drink and drink and drink and I never get drunk – just sick. Bit of a bummer really," she sighed. "It means I remember everything the next morning. With distinct clarity. Hideous."

"Yes, ma'am." The barman began to slowly unscrew the lid of the bottle.

"And I want it in one of those triangular glasses with lots of umbrellas and pieces of fruit. And after that, you can fix me an orange one. Orange curaçao. You see," she said triumphantly. "I do know what these drinks are called."

"Yes, ma'am."

She squinted at him. "God, you're boring. You ought to get a life. A high life like me." She hitched herself more firmly onto the bar stool, resting her freckled elbows on the sticky surface of the bar. "I know all the stars, you know," she continued. "Courteney O'Connor thinks she's my new best friend. And Luke McFadden, the star of *All That She Wants* – he's *desperate* to be my lover. Totally head over heels for *me*. People are so jealous. I'm having such a wonderful time . . ." A tear began to trickle down her cheek. "Everyone wants to be me . . ."

The barman slid her cocktail across the bar. It had more fruit than Mr Del Monte saw in a year, several umbrellas and a thick coating of blue sugar crystals around the rim of the glass. He went back to frenziedly polishing glasses.

At least she was giving the barman something to do, Shelby reflected sadly, wiping her eyes with the back of her hand. So she wasn't entirely useless. The poor man must have been very lonely, tending a bar with no customers, hidden here in the garden until she had happened upon him, still frantically searching for the way out. If only he would be a bit more sympathetic instead of glaring at her as though she was about to throw up in his fountain.

Shelby rested her chin on the back of her hands and wondered where everyone else was, and if they were having as much fun as her. Even in the garden she could hear the music pounding from the ballroom. It was lucky Ross didn't have neighbours.

" *I want to see the sunshine after the rain,*" she began to sing along. It summed her life up really. *"Where is the silver lining shining at the rainbow's end . . ."*

"I didn't know you could sing," said a deep voice, some way above her head.

Shelby didn't look up. Right now the rows of multi-coloured alcopops seemed to be dancing along with the music and she had a nasty feeling that if she made any sudden movements she was likely to fall right off her bar stool and into his arms. And her love life was in enough trouble to add any further complications. She had no need to look at him anyway. She only had to look at the barman's flabbergasted expression to know who it was.

"Hello, Luke," she said.

"Mr McFadden," stammered the barman, looking at Shelby with renewed respect. "May I get you a drink? Champagne perhaps?"

Luke slid onto a bar stool. "I'll have the same as the lady." And then he caught sight of the transparent blue liquid in Shelby's glass. "Or perhaps I won't. Do you have any Chardonnay?"

"Yes, sir." The barman bent to rummage in the small fridge behind him.

"What the hell have you got in that glass, Shelby?" asked Luke in an undertone. "It looks like methylated spirit!"

"Don't you think it's pretty?" She ran her finger around the top of the glass, scooping up the blue sugar crystals, then licking them off with a small pink tongue. She plucked a cherry from one of the many protruding cocktail sticks and popped it into Luke's open mouth.

Luke regarded her worriedly. She was being nice to him. There must be something seriously wrong.

"Shelby," he said, "how much have you had to drink?"

"I don't know." She looked helplessly at the barman.

The barman, pouring Luke's bottle of wine, began to reel off a list.

"OK, OK," said Luke, holding up his hands, "I get the general idea. Do you have any coffee?"

"Yes, sir."

"Then I'll have two black coffees, please," said Luke. "Forget about the wine – have it yourself if you like."

Shelby looked sulky. "I never stop *you* having fun."

"It might be fun now but at five o'clock in the morning it's hell. Trust me, I know."

The barman placed two steaming black coffees in front of them, stuck the wine back into the fridge, and lingered for the next exciting development.

Luke frowned at him. "Isn't there something you could be doing?"

The barman wrung out a cloth and began to sulkily wipe down the counter-top at the opposite end of the bar.

"Shelby," Luke said quietly, "have you been out here all this time?"

She regarded him thoughtfully, her emerald eyes huge in her little pale face. Her eyeliner had smudged, he noticed, making her appear curiously vulnerable. He wondered if she had been crying, and who had caused it, and was surprised at the surge of anger which tore through him at the thought that it was probably Ross.

"Most of it," she admitted. "I'm sorry, were you looking for me? Have you been pestered by lots of women wanting to sleep with you?" She managed a lop-sided smile. "I hope you copied their telephone numbers down correctly."

Luke glanced up at the barman. It didn't look as though he could hear but . . ." Hurry up and finish your coffee, Shelby," he said sharply. "I'm taking you home."

She frowned. "Will we be able to get a train this late?"

"I meant to the hotel."

"I'm sorry you haven't enjoyed your birthday party."

He sighed. "I hardly knew a single person there. And Ross inviting *Hello!* was the final straw. To him, the whole thing was just a public relations exercise to claim back on tax. I swear, this is the last film I do with him. Hypocritical bastard."

Shelby picked up a cocktail stick and began to stab listlessly at one of her discarded cherries. "The more you antagonise Ross, the longer the filming takes, the more the bills run up, the grouchier he gets. He's in trouble with the Americans for overspending already. There's only ten more days 'til the end of filming. Don't let it all fall apart now."

He watched her playing with the fruit from her drink, pulling out the cocktail sticks then jabbing them back in again, almost as though it was a voodoo doll. Poor Ross . . . he almost felt sorry for him. But only almost.

"Are you in that much hurry to go home?" he asked.

She looked up, cocktail stick paused in mid-jab. "I didn't mean –"

He gave a wry smile. "Not quite what you imagined,

is it? People always think that acting – filming – is so glamorous, so much fun – the dressing up, the fake blood, the parties and premieres. But the truth is, it's a God-awful bore, working with people you wouldn't even want to speak to ordinarily, who say 'you were great' to your face, then leave your best scenes on the cutting-room floor, and tell the world how they're never going to work with you again because you were such hell."

Shelby stuffed the fruit back into the cocktail and pushed it away from her, watching the barman clear it before she could change her mind, tipping the fruit into the bin and the liquid into the slops tray.

"Irving always said location filming was like being in one big happy family."

"Yeah, the Borgias." He sighed. "I suppose you'll be glad to be shot of us all? Me in particular. We didn't get off to a terribly good start."

She smiled warmly, the smile just visible through the curtain of gleaming auburn hair. "You're all right."

"I'm just misunderstood?"

"Oh, I understand you all right!"

"Look," he began quickly, "I've got to explain something to you. I know the papers all talk about me as though I'm sex on a stick – but the truth is –"

"Luke," she said wearily, "it's a free country. You can bonk who you like. I don't care who you have sex with."

Hell, why was this all coming out so wrong? "Shelby – about Ross –"

She chuckled. "I hope you haven't been having sex with *him*."

Her face was smiling but her eyes were so sad he just wanted to take her in his arms and smooth all the hurt away. "Shelby –"

"I don't want to talk about Ross," she said quickly.

"It's about Paige actually –"

"And I certainly don't want to talk about her."

"Paige was once engaged to Ross," he said calmly.

"*What?*"

"How do you think he got that broken nose?"

Shelby regarded him disbelievingly. "Paige hit him?"

"*I* hit him," said Luke. "Paige caught him *delicto flagrante* with some extra. She was distraught."

"You seem to spend most of your time comforting his ex-girlfriends." Her voice was stony.

Where's my scriptwriter? thought Luke frustratedly. How can I make her see that I don't just want to get into her knickers – even though I do. That I'm not just some lazy bum of an actor, I'm as intelligent as Ross, almost as rich, but twice as pretty and a much nicer person and oh fuck, I think I'll just shoot myself and save on the angst.

"I should have listened when you tried to warn me about Ross," said Shelby sadly. "It was entirely my fault. Irving got me this job and I thought it would be a terrific laugh – which it is sometimes," she added earnestly. "And I didn't mean to fall in love with Ross but he's so . . . he's so . . ."

"He's very so-so," said Luke caustically.

"You know he's with Paige at this very minute?"

Who gives a shit? thought Luke.

"Luke?" said Shelby.

He glanced up. Suddenly she sounded very tired.

"Yes?"

"Could you take me back to the hotel?"

Chapter Seventeen

They followed one of the little gravel pathways, along lawns so neat they could have been trimmed with nail scissors. They didn't dare walk on the grass. The path wound through herbaceous borders and a dark shrubbery, until they suddenly came up against an old stone wall.

"Which way?" asked Luke wearily. Only Ross would have a garden so big one required an Ordnance Survey map just to find the front gate.

But Shelby was staring at the lichen-stained wall. A secret garden . . .

"Left or right?" prompted Luke, then turned to find he was talking to thin air. "Shelby!"

He caught a glimpse of auburn hair to his left and ran after her. The path followed the length of the wall, then around the corner. He caught up with Shelby just as she ducked under an old archway, draped with honeysuckle and the leaves of a wild rose. The flowers were still in tiny pink buds.

As Shelby hurried up the worn steps, her high heels caught, causing the brick to crumble and she was sent sprawling across the flagstones. In a moment Luke was beside her, carefully helping her to her feet.

"Are you hurt?"

"I'm fine," she muttered crossly and pulled away her hand.

"Your tights don't look very well."

She glanced down at her legs. Her left knee had a large hole and a ladder disappearing up her thigh. "Oh bugger," she grumbled and, hitching up her short skirt, she tugged her tights off, chucking them into the bushes.

Luke was alarmed. A couple of drinks and she had turned into Gypsy Rose Lee . . .

"Wow!" she said, moving away from him. "A swimming-pool!"

Luke followed her into the walled garden. The space was almost entirely occupied by an elderly swimming-pool, circa 1920. It was long and narrow, the water a very dark and uninviting green, and surrounded by large uneven flagstones, which looked as though they had been pinched from somewhere else. There was a encircling garden, crammed with old-fashioned shrubs and flowers that were just coming into bloom – a peculiar jumble that had perhaps been chosen for their scent, rather than their colour co-ordination.

"Dare you to a swim?" said Shelby.

"What?"

She put her hand up to the neck of her dress and, unzipping it, kicked it into the flower-bed.

Luke realised his mouth was open. "Shelby! What the hell do you think you're doing?"

Shelby looked at him and laughed. "But Luke, I thought you *wanted* to see me with my clothes off?" And, taking a run at the pool, she yelled, "Surf's up!" and jumped in.

A huge wave of chlorinated water surged up over the side and drenched him. *Shit!* What the hell was he supposed to do now?

Shelby surfaced, her long, marmalade hair plastered to her face, then flipped onto her back and began to lazily float. "Come on in," she said. "The water's lovely."

Christ! thought Luke. Just how much has she had to drink? He was torn between his baser instincts and an overwhelming desire to protect her. He was getting soft in his old age, he decided. One thing was for certain, she couldn't stay in the pool after the amount of alcohol she'd put away. It would be dangerous.

She began to idly flick water at him. "Chicken!" she taunted. "*Cluck, cluck, cluck!*"

Luke slowly stripped down to his sensible navy boxer shorts to launch a rescue attempt. As his skin became exposed to the cool spring air he felt it form into millions of goose-pimples. Despite being voted 'Most Fanciable Person' in one of the teenage rags last year, he felt extremely self-conscious.

"Now don't get any ideas," he told her, attempting to bluff his way out of it. "I'm on my best behaviour."

"Of course you are," she grinned.

He padded round to where she was floating, staring

down at that delicious body. Because she was small and slight he had not realised how shapely her legs were. And her skin, pale and ethereal; the moonlight turning her hair to bronze. She looked like a creature from mythology.

Involuntarily his eyes travelled the length of her body, across her flat stomach, towards the gentle swell of her breasts. *Oh God, he was supposed to resist making love to this?* Luke abruptly dropped into the icy water, trying to cool the blood rushing through his body. *What the hell did he think he was doing?*

He opened his eyes and could see nothing. The underwater lights remained dark. So he quickly surfaced, the shock of the cold water making his skin tingle but having absolutely no effect on his ardour. He pushed his hair from his eyes, and was startled to find Shelby treading water not two foot away.

"Hi!" she grinned. "Race you to the other end?"

"Do you think that's a good –" he began, but she was already off, and it was all he could do to keep up, watching her body zip effortlessly through the inky-black water.

She won, of course. He was too busy attempting to get a grip on his hormones. They swam at a more leisurely pace back towards the deep, shadowy end. Luke made a heroic grab for the edge – despite his matinee-idol appearance he was desperately unfit. Shelby was already there, grinning delightedly, droplets of water sparkling on the tips of her eyelashes.

"Beat you!" she said. "Twice! You're hopeless! No

wonder Ross hired a diver for the lake scene at Prior Park. I'm surprised he didn't make you wear arm-bands."

"Thank you," said Luke sarcastically. There was a three-inch ledge running all the way around the pool. Shelby, standing on it, could just about keep her head and shoulders above water. For a moment he considered pulling her off. He always had been a bad loser. A *sad* loser, he reflected, treading water beside her. "Adrian Moorhouse could have filmed that scene and Ross would still have hired a diver. It's the law."

She wasn't listening. "Isn't this beautiful?" she sighed, gazing up at the moonlight. "I can't imagine why Ross doesn't live here all the time? Why shack up in some grotty hotel, even if it is five star. It's not the same as being at home. And this is heaven."

"Perhaps he wants to keep an eye on us?"

Shelby, having grown bored, kicked away from the side and floated on her back, her hair trailing in the water, the water rippling across her body like liquid silver. The black bra and briefs covered her quite decently, more was the pity. He quelled the desire to rip them off but found himself catching hold of her foot and tugging her back towards him all the same. She didn't resist. She didn't even move. He allowed his hand to trail further up her leg, pausing on her thigh. Still, she did not make a sound. She had her eyes shut and a smile curling her lips. Had she even noticed?

Avoiding her briefs, he swirled patterns on her tummy with his index finger. She even had freckles there, he realised, fascinated. Did they go all the way? He trailed up towards her breasts, bottled out and dipped his finger into the little puddle around her belly-button instead. She gave a gentle sigh.

It was no good, he was not a gentleman and his self-control only went so far. He slid his left arm under her back and pulled her against his body, feeling the coolness of her skin against the length of him. He had a fleeting glimpse of very sober green eyes, fringed with ginger lashes and the clumpy remains of brown mascara, before he kissed her.

Tentatively at first, then more boldly, she flicked her tongue into his mouth, holding tightly onto his shoulders, digging her nails into his flesh, trying to prevent herself from sinking beneath the water.

"God, Shelby," he groaned, burying his head in her neck, "do you realise what you're doing to me?"

"I have a pretty good idea."

"Do you want me to stop?"

"Could you?"

He was dreaming this. He must be. In a moment he would wake up and find the bedsheets damp and that he was trying to make love to his pillow. He rested his forehead on hers and wallowed in those beautiful eyes. He wanted this moment to go on forever. No, he didn't. He wanted to haul her out of this damn pool, which was distinctly hindering this seduction, lay her in the moonlight on those cold wet flagstones and –

"Aren't you going to kiss me again?" asked Shelby innocently.

He frowned. He was used to receiving instructions from his director but not from the woman he was contemplating making love to. "Depends," he said stiffly, "on whether I survive the experience."

"Oh, Luke," she said scornfully, "why don't you learn to live a little?" And suddenly he felt two cold hands disappearing into the back of his boxer shorts. She laughed at his indignation. "It's like having sex with a choirboy!"

He firmly pulled her hands out. "Have you had sex with many choirboys?"

"Have you?" she returned coolly.

"Are you drunk?"

"*Moi?*"

"*Oui.* You're behaving very strangely. Now either Ross has been lacing his Veuve Clicquot with LSD, or I've just slipped through the looking-glass."

"Why don't you just slip into me," she murmured, and slid the boxer shorts over his hips.

He held her at arms' length. "Shelby, don't do this to me. It isn't fair."

"I know," she said and kissed him again.

It wasn't right. She had admitted that she loved Ross – so why was she making love to him? He didn't want another Paige to rot up his life. He had to stop it now, while he still had the strength. Except he didn't have the strength. He was drowning in his emotions.

Before Luke realised what he was doing, he pressed his mouth against hers, wrapping his arms so firmly around her slender body there was no way she was going to get away. Although she showed no signs of wanting to escape. Her fingers were entwined in his hair, her legs wrapped around his hips, to avoid sliding beneath the water. He kissed her more slowly, drawing the sweetness from those lips, his fingers sliding along her spine until he found the catch of her bra and undid it with practised ease, all those fumblings behind the bike-shed in his youth finally paying off.

Her breasts grazed against his chest and he slid one hand down her ribcage to gently caress them, his thumb moving across a nipple, already hard from the cold water. Unable to bear it any longer, he bent his head to draw it gently into his mouth.

"Luke!" squealed Shelby. "Someone's coming!"

Yes, me, he thought disorientatedly, closing his eyes, pressing his head on her breastbone, letting his tongue slide across her wet skin tasting the chorine – and her.

She was pushing against his shoulders. "I mean it, Luke. Someone's walking along the path. I can hear voices!"

Luke raised his head, forcing his brain to focus. The anxiety in her eyes was very real. And now he too could hear a voice, deep and male, drawing steadily closer. They waited, silently, hardly daring to breathe. Footsteps echoed on the flagstones, from the opposite side of the wall, moving slowly along toward the crumbling steps. Then pausing.

"Shit!" said Luke. "We have to get out!"

She put a hand on his shoulder. "It's too late! They're coming in here!"

"Make for the diving-board. The water is in shadow there. We can hide. Unless you have a couple of straws?"

"Who do you think I am? Ursula Andress?" She grinned impishly and turned away, half-swimming, half-wading through the water toward the diving-board.

Luke made a grab for her bra as it sailed past but it was too late. It was floating off to the centre of the pool and there wasn't a damn thing he could do about it. Careful not to ripple the water more than he could help, he adjusted his boxer shorts and slowly edged along the ledge to where Shelby was waiting beneath the diving board.

"Duck right down in the water," he advised, and moved closer to her. "And for Christ's sake stay behind me. Your hair is shining out like a bloody Belisha beacon."

Shelby gripped onto the side of the pool as they huddled together in the small shadow created by the diving board. He felt cross and embarrassed that he had allowed himself to get into this mess. And cold. He was too old for this sort of thing, he thought. Why take the risk when he had a perfectly good suite, with a Jacuzzi, in a comfortable hotel? He was crazy.

A man walked through the archway to the pool. He was holding the hand of a woman wearing a green sheath dress, split up to the thigh. Oh *shit*! Ross and Paige. Did somebody up there hate him? Luke fervently hoped they were not going to strip off and dive in too. He was in no mood for an orgy and the sight of Paige with lover-boy might send just Shelby into orbit. He watched sullenly as Ross sat on the low wall that surrounded the flower bed and lit up a cigarette. The guy was a walking advertisement for the tobacco industry.

"Why don't we take off all our clothes and dive into the pool?" Paige was saying huskily. She attempted to sit on his lap, pressing herself against him. But as Ross made no move to slide his arm around her waist, the satin of her dress kept causing her to slither off.

She'd never been that decadently wanton with him, thought Luke. Strictly missionary position with the lights off and her nightdress on.

The moon glided out from behind a cloud. It was like a spotlight trained right on the glassy water. He shrank further beneath the surface, praying they wouldn't be seen. The chlorine was beginning to get up his nose, making him want to sneeze. He could feel himself shiver with the cold. It was only April, for Christ's sake! And the expectation of being caught was absolute torture. Why hadn't they just brazened it out?

"Ross?" prompted Paige fractiously.

"Too bloody cold," muttered Ross, who seemed to have been in a trance. He stubbed his cigarette out in a flurry of orange sparks and abruptly stood up.

Thank you, God, mouthed Luke silently. Thank *you*!

"Party-pooper," muttered Paige, bending to trail one elegant hand in the water. "It's quite warm. Are you sure I can't entice you?"

"No." His voice was harsh.

Again Luke marvelled how Ross could treat all women like shit and still have them crawling after him for more.

Intently watching his hated rival, Luke hadn't realised Paige had walked the full distance along the poolside. She was now a mere couple of feet from him. Couldn't she hear his laboured breathing, see it rippling across the water? All she had to do was turn her head . . .

Shelby's bra drifted past.

Paige, her long red nails snagging on the black lace, fished it out and shook off the water. "Ugh!" she said, when she realised what it was, dropping it onto the ground. "How disgusting!"

Ross picked it up between forefinger and thumb. Luke closed his eyes. How familiar was Ross with Shelby's underwear? Did he recognise it?

"Fucking exhibitionist," he grunted, dropping it into a bin.

Obviously not.

"That means I'll have to have the whole pool drained and cleaned."

Shelby prodded Luke in the back. "Can he see us?" she hissed.

"No, but he'll bloody well hear you if you don't shut up!" Luke clamped his hand over her mouth. "Keep quiet!"

Ross hadn't seen them but it appeared he had noticed something else. Slowly he bent and picked up Shelby's dress, from where it lay on a crumpled heap in the flowerbed. He held it up to the light.

"Somebody's been having a good time," said Paige grumpily.

Luke squeezed himself further against the side of

the pool. His thighs were pressed hard against the back of Shelby's legs, her bottom was curved up into him. Oh fuck, what a time to get an erection.

Ross dropped Shelby's dress back onto the soil. "Come on, Paige," he said flatly, turning back towards the archway. "Let's go."

"About time," muttered Paige, hurrying after him. "I don't know why you wanted to come in here anyway. Let's return to the party and dance." She fumbled for his hand but he shook it away, striding off down the garden path and into the darkness. Paige took one last puzzled look at the pool, then hitched up her tight skirt and teetered after him.

For several seconds Luke remained frozen, his heart hammering against his ribs, then, when he was sure they had left, he relaxed. Releasing Shelby, he quickly climbed out of the pool.

"Have they gone?" asked Shelby.

"Yes, they've gone." He held out his hand to haul her up onto the side. "And I think we ought to go too. Put on your clothes."

Shelby wrung out her bra but did not bother to put it back on, just stepped into her dress and turned around for Luke to do up the zip. He did so – in silence, then collected his own clothes. "OK," he said, "have you got everything?"

"Yes. Luke, about what happened in the pool –"

"I don't want to talk about it."

"Luke –"

"Leave it."

They walked back through the gardens in silence.

Shelby because she was bitterly ashamed of her behaviour. And Luke, because he realised that Ross, looking directly into the shadows beneath the diving-board, had seen them.

And had not said a word.

Chapter Eighteen

As Luke and Shelby walked silently along the moonlit path they met Courteney meandering out of the shrubbery – and absolutely no sign of Bruno. Courteney was no longer wearing her silver dress, instead she proudly sported a T-shirt bearing the legend *The Full Monty*. Her long tanned legs stretched endlessly from beneath it and Luke had the distinct impression that she was no longer wearing knickers.

"Oh shit!" he muttered.

Courteney was swinging a petal-less tulip in her hand. "Hi y' all," she grinned. "Excellent party!" And slid gracefully into a unconscious heap.

Women! thought Luke irritably. Why did they drink so much when they couldn't hold their liquor?

Shelby lightly slapped Courteney's face. Getting no response, she shrugged helplessly in his direction. "Out cold."

Realising Shelby was expecting him to do something

macho, he flopped Courteney's arm around his neck and heaved her over his shoulder in a fireman's lift. Christ, she was a dead weight. Any vertebrae that had survived the years of rugby at college should now be well and truly shagged.

"We'll take her back to the hotel," he said and staggered off down the path, hoping to get a speed up before he keeled over into the shrubbery. Rock Hudson had always made this look so *easy* . . .

Shelby was still peering into the shrubbery. "What about Irving? We can't leave him stranded here."

Did he look like Search & Rescue? "Irving can take care of himself."

* * *

The only member of staff still awake at the hotel was the duty manager. He sat behind the reception desk, his nose buried in a copy of Andy McNab's *Bravo Two Zero* and did not even bother to look up as he tossed them their room keys. Amidst much huffing and puffing, Luke hauled Courteney up the stairs to her room. They tucked her into bed, still wearing Irving's T-shirt, dropped her room keys beside her and the door locked itself behind them.

Shelby quickly inserted her key into the door to her suite. "Goodnight, Luke."

Luke snatched her keys. "You're not escaping that easily." He propelled her along the corridor to his own suite next door. "We've got to talk."

Shelby hated that expression. It reminded her of

teachers returning homework; her father finding out she had spent the night with the groom from her mother's stables; and her last serious boyfriend – shortly before he chucked her. In fact the words produced a horrible churning sensation in her stomach that could not all be apportioned to the amount of liquor she had guzzled.

The effects of the alcohol were beginning to wear off. As she remembered everything that had happened, her face burned with shame. It would not be Luke's fault if he had got the wrong idea and thought he could take over where Ross had left off. How could she have let things go so far? Yes, it had felt nice. Yes, it had seemed so right. But she couldn't jump into a relationship with Luke – for one thing they had to work so closely together. And, she admitted despairingly, she was still in love with Ross.

What a hopeless muddle – and she only had herself to blame.

"Coffee?" asked Luke as she sat on his sofa, squashing herself into the furthest corner.

"I'm sober," she replied sulkily.

"It was a question not an accusation. I'm trying to be polite."

"OK, black with one sugar." She made an effort to sound less cantankerous. "I hate those little plastic UHT things, don't you?"

Luke grinned and pointed to a small white cupboard behind him. "*Voila*," he said, throwing open the door to reveal bowls of salad, jugs of orange juice and several bottles of half-fat milk. "I have a fridge."

How the other half live, thought Shelby grumpily. "I hope you'll be very happy together."

He gave up and turned away to make the coffee. "What happened tonight? Between you and Ross?"

"Nothing."

"Sure. Next you'll be saying you only pounced on me because of PMT. Or maybe the alcohol was talking. I should get you drunk more often. The most outrageous alter ego emerges."

She cringed. "Luke, I'm sorry –"

"Don't say you're 'sorry'. You make it sound like a mistake."

It *was* a mistake, she thought wretchedly. "I didn't mean to lead you on. I've always despised women like that. Those stupid creatures who leap into bed with all and sundry and then blame it on alcohol when their conscience catches up with them."

"And you regret it?"

She could not look at him. Coward, she told herself. "I regret leading you on."

"How did you feel when I was kissing you?" Then, when she failed to respond, "Did you enjoy it?"

The Spanish Inquisition. "Well, yes, but that's not the point –"

"That's exactly the point!" His fist came down on the sideboard, rattling the china cups. "If we hadn't been interrupted –"

"I've said I'm sorry! What more do you want? For me to write it out one hundred times?"

For a moment he did not reply. Then, wearily, "Perhaps you'd better go."

"I just wanted to explain – Luke, I'm not into one-night stands. I'm not proud of my behaviour. It's just –" She broke off. "Oh God, it's all such a mess. Do you want me to resign? I'll call John in the morning, see if he can get Charles Smith to come and take over." She jumped off the sofa and was halfway towards the door when he suddenly caught her arm.

"No! *You* might be able to switch your emotions on and off like a fucking light bulb but I –" He released her, just as abruptly. "You really have no idea of the effect you have on me . . ."

She looked up into his eyes and the raw emotion made her catch her breath. He's an actor, she told herself. He's pretending. But surely some emotions could not be faked . . .

His finger trailed down her cheekbone. "Such beautiful skin," he murmured, so softly she could hardly hear the words.

"Luke . . ."

He was bending his head towards her, as though in a trance. She should move away, leave, before she made a whole barrow-load of mistakes she would have to later apologise for, and yet somehow she couldn't. His lips met hers, warm and gentle at first, then more demanding, and then something seemed to catch alight, a flicker rose up from her toes and without realising it she was kissing him back, with passion, with urgency, and this time she couldn't blame the drink. She couldn't even blame herself. Her senses seemed to have declared themselves an independent state and cut off all diplomatic contact with the rest of her body.

There was a piercing scream. A bucket of water couldn't have been more effective. Shelby's police training went onto automatic pilot and she pushed Luke away, her eyes wide and disturbed.

"What on earth was that?"

Luke pulled her back into his arms. "Mice."

She fought him off. "Are you crazy? It sounded like someone was being brutally murdered." Shoving him back against the wall, she wrenched open the door.

"Shit, shit, shit!" Luke punched the wall in frustration. "Back to fucking square one."

As he followed Shelby out into the corridor, he collided with Kit. "Was that you?" he asked ill-temperedly. "Another of your stupid jokes?"

Kit's attention had been transfixed at the sight of Shelby emerging from his best friend's bedroom at three-thirty in the morning, even if she was fully dressed. In fact, he was so gobsmacked, he failed to make any smart remark involving the words 'pot', 'kettle' and 'black'.

"I don't think so. I would have noticed."

"So why are you standing here? Your room's on the next floor."

"Eh? Oh . . . er, I was just passing . . ." said Kit airily. "Trouble sleeping, you know?"

"You're bed-hopping."

"Why do you always have to make it sound so tacky? Besides, *you* can talk."

Someone screamed again. "It's coming from Courteney's room," cried Shelby, tearing off along the corridor.

"It's like that game," said Kit brightly, "Murder in the dark."

Luke glared at him. "Make yourself useful and call hotel security."

Kit watched Shelby attempting to smash down Courteney's door with her shoulder. "Who needs security when we've got Shelby?"

Paige's bedroom door flew open. "What the fuck is going on?" roared Ross.

Beside him was Paige. As soon as she realised they had an audience she hooked her arm possessively around his waist.

Kit smirked. "Hullo, Ross, working late again?"

Paige was still wearing her emerald sheath dress, although it appeared to have been done up in a hurry and was sliding off her shoulders. Her blonde hair cascaded around her shoulders like Veronica Lake, two millimetres of brown eyes were revealed between sweeping black lashes as she looked Shelby up and down and recognised her burgundy jacquard dress.

False eyelashes, thought Shelby nastily, feeling her stomach fall away with pure hatred and jealousy. "Courteney's in trouble," she said out loud, rubbing her aching shoulder. "Luke was about to break the door down."

"The hell he is," growled Ross. "Any damage to hotel property comes out of my profits."

Bruno emerged from the shadows. "What's going on?"

"We heard screaming from Courteney's room," explained Shelby, wondering why it had taken so long for him to appear, when his own room was only next door. "But we can't get in."

Bruno threw his considerable bulk against Courteney's door. There was the sharp crack of splintering wood and the door swung open, crashing against the wall on the other side. Bruno fell in.

"Great," muttered Ross, surveyed the wreckage. "That's absolutely *great*."

Everyone else ignored him and charged in.

Courteney was crumpled up on the bedroom floor, her whole body wracked by hysterical sobs. Bruno gathered her into his arms, stroking her hair, muttering soothing words, gently rocking her, calming her down.

At least she was not the only one to let her professionalism slip, thought Shelby – yet she was not really surprised. Was there any man who wasn't madly in love with Courteney – including her own brother?

"On the bed," sobbed Courteney, "it's on the bed."

On the plump pink pillow Shelby could see a small bundle of black feathers. On closer inspection it was a bird's head, perhaps a crow, most certainly dead, probably for some time – as the tiny bones of the skull gleamed through the dull, matted feathers. It had been roughly severed from the rest of the body but there was no blood. Still, Shelby felt her stomach heave and turned away.

"That wasn't there earlier," she said to Luke. "Someone's been here. We'll have to call the police."

"No," said Courteney abruptly. She pushed Bruno away and stood up, albeit shakily. "They'll think it's just a publicity stunt. They won't take any notice – and then the papers will find out . . ." She paused to take a deep breath. "They're already slagging me off, saying I'm crazy, unreliable, and – and a terrible actress . . ." She bit her lip, struggling for control.

There was a strong willpower behind those baby blue eyes, decided Shelby. Courteney O'Connor might have received an unpleasant shock but there was no way *she* was going to be a victim.

"Of course we must call the police," muttered Ross irritably. "There's the ramifications on the hotel's security."

Shelby had expected a little more in the way of sympathy. Perhaps Ross just wasn't the sensitive type.

She watched him turn his temper on Bruno. "And I might ask where you were?"

Bruno opened his mouth but was not given the chance to explain.

"From now on," said Ross, "you sleep on the sofa in Miss O'Connor's sitting-room."

Bruno inclined his head, so slightly it was almost

insulting, although Shelby had the impression he'd rather punch Ross's lights out. Ross really needed to work on his people skills.

"No," said Courteney firmly. "I can't stay here. I quit the film. I don't care if you sue me, Ross. I'm not staying in this room another second!"

* * *

Wednesday

So Courteney spent the night in Shelby's bed while Shelby spent the night on her sofa and then had to wait forever to use her bathroom the next morning, listening to a hungover Courteney throwing up. At least it made a change from having to listen to Luke.

Courteney finally emerged, way past her 6.00 am call, looking pale and wan. She gulped down a couple of vitamin pills with some freshly squeezed orange juice, with which one of the waiters had just staggered up the stairs, and went to chose an outfit from her huge collection of clothes, now crammed into Shelby's wardrobe.

Shelby had an easier choice. Her black suit or her purple suit. She laid out her black jacket and trousers on the bed before nipping into the bathroom for a shower, prior to Courteney thinking of some other expensive cream to lather into her voluptuous body. Watching Courteney wander around in the nude had made Shelby feel like an anorexic stick insect.

As she took a swig of Courteney's untouched coffee

– seemed a pity to waste it – she noticed a white envelope propped up against the little glass vase on the breakfast tray, beautifully inscribed in purple italic handwriting.

"Aren't you going to open your post, Courteney?"

The actress shrugged. "I know what's in it."

"Your overdraft?" teased Shelby, taking another sip of coffee. "Fancy writing for a bank manager."

"It's fan mail – if you could call it that." Courteney shuddered. "Pretty sick fan."

Shelby's heart skipped a beat as she picked up the envelope. "May I?" she asked politely.

Courteney stepped into a pair of Earl Jeans and lay on the bed to zip them up. "Be my guest."

Shelby ripped open the envelope and pulled out the thick sheaf of paper within, laying it on the dressing-table. She had half-expected letters cut from newspaper but instead found several sheets of expensive writing-paper, beautifully inscribed in violet ink. It was only as she began to read the closely written words that she realised what the letter contained. It was obscene, in the realms of fantasy – yet curiously childish, perhaps written by someone in their teens, or educationally backward. No wonder Courteney had not wanted to open her post. It would make anyone paranoid.

Vaguely Shelby remembered a training module on handwriting at her police college, but she was damned if she could remember any of it now. She had dismissed the whole course as a load of New Age codswallop.

"This is horrible," said Shelby, shoving the paper back into the envelope, unable to read any more. "Do the police know?"

"Ross knows," said Courteney indifferently, tugging a pale pink cashmere sweater over her head and emerging with her hair sticking up in soft blonde spikes. "I received a death certificate in my last week at Shepperton. I wanted to quit but he threatened to sue me."

"How very understanding of him!"

Courteney shrugged. "All he cares about is his movie. I should have guessed what I was letting myself in for when I signed the contract. Big mistake. But you know what Ross's like when he wants something. So damned persuasive. He makes you feel like you're the only person in the world."

Shelby shivered. Had Ross slept with Courteney too?

"Look at poor Octavia," added Courteney. "She was terrified of horses and Ross still insisted she did that fox-hunting scene. He could have used a stunt double – hell, he could have used a stuffed horse. He's a cold-hearted bastard. Well, what goes around comes around. And I hope I'm there to see it."

Shelby felt she really ought to defend Ross but, before she could speak, there was a sharp knock on the door.

Courteney glanced at her watch, a tiny gold and diamond affair. "That'll be Bruno. I reckon they could set Big Ben by Bruno."

As she showed no sign of moving, Shelby opened the door. Reduced to the role of lady's maid in my very own room, she thought sourly. She was annoyed further to find Bruno hovering in the corridor, desperate to check that his charge had survived the night. She had to flatten herself against the wall to allow him to squeeze his bulk along the short narrow passage to the sitting-room.

"I'll be with you in a moment, Bru," called Courteney, wandering from the bedroom as she applied yet another sticky layer of lip gloss.

"The police are downstairs," he said to Shelby, uneasily shifting his weight from foot to foot. "The hotel manager called them last night but they were too busy to turn up until this morning." His scathing tone revealed exactly what he thought about the local constabulary. "They want to talk to Miss O'Connor."

"No way," said Courteney, bolting back into the bedroom. "I'm not talking to the police."

Shelby jammed her foot in the door before Courteney could lock herself in and she was reduced to flopping sulkily onto the bed.

"Did you know about Courteney's hate mail, Bruno?" asked Shelby

"Shelby!" wailed Courteney. "That was in confidence!"

Bruno frowned. "What hate mail?"

Ignoring Courteney's protestations, Shelby handed it over. Bruno read the letter in silence, his face looming blacker by the moment. He appeared visibly shaken. "Has Miss O'Connor mentioned the nut that's stalking her?"

"Only a teensy weensy one," said Courteney. "Not worth bothering about."

"Mr Whitney told me about this guy who used to lie in wait outside Shepperton Studios," explained Bruno. "Just a skinny little kid, eighteen or so. But Mr Whitney was concerned enough to hire me. Miss O'Connor declined police involvement in case the newspapers blew the incident out of proportion."

"What did he do, this 'teensy stalker'?" Shelby asked her sarcastically. "Follow you back to your hotel? Pop up in your favourite restaurant? Meet you, accidentally-on-purpose, in your local shop?"

Courteney squirmed and studied her loafers. "Something like that."

"Bloody hell! Do you want to wake up and find yourself dead? Brutally murdered and dumped in a ditch?"

"All actors have stalkers! Women are always sending Luke their panties in the mail."

"Frilly knickers are one thing. Bits of seriously dead bird quite another. *Someone* was in your room last night, Courteney – am I getting through to you? *Someone* put that bird on your pillow while you slept. You could have been *killed*."

"I thought you were my friend! Why are you so horrible?"

"I'm trying to save your life. We both are." Shelby resisted the temptation to slap her and looked imploringly to Bruno, who merely gave her a dirty look. She found it exasperating that Courteney, quite capable of being a tough cookie when she put her mind to it, always switched into Shirley Temple mode when under personal attack. Any minute now Shelby fully expected her to launch into 'On The Good Ship Lollipop'.

There was another knock on the door. It was Ross. As Shelby opened the door he barely glanced at her, muttering, "Can I come in?" to the space above her head.

"Sure," Shelby threw open the door. "Open house."

Courteney lifted her head. Her aquamarine eyes luminous with tears, slickly glossed lips trembling. Why can't I cry like that? thought Shelby in irritation. Why do I go pink and blotchy with a runny nose?

Ross folded his arms. "What's the matter, Courteney?" he asked, his voice distinctly unsympathetic. "I thought you'd have got over last night by now."

"I don't want to talk about it!"

"The police do. They're downstairs right now."

Courteney screamed. "I don't want to speak to them! Make them go away."

Ross made a sound of impatience. "What's your problem, Courteney? You're the victim here. Why are you so afraid of the police?"

"I'm not afraid of the police – it's just – well, they won't take me seriously."

"Of course they will. Look, Courteney, I've just spent the morning getting your suite changed to a double so that Bruno can sleep in an adjoining room, arranging for you to have another bodyguard –"

"*Another* bodyguard!" chorused Shelby and Bruno.

"I don't *want* another bodyguard!" Courteney picked up a bowl of potpourri and hurled it at Ross. "I never wanted a bodyguard in the first place." A hairbrush followed the potpourri. "I'm fed up with your rotten stinking film." A plastic plant, a gold-framed photograph, Shelby's Walkman – which luckily bounced safely onto the sofa. "I want out of my contract!"

Ross, Bruno and Shelby took refuge behind the sofa. Fruit, the TV remote control, even her mobile phone flew through the air until finally Courteney ran out of things to throw and burst into angry tears.

"Fuck you, Ross Whitney! I'm catching the first plane out of this backwater! I'm going *home* and shove your damn movie!"

Chapter Nineteen

The two police officers were waiting to interview Courteney in a pretty little sitting-room which was part of the hotel's function suite. Decorated in cool shades of blue and green, there were Monet reproductions on the walls, plastic foliage gathering dust around the Georgian windows and embroidered waterlilies embellishing the sofas. The officers lingered directly beneath a huge silver plate, hung lopsidedly on the wall. It depicted the head of Oceanus and bore a curious resemblance to Floyd after too many nips of whisky.

The officers were talking quietly with Ross and lapsed into silence as Shelby entered, trailing the rebellious Courteney closely behind – with Bruno bringing up the rear. Shelby met Ross's enquiring gaze head on. She wasn't one of his pathetic nineteenth-century heroines, crumbling into a weeping soggy mass at the first sign of adversity. No, siree. Let him lay all the wives of Bath if he so desired, and the husbands too. She would show him that she didn't give a damn.

As Courteney was introduced to the officers, Ross caught hold of Shelby's wrist and pulled her to one side. "We've got to talk," he hissed.

Another one! thought Shelby irritably. "Get your hands off me!" A swift downwards jerk of her wrist and she was free. "We have nothing to talk about." And she stalked away, leaving Ross nursing a wrenched wrist.

Shelby knew Ross had left when the door snapped shut. It was the nearest his usually iron control would let him get to an outright slam. She wondered why he was so rattled. Surely the prat had not thought she would happily share him with Paige? Did he think she had no self-respect?

One of the officers, a rather intimidating woman in a bright red suit, introduced herself as Detective Sergeant Nadia Meyer. She had glossy black hair, drawn off her face into a thick ponytail, mahogany eyes and the sort of bright red lipstick that would make Shelby look like Morticia Addams. As Shelby mentally appraised her, thinking how the DS was a dead ringer for Paloma Picasso, she suddenly realised Nadia Meyer was doing exactly the same thing to her.

DS Meyer broke the stare first, with a wry, acknowledging smile, and nodded to her younger male colleague to make coffee. Shelby slid into the seat next to Courteney, much to Bruno's chagrin, and noticed the young actress had finally stopped trembling. It could be the ambient surroundings – chosen to put Courteney more at ease than a tense question-and-answer session in the interview room of the local nick. More conceivably it was the dashing young Detective Constable, who had blond hair and dark brown eyes, which were currently gazing at Courteney in a very soulful fashion. His suit was well-cut and looked as though it far exceeded the wages of a mere DC. And, as Courteney's gaze flicked towards his hands, he plainly wasn't wearing a wedding band.

DS Meyer smiled at Shelby. "So, you're the bodyguard?"

"*I'm* the bodyguard," said Bruno. He took DS Meyer's hand and shook it firmly, almost crushing her long narrow fingers. "Bruce Hargreaves, Ma'am, known as Bruno." Standing briskly to attention, he very nearly saluted. Shelby studied her feet, trying to keep control over her desperately twitching mouth.

"Ah yes," DS Meyer consulted her notes and surreptitiously stretched out her fingers. "You're both employed by the John Ivar Security Agency?"

"Yes, ma'am."

DS Meyer's lips began to twitch too. "You can sit down if you like," she offered. "Would you like coffee?"

"No, thank you, ma'am. I shall stand."

Shelby leant over and poked him in the ribs. "Oh sit down, Bruno. Don't be such a martyr."

Bruno gave her a withering look, which was totally wasted, as Shelby had just dived hungrily on a plate of chocolate biscuits. With all the excitement this morning she never did get around to breakfast.

"I'm Shelby Roberts," she explained to DS Meyer.

"I'm actually Luke's minder but I came along to keep Courteney company." (And prevent her sprinting off to the nearest airport.)

DS Meyer nodded. "Ex-Tactical Firearms Officer."

Shelby's biscuit broke in two, scattering crumbs across her skirt and onto the carpet. "That's right," she replied warily.

"I understand you were first on the scene when Miss O'Connor found the bird in her bed?"

"I heard her scream but it was Bruno who smashed down the door." Shelby watched as the blond Detective Constable, reluctantly tearing himself away from Courteney's huge turquoise eyes, began to scrawl out a statement. He could have been writing a novel. Shelby tried not to appear as though she was trying to read it upside down.

"We'd like to interview both yourself and Mr Hargreaves later this morning," added DS Meyer. "If that would be convenient? I have cleared the request with Mr Whitney."

"Sure."

DS Meyer held out the plate of biscuits to Courteney, in a vain effort to catch her attention. "Perhaps you could tell us what happened, Miss O'Connor?"

Courteney took three bourbon creams, stuffing one into her mouth before replying. "Well," she said, still dimpling at the handsome DC. "I went to sleep, I woke up, I saw that disgusting dead bird and then Shelby, Bruno and Luke turned up."

"Approximately what time did you go to bed?"

"Erm . . ." Courteney shot a sideways glance at Shelby.

"Luke and I left your room at about three," said Shelby helpfully. "Perhaps it was shortly after that?"

"Yes," agreed Courteney gratefully. "It was shortly after that."

The DC patted her hand consolingly. "Don't you worry, Miss O'Connor. We'll find the culprit. Britain is very sympathetic to the victims of stalking. This man will be in a lot of trouble when we catch up with him."

DS Meyer regarded him with irritation. "We haven't yet established that Miss O'Connor has a stalker –"

"Oh, but I *have*!" said Courteney, all big eyes and trembling lower lip. The DC took her hand in a comforting manner. "Just a little one though," she assured him. "I don't think he really means to hurt me."

Shelby glanced at her watch. They were going to be here all day at this rate and there was no way she was about to sacrifice lunch.

"What about the kid at Prior Park?" she asked. "The one in the red jersey?"

A tiny frown creased Courteney's forehead. "*What*?"

"And the kid at Shepperton," added Bruno, anxious to get his halfpenny worth in. "He trailed you around all day. That's why Firestorm hired me," he added to DS Meyer. "This teenager was following her around like a puppy-dog, writing all these love letters. I bet he wrote the hate mail too."

"He didn't write the hate mail," Courteney dismissed Bruno airily. "He wouldn't have done that. It must have been someone else. This boy was sweet."

"Did you talk to him?" asked Shelby incredulously. "You did, didn't you? Jesus, Courteney! A dead bird in your bed? You got off lightly! You could have been lying at the bottom of the River Avon!"

"I can swim!" grumbled Courteney.

"With rope around your ankles?"

"Miss Roberts," intervened DS Meyer, "perhaps if we could concentrate on the matter in hand?"

"Sorry!" Shelby bit defiantly into another biscuit. "I don't mean to butt in. Force of habit. I can leave if you like?"

DS Meyer ignored her and smiled encouragingly at Courteney. "Do you know the name of this boy who has been following you?"

Courteney's eyelids flickered. "No."

"What does he look like?"

"Typically English. Brown hair, brown clothes, pale skin, pale eyes."

"Was he wearing a red sweater?" asked Shelby.

"No, he was not wearing a red sweater!" snapped Courteney. "What is it with you and red sweaters?"

Shelby caught sight of the DS's expression which plainly told her that one more remark out of line and she'd be out of the door. She looked at her watch again. Hell, it was almost lunch-time. What a complete waste of a day. Thank heavens she was getting paid.

"Miss O'Connor," continued DS Meyer patiently, "when did you first notice this boy following you?"

"At Shepperton. Fans would hang around the gate and that's when I noticed him. He asked for my autograph. He was respectful, quiet. I liked him." She thoughtfully chewed over the last biscuit. "Then he started popping up all over the place. It got kinda weird."

DS Meyer pushed the plate of biscuits back towards Courteney. "Was it then that you started receiving death threats?"

Courteney squirmed. "They weren't death threats exactly, although I did receive a death certificate through the mail and a wreath of red roses – oh, and lots of letters saying what he'd like to do to me in bed. Harmless fantasy stuff."

"Harmless!" scorned Shelby.

"Well, they didn't contain any reference to leather, chains or bondage," retorted Courteney, "so I thought they were harmless, yeah! You should have met some of the guys I've dated. The last one liked to tie me up and –"

"Are you in a relationship now, Miss O'Connor?" interrupted DS Meyer.

Courteney smiled beatifically. "Irv and myself are now considered an item."

The DC paused, pen in mid-air, "Do you think he would –"

Shelby glared at him. Irving, a psychotic stalker? One more remark like that and the DC would find himself lying on the terrace, wearing one of those Monet reproductions around his neck.

Courteney laughed. "Are you crazy? Irving's into the environment and animal rights. The sort of guy who spends half an hour trying to catch a bug instead of just squishing it with his heel? He sure isn't going to rip the head of some little old bird."

Ds Meyer sighed. "We've got the forensic people checking your room, dusting for fingerprints, that sort of thing. We've checked to see if anyone asked for your key last night, or if strangers were seen hanging around. The manager told me they have increased security since you film people moved in." She glanced towards Shelby. "I understand Mr McFadden has had problems with tabloid journalists?"

Understatement of the year, thought Shelby. "So," she asked, "if Courteney's stalker didn't use a key and didn't break in, how did he get inside?"

"It certainly is puzzling, Miss Roberts."

Which means you have a pretty good idea but you're not going to tell me, realised Shelby, and wished she hadn't made the wisecracks. Not the way to endear oneself to the local CID. Too late, she remembered the CID never did have much of a sense of humour, unlike Traffic, who were great ones for whoopee-cushions, potatoes in exhausts and tiny pebbles hidden behind hub-caps.

DS Meyer handed Courteney the last chocolate biscuit. "I understand the hotel have arranged for you to have another suite, one with extra rooms for your bodyguards?"

"Yeah." Courteney didn't look terribly thrilled.

"Would you like me to arrange police protection too?"

"What's the difference?"

"Plainclothes officers carrying guns. We'll fix panic buttons and give you a hand-held alarm too – instant contact with the police station."

"Armed guards? Like I'm the President or something?" Courteney burst out laughing. "You've got to be kidding me!"

"It's up to you."

"No way. I never wanted a bodyguard in the first place. Jeez, are you guys determined to stop me having fun?"

DS Meyer shrugged. "We're just trying to protect you, Miss O'Connor."

"I'm not in any danger," repeated Courteney firmly. "Filming wraps at the end of next week, then I'm off to Cannes to promote *A Midsummer Kiss*, then home to Savannah. This stalker isn't going to follow me to the US. He's only a kid. He wouldn't be able to afford the ticket."

"I can only repeat that it's your own decision."

"I don't want an armed guard."

"Fine." DS Meyer gathered her notes together and slid them back into her briefcase. "I think that's all the questions I want to ask you, Miss O'Connor. Thank you for sparing me the time from your busy schedule. If I think of something else, I know where to find you."

"Sure. Er, thanks."

As Shelby got up to follow Courteney and Bruno to the door, DS Meyer deliberately stepped in front of her. "Could I have a quick word, Miss Roberts?"

Shelby sat down again, looking longingly at the

scattering of crumbs across the plate in front of her. If she got any thinner her breasts would start to grow inwards. Her stomach gave an ominous rumble.

DS Meyer waited for the DC to close the door. "Do you have any feelings on this matter?"

"What sort of feelings?" asked Shelby guardedly.

"That things are not quite what they seem?"

Shelby had no patience for guessing games. "What are you getting at?"

DS Meyer sighed. "Is Courteney O'Connor telling us the truth?"

"About the stalker?"

"About everything."

"You think she would lie?" Shelby was taken aback. "About something like this? You didn't see her last night. She was hysterical. Maybe she is capable of writing a few dirty letters to herself – but ripping the head off some bird? That's sick."

"It was only a suggestion." DS Meyer seemed surprised at her fervent tone. "We have to cover every angle. Even you must be aware that sometimes the theatrical profession use every means to ensure the best publicity available."

"Just what are you insinuating?"

"Or perhaps it was intended as a prank? Luke McFadden is well known for his practical jokes. Didn't he gift-wrap a stuffed rat for some actress who irritated him?"

Shelby suppressed a smile. It wouldn't surprise her in the slightest. "I agree that Luke has a juvenile sense of humour but he wouldn't be so cruel. Besides, he likes Courteney. Everyone does."

"How about Mr Whitney?"

"Ha! He's spending all his time trying to keep us *out* of the tabloids. You think Ross would really go to all that trouble for a few extra column inches when he already has journalists coming out of his ears?"

"It was only a suggestion, Miss Roberts."

"It's costing him a fortune to hire additional security. Bruno and myself are on several hundred a day, plus expenses, and Firestorm hasn't really got the money to burn. This is their first 'blockbuster'. Ross is on a tight budget."

"Good publicity though. An actress with a bodyguard has status. The more bodyguards, the more status. Think about it. If you saw Bruce Willis at your local pub, all on his own, would you look twice? Would you think you had made a mistake, that he was just a lookalike? How about Bruce Willis with a dozen minders? You'd notice him then. And if there was a scuffle or two, more people would notice, word would spread. Front page news, Miss Roberts. Priceless publicity for the sake of a few hundred pounds."

"No," said Shelby resolutely. "It's not true. You didn't see Courteney last night. She was terrified, a gibbering wreck – Ross wouldn't do that to her."

"Surrey Constabulary faxed me a copy of this." DS Meyer handed her a formal-looking certificate sealed in a plastic envelope. "It's the death certificate Miss O'Connor received a month or so ago, while she was working at Shepperton. Do you notice anything odd about it?"

Shelby took it from her. This was such a waste of time. "Well, it has Courteney's name on it, and Courteney plainly isn't dead, and there isn't a date of death, which is understandable and . . ." Shelby paused.

"Yes, Miss Roberts?"

"It's an *American* death certificate . . ."

"Got it in one."

Chapter Twenty

By the time Shelby arrived on set it was twelve-thirty and the cast and crew had broken for lunch and returned to their trailers at 'base'. The weather was so sweltering, most had flopped outside and were sprawled across the grass of the Royal Victoria Park, on a patchwork of rugs, coats and plastic carrier bags, knocking back little bottles of mineral water and making serious inroads into the caterer's cod and chips.

The crew smoked and swigged the occasional beer – when they thought Ross wasn't looking, and attempted to outdo each other's dirty jokes. The 'Talent', still in their costumes, murmured occasional polite comments but mostly had their heads buried in a book or a copy of their script, unwilling to lose the momentum of the morning. The bright gaudy carnival they created caused a steady influx of spectators into the park as word spread throughout Bath.

Lúke had got used to living his life in a goldfish

bowl years ago and just pretended they weren't there, leaning over to pour Shelby a drink of mineral water in a plastic cup and to poke disinterestedly at his salad. The caterers had not quite got the hang of Luke's salads. Limp sticks of carrots, stringy green celery and a large tomato, all sitting on a bed of iceberg lettuce that he wouldn't give a tortoise for the fear of upsetting the RSPCA.

"How did it go?" asked Luke, stretching himself out on the newly mown grass, spurning a corner of Shelby's tartan rug, oblivious to the cuttings slowly congregating on the back of his dark 19th century coat and the herds of panting women not ten feet away, psyching themselves up to ask for his autograph.

"Weird being on the other side of the interviewing," replied Shelby, tucking into a plate of chips and hoping he wouldn't start interrogating her as well. She was still trying to get her head around DS Meyer's suggestion that Courteney was stalking herself. She thought of 'Billy the Kid' – and, more importantly, the run-in she'd had with him by Queen's Square, when he had suggested Courteney had paid him to fire a gun at her – and miss.

Shelby rolled onto her tummy, kicking her feet up behind her, and stared up at the beautifully symmetric arc of the Royal Crescent, oblivious to Luke's scrutiny, and attempted to rationalise events so far. It was just too weird. Why would Courteney want to stalk *herself*? For attention? She already had plenty of that. Courteney only had to show up on set and the entire crew dissolved into a blissful puddle of goo. They were all madly in love with her, including Jasper, and he was supposed to be gay.

Luke, watching her shovel greasy chips into her mouth like a failed dieter after a week on Slimfast, handed her the ketchup.

"Ta," she mumbled, her mouth full and, giving the bottle an enthusiastic squeeze, splattered red gunk across her cardboard plate.

"You looked as though you needed it," he commented dryly. There must have been over twenty women, gazing adoringly at him, desperate for one look, one word, something to show he'd noticed them, and *he* couldn't take his eyes off the only woman who didn't give a toss whether he was there or not. "I'm sure there's peanut butter and jam around here somewhere."

"I haven't had any breakfast," protested Shelby, indignant that he was comparing her with Courteney. She noticed he was picking away at his usual salad with a distinct lack of enthusiasm. "Would you like a chip?"

He regarded the crimson glutinous mass congealing on her plate. "I wouldn't dream of coming between you and your lunch." He slid his plastic cutlery together and was about to tip the whole lot into the black plastic bag serving as the bin, when Shelby seized the tomato as it rolled across the plate.

"Sorry," she said, catching sight of the astonished look on his face. "Did you want that?"

"Help yourself," he sighed. "I'm off to see Kit for a touch-up."

"OK," she said. "I'll just finish this and I'll be right with you."

Having been passed over in favour of a greasy chip, Luke felt suddenly deflated. She couldn't even be bothered to jump on the double entendre.

Last night might never have happened.

* * *

Luke regarded his handsome countenance with disfavour. Even in the harsh white lights of the Make-up trailer he looked devastating.

"Well?" Kit, prodded his collar bone with the end of the comb. "What do you think?"

"It's all right," said Luke and automatically reached for the hairnet to preserve his black curls.

Kit slapped the back of his hand with the comb. "Are you trying to do me out of a job? There's a storm brewing. If it's not done properly you'll end up looking like Scary Spice."

"In a fluorescent pink hairnet?" scoffed Luke. "More like Ena Sharples. Why don't you invest in more macho colours?"

"And what, pray, is macho about a hairnet?"

But Luke, glowering at his reflection, was no longer listening. "Where am I going wrong, Kit? I thought I'd got women sussed but it's as though they come from another planet."

"It's taken you twenty-nine years to work that out? Why do you think I'm gay?"

Luke failed to smiled. "I'm rich, I'm famous," he

sighed, "some women think I'm a complete hunk. I like children, I respect old people, I'm kind to animals. I can be sensitive if I put my mind to it, I have a terrific sense of humour – usually I have to fight women off. I just don't understand it. What is it that women like in a man? What more do they want?"

"Even Freud couldn't come up with an answer to that one, so why ask me?"

"You do their make-up – don't they confide in you?"

"You're getting muddled with hairdressers. Actresses are usually too concerned about whether I've got their lip liner symmetrical. Is this a hypothetical question? Or are we talking about one woman in particular?"

"You have to ask?"

"Not really." Kit clicked on the kettle to make a pot of tea. "Shelby the Shadow, right?"

"Last night, we were so close – everything was going perfectly. Picture a beautiful walled garden, the scent of flowers on the breeze, a cool moonlit pool . . ."

"Spare me the gruesome details."

"And today it's like nothing happened. As though I woke up in the shower and it was all a dream. Yesterday it was *From Here To Eternity* in Ross's swimming-pool and today it's *The Big Freeze*. He's got to her again, I know he has. I don't know how, but in some way –" Luke broke off and thumped the counter, rattling all the jars of cream and sending Kit's make-up brushes cascading onto the floor. "Christ, what do women see in that bastard?"

Kit wearily picked up the brushes and placed a cup

of tea in front of his friend. "Several million a year, a house in the country and his very own film company. Have you never heard of the casting couch? He'll be offering her a bit part in one of his films. Never fails. How do you think he landed that earl's wife in Scotland? With a shrimping net and a gaff?"

"Shelby isn't like that."

"Oh no? I'll tell you what Shelby sees in Ross. He's mean, moody and magnificent. It's the caveman thing. For all their squeals of equality, women just want some hunk to drag them back to his cavern. Why do you think these costume dramas are so popular – apart from the breeches? It's because it was the last time women could be swept off their feet without feeling as though they were betraying the sisterhood. Ross is just the type of man that women adore. An arrogant, upper-class shit who treats women appallingly. You know the type, you've played them often enough – Heathcliff, Byron, erm . . . Rupert Campbell-Black . . ."

"I can do that."

"But can you keep it up for the next fifty years – or only to the first alimony cheque? That's where you came unstuck with Paige. You fell in love with the plucky heroine from *All That She Wants* and Paige lusted after the macho hero trying to save her from a psychotic murderer. As soon as the director yelled 'cut', the credits went up, the lights went on and you were all out of popcorn. Leave the acting to Kenneth Branagh. Just be yourself."

"I tried that and ended flat on my back – twice. And it wasn't in bed."

"I suppose you could say you fell for her then," smirked Kit then, catching sight of Luke's expression, added hurriedly, "OK, I guess you couldn't."

But Luke was gazing through the net curtains at Shelby, now chatting patiently to his fans, answering the daftest questions and collecting up autograph books for him to sign. "So, what sort of man do you think Shelby wants?"

Kit regarded him pityingly. "Ross Whitney. Producer, director and all-round bastard."

* * *

They were filming in The Circus, one of Bath's more spectacular follies – an inside-out Roman colosseum, designed by John Wood, who had also been responsible for the Queen's Square. The curved facades were elegantly embellished with Doric, Ionic and Corinthian columns, like the layers of a wedding cake, and topped by a row of huge stone acorns rather than a bride and groom – an oblique reference to the legend of Prince Bladud and his pigs.

The set designer had arranged for 70 tonnes of two inch gravel to be laid over the part of the road they were filming in, to hide the tarmac and white lines, and a number of residents' doors had been covered in cream latex to fit the appearance of genuine early nineteenth century.

The weather was scorchingly hot, and by the mid-afternoon a sirocco had got up, blowing the dusty gravel in everyone's eyes, creating havoc with the actresses' neatly pinned wigs and Luke's Regency curls. Kit was in a foul temper and the Unit Nurse had a full-time job dispensing eye-drops, particularly to those who were wearing contact lenses. Ross had been smart enough to wear prescription sunglasses, which he dangled between forefinger and thumb every time he wanted to squint down the camera viewfinder. Aviator Ray-Bans had not been available in 1815 and Luke had to suffer the grit along with everyone else.

Paige was lording it up in a pink and orange striped deckchair and had conned one of the more timid extras into holding an enormous golfing umbrella over her head, to protect her complexion, even though she was sitting under one of the huge plane trees and so was therefore in the shade. Any moment, Luke expected the extra to be swept off her feet and over the rooftops of Bath, like Mary Poppins. The tourists weren't pleased either. They were straining over the crowd barriers, dividing the central green into two, clicking furiously with their Nikons, and all they could see of Paige was the occasional glimpse of a blue Empire gown and a pair of dusty lace-up boots.

Kit and Dulcie were hovering with their toolkits, reapplying lipgloss and repairing smudged eyeliner, powdering running noses and sunburnt bosoms with equal aplomb. Ross had organised yet another press call and Irving was attempting to file the cast into two demure lines, rather like school Photo Day, with Luke towering over everyone else at the back and Courteney wisecracking at the front. And ensuring the photographers got a lovely background of eighteenth-century architecture and not two hefty grips leaning against the black painted railings, swigging cans of suspiciously aromatic cola and swapping ribald comments with the gang of female students who had a flat on the third floor and were leering out of the window at Luke. Luke, however, was watching Ross wait until everyone else was occupied, before walking across to Shelby who was leaning up against one of the massive plane trees, listening to Oasis on her Walkman. Luke clenched his fists and wished he still had his contact lenses in so that he could lip-read.

"Luke," called one of the photographers, dragging his attention back to the press call, "could you do 'mean and moody' for me? Hold it! That is absolutely perfect!"

* * *

Shelby, keeping a watchful eye on the press call, did not see Ross approach until it was too late and was unable to retreat because of the huge tree behind her. So she gritted her teeth, folded her arms protectively across her chest and dared herself to stare defiantly up at Ross. Although, as he was wearing mirrored sunglasses, all she could really see was his Cossack bone structure and a distorted reflection of herself. As he leisurely removed the Ray-Bans she could see his charcoal eyes were frostier than usual and her heart sank. Why couldn't he just leave her alone?

"Why are you avoiding me?" asked Ross, calmly unhooking her earphones so that she couldn't pretend she was unable to hear him above Liam Gallagher.

"Because I don't want to talk to you," replied Shelby. "Go away."

His mouth lifted into a crooked smile. "My film set."

Her face burned. He was quite entitled to give her the sack for that last remark. "So move aside and I'll go."

"You're not going to do one of those Grrrl Power kicks and send me flying like poor old Luke?"

The Walkman rattled away to itself. Ross must be taking the piss, she thought. Didn't he know 'Grrrl Power' was for eight-year-olds? "Did you want me to?" she returned stonily.

"Not particularly. I'm supposedly the director of this shoot. I do have a certain image to perpetuate."

She glanced at the Ray-Bans. "I can tell."

The smile which had been hovering on his lips, disappeared into a hard line. For a moment there was silence between them, broken only by the gale shaking the plane trees like giant maracas, shredding great clumps of greenery over the heads of the nearby actors, ruining the photographers' shot, and sending Paige's empty deckchair scurrying across the grass like an amorous crab.

"What gives between you and Luke?" he asked.

"Not knicker elastic if that's what you're implying!"

"I just don't want to see you getting hurt. Luke has a reputation for falling for his leading ladies, that's his style of er, acting. He keeps in character even when the cameras aren't rolling."

"*Last* week you said Luke *couldn't* act."

"He peddles a version of himself," conceded Ross, "like all the big stars. Technically, I suppose you could call that 'acting'."

She glowered at him. "I'm not Luke's leading lady. I'm only his minder."

"Oh, you're more than that."

Shelby paused, considering the ambiguity of the remark. More than what? Did he mean she was virtually Luke's baby-sitter or that she meant more to Luke than just employer/employee relationship? Or wasn't Ross talking about Luke at all?

"There is nothing between me and Luke," she said slowly.

For a second there was a flicker of something behind the ice in his eyes and then he said, as though the words were being dragged from him, "I saw you. In the pool . . . with him."

She smiled sardonically. In a lovers' tiff, nothing could beat the cheap thrill of one-upmanship. "How nice for you. Did you enjoy the show?"

"*Shelby*!"

She became aware that to her right, the photo shoot was breaking up, the photographers packing large expensive cameras away into leather cases, the actors meandering over to the refreshment table, Paige stalking determinedly in their direction, brutally kicking aside the fallen branches with her blue suede boots.

"I think your leading lady needs you," said Shelby.

"Fuck my leading lady." The words came out as though he were spitting bullets.

"I thought you already do," returned Shelby sweetly.

He grabbed hold of her arm.

"Let go of me! People are staring."

"I don't give a shit."

"Let me rephrase that," she said quietly. "Let go of me or I'll *make* you let go of me. Do you want to look a complete prat?"

He released her. "You couldn't make me feel more of a prat than I already do." He watched Paige being cornered by a reporter from *The Bath Chronicle*. "I'm crazy about you."

Shelby burst out laughing. "Bollocks!"

It had not been the reaction Ross had anticipated. Disconcerted, he ran his hand through his hair, unwittingly spiking it up. "Why don't you believe me?"

"Because you're lying! I saw you with Paige! Do you think I'm stupid? You get out of bed with me and leap into bed with her."

"I didn't leap into bed with her. I just spent the time talking her through her part. She's not relating to Luke. He's already started winding her up. Actresses have no self-confidence as it is. I have to keep telling Paige she's beautiful, sexy, a terrific actress . . . With any luck she might start to believe it."

"Are we talking about the same Paige? This is not a woman who is lacking in self-confidence. She must have made dozens of films over the last few years. Without you."

"Dozens of *unsuccessful* films," Ross pointed out. "But as soon as *All That She Wants* hits the cinemas

Paige Lorraine is going to be a huge star. She turned in a terrific performance, due to the fact she was blindly in love with Luke. This time she is not in love with him. She hates him. So far, their on-screen embraces have all the passion of a gutted fish. They've got a sex scene next week. Somehow I've got to coax a virtuoso performance out of her. If that means pandering to her I shall. I've invested millions in *Midsummer Kiss*. If the film flops Firestorm goes bust and so do I. Manipulating Paige is a small price to pay for success."

"Is that what they call prostituting one's art?"

The shutters came down over the blazing, passionate eyes. "I didn't expect you to understand."

"No," she said flatly. "I don't. You lie to Paige, you lie to me, and this is all right by you? You make a tomcat look like the Archbishop of Canterbury."

The charcoal eyes darkened dangerously. "Deception is what the cinema is about. Everyone pretending to be something else. Luke isn't a nineteenth-century aristocrat with fifteen thousand a year; he's the son of a country doctor and could clear several million a picture if he moved to LA and stopped clowning about. Courteney isn't a virginal English rose; she's a spoilt child star from Savannah, who's had more men then you've got freckles. Paige is not a spurned mistress, plotting her revenge; she's an ambitious wannabe who will do anything, *anything* to be famous. Even dump her fiancé at the altar if it guarantees her picture on the front page of tomorrow's papers."

"That's a *horrible* thing to say."

Ross shrugged. "It's the truth."

Shelby glanced back at Paige, who was watching Ross with a very predatory look in her eye, while simultaneously providing an endless stream of bitchy quotes about her co-stars for the star-struck young reporter interviewing her.

"It's the premiere tomorrow night," said Ross. "For *All That She Wants*. Forget Luke. Come with me. I'm chartering a helicopter. It'll be much more comfortable than the train."

"May I remind you that officially I'm Luke's minder. Where he goes, I go."

"So I'll offer him a lift too."

Shelby laughed. "Now that's what I call a sacrifice."

* * *

Paige finally escaped from the reporter by pleading that she was desperate to use the bathroom and turned to walk smack into Luke.

"Why don't you fucking look where you're going!" she screamed, her temper already frayed by the heat, dust and wind, and unravelling completely at the little tête-à-tête she had witnessed between Ross and that horrendous, freckled creature.

"Sorry," said Luke, looking down at her with reddened watering eyes, despite half a bottle of Murine he'd tipped in when the Unit Nurse wasn't looking. "I can't see a damn thing without my contact lenses."

"Then put your damn glasses on, you asshole!" Paige's refined Boston vowels disintegrated along with her self-control. "You always were a vain, conceited, egotistical, prat!"

"Thank you," said Luke and had another attempt to squeeze past her. He only succeeded in tripping over the knotted roots of the plane trees and had to grab wildly at the trunk to avoid falling over.

"That red-headed tart –" began Paige spitefully.

"Ross?"

"Your *bodyguard* – is supposed to be looking after *you*. Why is she always hanging around Ross? It's embarrassing. Surely she doesn't think he would be interested in her? And she talks like a damn hillbilly."

"He hired her," shrugged Luke.

"Well, he can fucking well unhire her. Some girls will do anything to be in the movies. She's not even a good bodyguard. Look at that Bruno guy; he never leaves Courteney's side. *He* doesn't go to parties, or try to mix socially with us. She should be more like him."

Luke shuddered. "No, thank you. If I've got to be saddled with a minder, I would much rather have one as sexy as Shelby, than be stuck with that revolting gorilla."

"Men!" spat Paige, her black ringlets bobbing with rage. "You're all the same. Tits and ass. That's all you care about."

"Sorry," he smiled helplessly. "It's in the genes!"

"So long as it stays in the damn jeans!" snapped Paige and marched off towards Ross.

Ross saw her coming and dived off for a conference with Irving and Jeremy. Shelby neatly ducked behind

Louise Marley

the tree, waited for Paige to storm past, and then doubled back to Luke. So that when Paige finally ended up beneath the plane trees all she found was a little blonde girl holding out a scruffy exercise book.

"What do you want?" growled Paige.

The girl took a worried step backwards. "Er, please, Miss Paltrow, if it's not too much trouble, may I have your autograph? I thought you were fantastic in *Shakespeare In Love* . . ."

294

Chapter Twenty-one

Thursday – London

"There is no way you are going to a West End premiere dressed like that," said Courteney.

Shelby glanced down at her new black trouser suit. It had been bought for her by John Ivar. It was exactly the same as his other minders were wearing and, more to the point, "It's Armani," she protested. "You can't get much smarter than that!"

"He must have been having an off-day."

Courteney herself was wearing a glittering crimson creation, slashed to the waist at the front, which had been lent for the night by a famous designer. Only double-sided sticky tape adhering her voluptuous breasts to the fabric was preventing them from popping out. She casually dropped a platinum and ruby necklace easily worth several hundred thousand pounds around her neck, then spoilt the effect by fixing two diamanté clips, which looked as though they'd come free with a Barbie doll, in her pink-streaked hair.

"I'm a bodyguard," said Shelby, "not a supermodel. This is the uniform. It comes with the job. Bruno and John will be wearing the same."

"The Men in Black," derided Courteney.

"Thank *you*!"

But Courteney was regarding her in much the same way as a Fairy Godmother would regard Cinderella. Shelby's heart began launching the lifeboats. Courteney might not have a magic wand but she had an awful lot of clothes . . .

"You know," she was saying idly, "I'm sure there's something in my closet you can borrow."

Shelby watched Courteney disappear into her bedroom. She had only popped into Courteney's suite to let her know Bruno was waiting outside, pacing the corridor and driving the other guests crazy – not to experience a makeover. But somehow she had become Courteney's new best friend. The lines between employer and employee had become blurred, just like they had between her and Luke – and Ross, and just about everybody really. Shelby pulled a face at herself in the mirror and, not for the first time, wished herself back in the police, where no one would have the impertinence to suggest wearing a Dolce & Gabbana ballgown to a drugs raid.

Courteney returned, trailing a long gown enveloped in a plastic cover. She hung it on the wardrobe and excitedly unzipped it. "What do you think? Sexy, isn't it? I bought it by mistake. Brown – I mean *chocolate* – isn't really me, but it'll look excellent on you. Why don't you try it on?"

Shelby was tempted. Surely it wouldn't hurt? And the dress was beautiful – iced coffee satin, shimmering with delicate embroidery. She slipped it over her head and felt the material caress her skin.

Courteney zipped it up before she could change her mind. "It sure looks great – and I've a jacket you can have too."

Shelby surveyed her reflection. The gown was high-necked, sleeveless, very long and very impractical. If she tried a karate kick her foot would either go straight through the satin or she'd end up flat on her face. Although, after two weeks working for Luke, the only people who had come close to murdering him had been herself and Ross.

She searched for an excuse to let Courteney down gently. "It's not Chanel and worth the Brazilian National Debt?" she asked, twirling around in front of the mirror, reluctantly admiring the way the dress clung to curves she didn't know she had.

"£778 sterling – practically free! And designed by English Eccentrics!" Then she added with a huge lipsticked grin, "So it's absolutely perfect for you."

* * *

Luke, Shelby, Courteney and Bruno had travelled to London, first class, on the train, arriving at Paddington just before lunch. They caught a taxi to their hotel and got there at the same time as Ross and Paige, who had journeyed by helicopter and hired limo. It did not appear to have been a happy trip. Ross was chain-smoking. Paige was complaining bitterly that they were booked into a mere five-star hotel in the West End, instead of Mayfair.

"It'll be full of damn tourists," she was complaining, "on their way to see an Andrew Lloyd Webber."

Luke, Courteney and Paige spent their afternoon providing sound-bites for journalists to publicise *All That She Wants*. Each journalist was allocated twenty minutes and all Luke was given to drink was mineral water, so it was very difficult for him to keep a hold on his temper when he was asked, over and over again, "What's it like working with Paige Lorraine?" usually accompanied by a smug grin. Or, "How about those fights with Ross Whitney?" Innocent look –"Is it true you've walked out on *Midsummer Kiss*?"

It was almost a relief to be asked by some bored American, "So, tell me again, *who* are you?"

The British Press, attempting to find a new angle and bearing in mind Luke's reputation, were very interested in Shelby, who sat in one corner looking bored, ignored by Fiona and the bevy of PR girls fawning around Luke. Oblivious to the scrutiny of the journalists, she slid Luke's sunglasses onto her nose so that she could have a snooze without anyone noticing.

Despite the utter boredom of the afternoon, Shelby found it difficult not to get excited at the thought of a real live West End premiere. There was a constant stream of flowers, good luck cards and faxes through to Luke's suite. Fiona had sent up a long list of instructions – what to do, when to do it, what to say, and who not to say it to, although Luke, remaining his usual laid-back self, had promptly torn it up and flushed it down the loo.

"Was that wise?" murmured Shelby.

"Best place for it." Luke grimaced at the Jane Austen style ringlets his hair had degenerated into without the skilful administrations of Kit. "At least there's a free movie at the end of all this. Pity it's got me in it though."

Shelby confiscated his electric razor just as he was about to give himself a No 1 cut and, as he disappeared into the bathroom for an illicit swig of Chardonnay as consolation, she entertained herself by reading the faxes and the cards that accompanied the dozens of extravagant bouquets. A lot were from toadies inside the industry, some were from women with names such as Laura or Charlotte or Kate, but she found herself gasping at the many famous signatures. Did Luke really know all these people?

She was just eyeing up a peculiar dead-twig arrangement from Paige, and wondering if she really had sent them/picked them herself – or if it had been another of Fiona's PR jobs, when there was a knock on the door. Shelby answered it, expecting Ross, but found John Ivar, his middle-aged spread surprisingly distinguished in his Armani suit, accompanied by an identically dressed, black minder.

"Shelby," beamed John, "this is Charles Smith – you haven't met, have you? He's Luke's other minder but I've asked you both to work tonight because of the crowds expected outside the cinema."

The black man smiled, revealing a mouthful of gold teeth.

He must be over seven foot, realised Shelby in awe. She wondered if he played basketball, but was able to refrain from asking. This was not the sort of person to upset. Although Charles's head had been shaved completely bald, he had a goatee beard, and was roguishly handsome. And those teeth must be worth a fortune. Would he clean them with Colgate or Duraglit? That was some shine.

"Hi," he said in a deep rich voice, which sounded as though it was rumbling up from beneath their feet. "Call me Shark."

Shark? But –" *Shut up, Shelby, shut up,* she told herself irritably. If the guy wants to call himself after a fish, who are you to argue?

John Ivar handed her a small box. For one moment she thought he was giving her a present but, as she thanked him, she realised it contained a communications earpiece, several lengths of wire and a small microphone to conceal up her sleeve. "Will I be able to get Capital FM?" she asked.

But John appeared to have had a tiring day and merely said, "Charles will show you how to work it. It's dead simple." Then, as he turned to leave, his eyes swept over her long satin gown. "Don't you think it's time you changed out of your glad rags and into your suit, lass?"

* * *

It would have taken only a few moments to walk round to Leicester Square but queuing with all the other limousines it took almost twenty minutes. Ross and Paige were in the car in front and their driver had to give them a headstart to make sure they were clear before dropping off Luke, Shelby and Shark.

Shelby pressed her nose up against the smoked windows. As they turned the corner of the square she suddenly saw all the people, the cameras bulbs flashing, the TV cameras and film crews fronted by cloned female presenters not much older than herself, with identical blonde flick-ups and 'funky' black dresses. And everyone was split, like Moses's Red Sea, by the inevitable crash barriers and a chain of policemen in yellow fluorescent jackets guarding that hallowed crimson carpet.

Shark opened the door and Shelby slid out next, blinded by flashbulbs, deafened by the overwhelming roar of the crowd. She could hear the nearby photographers, all with little press passes around their necks or clipped onto their belts, muttering, "Who's she?" "Another of Luke's harem, I suppose." "Wonder how long she'll last?" and taking her picture regardlessly.

Shark placed a reassuring hand on her shoulder. "Earpiece OK?"

Which Shelby took to be shorthand for, "Are you all

right?" She nodded and then stood aside to allow Luke to get out, standing between him and the crowd, her eyes sweeping over the mass of faces looking for something – *anything* – out of the ordinary.

As Luke stood on the pavement and waved cheerfully, a deafening cheer went up, the (mainly female) spectators surged against the barriers and the police officers had to lean into them to prevent them from going over.

Someone closed the door and the limousine glided away, another identical one drawing up in its place. "Could you please keep moving, sir?" muttered one of the cinema staff.

Shelby could have kicked herself. She should have been the one to say that. Instead she felt like some fluffy bunny caught in the headlights of a juggernaut. She found her legs shaking as she tried to keep up with Luke and Shark, striding across the red carpet towards the cinema. It seemed to stretch for miles.

She jumped as someone thrust an autograph book across the barrier, between the shoulders of two burly policeman, and was terrified to realise that if she had been armed, her first reaction would have been to shoot them. As Shark calmly passed the book on to Luke and he exchanged a few kind words with his fan, Shelby found she had broken into an icy sweat. Was it her police training that made her so paranoid, making every sudden movement a potential assassin?

"Luke! Luke!" It seemed half of London had taken up the chant. She felt as though the crowds were closing in on them.

"Over here, Luke!" A thirty-something blonde in a tight sapphire-blue dress barged between her and Luke, trailing a scruffy youth with a camera, and shoved a microphone in his face.

The blonde pouted ingratiatingly. "Hi, Luke, I'm Ella Carmichael from *Prime Cuts*. You're live on CLTV and I'd just like to ask you if it's true that you and Paige Lorraine have secretly married?"

Luke had to duck to avoid being brained by the camera. He smiled politely although his eyes were hard. "I'm still single."

"But it's true she's pregnant?"

Luke, for once, was speechless. The cameraman zoomed in for a close-up.

Shelby hauled the youth back by the scruff of the neck. "Don't go shoving your camera in people's faces. It isn't polite." She glared at the blonde. "Would you please give Mr McFadden some space? This is a film premiere not a rugby scrum."

"And who the hell are you?" sneered Ella Carmichael. "His bodyguard?"

"Got it in one, so would you please let us pass? He doesn't want to talk to you and you're holding everyone else up."

Ella recovered quickly and, twisting her cameraman's head so that he was pointing the camera at Shelby, repeated, "His bodyguard, eh? What a simply *wonderful* job. And such a *splendid* body to guard. Tell us more – you're live on CLTV!"

Shelby gritted her teeth. All that peroxide must have

leaked through to the woman's brain but at least Luke had managed to escape and was now chatting happily to a teenage presenter from the BBC.

"So what's your name, Miss Bodyguard?" sneered Ella. "And how long have you been dating Luke McFadden?"

"*Dating*?" Shelby blinked. "Are you *crazy*? I mean, we have a purely professional relationship."

"Yeah, *right*!" And both Ella and her cameraman began to laugh.

Shelby merely flicked her a 'v' and followed Luke, who was now almost at the cinema entrance and had paused to shake hands with more of his ecstatic fans, sign a few autographs, make polite conversation. Shelby watched, her heart in her mouth at all the women clamouring for him.

"Watch the hands, watch the hands," she murmured to herself. But there was so many of them, all thrusting biros and pencils at Luke, which could so easily be a knife or a gun . . .

Courteney was now walking up the carpet behind them, accompanied by John Ivar and Bruno, their eyes constantly moving, checking the crowd. Despite several TV crews lunging forwards, the minders just propelled Courteney onward and upward along the red carpet and towards the cinema.

It was then that she saw him, on the opposite side, one face amongst thousands. Pale eyes and pale skin, brown hair and red sweater. There was perspiration on his upper lip and a certain look of bravado masking his fear. Their eyes locked. Then he grinned, blowing her a kiss, before turning away, squeezing his slight frame back through the thronging fans.

"Shark!" cried Shelby but he had moved protectively to Luke's other side and could no longer hear her above the screams of the crowd. Remembering her earpiece, Shelby raised her hand to her mouth, and hissed, "Shark!" into the tiny microphone.

"What's up?" his voice crackled in her ear. She had to stick her finger into the other one just to hear him.

"I've seen him!" she cried. "I've just seen Courteney's stalker!"

"Shit. Get Mr McFadden inside. I'll call the police," and Shark snapped his fingers as though summoning a maître d'.

"No time! You take Luke. I'll go after the pervert," and she hitched her dress up around her waist, giving several hundred people and five TV cameras a glorious flash of white silk knickers as she hurdled the nearest crash barrier and landed on top of a gang of surprised teenagers.

Luke stuck his head over the crowd barrier. "Shelby! What the hell are you doing?"

Shelby emerged, flustered and bedraggled, "I'm OK," she called. "I'll catch up with you later!"

Struggling through the crowd of film fans was a bit like repeatedly hurling oneself at the Berlin wall. It took a while for the idea to spread that she was actually attempting to get out, before they grouped together, bundled her up and spat her out onto the Siberian wastelands behind.

Shelby picked herself up from the filthy pavement, cursing at a piece of bubble-gum which had adhered to her bottom, and hurtled after the youth in the red sweater. It was not yet dark and he was easy to spot, particularly as they were the only people moving away from the cinema. As though aware he was being watched, the youth twisted his head and saw her, his foot stumbling off the kerb. But he regained his balance and sprinted off in earnest, disappearing into the theatre crowd thronging the West End.

Shelby realised he was heading towards the subway and crossed the road to head him off, praying he wouldn't look around. He did, but did not spot her and thinking he had lost her he slowed, a big grin spreading over his pock-marked features. Shelby dived at his ankles and he crashed onto the pavement. Unable to put out his hands because of something he was holding tightly to his chest, his face slammed into the concrete.

Seeing dark red blood seeping across the pavement in spidery rivulets, Shelby slowly rolled him over, terrified that she'd cracked his skull open. But it was merely his nose, bleeding profusely, although it did not seem to be broken. He looked at her with tears in his eyes, his fingers gently feeling his split lip.

"What the fuck are you doing?" he wailed. "Get off me!"

Shelby stared at the unfamiliar face. "Who the hell are you?"

"You're crazy, lady. All I did was wink at you. Why d'yer run after me like that? I wasn't gonna rape you or nuthin'. Can't a guy wink at a girl, without her breaking his nose?"

"Oh, stop whingeing. You've only got a nosebleed." She handed him her handkerchief. "I'm sorry, I made a mistake. I thought you were someone else."

He dabbed fretfully at his nose. "Let me guess, your ex-boyfriend?"

"I said I was sorry!"

"I don't know where you're from, lady, but this is London and we don't bloody jump on people and break their fucking noses. You know, I'm gonna sue you. I'll sue you for every –"

"Can I be of assistance, ma'am?"

Shelby looked up at the sweating policeman and recognised him as one of the officers making up the cordon around the cinema.

"Oh Christ," wailed the youth, closing his eyes and collapsing back onto the pavement. "It's a bloody vendetta!"

"Mistaken identity, officer," she said. "I thought he was someone else."

"Oh, I wouldn't say that." The officer bent to pick up a leather handbag lying on the pavement. "You started shopping at Prada, Darren?"

"It's not mine," mumbled the youth.

The officer held the bag out to Shelby. "Ma'am?"

Shelby stared at it incredulously. "I've never seen it before . . ."

The officer smirked. "Up to your old tricks, eh, Darren? OK, you're nicked."

"But it ain't fair! She kicked *my* head in – totally unprovoked – like fucking Bruce Lee. Why ain't cha nicking her?"

"Do you want me to give you a statement?" asked Shelby. "It's just –" she looked down at her beautiful embroidered dress, realising she now looked much like the 'before' picture for Cinderella. "I'm supposed to be somewhere else . . ."

"No problem. I know John Ivar. I'll catch up with you later."

Shelby walked back to the cinema. The crowds were still there, the TV cameras and pressmen, but there were no longer any limousines drawing up or celebrities sauntering up the red carpet and there was no longer any excitement. The fans were just chatting quietly amongst themselves.

Shelby had to fight her way through to the front. No one was going to give up their hard-won place easily. But as she attempted to clamber over the crash barrier she was pushed back into the crowd by a policeman.

"I was invited!" she shrieked indignantly.

The officer laughed. "And I'm Barry Norman."

"I've got a pass!" She dived down the front of her dress and hauled out her little plastic pass, in the shape of a gold CD, waving it before his eyes. "See!"

The officer's face dropped. "Honestly," he grumbled, hauling her over the barrier. "Why couldn't you use the front entrance like everyone else?"

Shelby scrambled across the red carpet and fell through the door, worried she had missed the start of the film and that they wouldn't let her into the auditorium. But the TV people were still doing interviews and, as she bounced off a couple of security men, she spotted Luke and Ross, towering above everyone else. Ross was earnestly explaining camera angles to some bored GMTV presenter, Luke was providing 'an interesting background' while waiting his turn, and trying desperately not to catch the presenter's eye – they were old friends – in case they both burst out laughing.

Suddenly she found herself nose-to-nose with an Armani suit. Fearing she was about to be thrown out, she began to hastily explain about the handbag snatcher and mistaking him for a stalker, then realised she was looking at Bruno.

She patted his shoulder. "So it was lucky that it all turned out all right, eh?"

He did not smile. "You always have to play the hero, don't you? Didn't you have *any* training before you took this job on?"

Well, if that wasn't the final straw! "Listen, Buster, I *was* a police –"

"You're a fucking liability," he snarled, disappearing into the crowd.

"Jesus, Shelby," said Luke, sliding one arm proprietorally around her shoulder. "Where have you been? I was worried about you."

"Well," began Shelby, still shaken by her encounter with Bruno, "Erm . . . it's a long story."

"Oh, Shelby!" Courteney squeezed through the crowd

of stunned celebrities, "What have you done to your dress?"

Shelby glanced down. The beautiful coffee satin was smeared with dirt and oil and blood from a graze on her elbow. The skirt was ripped all the way up the right-hand seam, practically to her white knickers.

"Oh damn!" she said. "I knew I should have worn my suit. I'll pay you back, Courteney, promise!"

"Well, you certainly can't enter the auditorium like that," said Paige, her voice taking on the cold edge of steel. "You'll have to go back to the hotel and change." Ross received a bony elbow in his ribs. "Won't she, darling?"

"I can fix it," said Shelby quickly. "Does anyone have a safety-pin?"

Paige smiled evilly. "Do I look like the sort of woman who would carry a safety-pin?"

"Here you are," said Fiona, Ross's PR girl, pulling a handful of safety-pins from a tiny, quilted Chanel bag. "I have a sewing-kit too. Would you like to borrow it?"

"Thanks but I can't sew!" Shelby quickly fastened the two safety-pins in the top of the split to prevent it going any further. "There, that's fixed it."

"Oh yes," agreed Paige, "that's finished it off completely."

"Why aren't you wearing your suit?" asked John.

"Ah," said Shelby fretfully, sensing a rather messy dismissal was imminent. "That's a very good question. And if you give me long enough, I'm sure I can come up with a very good answer."

John began to laugh.

"Calamity Jane!" grinned Luke, affectionately slapping her on the back and almost sending her on a collision course with a life-size cardboard cut-out of himself. "I can't take you anywhere!"

Chapter Twenty-two

Friday – Bath

Floyd Mulligan stood on the pavement of The Circus, holding tightly on to his stove-pipe hat to prevent it blowing off and scudding across the gravel – mainly because if he thought he had to unsteadily retrieve it from the green, he might collide with one of the plane trees.

The two patches of high colour on his cheekbones, which Dulcie kept smothering in sunblock, were actually due to copious swigs of Glenfiddich. To hide the smell he was crunching Extra Strong Mints, which made the whisky taste disgusting but he wasn't going to risk Ross getting a whiff.

Floyd needed this job. He hadn't had a hit film in ten years and as far as Hollywood was concerned he could have been dead. Desperate for money, his last job – panto in Birmingham – had been eighteen months ago. It had been toe-curlingly embarrassing. The audience had not the faintest idea who he was and were only interested in the ex-Page Three bimbo – totally miscast as Snow White – who spent every evening and mid-week matinee flirting with the director and making up her lines as she went along.

Floyd watched the elegant horse-drawn carriage, with Courteney inside, lumbering around The Circus for the third time, bumping over the ridge where the gravel ended and the tarmac began. As it passed him by, and out of the shot, a thick cloud of dust rose up causing him to have a coughing fit. He'd had a bout of pneumonia just after Christmas and even after all this time the cough still lingered.

Irving, standing across the road with a loudhailer dangling from his hand and both a walkie-talkie and a mobile phone shoved into the pockets of his jeans, hopped between the piles of steaming manure left by the horses, to bang him on the back. Floyd swallowed three mints in one go.

He glanced up, his eyes still watering, "Are you sure this is a little Regency romance? Or is Ross secretly re-making *Lawrence of Arabia*?"

"I'd keep your voice down if I were you," said Irving, taking a swig from Floyd's silver flask. "He's already sacked a couple of the extras for whingeing."

"I'm not surprised; even the horses are better treated than us. After every scene they're returned to their nice cool loose box and given a long drink."

"If you want to sit in a horse box go right ahead." Irving held the walkie-talkie up to his mouth. "OK guys, you can restart the traffic." He then waved to the silently watching crowd. "Thanks for being so patient!"

Floyd watched another tour bus drive past, the occupants excitedly pointing and waving at Courteney, who blew kisses back. No one noticed him. Despondently he took another swig of Glenfiddich and found Irving had polished it off.

"If one more person asks me what we're filming, I'll scream," muttered Irving, glowering at a couple of loitering tourists so furiously that they scuttled away. "I don't blame Luke for lying low this morning. Ross is in a terrible temper, Jeremy's threatened to resign and Kit's had a fight with Elliott, the wardrobe master. Make-up on shirt collars – I ask you!" Irving rolled his eyes heavenwards.

It was unlike Irving to be indiscreet, realised Floyd. This was not a happy shoot. At least when Luke was here he kept everyone in stitches but Luke wasn't due on set until that evening. Floyd fiddled restlessly with the empty silver flask in his pocket. He hoped the bulge wasn't too noticeable. At his age he could hardly blame it on a rampant erection.

Wistfully he watched a gang of pretty young girls swarming around Dean – the young pop star playing the villain – clamouring for his autograph. One never appreciates adulation until it's gone, he thought sadly. Or adultery come to that.

In the distance a house alarm began to ring shrilly. "Ir-*ving*!" shrieked the walkie-talkie in perfect harmony.

Irving pulled it from his jeans pocket, holding it up

to his ear, just as it squawked again. Debating whether to toss it over the railings and into the basement of the nearest house, he decided diplomacy was a better option.

"Lots of interference, Ross!" he shouted, blowing a raspberry against the walkie-talkie. "You're breaking up!" His mobile phone began to ring. Irving switched it off and surreptitiously placed a small Lucozade bottle in Floyd's pocket. "Brought you a top-up. Couldn't get Glenfiddich though, just regular whisky disguised in a bottle of pop."

Floyd patted his shoulder. "You're a lifesaver, boy. Here, have an Extra Strong Mint."

The alarm stopped as suddenly as it had begun.

"Action!" yelled Ross, casting a vile look in Irving's direction.

"I think he wants you to stop the traffic," murmured Floyd.

"Let him stop his own bloody traffic." Irving leant calmly against the railings, crunching on his mint. "I'm tired of being his gofer. We've been working on this film for three bloody months and I can count the number of scenes I've directed on one hand."

There was a violent crack of thunder, which made both of them jump.

"Amazing special effects," said Floyd in awe.

"I don't think that was one of ours."

The heavens opened and down came the rain – thick, fast and icily cold.

"Hell," said Irving, watching the imported gravel

turn into a quagmire and gradually wash down the hill.

"Excellent weather machine," said Floyd, taking a long swig of Lucozade-flavoured whisky, watching the raindrops shimmering silver-blue. "Very realistic rain. I'm quite soaked through." He took another gulp. "Bit cold though."

"I think it's hail."

"I think you're right. Ah, the joys of British summertime." Floyd handed over the bottle of Lucozade. "Care for a nip, dear boy?"

Not even bothering to glance in the direction of the frantically gesturing Ross, Irving took it. "Don't mind if I do."

* * *

Shelby took a hairpin and inserted it into the lock. A quick flick of the wrist and the catch clicked. With a smirk she pushed open the door; so nice to see she hadn't lost her touch. Moving softly into Courteney's old suite, she trailed a finger across one of the smart green suitcases stacked in the centre of the room. Real leather. All sizes. All matching. They must have cost a fortune.

Deciding to search the cases last, Shelby entered the bedroom. The linen had been removed for cleaning and the shallow drawers on either side of the bed were empty, apart from a stick of chewing-gum and a souvenir pen from Disney World rattling around at the back. The maid must have missed them. Shelby ignored the chewing-gum but stuck the pen into her pocket. It was probably the closest she'd ever get to Florida.

Shelby bent to peer under the bed. Nothing. Then checked each of the wardrobes. More nothing. This was a serious waste of time. Despondently she wandered through to the bathroom. That had been cleared too. She had got here too late – she should have done this Wednesday, perhaps borrowed the key from reception on some pretence . . .

A key rattled in the outside door.

Shelby crashed backwards onto the balcony, tangling up with the curtains, only managing to kick her leg free and hop from sight as the maid walked in, balancing a pile of fresh laundry, closely followed by one of the hotel porters. He came directly into the sitting-room and stooped to collect the suitcases.

Shelby watched him in frustration. "Damn and blast!"

The maid emerged from the bathroom, trailing a toilet roll. "Did you say something?"

"Not me." The porter slowly replaced the suitcases onto the floor and looked about him. His discerning gaze took in the open drawer beside the bed, the French windows slightly ajar, the net curtains fluttering in the wind.

Shelby flattened herself against the wall, holding her breath. It had started to rain. She could hear her heart beating an accompanying bass rhythm in her chest. If the porter came onto the balcony . . . Go away, she pleaded silently. Just pick up the suitcases, open the door and walk away. Don't be a hero.

"It could be that film star's stalker," whispered the porter.

"St-stalker?" The maid's voice trembled.

"*Miaow!*" said Shelby desperately.

"You fetch security," instructed the porter. "I'll check it out."

"Be careful . . ."

Shelby risked a peep back into the sitting-room, saw the maid sliding nervously out of the room and the porter pick a large vase. This was getting out of control. She should have shown herself as soon as they had appeared. Maybe there would have been a few recriminations but compared to this! And there was nowhere left to hide – short of dangling herself by her fingertips from the balcony, or shinning up the drainpipe onto the roof.

She could hear the porter's heavy footsteps clump into the bedroom. The next stop would be the balcony. She had to get out of here.

Shelby scrambled up onto the balustrade. She looked across to Ross's balcony and bit her lip. She did not want to do this. She really did not want to do this. Four feet across the gap. She looked back to the flagstones. Or twenty feet down if she failed – and a hell of a headache.

No choice. Shelby jumped. For a second it felt as though she was flying – she felt the breeze, slight spots of rain against her face, as she landed on Ross's balustrade. A stone shifted, sending her off-balance. She made a desperate lunge but her fingers scraped impotently across the stone and she was snatching at thin air, before one hand grabbed at the jutting edge of the balcony. Her arm was nearly wrenched from the socket, every single nail seemed to rip, but her descent was halted abruptly. She swayed, twenty foot above ground.

Shelby closed her eyes and waited for her heart to stop breakdancing against her ribcage. "Thank you, God," she breathed, and swung up her other hand to grab at the balcony. Kicking her legs wildly, and hoping no one could see them through the windows of the restaurant below, she managed to lever her elbows onto the edge and caught her arm around a stone column. Swinging her foot up onto the stone, she pulled and pushed herself up and over the balustrade and fell over onto the balcony, crashing onto her knees, her hands scraping across the rough stone. Thank goodness she was wearing jeans, pity about her palms though. There were several nasty cuts where the skin had peeled back, leaving bare bleeding flesh.

Shelby winced as she picked out a couple of crumbs of stone. It stung like mad, a steady tingling burn. Just call me Cat Woman, she thought grimly.

Peering through the balustrade, she could see the porter had walked out onto Courteney's balcony and was staring down into the garden, scratching his head. She was just congratulating herself on her narrow escape, when she realised she could see right into Ross's sitting-room and he had just walked through the door.

Shelby yelped and scooted backwards away from the window, prostrating herself on the wet flagstones.

There was no way her nerves could bear another wild leap across the balcony. Besides, the porter was still loitering with his vase. After about five minutes of hell, she stuck her nose between the gap in the curtains. Ross had gone into the bedroom.

Some masochistic streak made her commando-crawl across to the bedroom window. There was the seat where they had made love and the huge double bed where they had also made love. Wouldn't it be wonderful to just go back in time, to those couple of days when she had been so happy . . .

Ross had not seen her. As Shelby watched, he flung clean clothes onto the bed and undid the buttons of his shirt, then threw it in the vague direction of a laundry sack, and unzipped his jeans. She allowed her eyes to travel across his beautiful body and cursed herself. She was like a bloody addict. Always wanting one last fix. She wasn't safe to be let out. She needed a cold shower and several pints of bromide.

"This is mere lust, Shelby," she muttered to herself. "Complete, adulterated lust."

"What are you doing here?"

Shelby froze at the note of contempt in his voice and slowly looked up. What could she say? What possible excuse was there?

But the balcony was deserted. So she was going crazy now too?

"I came to check that you were all right."

Paige. Her bloody Nemesis. Shelby slowly crawled back to the French windows and peered through.

There was Ross, a hopelessly inadequate white towel around his hips, one hand resting on the door to the corridor. "Come in if you must," he grumbled. "But I don't have the time for small talk. I was about to shower, then watch yesterday's rushes. You'll be very bored."

But it wasn't Paige who wandered into the sitting-room and helped herself to a drink from the minibar. Shelby stared incredulously at the distinctive orange bobbed hair glinting in the light of the overhead chandelier. *Dulcie . . .*

"The scenes that Irving directed while you were in London?" Dulcie's voice had only the tiniest tremor to betray her nervousness and she quickly took a large swig of her drink. "He told me they went quite well."

Ross took the drink out of her hand and placed it onto the sideboard.

"I – I hadn't finished . . ."

"If you wanted a drink you could have gone to the bar. Why are you really here, Dulcie?"

She licked her lips nervously. "You seemed . . . upset. I thought I would . . . check that you were all right."

Bollocks, thought Shelby. *You just want to get into his boxer shorts.*

Dulcie ran one purple-tipped finger down Ross's bare arm. "I know LA are hassling you about the budget –"

"I'm all right."

Dulcie appeared crushed but still she didn't move away.

How can she throw herself at him like that? Shelby

wondered. Can't she see he doesn't want her? Has she no self-respect?

"So why did you really come here?" Ross began to deliberately undo the buttons on Dulcie's black crocheted top.

Dulcie moaned softly. Shelby found herself digging her broken and bleeding nails into the palms of her hands.

"How much do you really want me, Dulcie?" Ross asked coolly, stroking one finger along the curve of her voluptuous breast.

"I . . ."

"You've always loved me. Even when you had that schoolgirl fixation on Luke, you wanted me. Do you deny it?"

"I . . ."

"Oh, stop stammering and get into bed," said Ross. "If you're that desperate, all you have to do is ask. The role of simpering Barbara Cartland heroine doesn't mix with black fishnet and purple nails."

Dulcie didn't move. "I'm not your paid whore."

"I know," said Ross, sliding his finger down between her breasts. "But wouldn't you like to be?"

Shelby felt the hot wet tears sliding down her cheeks but could not make a sound. How could she have loved such a callous bastard?

There was a sudden hammering on the door.

"Christ!" said Ross. "Who else have you invited?"

Dulcie looked as though she might burst into tears.

Ross's face softened. "It's probably Jasper with another

location problem. Go into the bedroom. I won't keep you."

Dulcie obediently trotted into the next room. Ross waited until the door closed before he opened the one which led into the corridor.

Courteney flew at him, her fists flying, pummelling effectively against his chest. "It's happened again!" she cried. "So much for your damn bodyguards!"

"What's the matter now?" asked Ross, wearily disengaging himself.

She thrust a piece of paper into his hand. "This."

Ross frowned. "What is it?"

"Can't you see?" Courteney's voice began to rise hysterically.

"I can see it's a photograph," said Ross, "But it looks more like a blown-up negative. A very poor one. All I can see is snow."

"It's an ultrasound scan. That bastard sent it to me in the mail. Can you see what it is? It's a baby!" She began to cry. "That pervert has sent me a picture of a baby. He means to kill me, Ross, I know he does. What am I going to do?"

"I don't understand. Is this supposed to be significant?"

"Of course it's fucking significant!" screamed Courteney. "Look at the date. The name of the clinic. It's *our* baby. The one you made me terminate."

Chapter Twenty-three

It was several minutes before Shelby realised Ross had bundled Courteney out of the suite, presumably to her new suite several doors down the corridor – he was only wearing a towel after all. After another ten minutes, Dulcie came back into the sitting-room and left. She was crying, Shelby realised, and felt sorry for her.

Waiting another five minutes to be certain Ross was not coming back, Shelby slid open the French windows and, running lightly across the sitting-room, opened the door to the corridor. All clear.

Unwilling to return to her own apartment, in case she met Ross, she walked slowly down to the bar with the intention of ordering a large drink to assuage her guilt and thoroughly submerge her sorrows. She was in such a trance she almost ended up in the leisure complex by mistake.

Ross was sleeping with herself, Paige, Dulcie *and* Courteney? It was a veritable harem. He was the one who needed the cat-flap fitted to his door. Where the hell did he find the *energy*? It would have been ludicrous – she might have laughed if someone else had been his victim – but to find she had been treated so badly by someone she loved – and she had *told* him she loved him.

She was stupid, stupid, stupid – and she hadn't the vocabulary to describe what she felt about *him*. 'Bastard' suddenly seemed hopelessly inadequate. Why were there so many derogatory terms for women, yet a distinct shortfall when it came to men? Because women always believed the best of their men, falling for their lies every time?

Shelby cursed herself. So much for her fine judgment of character. She might be able to spot a criminal at thirty paces but when it came to a love-rat she needed a white stick. She cringed as she remembered the excuses she had made to herself for Ross's cruel behaviour – when all the time he had just been your typical cold, heartless . . . er, bastard. She had thought Luke to be the womaniser. Ross made Luke look like a Cistercian monk.

Shelby sat abruptly on a bar stool and ordered a double whisky. The bar was reasonably busy, the bad weather having driven everyone indoors until the restaurant opened. Floyd and Irving were there, lining up their glasses on the piano, drunkenly singing 'We're a couple of swells'. Although their clothes were dry, their hair was plastered to their heads.

Not wishing to be alone with her vengeful, self-pitying thoughts, Shelby picked up her drink and wandered over. "Has it been raining?" she asked, purely to start a conversation.

"Has it been raining!" scoffed Irving. "It's like the bloody monsoon season in town."

"On our return," said Floyd, "we passed an elderly gentlemen loading animals into an enormous boat. Two by two."

"All our imported gravel washed away," added Irving. "The Council are furious with Jasper. He's onto Bristol Airport every half-hour checking the weather report. We're supposed to be starting a night shoot at six."

By supreme effort Floyd was able to get Shelby in focus. "Why are your hands purple?"

Shelby looked down. Red and raw from her accident earlier, her hands were also covered in mauve paint. "I don't know – I don't remember –"

"Maybe the dye is coming out of your jeans?" suggested Irving.

"But my jeans are blue –" began Shelby until she noticed the dark stain spreading across one hip and down her thigh. She stuck her hand in her pocket and took out the Disney World pen. It was smashed to smithereens – she must have landed on it when she crashed onto Ross's balcony. "It's not paint," she said slowly. "It's ink."

Irving laughed. "Violet ink? You're such a pseud, Shel. Why can't you use a Bic biro like everyone else?"

* * *

By five o'clock that afternoon the sky was a gorgeous cerulean blue. After a lumbering coach ride along winding narrow lanes, bordered by acid-green hedgerows adorned with blossom like great drifts of snow, the cast arrived at the set late, the driver having got lost three times. Ross was already pacing up and down the location, frantically puffing away on a cigarette, trailed by a rather green Irving.

Shelby stuck her face against the coach window. Lots of grass, trees, wild flowers and a fast-flowing river. "Where are we?"

Luke blearily consulted his script. "A Field In Somerset."

"I mean really."

"A field in Somerset? Or maybe Wiltshire? After we drove out of Bath, I wasn't really paying attention. Did we turn left or right?"

"You were asleep!"

"As Ross intends to keep me up all night, I thought I ought to get some kip in."

"You've been in bed all day."

"I know," Luke winked. "Which is why I need to catch up on my sleep."

The guy was incorrigible! As they jumped off the coach, Shelby admired his long legs displayed to perfection in early 19th century breeches – and Nike trainers. Every (other) woman's fantasy, she thought and yawned. Perhaps she could do with a good night's sleep too.

Elliott, the wardrobe master, a distinctly harassed

expression on his ferrety face, handed Luke a stove-pipe hat and full-length coat before he even got near to the trailers. "Sorry, with so many extras, wardrobe's a full house."

"You wouldn't find Hugh Grant getting dressed in a field," grumbled Luke, sulkily putting them on. "A coat, waistcoat, shirt – hell, I'm going to be boiling."

"You won't," replied Elliott, in his curious squeaky voice. "Jasper says it's going to rain. Absolutely tip down."

"At least it will save on the weather-machine. Has anyone plucked up courage to tell Ross? I understand this afternoon was a . . . er, wash-out."

Elliott reached into his cardboard box and handed Luke a pair of riding-boots. "Do you think we have a death wish?"

The crew had not had the luxury of a break following filming in The Circus and had moved straight here to set up the equipment. Luke and Shelby walked down the hill, past special effects assistants soaking the grass with hosepipes and setting up a network of sprinkler systems.

Further along, the lighting technicians were positioning the huge arc-lamps, their thick cables nestling in the long emerald grass towards the generators, like great sleeping adders. The lighting gaffer was rearranging the lights, creating a romantic moonlight diffusion, with the lighting director standing below and yelling, "Left a bit . . . right a bit . . . oh bugger, you had it just perfect then!"

"Is it the bum shots tonight, Luke?" asked Shelby casually.

Luke shuddered. "Are you serious? God knows what wildlife is lurking in that long grass. Bum shots are next week, in a sumptuous four-poster bed, with soft lighting, sweet-scented flowers and edited together with lots of romantic and meaningful background music."

"And the sweaty crew squashed in beside you, a boom two inches from your nose and a camera up your bottom," grinned Shelby. "You know," she added idly, the whisky still capering about in her veins, "I always fancied making love in the great outdoors – provided no one else could see me," she added hastily.

"I shall bear that in mind," said Luke. To make her laugh, he began to tell her of the first love scene he had filmed, for the BBC. "There we were, crammed into this tiny, grotty, high-rise flat, with a skeleton crew to protect the actress's modesty – funny how no one ever thinks the actor might get nervous about showing *his* tackle. I ripped off my trousers and was just about to er, do my duty, when there was a terrific whoop from outside and there were hundreds of women waving and screaming out the windows of the tower block opposite. They could see *everything*. I've never been more embarrassed in my entire life."

"Perhaps you should have sent a grip round to make a collection," she teased him. "It must have been worth a couple of quid at least."

Luke grinned and pretended to cuff her.

She watched a huge horse box swing through the

gate and into the field, churning up all the mud, almost taking out half the hedge as the driver misjudged the gap and nearly collided with a man fiddling about with what looked like a steam-engine stuck on a trolley. "What's that?"

"It's a smoke machine. Amazing contraption – belches out smoke like a fire-breathing dragon."

"Just like Ross," murmured Shelby and frowned. Bang went her resolution not to even think about him.

Luke glanced curiously at her but said nothing.

Courteney was standing in the middle of the field in a white lawn nightdress while Ross walked around her and Elliott stood nervously chewing on his lower lip.

"Are you sure this isn't going to go transparent when it's wet?" asked Ross.

"Depends on what you mean by transparent?" wavered Elliott timidly. "You'll see the outline of her figure."

"Is she wearing underwear?"

"Are you wearing underwear, Courteney?" whispered Elliott.

"Depends on what you mean by underwear," sniffed Courteney.

"Bra, knickers, thermal vest –" reeled off Ross irritably.

"I'm wearing panties."

Ross scowled. "You're supposed to be a virginal Regency heroine, not Miss Wet T-Shirt circa 1985. Put some clothes on."

"Sure. You just wait here and I'll go dig out my twin-set and pearls."

Ross returned behind the camera and raised a megaphone to his lips. "OK, after Miss O'Connor has run over the hill doing the usual pathetic heroine stuff, we'll have the hounds, then Dean. Dean, you pause on top of the hill, the horse has been trained to rear, just watch that pretty nose of yours. Then we'll do the next scene with Floyd jumping from the barge to rescue Courteney and Dean setting about him with his whip."

"Kinky," said Floyd, still floating three inches above the ground on Glenfiddich. "Does he get to wear black rubber too?"

Ross ignored him. "Where's special effects? I want wispy mist curling up from the river – ethereal but, at the same time, sinister. I do not want a Sherlock Holmes pea-souper."

Shelby sank down into Courteney's deckchair, next to Luke. She had the suspicion that Luke, wearing sunglasses and resting his head on his hand, had fallen asleep again and so did not bother to exchange conversation with him, just watched as the special effects men soaked Courteney, and Kit painted her suntanned face white and pencilled black circles under her eyes. Shelby yawned, wishing she had brought her dark glasses. It was an effort to keep her eyes open. God, filming was boring.

Ross glanced up at the fading light. "OK, Action."

* * *

Four hours later and they were still shooting the same scene, albeit from the third camera angle.

"Come on, Floyd," grumbled Ross. "You're not putting your back into this. Don't pluck timidly at the horse's bridle, grab it, yank its head down. You want to stop this monster from ravishing your daughter."

"I want to stop this monster from trampling all over me," complained Floyd. "I'm sure the damn creature has broken my toe. Can't you get a stuntman?"

"It's a close-up."

"Well, can't we have a break? We've been doing this scene for almost four hours."

"I want to get it into the can before eleven-thirty."

"What time is it now?"

"Ten-thirty."

"But that's another hour!"

"For Christ's sake, Floyd, stop whingeing. I think I'm going to have to drop Luke's scene. I don't want this evening to be a complete waste of everyone's time."

Kit tiptoed over and dabbed at Floyd's make-up.

"Action!" yelled Ross.

Dean cantered down the hill after Courteney, who disappeared off camera as Floyd suddenly appeared in front of Dean's horse, half-heartedly waving his hurricane lamp. "Stop, you bugger!" he hissed under his breath.

Dean's horse reared up on cue. Floyd attempted to grab at its bridle, missed and staggered forwards, desperately trying to avoid going flat on his face. He fell into the arms of Courteney, giggling helplessly.

"Shall we dance?" he asked to her bosom.

Courteney laughed and heaved him back onto his feet. "They haven't been introduced to you."

"Hello, boys," said Floyd and was about to happily bury his head when Ross got him by the scruff of the neck and hauled him out.

"Cut," said Ross wearily. "And Floyd, one more trick like that and you're fired. It's sexual harassment. The next actress might not have Courteney's warped sense of humour."

"I feel faint," gasped Floyd, suddenly sitting onto the grass.

"Lack of oxygen," muttered a grip and the crew laughed.

Ross regarded Floyd with dislike. "Are you drunk again?"

"I don't –"

"Save your breath, Floyd. It takes more than a couple of mints to hide the stench. Everyone knows I do not tolerate alcohol on the set. Don't you want to work? Are you trying to goad me into giving you the sack?"

"My arm aches," grumbled Floyd. "This wretched heavy coat – has cut off the – circulation."

Shelby knelt beside him. "You look terrible," she said sympathetically. "Would you like me to get you a drink or something?"

Floyd clutched wildly at her hand. "I can't . . . breathe . . ."

Courteney glanced at Ross. "Perhaps we should just take a break? I feel tired too. We have been working all day."

"So have the crew," snapped Ross. "And they know better than to whinge."

"They're paid overtime and they belong to a union," Courteney pointed out.

"And what's Equity? A dating agency for insurance salesmen? Get up, Floyd," he added, although not unkindly. "You'll be all right. Do you want a glass of water?"

"You don't think I'm wet enough?" managed Floyd.

Shelby stood up and held out her hand. Floyd grasped it gratefully. Then clutched at his chest and collapsed back onto the grass, taking Shelby with him.

"Floyd?" Shelby scrambled to her feet. "Floyd! What's the matter?"

Floyd gurgled indistinctly.

"Oh God, I think he's having a heart attack – Floyd? Can you hear me? Is it your heart?"

Shelby, bent over Floyd's prostrate body, tried to stay calm. First you had to check the airway wasn't blocked. She tilted back Floyd's head. Then check breathing . . . Shelby pulled her hair out of the way and placed her ear over Floyd's mouth. She nearly gagged at the terrible smell of stale alcohol but there was no breath coming from those blue lips.

Vaguely she was aware of Irving stammering into his mobile phone, as she pressed her lips against Floyd's and breathed for him. She watched as his chest rose and lowered, then tried again, checking his pulse – not even the tiniest flicker.

Ripping open Floyd's waistcoat, she felt for the place where the ribcage and the breastbone met, measured two finger-widths back up and began to compress his chest with her heel of her hand. Courteney was crying in the background. Luke had wrenched the mobile phone from the panic-stricken Irving and was barking instructions at the operator.

Shelby completed the fifteenth compression and then moved back to Floyd's head to check his breathing. Nothing. She tried again, twice, then checked his pulse. A faint flicker, but he still wasn't breathing. Oh God, it was hopeless.

"Don't give up," said a voice close by her ear. It was Luke.

She sat back on her heels. "I think he's . . ." she hardly wanted to utter the word. She closed her eyes. "I think . . . he's dead . . ."

He patted her shoulder. "The ambulance will be here soon. You're doing brilliantly."

But he's dead! she wanted to scream. What's the point? I've failed, like I failed in everything else I've ever done. But, as though on automatic pilot, she bent to commence mouth-to-mouth again, trying to shut out the thought that she was merely wasting her time.

After what seemed an eternity, she realised she could hear the far-off wailing of sirens, then closer, as an ambulance bumped over the field and two paramedics in green and yellow uniforms jumped out and ran towards her . . . just as Floyd began to breathe for himself.

As she watched the paramedics take over, carefully transferring the still unconscious Floyd to an ambulance, she felt suddenly faint and sat on the soaking wet grass in case she keeled over.

"It's over now," Luke said softly. "You saved his life."

Shelby felt numb. "I want to go to the hospital," she heard herself saying. "I want to make sure he's all right."

"Of course," said Luke. "We'll all go together in Ross's car."

"Are you crazy?" said Ross, his voice harsh. "We've got to finish this scene."

Luke stared at him. "Your father has just had a heart attack and you want to complete the scene?"

"Floyd would understand."

Luke shook his head. "Well, *I* don't understand. Come on, Shelby. We'll borrow someone else's car."

"And how am I supposed to finish? I can't work around both you and Floyd."

"You could always come with us."

"If you leave this film set, you're fired."

"So fire me," said Luke.

Chapter Twenty-four

"I hate hospitals," said Shelby.

Me too, thought Luke but remained silent. Shelby was babbling enough for the two of them. She was trying to stay calm, to sit still, but he watched her relentlessly pacing up and down, forever asking him the time – as though Elliott would let him wear a watch with period costume – and pestering any passing nurse for an update

To take his mind off the sickening fear gnawing away at his insides, Luke had a tattered copy of *Bella* magazine on his lap, open at the problem page, but found he just kept reading the same line over and over again – about some poor cow whose husband had left her for her best friend, although he kept coming back for sex. Did this mean he really loved her?

Luke glanced at Shelby, now motionless, apart from her twisting hands in her lap. Her face was so pale her freckles had practically disappeared.

Ross stalked through the waiting-room once, also resembling one of the living dead, on his way to harass one of the doctors. Luke watched Shelby's eyes cloud with anguish as Ross ignored her calling to him, although, to be fair, he probably hadn't heard.

Why do fools fall in love? thought Luke bitterly.

Shelby restlessly stood up. She hesitated, biting her lip, before asking Luke, "Would you like a cup of coffee? It'll help you keep awake." Without waiting for him to answer she almost sprinted off towards the coffee machine – the same direction that Ross had taken.

"Damn, damn, damn," said Luke and hurled the *Bella* magazine across the room, decapitating a yellowed coleus and waking up an elderly gentleman who had fallen asleep over a copy of *Cosmopolitan*.

Luke swopped it with *Bella* while the old dear was still trying to work out where he was and what day it was. *Thirty Things You Didn't Know About Orgasms*, screamed the fluorescent orange headline across the incongruously virginal model on the cover. Oh yeah? But he thumbed through the pages to find it just the same.

Shelby found Ross slumped against the coffee machine, his spectacles swinging from one hand, the other across his face. At first she thought he had fallen asleep on his feet, like a horse, and tiptoed quietly away.

"Shelby!" he called brokenly.

She reluctantly turned but remained rooted to the spot. "How's Floyd?" she muttered.

"They've had to restart his heart three times."

Ross's voice choked. "I had to leave. I couldn't stand it any more. All those machines bleeping, the wires – God, it was awful." He rubbed the heel of his hand into his reddened eyes. "At the moment he's stable but they think he might still have another attack."

Shelby hesitated, then walked over, placing her hand on his shoulder. It was horrible to see his defences come crashing down, to see he had his vulnerabilities just like everyone else.

Ross didn't flinch from her touch – he didn't seem to notice, just blinked ferociously at the moisture gathering in his eyes. "I never realised I cared so much for the old bastard," he croaked, replacing his spectacles, looking more like the old Ross. "I haven't cried since my prep master gave me six of the best for setting up a ciné camera in matron's bedroom. How was I to know he was fucking her?" Ross searched his pockets for cigarettes but only found an empty packet. In despair, he scrunched up the box and flung it into the waste-paper bin.

"Floyd *is* your father. It's natural to feel anxious." Shelby wondered if she should volunteer to fetch some more cigarettes from the shop but thought it unlikely, even if it was open at this hour, that a hospital would sell them. Besides, she had no desire to encourage him to smoke.

"Anxious!" Ross slid down the side of the coffee machine until he was sitting on the bright orange carpet. "The bastard's last memory is of me cursing him. I know we've had our differences but I always thought – I thought that someday –" He slammed his fist back against the machine. "But now there's no fucking time!"

Shelby crouched beside him. "Floyd will be all right. He'll be fine. Lots of people have heart attacks and pull through."

"Not four massive attacks. Not at seventy-three. Jesus, why the hell did I hire him? He was far too old for the rigours of this shoot. And I didn't make it easy for him. I tortured him. I didn't want people thinking I'd given him the role because I felt sorry for him. Because he was my father."

Shelby fumbled in her pocket for change and shoved £4.75p into the coffee machine without realising, just desperate to get two coffees to take Ross's mind off Floyd. Most of the liquid bubbled over the edge of the plastic cups and into the slops tray. She also forgot to programme in milk and sugar.

Ross didn't appear to notice, just clutched at his coffee like a drowning man would clutch at a lifebelt and drank it down in one go, regardless of the scalding heat. He must have asbestos lips, thought Shelby in awe. She handed him her coffee too but he waved it aside.

"I never saw much of Floyd when I was growing up," he said, almost to himself. "I was shunted from aunt to aunt – if I wanted to see either of my parents I would have to buy a ticket for the cinema. Tragic, eh?" His voice was bitter.

Shelby took a sip of her coffee. It was disgusting;

she slipped it onto a windowsill in case Ross should want it later. "Didn't you see him at all?"

"How? When he wasn't filming he was performing on stage, or jetting around the world, yet another glamorous wife on his arm, cuddling yet another gorgeous baby. I only ever saw him in the newspapers, playing at happy families, but not with me. He didn't need me. He had seven other children, four of them boys. I was replaceable."

"Bollocks, look at all you've achieved! Floyd must be very proud of you."

"And did *he* tell you that? I thought not. It's easy to achieve things when you're rich," Ross's voice was harsh. "Floyd fought his way up the hard way. First as a child performer in variety, then in the fledgling British cinema. He even had chart success in the fifties with his music. He just kept reinventing himself, much as he's doing now. You've got to admire him for that. He just keeps starting over. And in thirty years what have I done? I set up a film production company with my mother's money."

"You're talented," protested Shelby. "You're a brilliant director."

"How many directors do you know?"

"The crew think you're great."

"They hate my guts!"

"But they respect you."

"How can I expect anyone to respect me when I don't even respect myself. I've been a complete bastard to every crew I've ever worked with and every woman

I've ever slept with. I tell myself it's to achieve the best performance but really it's just to see how far I can go, to see what reaction I'll get. To see just how much they can stand before they reject me like my bloody father did."

"Relationships are something you need to work at," said Shelby, wishing she could offer more help than just utter platitudes. "Real life is not like you see in the movies."

He smiled ruefully. "Why do you think Hollywood blockbusters are so lucrative? I know my personal life is a complete disaster and I know that when it comes to the crunch I suppose I'll never love a woman as much as I love making films. Transforming three months of blood, sweat and celluloid into a hundred and twenty minutes of escapism – sex doesn't even come close."

They became aware of footsteps along the corridor. Shelby turned, expecting to see Luke, but it was a young male doctor, who looked even rougher than Ross, his face pale and sweating, patchy stubble beginning to emerge on his chin. He didn't look old enough to shave, thought Shelby, let alone operate.

"Mr Ross Mulligan?" he asked.

Ross gave a wry smile. "That's me."

"Your father is stable but still unconscious. We expect him to come round soon, although we need to keep him in intensive care for a few days. Would you like to see him?"

"Yes." Ross glanced at Shelby. "Would you come with me? Please?"

How could she resist those beautiful grey eyes, even if they were bloodshot and ringed with black circles. Shelby looked at the doctor. "Is that all right with you?"

He nodded wearily. The poor man looked dead on his feet. "Yes, but only for five minutes. You can stay longer tomorrow."

Floyd was in a little ward by himself, or perhaps it was a recovery room. There was a black nurse sitting at a desk a few feet away, hunched over some paperwork. She looked up as they entered, smiled encouragingly, mouthed: "Five minutes," and then held up her hand in case they couldn't lip-read.

Ross nodded and, taking Shelby's hand, led her around the bed to where there was a threadbare easy-chair – but only the one. Despite her protests he pushed her into it. The nurse looked up at the commotion and frowned.

Shelby was shocked at how pallid and wan Floyd was. And so very old. She knew he was well over seventy but he had always been so full of the joys of life – and the joys of Glenfiddich – that she hadn't appreciated his age. His white hair was in soft spikes around his head like a baby's. His skin was dry, papery, threaded with blue veins, his usual ruddy cherubic cheeks had blanched. He was an elderly man and very ill.

Ross stared down at his father, his fingers digging into Shelby's shoulder, his face inscrutable. Shelby patted his hand. "He'll be all right," she whispered, as though saying the words out loud would make them true. "Don't worry. You'll soon be fighting each other again."

"How could I have pushed him?" Ross's voice cracked. "I just kept on and on at him. I thought he was just playing the fool but instead he was ill. He had been ill all the time. The staff found a phial of drugs in his pocket as well as the flask of whisky. He knew he had heart problems but he never told me. He never told anyone."

"Because you wouldn't have hired him if he had. He needed the job, he needed the money, so he lied."

"I knew he was an alcoholic. I could have done something about that."

"What? Fired him? He'd have been well chuffed."

"I could have tried to help him! Instead I just hoped it would go away."

"You're here now, aren't you? If you hadn't have cared, you wouldn't have come."

"You mean if Luke hadn't threatened me."

"Oh God, I'd forgotten about Luke – he's still waiting for his coffee. He'll have wondered what's happened to me." She stood up, the chair scraped along the lino, echoing around the empty room.

The nurse glanced up. "I'm afraid you'll have to leave now," she said. "But you can come back tomorrow. Why don't you go home and have a nice sleep. We'll call you if there's any change."

"You think he might deteriorate?" Ross asked anxiously.

"That wasn't what I said," reproved the nurse.

"I'm going to stay all the same," said Ross firmly.

"Not in here you can't."

"So I'll wait in the corridor."

The nurse scowled at him. Then she relented. "I'll see if we can find a camp-bed for you."

"Would you like me to stay with you?" asked Shelby, as the nurse picked up her telephone and dialled for a porter.

"No. You go and get some sleep – but thanks for the offer."

"Will you be on set tomorrow – I mean, today?"

"I doubt it. Tell Irving he's in charge. Hire and fire at will."

Shelby smiled. "Can you honestly imagine Irving firing anyone?"

* * *

Luke was pacing the waiting area. "Where the hell have you been? I've been worried sick. Has something happened to Floyd? Is he . . . is he dead?"

"Floyd's fine." Shelby was so happy she hugged him. Luke, not one to miss an opportunity, hugged her back. "I've seen him. He's got to stay in intensive care for a few days, to make sure he doesn't have a relapse."

The grey lines of tension mapping Luke's normally cheerful face faded away into a huge grin. "Can I see him?"

"It's family only. I got in because I was with Ross."

Luke's eyes narrowed. "Oh yes? Where, pray, did you meet Ross?"

"At the coffee machine. You remember? I went to fetch a drink? The poor man was distraught. He had completely gone to pieces."

"Yeah, distraught that he's just lost one of his leading men and it's too late to find a replacement."

"That's a horrible thing to say! You didn't see the state Ross was in. I really had to calm him down. He's going to spend the night here, on a camp-bed," she added defiantly, "and Irving's going to shoot the rest of the film."

"Fuck me," said Luke. "I take it all back."

* * *

It proved impossible to entice a taxi to the hospital at half-past three in the morning, so in the end they had to pinch one that had just dropped an expectant mother off at the Maternity Unit.

"But the lady's not sure she's in labour," protested the driver. "I might have to take them back home."

Luke brandished a wad of tenners.

"But she looked pretty far gone to me," added the driver. "Hop in."

As they stood in the hotel reception Shelby looked up at the long flight of steps and wondered if it really was worth going to bed for what would amount to little over an hour's sleep.

"How about a drink?" suggested Luke.

"OK," said Shelby, following him upstairs to his suite, unaware of the intense interest of the duty manager who had, until then, been dozing behind the reception desk. She'd never get to sleep now anyway. "A hot chocolate would be great," she added, as Luke unlocked the door to his suite. "It'll help relax me."

"I was thinking of something a bit stronger." Luke began to count out the contents of the minibar. "One for you, one for me . . . Let's get uproariously drunk."

"In two hours Baz will be hammering on that door, to drive us to the shoot."

Luke raised one of the bottles as though in a toast. "Two hours' valuable drinking time."

"We've just come from the hospital," she said coldly, "Where poor Floyd has just suffered four heart attacks."

"Caused by a heart problem," said Luke reasonably. "You told me yourself."

"But all that alcohol wouldn't have helped." She shuddered. "I bet his liver looks like a pickled gherkin."

"I believe everything is fine is moderation."

"So speaks the great vegetarian."

Luke looked sheepish. "A vegetarian diet makes my skin look clearer and younger. Why do you think I drink gallons of spa water? You don't think I actually like the stuff?"

"To wash down the gallons of Chardonnay?" she suggested sarcastically.

"To keep spots at bay." He pulled off his long coat and waistcoat, threw them in the vague direction of the bedroom and, picking a thick blue jersey off a chair, slid it over his head. He had to sit down to haul off his boots.

"Sorry I'm such a bitch," she sighed as he went back to the minibar. "I'm still worried about Floyd."

Luke ripped the lid off a Baileys miniature and, pouring it into a glass, added a couple of chunks of ice from the tray in his fridge. He handed the glass to Shelby. She took it reluctantly and watched as he poured himself a brandy and sat next to her on the sofa.

She took a sip of her drink. God, she was so tired she could hardly keep her eyes open. How the hell was she going to get through tomorrow? As her head nodded she discovered she had snuggled into Luke's blue fisherman's jersey. He felt warm and reassuring. The awfulness of the hospital began to recede. She watched him swill his brandy around his large round glass. It looked like Mystic Meg's crystal ball. She wondered if he could tell her future.

He suddenly realised she was cuddled up against him and regarded her suspiciously. "What are you up to?"

"Sorry," she yawned. "Don't get the wrong idea – I'm just so tired and depressed –"

He gave a short laugh. "So you thought you'd give yourself an excuse to throw me across the room to cheer yourself up?"

"Oh shut up," she sighed. "I'm tired of fighting."

"Me too."

There was something in his voice that caused her to glance up into his intense blue eyes and quickly look away again. Why was it, whenever he looked at her like that, she was transported right back to the night of his birthday and Ross's swimming-pool. She felt her cheeks begin to glow. Still, she wondered how she would react if he kissed her now? Would she really throw him over the sofa, or merely kiss him back. He certainly had very kissable lips. And eight million BBC2 viewers could not be wrong.

He drew her closer. "OK," he said amicably. "One cuddle and that's your lot."

* * *

Saturday

Two hours later, they awoke to find Baz hammering on the door. "Oy, Luke! Are you all right? The minibus leaves in ten minutes."

"Oh my God!" Luke launched himself off the sofa and began scrambling around on the floor, searching for his boots. "We fell asleep!" And, as he caught sight of Shelby's amusement, added, "I suppose you realise that's my reputation gone for a Burton?"

"Oh yes," Shelby smiled sleepily. "We'll have to get married now."

Luke emerged from behind the sofa, a dusty boot dangling from one hand. "Shelby . . ."

Baz thumped on the door again. "Can you hear me, Luke? Are you in the bog?"

Saved by the Baz, thought Shelby gratefully. "Just coming," she called, avoiding Luke's scrutiny. "Give us five minutes – we'll meet you in the car park."

"Sure thing . . . *Shelby* . . ." Even through two inches of oak, Barry's voice dripped innuendo. "You chaps take your time. No hurry . . ."

"Smart one, Shelby," muttered Luke, crawling

beneath a chair for his other boot. "Now the whole world knows we spent the night together."

"Perfectly innocently!" Furious at herself, she tossed over his script. "Can't you hurry up? Baz will think we've gone back to bed for an encore."

"It's all right for you. You're already dressed."

"In exactly the same clothes I was wearing yesterday!"

Luke's smile was lazy. "Ah, but you're a woman; it's different for a man."

"I'm going to brush my teeth," she said crossly. What did he care for her reputation? After all, to the rest of the crew she was just another notch on his increasingly distressed bedpost. "I'll meet you in the car park too."

He feigned anxiety. "But what if I get kidnapped between here and reception?"

Shelby grabbed her rucksack and headed for the door. "No such luck!"

Chapter Twenty-five

Ross did not leave the hospital until the late afternoon. Instead of dropping in on the filming in Bath, he returned to the hotel for a long hot shower. Unable to sleep, he decided to watch the day's rushes, which Irving had simultaneously filmed onto video and left at reception for him. His mind was constantly turning over, so that it took him several minutes to realise the TV screen had gone blank, and that was only because the tape had rewound, causing the machine to clunk off, leaving a mass of snow and static on the screen.

Ross picked up the remote control and switched the video back on, pushing the tape in with his foot. Then, as the first scene began to play, he drained his whisky before pouring another. As he tossed the empty miniature into the bin, there was a knock on the door.

"Hi, Ross," said Irving, sliding his blond freckly head through the door. "How's Floyd?"

"Fine."

"That's great. The crew will be delighted. He's very popular, you know."

Ross ignored him, hoping he would take the hint and leave him alone.

Irving boldly took a step into the sitting-room. "Erm . . . sorry it's so late. I wondered if you'd had the chance to view today's rushes?"

"Three times."

Irving hovered uncertainly, perhaps realising Ross was in one of his moods. "I thought the first scene went brilliantly," he managed eventually, walking off towards the window to avoid eye contact. "Um . . . the second had to be reshot several times but I think it will come across better with careful editing –"

Ross handed him his glass tumbler to shut him up. "Have a drink."

Irving took it dubiously, peering into the amber liquid. "Ah . . . thanks, Ross."

Anyone would think I was trying to poison him, thought Ross irritably. "And sit down. You'll wear a hole in the carpet with your pacing."

Irving obediently sat in one of the large squashy armchairs, his feet only just reaching the floor, and took an unenthusiastic swig of the whisky.

"Irving, you are a terrific 1st AD –" Ross paused, aware that the vindictive note was apparent in his voice, "but basically you're a crap director. We're re-shooting everything."

Irving stared silently at him, with green-gold eyes that were so like Shelby's. Even his lashes were the same sandy colour. "I don't understand –" he stammered, looking not unlike somebody's pet pooch which had just been delivered of a hefty kick. "I didn't think it was that –"

"Your direction was all over the place. Luke was so wooden he could have had dry rot and Paige incapable of seducing Casanova. You failed to inspire the actors, translate the author's dreams to the camera – in short, it's a disaster."

Irving's fingers tightened on the glass, turning the nails almost white. "You can tell it to me straight, Ross," he said, in a sharp, tight voice. "I can take it."

A faint smile turned up the corners of Ross's mouth at the uncharacteristic sarcasm. "I am telling it to you straight. You're a friend and I don't –"

"Bollocks," said Irving suddenly, reminding Ross forcibly of his sister. "Don't bring a mythological friendship into this." He broke off, struggling for his usual self-control. "Besides, I don't believe the filming was that bad. Sure, there may have been a few flaws, I'm not as experienced as you, but I'm not a raw beginner either. I've directed before –"

Ross, growing bored with the entire subject, attempted to speed things along with a few insults. "Yes, action scenes with the 2nd Unit and beer advertisements."

"Don't play the snob with me," retorted Irving. "Until a few years ago this country barely had a film industry. Advertising was about the only work anyone could get. You yourself started out the same way." He frowned. "You know what I think?"

Ross poured himself another drink, wishing Irving would just storm off and leave him alone. "No, but I'm sure you're about to enlighten me –"

"I think today's filming was perfect – nothing wrong with it. You're just such a control freak you cannot bear to see anyone else succeed. You're the director, you're God, and woe betide anyone who attempts to usurp you."

Unable to believe what he had just heard, it took a while for Irving's words to sink in. "Thank you for sharing that thought with me, Irving."

Irving, however, was warming to his theme. "I feel sorry for you, I do really. It's such a shame. You've put together a great team for this production, if only you'd delegate, inspire us to excel, but no, you have to do everything yourself, keep us all in our place."

"Ah well, come the revolution, citizen –"

"Oh fuck you, I quit! I'm just wasting my time trying to reason with you. Have another drink, the budget sheet won't look so bad; finish the bottle, you can see that BAFTA on your mantelpiece already. I wish you all the best, Ross. It's lonely at the top, particularly when you've pushed everyone else off."

Well, he had certainly pushed the amiable Irving too far. But it wouldn't take much to bring his wimpy 1st AD back to heel. "May I remind you you're on contract to finish the film?"

"For a week's work?" derided Irving. "I'm sure you can cope without me."

"I'll sue."

"Go ahead," said Irving and marched out, slamming the door behind him.

"Always the theatrical." Ross turned back to the TV screen just in time to see Luke leap unenthusiastically on top of Paige. Paige slapped him, a move which was not actually in the script, and began screaming abuse. Ross sighed and raised his glass in toast.

"I name this film a crock of shit and God bless all who sink in her."

* * *

Sunday

After a half-hearted lie-in, Shelby dressed in jeans and wandered down to breakfast, picking up a copy of *The Mail On Sunday* as she passed reception.

"Hello, Miss Roberts," said the waiter. "Would you like a seat by the window this morning? It's a lovely day."

Shelby regarded him suspiciously. He wasn't usually this attentive. Perhaps he had been on a customer-service training course.

"Well, I usually –"

"It's vacant," he smiled winningly, before holding the chair out for her.

She shrugged and sat down, aware she was attracting attention.

"Will Mr McFadden be joining you?" enquired the waiter, as he straightened the cutlery and perked up the dropping flower arrangement.

This was a bit much to comprehend first thing in the morning. "Dunno," she replied, wishing he would go away and just leave her to it. "Perhaps."

He handed her a menu. A menu? For breakfast? This was a first.

After lingering for a few moments he said, "Perhaps I could fetch you fresh orange juice while you decide what to have?"

"It's very kind of you but I usually just go up and help myself –"

"I can get it for you, Miss Roberts." And he again smiled that insincere smile, favoured by American actors and newly elected Prime Ministers. "Just tell me what you'd like."

For you to bugger off, thought Shelby but really she felt too tired to argue. "Yeah, yeah, that'd be fine. Ta very much."

He flashed her another toothy smile and sprinted off towards the kitchen. Shelby spread the newspaper out on the table beside her, so that she wouldn't have to make polite conversation with anyone else. One week to go, she reminded herself. You just have to stick with it for one more week . . .

Skipping the headlines – usual boring political sleaze – she turned to page three and was confronted by a full-page colour photograph of herself.

At first she did not realise it was her. Just noticed that the rather attractive redhead had a burgundy jacquard dress just like hers. Then that the redhead was cuddled up in an embarrassingly familiar way against Luke, who admittedly looked the most cheerful she'd seen him look in a long time. The accompanying headline caught her eye.

All That She Wants, it said, (the title of Luke's last

film). *'Martial arts expert and firearms crack-shot Shelby Roberts (26) . . .'*

Shelby scowled. "I'm twenty-four, you bastards."

' . . . has just landed the most eligible man in show business, hunk Luke McFadden'.

"Like he's an out-of-control plane or something."

'Employed as Luke's bodyguard, it did not take ex-WPC Shelby long to work her way into Luke's heart.'

"God, who writes this drivel?"

'Luke's fiancée, American heiress and actress Paige Lorraine, was last night said to be devastated. Although she jilted him at their Christmas wedding, Paige had always hoped for a reconciliation. Until recently, Shelby Roberts was said to have been dating millionaire Ross Whitney, who is directing Luke's latest film, A Midsummer Kiss, *based on the best-selling Regency romp by Marina Grey.'*

"Oh God," said Shelby. "Oh hell, oh shit, oh bugger –"

"OJ?" enquired the waiter, materialising at her elbow with a glass of freshly squeezed orange juice.

Shelby almost hit the ceiling. Attempting to hide the story she abruptly turned the page, only to be faced with more lurid headlines and, horror of horrors, an old school photograph. Pigtails, freckles, gap-teeth . . . Dumping her rucksack on top she attempted to smile brightly at the waiter.

"Er, orange juice, Miss Roberts?" he repeated.

"Could I have some vodka in that, please?"

"Sorry?"

Shelby ferreted around in the rucksack and, heaven, found a crumpled fiver. She shoved it at the waiter.

"An inch or two of vodka in the bottom of that glass and I'll be your friend for life," she whispered and tapped her nose conspiringly.

The waiter hurriedly backed away.

Shelby dropped her rucksack on the floor and picked up the newspaper, effectively hiding behind it. Turning back to page three, she studied the photograph. It must have been taken on the night of Luke's birthday party, when he was fooling around in front of the official photographer. It was a brilliant picture of her, she looked almost pretty – perhaps they had touched it up in some way? Apart from the fact she was nearly a foot shorter than Luke, she could have been a supermodel. All she need was a bare midriff and a diamond through her navel. Luke was leaning on her shoulder, one of his silly besotted looks on his face – no wonder people thought they were 'in lurve'.

Shelby turned the page and found lots of lurid revelations about her skinny-dip in Ross's pool. Most of it was untrue but one thing was certain. The story could only have come from Paige.

Furiously Shelby stuffed the newspaper into her rucksack and came face to face with Ross, sitting across from her, nursing a large mug of steaming coffee. Her vodka and orange had materialised too, without her realising it.

Too angry to be polite, she snapped at Ross, "How long have you been sitting there?"

Ross shrugged. "A few minutes, does it matter? I didn't like to interrupt. You seemed engrossed."

"Incensed more like!" Shelby dragged the paper out from her bag, tearing the pages, and tossed it across the table to him. "Have you see this?"

"A version of it," admitted Ross, breaking off a piece of croissant and toying with it. "I'm afraid the story is in all the papers. It must be a poor week for news. Someone must have leaked the photos from the *Hello!* shoot."

Shelby suddenly realised how terrible he looked and felt sorry for him. "How's Floyd?" she asked. "Have you had an update from the hospital?"

"He's fine. Twenty-four hours after a near-death experience and he's already in trouble for pinching a nurse's bottom and sharing a bottle of Glenfiddich with some young and impressionable student doctors."

Shelby laughed. "I'm glad to hear it."

He smiled wryly. "You won't be when you hear my next piece of news. There are reporters camped outside the gate. They are even trying to get into the hotel, although security has managed to thwart them so far."

Shelby stared at him. "Because of this stupid article?"

"I've already released a denial, but of course this is far too good a story for them to pass up. I've been on the phone to John Ivar and he's sending Shark to take over. You're welcome to return home if you wish – you'll still be paid – but I think your best bet is to remain with us. We can handle everything."

"The bodyguard needs a bodyguard? It's ridiculous! Why do these people believe such lies? Can't they accept the truth?"

"The truth is boring."

"I'm sorry to bring all this upon you."

Ross shrugged. "I feel partly responsible. I'm sure it was Paige venting her spleen which set them off in the first place."

"The bitch," murmured Shelby, then felt as though her face had been smothered in Deep Heat. "I mean –"

"I'm calling an emergency meeting," said Ross. "Anyone found speaking to the press, unless through the official channels, will be fired."

"Good," said Shelby.

"I'm also cancelling leave. We've got to reshoot yesterday's scenes."

"Oh, Irving will be disappointed! Does he know?"

"Yes, he took it in good part. We had a few technical problems, lighting and sound – the set was so dark."

The waiter moved silently up beside them. "So sorry to interrupt, Mr Whitney. We have the call you were expecting? You can take it in the manager's office or we can patch it through to your room?"

Ross sighed. "I'll take it in the manager's office."

Shelby didn't bother to watch him go, just took a large gulp of her drink. The alcohol kicked in, warming her stomach, calming her nerves but leaving her feeling slightly sick. It was no good. She was going to have to jack this job in. She was turning into an alcoholic.

"A bit early in the morning, isn't it?" said Luke, tapping one finger against her glass.

Shelby jumped – she hadn't even heard him approach and there he was, comfortably sitting opposite, the waiter fawning around with jugs of coffee and orange juice. She glared at him. He was like the sanctimonious angel in one of those old *Tom and Jerry* cartoons, who sat on Tom's shoulder dishing out unwarranted advice. Besides, she thought sourly, he was a right one to talk.

"For orange juice?" she said, feigning innocence.

"For vodka," he said uncompromisingly.

It wasn't worth making an issue out of it. Sulkily she pointed out the lead story in the newspaper. "I have a good excuse."

He barely glanced at the paper. Instead, regarding her intently he said, "I thought you'd finished with Ross?"

She felt the fury well up inside her. Considering he had played fast and loose with half the women on the set – much the same as Ross really – how dare he talk to her this way? "My private life is not your concern!"

Luke turned to look out of the window. Some old grannies were taking their coffee on the terrace and when they saw him they started waving enthusiastically. Luke didn't even notice. "I don't want to see you getting hurt."

Shelby felt the irrational need to hurt. "You mean you can't bear to see Ross succeed where you failed."

His fierce blue gaze whipped back to her. "I'm not like that!"

"What about the way you dumped poor Dulcie? She was devoted to you."

Luke snorted. "I have never slept with Dulcie."

"And I'm the Christmas Fairy," said Shelby.

A glimmer of a smile passed across his face. "Don't let's fall out over something so stupid. We've only a week of filming to go."

"I'm counting every second!" Shelby pushed back her chair. Grabbing her rucksack and then, as an afterthought, the newspaper, she marched out of the dining-room.

As Shelby walked through reception she bumped into Ross coming out of the manager's office. "Quick call," she said.

He was frowning. "It was certainly very odd," he agreed. "The caller rang off just as I picked up the telephone."

"Really?" Shelby cast a suspicious look back in Luke's direction. "Why does that not surprise me?"

Ross followed her gaze and his mouth tightened. "We need to talk," he said. "There are too many misunderstandings floating about."

Her smiled disappeared. "There's nothing to talk about."

He cast a look around the reception. Apart from the girl behind the desk it was deserted. He pulled Shelby into the corner by the fireplace and lowered his voice. "I still have feelings for you, Shelby. I know I've behaved like a bastard, I have no excuse, I just feel that if we tried again –"

"You could have the opportunity to behave like a *complete* bastard? No, thanks. This isn't baseball. You only get one strike."

He smiled, although it was an effort. "You're right, this isn't baseball, but I'd still like another chance. Can we discuss it in private over a drink tonight?"

"You've got to be jo –" were the first words out of her mouth – until she noticed Luke appear through the door to the dining-room. She forced herself to smile encouragingly at Ross. "That would be lovely," she said. "I'll look forward to it."

Ross seemed surprised she had capitulated so easily. "My suite or yours?"

"Mine," said Shelby. At least that way she'd have some degree of control over kicking the bastard out.

* * *

That evening, as Shelby changed out of her work clothes into something more casual for her meeting with Ross, she could hear Luke and his cronies still frenziedly partying below. She had been glad to leave him in the capable hands of Bruno, whose nose had been severely put out of joint by the arrival of Shark and his easy-going flirtations with Courteney.

She pulled black jeans over a matching velvet body, pausing to frown at her concave stomach in the mirror opposite. "Just call me the Invisible Man," she murmured and threw on a pewter silk shirt to disguise it, not bothering with the buttons, just tying it loosely at the waist.

There was a sudden dull thud at the door and she opened it reluctantly, wary of the mood she might find Ross in. He was smartly dressed in white shirt and suit trousers but no jacket or tie, almost as though he hadn't finished dressing. Having never seen him wearing anything other than a plaid shirt and jeans, she was surprised. Perhaps he was going out later with Paige.

"Hi," she said. "Come in."

Ross gave an indistinct gurgle and fell through the door, landing by her feet. Shelby stared at him in shock. Was he drunk?

"Ross?" she said uncertainly. "Are you all right? If this is your idea of a joke –" She bent down beside him, about to prod him with her finger when she saw the bright crimson stain drenching his white shirt.

Shelby screamed but no one came running. She watched the blood drip, drip dripping onto the carpet. His eyes were closed, the colour had drained from his face leaving his skin grey. She stretched out one finger to gently stroke his cheek. It was cold and moist with perspiration. Then Ross groaned and the stark reality of it all hit her square in the face.

He was dying. And she was the only person who could save him.

Chapter Twenty-six

Luke sat on the bar stool slowly sipping his glass of Chardonnay but his heart wasn't in it. Alcohol just didn't give him the same buzz any more. All he wanted to do was go up to his room, learn his lines for tomorrow and sleep. He must be getting old.

He was surrounded by several men in suits, like an undertakers' convention, leaning menacingly on the bar, glaring at anyone who dared to venture into their territory. Luke felt the familiar dark cloud descend over him. All these security guys; it was ridiculous. He wasn't Michael Jackson. His fellow drinkers were the film crew and hotel guests, foreign tourists who couldn't tell him from any other two-bit English actor.

Bruno and Shark standing next to each other, emphasising their unequal heights, looked particularly ridiculous – like the Blues Brothers. He kept expecting them to break into song and tap-dance along the bar.

Luke poured himself another drink. Perhaps if he got completely rat-arsed his hallucinations might improve radically enough to include a few half-naked showgirls.

Kit, perched like a moulting cockatoo on the bar stool beside him, knew better than protest at the amount of alcohol he was consuming. Besides, Kit himself was on his sixth cocktail, having recently discovered banana daiquiris following a wild Caribbean night at one of the local nightclubs.

Seeing Kit stab a piece of banana as it floated past, Luke remembered Shelby drinking those peculiar blue cocktails, the night they nearly made love in Ross's pool. The way she had popped a scarlet cherry into his mouth, daring him to mischief. He closed his eyes, feeling the despair wash over him. How his ex-girlfriends would laugh if they could see him now. The heartbreaker with a terminally cracked heart.

He heard a sharp snap and found pink Chardonnay pouring from his fingers, thoroughly soaking his shirt, accompanied by a intense pain in his hand.

Kit was on his feet in seconds, shaking at his turquoise shirt. "Jesus, Luke! What the fuck did you do? You've just showered me in glass."

But Luke was staring blankly at his hand, then down at the shards of glass sparkling against the denim. *Pink* Chardonnay?

Kit firmly removed the broken wine-glass from Luke's hand. "You're bleeding."

It could have been Kensington Gore for all the effect it was having on him. "So I am," he said numbly, watching copious amounts of B positive slowly drip off the end of his fingers, splashing crimson dots onto the grey dusty flagstone below, until it resembled a painting by Damien Hirst.

"Well, do something," fretted Kit. "I don't like the sight of blood."

"It's not your blood, so why worry?" Luke looked vaguely about for a napkin. While he wasn't particularly bothered about bleeding to death, he would hate to make a mess for some other poor bugger to clean up.

Shark dunked Luke's cut hand in Bruno's glass of mineral water, embalmed it in floral paper napkins, then calmly wrapped a handkerchief around it. "You'll live," he pronounced with a golden grin, deftly tying off the knot and tucking in the ends.

"Thanks." Even Shark's handkerchief was black, realised Luke – colour co-ordinated with the rest of his wardrobe. He stood up to carefully shake the broken glass from his jeans and the barman appeared at his feet with a dustpan and brush.

He handed the barman a crumpled tenner. "Sorry."

The barman handed it back. "No problem, Mr McFadden."

Why did everyone have to be so nice to him all the time? In the old days he'd have been chucked out. It was nauseating. He made films for a living; he wasn't a brain surgeon; he didn't save lives; he just spent his working life pretending to be someone else and earning an indecent amount for it.

Suddenly he longed for the time, not so long ago,

when he was so desperate for work he would dress up as a burger to advertise his local fast-food chain. And girls would sleep with him because they loved him, or at least liked him, and not because they wanted to be featured in *Hello!* the following week.

He left the money on the bar. "I have a headache," he told Shark. "I'm going back to my suite."

Shark drained the remainder of his orange juice. "No problem, Mr McFadden."

"On my own," added Luke firmly. "Why don't you take the night off, see the Roman Baths, take in a movie. In fact, why not take the rest of the year off too. Consider yourself redundant."

"Mr McFadden?"

"I mean it. I don't need a bodyguard, I'm a crap English actor not some Head of State. No one is going to assassinate me. And if I can't handle the press, and a few over-enthusiastic fans, I had no business taking up acting in the first place."

Shark regarded him thoughtfully. "I'll escort you to the first floor, Mr McFadden."

Luke sighed. The guy obviously ran on Duracell batteries. "You can walk me to the staircase but don't expect me to kiss you goodnight."

There was a flash of gold as Shark produced another of his rare smiles. "I guess we have a deal, Mr McFadden."

Kit, who had rushed off to rinse out his shirt in the Gents', ran to catch up. "Hey! Wait for me! Where are we going now?"

"*I'm* going to bed," said Luke grimly. "I'm tired."

Kit was not impressed. "What's up with you? You used to be such a party animal."

"Mid-life crisis."

"You must be sickening for something," said Kit, then paused and smiled. "Or perhaps someone? A skinny little redhead?"

Luke did not even bother to reply, just strode up the staircase, two steps at a time, leaving Shark in reception and Kit puffing far behind. And as he rounded the corner, fumbling in the pocket of his jeans for his keys, he fell over Ross, bleeding all over the hall carpet.

* * *

Shelby and Luke sat silently in the ambulance as it hurtled down the hill through Bath. The blue light bounced off their white, pinched faces, as though they were wallflowers at some surreal disco. Shelby was holding so tightly to Luke's hand her nails had left little half-moon marks in his skin. He noticed her eyes never left Ross. She must really love him, he thought and blinked hard. Damn these wretched contact lenses.

The ambulance parked in the Accident & Emergency bay, and Ross, still hooked to a battery of drips, was whisked off towards the operating theatre. Luke bought Shelby a cup of coffee, which she didn't drink, merely chewed relentlessly on the plastic spoon until it finally broke in two. Luke, to try to take his mind off Ross, found himself leafing through the women's magazines again. It didn't matter which hospital they were in, they were all the bloody same.

Vaguely he was aware of a woman's high heels clicking into his viewpoint. Thinking she was a nurse, he jumped to his feet and found himself on eye level with the glamorous DS Nadia Meyer. Her sleek black hair was styled in its usual chignon. Her make-up was air-hostess perfect. Her resemblance to Paloma Picasso uncanny. She even wore the same colours – red, black and white. Considering she had been up all night, she looked as though she'd just stepped off the cover of *Vogue*. Luke felt extremely conscious of the fact that he looked as though he'd just stepped out of the nearest ditch.

She seemed surprised to see him. "Hello, Mr, McFadden. I didn't realise you were such a friend of Mr Whitney?"

Luke smiled non-committally. "I'm here to keep Shelby company."

Her brown eyes softened. "Finding Mr Whitney like that must have been a terrible shock for her. Have you any idea how he came to be in such a way?"

"How the hell should I know?" Even to himself his voice did not sound very convincing. Sheer tiredness and misery overwhelmed him. "That's your job, isn't it? To find out 'whodunit'?"

The brown eyes frosted over, her mouth tightened, the bright crimson lipstick disappearing into a thin angry line.

"Sorry," he muttered, running his fingers through his hair. "I'm so sorry. I didn't mean to be rude, it's just . . . well, I don't pretend that I like the bast – I mean,

Ross – but I wouldn't want him to die, not like this. I wouldn't want anyone to die like this . . ."

"I have to do my job, Mr McFadden. I'm sorry if it seems as though I'm trampling all over your feelings but I have to find who did this in case they do it again."

DS Meyer spoke as though explaining the mechanics of Play-Doh to a three-year-old. Luke slumped back into his seat without bothering to reply, in case he succumbed to his overwhelming temptation to wring her long, elegant neck.

She glanced across at Shelby, who was mindlessly shredding one of the yellowing house plants on the windowsill. "I believe Mr Whitney was found in Miss Roberts's suite?"

"*Outside.* Shelby opened her door and there he was, unconscious and bleeding. Are you suggesting she did it?"

"And you were with her?"

"Yes, we spent the evening together – that is, she's my bodyguard."

DS Meyer consulted her notebook. "According to the hotel manager, you spent the evening in the Neptune Bar in company with Charles Smith, Bruce Hargreaves and Christopher McKinley. He didn't mention Miss Roberts at all." She smiled kindly. "Perhaps you would care to revise that last statement?"

Luke stared at her. She didn't care about trampling over anyone's feelings. She was just pretending to be kind to lull him into a false sense of security, just like a fucking journalist. She was convinced Shelby had knifed Ross, perhaps due to a lovers' tiff, and that was what the bitch was out to prove.

"Shelby didn't stab Ross," he said firmly, trying to keep a hold of his temper. "You know she wouldn't. She's more likely to break his neck with a judo throw – why waste time with irrelevancies like knives?" He broke off as a thought occurred to him. "Have you actually found a murder weapon?"

DS Meyer smiled tightly. "This is getting us nowhere –"

Luke leant back in his chair. "Perhaps you'd better wait until Ross regains consciousness and then you can ask him yourself. Can I get you a coffee? How about a copy of *Woman's Weekly*? There's a fab knitting pattern on page 20."

DS Meyer ignored him and walked across to where Shelby was staring miserably out of the window, oblivious to any undercurrents swirling around the waiting-room. "Miss Roberts?" she said brightly. "Would you mind coming to the station to answer a few questions?"

Luke was between them in seconds. "Are you arresting her?"

"It is voluntary," said DS Meyer.

"Then she stays here!"

Shelby calmly laid her hand on his shoulder. "It's OK," she said listlessly. "We have to catch the person who did this. You stay with Ross. I'll be fine."

He took hold of her hand, encasing her cold fingers in his own. "Shelby, don't let them bully you into this. You don't have to go. Let them get a warrant."

She looked him straight in the eyes. "I'll be fine," she repeated firmly.

"Shelby –"

"This is something I have to do. For Ross."

* * *

DS Meyer drove Shelby to the police station in an unmarked car – perhaps it was her own – and escorted her into an interview room, bare save for a table, chairs – and tape recorder.

Shelby looked at it in surprise. "Are you sure you haven't arrested me?" she said, only half-joking.

DS Meyer smiled. "This is just an informal question-and-answer session. You can have a solicitor present if you wish?"

Shelby lowered herself into one of the chairs. "I have nothing to hide."

DS Meyer broke open some tapes, inserted them into the machine and pressed 'record'. Shelby confirmed her name and date of birth.

DS Meyer opened her briefcase and took out a small transparent plastic bag. "Could you take a look at this?"

"What is it?" asked Shelby, feeling the nausea rising within. She hoped to God it wasn't the knife which had so nearly killed Ross. But as she held out her hand she found she held the shattered remains of a cheap pen, sliding about in a small polythene bag. Clearly marked on one shard was 'Disney World'.

"Is it yours?" asked DS Meyer politely.

How on earth had the police got hold of this? The

last Shelby had seen of Courteney's violet pen was buried beneath a clump of make-up-stained cotton wool, at the bottom of her waste-paper basket. Shelby tried to read a motive in those slanting brown eyes. But the DS looked as enigmatic as ever. She'd make a terrific poker player.

"I thought we were here to talk about Ross?" she said at last, stalling until she could think up a reasonable lie.

"The pen, the stabbing, I believe everything is connected."

Bloody hell, the woman was good. It was almost as though she could hack into her mind. It was also extremely unnerving. Shelby wasn't so keen to be on the other side of the interviewing. But still, she had no skeletons in her closet, so why was she worried? She just had to remain calm and tell the woman the truth.

Shelby firmly handed back the pen. "This is Courteney's pen, not mine. I've never been to Disney World. I've never even been to America. Check my passport. I've visited Greece twice, plus Tunisia, Morocco and France on a day trip when I was fifteen." And that, at least, was the truth.

DS Meyer calmly placed the bag back on the table. "We believe this pen was used to write the hate mail Miss O'Connor has been receiving."

"You're probably right." Shelby, almost without realising she was doing so, picked the bag up again and turned it over in her hands. The ink was already staining the plastic violet. "I discovered the pen in

Courteney's bedroom," she found herself saying. "Tucked away in a drawer. I think she had forgotten it. Her suitcases were all packed ready for her to move to another suite but this had been left behind."

DS Meyer regarded her curiously. "Why were you in her suite? I thought you were Mr McFadden's bodyguard."

"Like you, I had my suspicions that she was stalking herself. Remember I mentioned the kid at Priory Park? The one in the red jumper? He told me Courteney had paid him to fire a gun at her and miss. Perhaps she's trying to get out of doing the film? I don't know how these things work but I assume if she just upped and left Ross would sue. He's like that." She paused for a moment. "The irony was, no one heard the gunfire – no one would have even noticed if Octavia's horse hadn't bolted – and the National Trust hadn't discovered a bullet hole in their precious Palladian bridge."

If DS Meyer believed a word she said she wasn't showing it. "Why didn't you say something at the time?"

"I just thought it was my overactive imagination. I needed proof. So I broke into Courteney's hotel room and found this pen. Like you, I guessed it had been used to write the hate mail. It was in one piece then – I broke it doing Tarzan impressions, jumping from Courteney's balcony to Ross's, to escape discovery by the hotel porter."

DS Meyer was staring incredulously at her. "You jumped from one balcony to another, just to get this pen?"

"Er, yes." Stated baldly like that, it did appear more than a little crazy. Shelby felt her face begin to glow. "It seemed like a good idea at the time," she said lamely.

"And you now agree that Miss O'Connor might have sent herself a death certificate and a funeral wreath? That she was capable of placing a dead bird on her own pillow?"

"That bit I'm not sure about. She seemed genuinely upset – but then, she is an actress."

DS Meyer smiled. "I know I said that last time – but, to be honest, I've seen her films – she's not that good."

"I still don't see how you can connect her stalker with Ross being stabbed."

"Me neither, but I'm working on it." DS Meyer switched off the tape recorder. "Meanwhile, you're free to go. Thank you for being so frank. Would you like me to drive you back to the hospital?"

They were letting her go? Just like that? "No thanks," she murmured, feeling that somehow it would betray Luke. "I'll get a cab from the train station."

* * *

Shelby walked slowly along the pavement towards the taxi rank, wondering why on earth she cared about Luke's hurt feelings, when she had never cared much about them before. The sun was just beginning to lighten the navy-blue of the sky and it was eerily quiet. No traffic, no tourists, no noise. Just the great pale buildings, looming over her like silent tombs.

She crossed the road to the station, not bothering to

press the light for the pedestrian crossing, or even checking for cars. It was like a ghost town. That's what Bath was, she decided. Some great relic from the past, one up from Stonehenge. Even the train station looked like a stately home.

Home. There's no place like home. Home is where the heart is. Shelby sighed. What wouldn't she give for a pair of ruby slippers!

There was a sudden noise, a rush of air, and a black BMW swished to a halt beside her. She recognised the car as belonging to Firestorm but instead of one of the part-time chauffeurs driving, it was Bruno.

"Good morning, Shelby," he said, and very nearly smiled. "Can I give you a lift back to the hotel?"

"Thanks," she said, fumbling with the door handle. "Did they drag you in for questioning too? DS Meyer must really be clutching at straws."

Bruno didn't reply. He seemed more interested in the catch on the door. "Is it jammed?" he asked, opening the driver's side and hurrying around to help her. Even this early in the morning he looked immaculate. Shelby wondered if he slept in his suit and tie. She couldn't imagine him wearing anything else, even pyjamas. "It does that sometimes. Here, let me get it for you."

Shelby stood aside while he tried the handle again and opened it. "There you go," he said, holding the door for her.

Shelby bent her head to climb into the front seat when suddenly a damp white cloth was thrust over her face. Shelby recoiled instinctively but fell against

Bruno's barrel-like chest. His thick muscular arms were around her like a bear-hug, pinning her arms to her sides. It was too late to struggle, it was too late to do anything.

As she began to feel sick and faint, she realised the cloth had been impregnated with a chemical – chloroform? Unable to loosen his hold on her, she resorted to using her teeth and nails, like any hysterical female, stamping on his foot, wishing she was wearing stilettos like Paige, but Bruno could have been Mount Everest for all the effect she had.

As she opened her mouth wider to scream, frantically turning her head from side to side, the cloth entered her mouth, making her gag. She tried coughing it out before it choked her but only succeeded in breathing more of the stuff in.

Whatever the chemical was, it soon began to take effect, making her vision appear as though everything was down a long black tunnel. Why didn't anyone help her? Couldn't they see she was being kidnapped in broad daylight? Why didn't someone do something? The police station was just up the road for Christ's sake!

Gradually her strength ebbed away, her legs buckled beneath her. She could hear her heart beating, her own laboured breathing then, like an old TV, the tunnel abruptly narrowed to a pinpoint of light and the world went black.

Chapter Twenty-seven

Shelby opened her eyes. It didn't make a difference. She could have been in the depths of Wookey Hole for all the daylight she could see. Hearing the gentle hum of an engine, the swishing of rubber tyres against tarmac, she realised she was lying on the back seat of the BMW. The skin around her nose and mouth felt sore and there was also something rough and dusty scratching against her face, making her nose tickle. Bruno had covered her head in what felt like an old dog blanket. She supposed she should be grateful he had not shoved her into the boot.

She sneezed and felt it ricochet back. Yuck. She had to get this thing off her face. Except her hands seemed to be bound behind her back . . . Shelby felt the fury scorch up her backbone. What the fuck did Bruno think he was doing?

The car swerved around a corner, bumped over uneven ground, braked and the engine was switched off. Shelby imagined a deserted lane, a dark, forbidding wood, where a body could remain undisturbed for months.

She lay perfectly still as the driver's door opened, her ears straining for the next sound. Bruno roughly grabbed her ankles, dragging her along the back seat and through the passenger door. Biting off a curse, Shelby deliberately made herself as heavy as possible, pretending to be still unconscious. She was damned if she was going to make it easy for him.

"Christ, for a little thing, you're a dead weight," he grunted, dropping her on the ground.

Shelby's face hit the deck, her teeth split her lip and she got a mouth full of dirty blanket. She began to choke on dust and blood and Bruno pulled the blanket from her head, taking a clump of hair with it. Her resolutions to remain calm floated off with the breeze.

"You bastard," she croaked, her eyes streaming. "What the fuck do you think you're doing? Has that brain cell of yours completely flipped out? Or do you get your kicks from tying up women?"

His lips twisted. "Like your ex-boyfriend, you mean?"

Ross . . . Her face coloured. *How on earth* – His words forced her to reassess the situation. She was not going to get out of here by antagonising him.

"Look, Bruno," she said sweetly, "just untie me. I don't care why you've done this; I just want you to let me go. OK? Just undo these ropes and let me walk away and I promise I won't tell a soul."

Bruno merely picked up the blanket, folded it neatly into four and placed it carefully on the back seat. After locking up the car, he conscientiously set the alarm. It was surreal. He could have been going on a picnic.

"Bruno, are you listening to me?"

"Yes."

"Then answer me!"

He crouched beside her, amused as she flinched away. "Your nose is bleeding."

"So is my mouth. Neither of which is surprising considering you've just slam-dunked my face into a field. Why are you doing this to me, Bruno?"

"Sorry," he replied. "It's not personal." But he made no move to blot away her blood with the immaculately folded handkerchief poking from his breast pocket.

That was crimson too, she found herself thinking. So it wasn't as though her blood would stain the silk . . . Shelby felt another surge of rage and kicked out with all she was worth. Her feet slammed into his waiting fist; his solid body didn't even sway. In fact, he seemed amused.

"Is that the best you can do?"

"Flat on my back and trussed up like a bondage queen? Yeah, that's the best I can do. So why don't you untie me and let's make it more even."

He stood up. "Sorry. No can do."

Shelby howled in frustration. As she lay on the ground, frantically trying to formulate an escape plan, she suddenly recognised her surroundings. Grass, trees, wild flowers and a fast flowing river. They were back in the same place where they had filmed on Friday. Where Floyd had had his heart attack . . .

Bruno saw her shiver. "You've finally realised where you are? Not very observant for a police officer are you?"

She forced her voice to remain calm. "I know you're Courteney's stalker . . ."

"And how long did it take you to come to that conclusion?" he scoffed. "You and the Jane Tennison wannabe, scurrying around, convinced the stalker was some mythical kid in a red jersey. I suppose that's what happens when the police hire women to do a man's job."

"It was you who sent the hate mail, the funeral wreath . . ."

"No, the silly cow sent them to herself. Some people will do anything for attention."

"But the dead bird? Surely Courteney wouldn't –"

"That was me," admitted Bruno, "and the photos of her shagging Irving too. Although God knows what she sees in that pathetic wimp."

"Photos?"

He smirked. "They didn't tell you?"

Obviously not.

What Irving and Courteney got up to in their free time was not uppermost in her mind at the moment. She shifted slightly, twisting her fingers back on themselves, frantically trying to lever off the rope that bound her wrists. Her face, though, remained the picture of serenity.

"Why are you doing this?" she asked Bruno. "Why would you want to stalk Courteney? Does it give you a feeling of power, frightening a world-famous film star half to death? Or is it all part of some larger plan? Are you jealous of her romances with Ross and Irving? Do you want her for yourself? That's it, isn't it? By making her reliant upon you for her safety and security, you're hoping she will fall in love with you? You want her to see you as some kind of hero – which is why you hate me – because I'm the kind of hero you'll never be."

"Quit the psychoanalysing," he snapped. "You don't know me. How can you possible comprehend what I want, what I'm thinking?"

Shelby allowed herself a small smile of victory. At last she had got under his skin. "It won't work, you know. Courteney's in love with my brother."

By virtually dislocating her thumb, she was able to force it between the rope, move it an inch across her wrists, across the fleshy part of her other hand, where it jammed, cutting off her circulation. Slowly, her hand began to go numb. She carried on talking, hoping Bruno would not realise anything untoward.

"Courteney, more than anyone, is not one to play the victim unless it suits her purpose. She's not the type to dream about Prince Charming sweeping her off her feet. You're deluding yourself, Bruno. Courteney's not holding on for a hero to make her life complete. She's doing it by herself."

"Like you?" he sneered. "Racing off after a bolting horse, capturing a mugger single-handedly, giving the

383

kiss of life to a drunk. Can you catch bullets between your teeth too?"

"Well, I wouldn't go that far –"

"You're always saving people in trouble." Bruno slowly bent down, until his face was a few inches from hers. "Tell me, Shelby, who's going to rescue *you*?"

"Rescue me?" Shelby laughed with a confidence she did not feel. "I don't need rescuing . . ."

Bruno slipped his hand behind her back, turning her over, and firmly pushed the rope back into its original position around her wrists. "No?"

Shit!

And with her arms thus confined, he was able to scoop her effortlessly into his arms, and stride down the hill towards the fast-flowing water.

Don't panic, she told herself, repeating the mantra that had served her so well during her years in the police. This is not a problem. This is an opportunity.

An opportunity to do what, for fuck's sake!

"Where are we going?" she felt compelled to ask – although she wasn't so keen to know the answer.

"I'm going back to the hotel," he replied. "You're going to the bottom of the River Avon. With rope around your ankles." He gave a short laugh as Shelby's face finally registered shock – and panic. "Weren't those your exact words?" he taunted.

"When the police were interviewing Courteney –" She broke off and attempted a crooked smile. "This is a joke, right?" Her words came out faster and more garbled as the reality of it all hit her in the face with the force of a breeze block. "As you chuck me in the river, John and Shark are going to jump out of the bushes with party-poppers and streamers and we'll all have a good laugh and then go down the pub. Right?"

"I don't joke," said Bruno. He stood on the very edge of the river, paused for an agonisingly long few seconds, then abruptly dropped her into the water.

Despite the warm spring weather the river was icy and such a shock it took all Shelby's self-control not to take a deep breath. She felt herself sink like a lump of concrete, bouncing off the bottom, jarring every bone in her body. She tried to dig her heels into the gravel and force her way back to the surface, which shimmered tantalisingly above her head, but the strength of the current dragged her along, through tangles of slimy weeds, slamming her against the rubbish rotting in the mud.

The water was so murky she could barely see a few feet in front of her face and she was thrown against an old oil can. The corroded metal slashed through her shirt, cutting a nasty zigzag wound into her arm and, in her disorientated state, all she could think was, 'Lucky I'm up to date with my tetanus shots . . .'

The water clouded with her blood but the pain sharpened her concentration. She tried to kick out for the surface but the slimy weeds were wound around her ankles and she was caught. She couldn't hold her breath for much longer. A thought flashed through her mind – she could use the edge of the oil can to cut the rope from her wrists. But just then the weight of her body dislodged the can from the silt and the current took it bobbing along the river bed and out of sight.

For a moment Shelby felt real terror. She was going to *die*? *Like this?*

Desperately she tried to kick out towards the surface again – but it was hopeless. The weeds around her ankles were holding her down and the current kept smashing her against the bank, knocking out what little air remained in her lungs in a flurry of tiny bubbles. Forced to snatch a sudden breath, she felt the grey river water being drawn deep inside her, choking her.

Then something grabbed hold of her belt and she was being dragged upwards. Her world exploded in a mass of light and sound and suddenly she was heaved onto the muddy bank and a man scrambled up beside her.

"Breathe, Shelby, breathe," he was saying, banging her on the back and pulling the rope from her wrists.

Through streaming tears she could see Luke, soaking wet, water dripping off his eyelashes and nose, his face a ghastly grey-green. He slapped her on the back again. *You're doing it all wrong*, she wanted to say, but her words came out as a peculiar gurgle and instead she puked up a lungful of dirty river water all over his jeans.

"I'm sorry," she croaked, her throat feeling as though someone had played noughts and crosses in it with a razor blade. She coughed and threw up again.

But Luke threw his arms around her, squeezing her tight, and covering her face in butterfly kisses. "Who cares! I've got you back and that's all that matters."

Unable to get her head around his sudden, overwhelming affection, she murmured, "Where's Bruno?"

"I tied him up with a length of his own rope and threw him in the boot of his car. Bloody pervert."

She was shocked. "Will he be able to breathe?"

"Who gives a shit?" Then he laughed at her expression. "I was *joking*! A policeman has him handcuffed in the back of a patrol car."

"Police?" she said vaguely. It was all too much for her to cope with. Where did his jokes end and the truth begin? "Are they here too? How did you find me?"

"I caught a taxi to the police station only to see Bruno bundling you into the BMW. So I said to the driver, 'Follow that car'. Except he thought I was taking the piss and chucked me out onto the pavement. Fortunately, darling Nadia came to the rescue – commandeered half the Avon and Somerset police force – and here we all are."

Darling Nadia? Surely he didn't mean –

"Hello, Shelby," said DS Meyer, the original lady in red, looming over Luke's shoulder. "For a moment we were really worried about you."

"Thanks," muttered Shelby, burningly conscious of being soaked with river water and covered in blood and sick. "Me too." She caught Luke admiring the police woman's long slender legs, stunningly displayed in black stockings and four-inch stilettos, which were slowly sinking into the soggy meadow, and was surprised at the streak of jealousy which shot through her. I bet 'Darling Nadia' doesn't get to chase many villains in those shoes, she thought enviously.

Shelby wiped the worst of the blood and mud from her face with her sleeve. "So, now we know – Bruno's the stalker. Did he stab Ross too?"

"Er, no." DS Meyer took a packet of paper tissues from her shoulder bag and handed them to Shelby. "It's like this. Shortly after you left, a young woman came into the station to confess it was she who stabbed Mr Whitney. At the very same time, one of my officers, waiting at Mr Whitney's bedside, telephones to inform me that while Mr Whitney has regained consciousness and is expected to make a full recovery, he has also made a statement to the effect that he actually fell onto a paperknife. He was not stabbed by some unknown assassin – the whole incident was an unfortunate accident."

Although relieved that Ross was finally out of danger, Shelby could not help but comment on the whacking great holes she perceived in this story. "He fell onto a paperknife?" she derided, remembering all the blood that had pumped from his wound. "What, after wedging it between the floorboards first?"

DS Meyer raised an elegant eyebrow. "And I thought I was a cynic."

"Who confessed?"

"Dulcie Gordon. A freelance make-up artist."

"*Dulcie*? *Dulcie* stabbed him? I don't believe it!" And then Shelby remembered the scene in Ross's bedroom, when Dulcie had virtually offered herself to him as a TV dinner.

"Apparently she had been having an affair with Mr Whitney and was jealous of the er, way in which he remained on good terms with all his ex-girlfriends."

"Tell me about it," sighed Shelby, allowing Luke to help her to her feet. He gently wrapped a blanket around her shoulders. For a brief moment, that small act of kindness almost caused her to break down completely.

"As we have no evidence, and of course without Mr Whitney's support, we cannot press charges," said the DS, "I would be grateful if you could keep it to yourself. Now, I'll get one of the lads to take you into hospital, get you checked over. Mr McFadden? I'm afraid I need you down at the station to give a statement. You can shower and change there."

Luke frowned. "Can't I just see Shelby's all right?"

"Er, no, sorry. We've got Mr Hargreaves in the back of the patrol car and if we want to keep him in the cells overnight we need your statement as evidence."

Luke ruffled the top of Shelby's head. "Will you be all right on your own?"

"Fine," she lied. "You know me. I'm an ex-police officer, a bodyguard. This sort of thing happens to me all the time." She attempted a bright smile. "I'm Errol Flynn in lipstick and short skirt."

Luke's eyes were warm with affection. "My very own Calamity Jane."

* * *

Shelby watched the acid hedgerows fly past. The young PC was taking her to the same hospital to which the

ambulance had taken Floyd two nights ago. She tried
to rest her throbbing head in her hands but found they
were shaking too much. She wanted to cry. What the
hell was happening to her? She bit determinedly on her
thumb, and tried to think of something else, blinking
away the tears pricking her eyelids. She couldn't break
down now. Not here. It would be too embarrassing.

"Are you OK?" asked the young PC, looking
concerned.

Or in other words, 'Don't you dare have a nervous
breakdown on my shift'. She stifled a hysterical giggle.
He reminded her so much of PC Wells.

"Yes," she muttered between gritted teeth. "I'm *fine!*"
She pulled the sodden blanket away from her shoulders
and tossed it onto the back seat. "Absolutely terrific. I've
been chloroformed, kidnapped, chucked into an icy river
and half-drowned. But I was rescued by a hero so I guess
that makes it all right – *of course I'm fucking fine!*"

"Sorry," muttered the PC. "I expect you're in shock.
It often happens like that – hits you later when
everything's OK."

Patronising weasel! She took a deep breath. "I'm
sorry if I'm taking it out on you, but I don't really want
to go to hospital. I just want a nice warm bath, some
chocolate, and twelve hours' sleep. Could you drop me
off in town? I'll find my own way back to the hotel."

"But my orders were –"

"To hell with your orders, show a little independent
spirit for Christ's sake! You're going back to the station,
aren't you? It's hardly out of your way?"

"But –"

"Tell them I put you in a headlock."

A glimmer of a smile appeared on his face as he surveyed her slight, bedraggled frame. "Right . . ."

He dropped her off outside the police station. She waited until he had locked up the patrol car and disappeared inside, and from there it was a short walk for her down to the train station. When she reached the pedestrian crossing she stopped. This was where it had happened. This was where Bruno had chloroformed her. She clutched onto the traffic light for support, feeling the city do a circuit around her.

"Get a grip!" she muttered fiercely. "Where's your backbone, girl? Your British stiff upper lip?"

Totally unaware of the curious glances she was generating, Shelby gingerly released her grip on the traffic-light and walked across the road, oblivious that the light was green and a car had to veer onto the traffic island to avoid her. There was a smash and tinkle of glass but Shelby heard nothing. She was concentrating on putting one foot before the other, watching the train station wobble closer towards her.

The lobby was heaving with tourists. All nationalities, all ages. She cannoned off several rucksacks to a chorus of disapproval but even if she had understood the languages she didn't hear anything. She just pushed to the front of the queue at the ticket office and emptied her purse on the counter. Pound coins, coppers and a shoal of silver spun in all directions, ricocheting off the floor. A couple of well-dressed, middle-aged ladies scrambled around picking them up for her, muttering about 'care in the community'.

Shelby ignored them. "I want to get as near to Calahurst as possible," she said to the clerk, "and I don't care if I have to ride in with the baggage."

Chapter Twenty-eight

Shelby arrived back at her flat in Calahurst just before lunch and was able to slip up the stairs without bumping into any of her neighbours. She turned the key in the lock, pushed against her door, which slid open an inch and then stuck firmly. She cursed under her breath. The joys of living in a Victorian house.

Shelby gave the door a hefty kick and it scraped inwards, just wide enough for her to squeeze through. The jam was caused by a sea of envelopes (mostly brown), junk mail and free newspapers. She picked up a handful of last reminders, groaned, and scattered them back on the floor. So much for her father's promise to forward her mail, and water her few remaining pot plants – they were probably now potpourri.

Slamming the door, she kicked the debris to one side, took the phone off the hook and, without getting undressed, climbed into bed and fell into a deep, thankfully dreamless, sleep. The events of the last forty-eight hours had been too traumatic for her to desire a repeat performance.

By the time she woke it was late afternoon. The sun, now low in the sky, glittered on the River Hurst far away in the distance and brought a warm glow to the mellowed brick houses along the High Street. She showered and pulled on a pair of shorts and T-shirt – such a relief to be out of those damn suits – and stumbled into the kitchen in search of lunch – or should that be dinner?

She used to keep several tins of food at the back of the larder for emergencies but, following the crises of Christmas, she was down to a rusting tin of chicken korma, six months out of date. Knowing perfectly well her bank account was empty, she dialled out for a pizza and a tub of chocolate ice cream, wantonly committing credit-card fraud. At least she'd be sure of regular meals and early nights in Holloway.

By six o'clock she was no longer hungry but was decidedly bored. If she had been in Bath, they would be filming the last few scenes; Luke and his motley gang of sparks and grips would be planning the night's pub crawl. But no, she wasn't going to think about Luke.

Which was easier said than done. Wandering into the kitchen, she found a dusty bottle of beer in the cupboard, still within its sell-by date, and stuck it into the freezer for a quick chill. What the hell she was going to do for the rest of the evening? The second she was alone with her thoughts they strayed. She only had to close her eyes and see the river bed, the reeds tangling around her legs; the horror when she realised she couldn't breathe . . . that she was going to drown . . .

Shelby rubbed her hand across her eyes to try to erase the memory. She had to do *something* to take her mind off it. The beer was still lukewarm but she opened it anyway, taking a large, thirsty gulp, feeling the bubbles explode against the roof of her mouth and flood down the back of her throat. Heaven.

She threw herself down onto the sofa and stared at the paler patch in the dust on the TV stand. If she had a TV she could watch one of the soaps or the late-night film. If she still had her VCR she could walk down to the local video store and rent out a blood and guts blockbuster – or even a soppy romance. She wasn't picky. Shelby kicked the coffee table in frustration. It was certainly no fun being poor.

As the table rocked she had a vision of Irving, diving to rescue his drink, as he sat in this very room three months previously. She winced as she recalled how she had pestered him to get her a job with Firestorm Productions. God, if only she had known what a total disaster *that* was going to be.

She took another sip of her beer, vaguely debating whether to pour it into a glass. She had plenty of ice jamming up the freezer. But it seemed a bit pointless now she had almost the finished the bottle. She also began to feel a bit piqued that Irving had left Bath for the US without letting her know. It wouldn't have taken him a moment.

It was also occurring to her that Irving was the proud

owner of six television sets and three video recorders. He was possessive of his belongings, true, but then Irving was thousands of miles away, safely tucked up in a film studio in LA . . . She smiled to herself. After all, what Irv doesn't see, his heart can't grieve after.

* * *

Irving's flat, in a beautiful converted Georgian town house, overlooked the Quay, just two doors down from their father's pub, The Parson's Collar. Shelby had no trouble gaining entry; she had a key and the code to Irving's alarm, and even the uniformed commissioner recognised her, barely looking up from his desk to nod a greeting.

She stepped into the womb-like confines of the shiny gold elevator and left her stomach behind as the elevator shot up to the top floor. Irving's plush penthouse was far nicer than her grotty flat. Perhaps she should just move in for a week or so. She bet he had more than a rusting tin of chicken korma in his larder.

As Irving spent most of the year circling the globe, 'roughing it' in hotels, he rarely took holidays abroad, preferring to veg-out at home. His hard-earned cash was spent on his apartment, particularly his state-of-the-art technical equipment. So Shelby was surprised to find the burglar alarm was not set. She was even more surprised to find the sitting-room light on, Andrea Corr singing softly on the stereo, champagne chilling in a bucket crammed with ice – and Irving and Courteney necking on the sofa.

Courteney saw her first and shrieked, pulling her red dress back up over her shoulders. Irving was on his feet in seconds, brandishing what looked suspiciously like one of Shelby's old judo trophies above his head.

Shelby could not help but burst out laughing. "Are you threatening to lay me out – or offering me a very large drink?"

Irving put down the trophy. "That little round brass thing beside the door is a bell," he said tartly. "Next time I would be grateful if you would ring it before breaking and entering." Shelby was still convulsed by giggles. "It's not that funny, you know."

"Oh Irving, you've cheered me up no end. I'm sorry. I thought you were in LA or I would never have burst in." She glanced across at Courteney, one of the world's biggest movie stars, her lipstick smudged, her dress sliding off one shoulder. She looked thoroughly rumpled and yet somehow rather pleased with herself. Shelby shook her head in disbelief. It was true! Courteney and *Irving*? Bloody hell!

Irving was also taken aback. "Why would I be in LA?"

"Ross said you had to fly out to sort out some business."

"Then he's telling porkies. I've resigned."

"Resigned?" Shelby regarded him blankly. "But why? You loved working for Firestorm Productions. It was your dream."

Irving replaced the trophy in the bookcase, next to the shields he had won at film school. He took his time re-arranging them all. "Ross scrapped the scenes I directed," he admitted eventually, perhaps realising there was no way he could get out of replying. "He said they were . . . crap."

Shelby smiled sympathetically. "Ross would never have been so cruel. You must have misunderstood his constructive criticism –"

Irving's freckles took on a distinctly pink tint. "Ross wanted to re-shoot a complete day's filming. My work may not have been perfect but it wasn't bad enough to do the whole thing over again. He's made me look an idiot, put Firestorm back a day, used up film stocks, not to mention more of his precious budget – and why? Because the prat is so bloody egotistical."

Shelby picked up one of the shields and read her own name on the inscription. Dear, sweet Irving – he had bought her judo trophies back from the pawn shop. He had even polished them. Trouble was, how would she ever pay him back?

"Ross is not egotistical," she said, sliding the shield back onto the shelf before Irving spotted her scrutiny. "A little *obsessive*, I grant you, but –"

"He's just misunderstood?" mocked Irving.

"What would Ross gain by not admitting the truth?"

"His leg over? He's hardly going to admit to firing the brother of his latest conquest. And don't look at me like that. I'm your brother. If I can't say these things to you, who will?"

"I don't need you to tell me how to run my affairs! For your information, I have Ross completely sussed as a womanising creep and he no longer features in my life."

"Thank God," muttered Irving. "I certainly didn't fancy him as a brother-in-law."

Courteney hastily sloshed some champagne into a crystal flute and handed it to Shelby. "Here, have a drink. You look worn out."

"Thanks," said Shelby, and blithely sat on the sofa, wedging herself between Courteney and Irving. "I certainly need it. You wouldn't believe what happened after you two left." As she knocked back the champagne as though it was 7-Up, she realised Irving and Courteney were looking at her expectantly. "No one told you? About Ross?"

"He's been sacked?" said Irving hopefully.

"He can't be fired from his own company," pointed out Courteney.

"He's in hospital," said Shelby. "Dulcie – who, apparently, is madly in love with him – stabbed him." She hesitated, reliving that awful moment. "He nearly died." Reflectively, she swilled the champagne around in her glass. Maybe he'll learn a lesson from this, she thought. That he can't just treat women like disposable characters out of one of his movies. Because real people are not going to keep to the script.

Slowly, Shelby began to tell Irving and Courteney about the last twenty-four hours, from when Ross had collapsed on the floor outside her room, his life-blood pumping out of him, to Bruno throwing her into the river.

Courteney stared at her in shock. "This is all my fault."

"How can Bruno turning out to be a psycho be your fault?" asked Shelby.

"He was my bodyguard."

"You didn't employ him."

"But don't you see? Ross hired Bruno because of all the hate mail – the death threats, the wreath." She paused, took a deep breath and said in a rush, "But I sent them to myself. I never did have a stalker. I made it all up."

"You *haven't* got a *stalker*?" Irving stared at her. "Can you run that by me again?"

Two spots of colour appeared on Courteney's cheekbones and her aquamarine eyes began to slide away from Irving's scrutiny. "I . . . er, don't have a stalker. I never did. I wanted to get out of my contract with Firestorm Productions. It's pathetic but true. I'm supposed to do three films. I've now made one and a half and the idea of spending another three months with Ross working on number three . . ." She grimaced and shook her head. "Jeez, it just doesn't bear thinking about. I wrote myself some hate mail, faked a death certificate and sent a funeral wreath to myself. I decided that if I was too much hassle Ross would get another actress. I sure didn't think he'd go hiring a bodyguard for me! I mean, it's not like I'm the President."

"Which was why you were so upset when Ross called the police to investigate," said Shelby.

"I guess the dead bird must have been Bruno's

work, to make me more vulnerable, more reliant on him, to prove I really did need a bodyguard. But the rest, well, I thought the police would find me out for sure."

Irving was finding it all too difficult to take in. Alice's trip through the looking-glass was a doddle compared to five minutes' conversation with Courteney O'Connor. The girl was not only on another planet, she was coming from a whole new universe.

"So how did you take the photographs of us? Did you have a camera on automatic timer set up in the bedroom?"

"Photographs?" said Courteney, baffled. "What photographs."

"Erm, we'll discuss it later." He hurriedly changed the subject. "If you didn't want to do Ross's films why sign a contract?"

"Ross romanced me, took me out for dinners, bought me flowers – of course, he was too clever to tell me he loved me, I just assumed he did. And just when I'd signed on the dotted line, the bastard announced his engagement to Paige."

And you discovered you were pregnant, thought Shelby.

"Why didn't you confide in me?" Irving was asking Courteney. "Instead of trying to tackle it all on your own?"

Courteney smiled, ruffling up his blond hair in an affectionate manner. "And what would you have done, Clark Kent?"

"Punched the bastard into his own technicolour sunset."

"Exactly, and then Ross would have taken you to court. You know what he's like. His Mama should have named him Sue."

Irving's doorbell suddenly blasted out its usual theme from *Star Wars* (his favourite movie), making them all jump.

"Who's that?" Irving looked at his watch. "Are we expecting anyone?"

"Try answering it," suggested Shelby. "Then you'll find out."

Irving got up, dropping the empty champagne bottle into the bin as he passed. "Bang goes my romantic night in," he grumbled. "Looks like I'm having a party whether I want one or not."

It was Luke. "Hello, Irving," he said. "I seem to have mislaid my bodyguard. Terribly careless I know, but if I promise not to do it again, do you think you could tell me where to find her?"

* * *

Calahurst was an old fishing village on the south coast which now made most of its revenue from the hordes of tourists which flooded the King's Forest every summer. It used to have a certain rustic charm but lately it had become too cute for its own good. Every other store was a 'ye olde tea shoppe' and if you wanted a loaf of bread you had to travel the five miles into Norchester.

After leaving Irving's apartment, Shelby and Luke walked around the horseshoe-shaped Quay until they reached the entrance to the River Hurst and stood looking out over the fast-moving current, which hardly affected the little boats in the harbour.

The spray began to collect on Luke's Predator Raybans like tiny diamonds. He was wearing them in case someone recognised him but, despite his gleaming beauty, no one gave him a second glance. The locals were far too used to the glamorous French and Italians Channel-hopping in their expensive yachts. The breeze whipping up from the coast blew his black Regency curls around his face and he cursed. "I can't wait until this picture's finished and I can cut it all off. My next job is playing second banana to Tom Cruise in a war film." He grinned self-deprecatingly. "I'm his handsome but reckless younger brother."

"Sounds like typecasting," she said dryly. "Do you get shot in the first reel?"

"Second – after I've blown up a German Intelligence HQ."

"Single-handedly?"

"Of course."

"And do you get the girl?"

"No," he sighed, looking back out to the river, where a beautiful yacht was bobbing up the river, perhaps returning from a pleasure trip to the coast. "I never get the girl. Please come back," he said, not taking his eyes from the yacht. "It's only a matter of days until we finish filming."

Although touched, Shelby had to ask, "Is it worth it? Just for three days?"

"It is to me," he said, finally turning away from the

river to stare down at her. For a moment her confused reflection was caught in the two black pools of his sunglasses and then he slowly removed them.

She was surprised at the dark circles beneath the red-veined eyes, the paleness of his skin. It was amazing what Kit could do with a bucket of Max Factor, she caught herself thinking, shortly before she made the mistake of looking directly into his bloodshot eyes. The raw passion made her catch her breath and she had to look away, her heart hammering. Luke? Luke really felt like that – about *her*?

It reminded her of the time she had turned up to take her English GCSE exam, after a weekend of frantic revising, only to discover it was History. Unable to look at him she concentrated on his hands instead, large and strong, gripping at the rusting black railings until the tips of his fingers had turned white. They were not like Ross's hands, but callused and rough. She quickly glanced away to the yacht before her thoughts could wander any further into trouble but it had gone.

"Did you ever see the film, *The French Lieutenant's Woman*?" she babbled, purely to break the silence.

"This isn't Lyme Regis and I'm not Jeremy Irons." One hand abruptly let go of the railings and clutched at her arm instead. His touch felt cold, and wet with the spray from the river. "I'd rather you didn't chuck me in," he said laconically. "It looks awfully chilly."

"I think I've had enough of rivers to last me a lifetime," she replied with some feeling.

"I'm sorry." Absent-mindedly, Luke began to

stroke her skin, up and down. "Me and my big mouth."

"Stop it."

"Stop what?" His palm stroked up her arm, his eyes never left her face.

"You . . . you know what I mean."

He took a step closer. There was only an inch between them.

She swallowed. It was like trying to gag a tennis ball. "Luke, I know you like me but I've only just got over Ross –" She winced at her choice of words – like Ross had been a bout of chickenpox or something.

Luke closed the gap between them, his hands sliding around to her back, caressing her shoulder-blades through the thin material of her T-shirt while his lips moved against hers, soft and persistent, as he pressed her back against the railings. She felt her hands involuntarily creeping up to tangle themselves in his hair as his lips became harder, his tongue exploring her mouth as she felt the fireworks slowly ignite and abruptly pushed him away.

"No!"

Luke gripped the railings again, his face a mask. "No, thank you?"

Shelby put her hands over her eyes. "I'm sorry!"

"Why must you keep saying that!"

She reeled from the vicious note in his voice. "You started it!"

Luke gazed down at the churning water. "Perhaps I had better just fling myself in and have done with it.

She smiled, unaware that it banished the sadness from her eyes.

Louise Marley

"Please come back," he said. "I promise to be on my very best behaviour. Scout's honour."

She played for time. "I didn't know you were in the Scouts?"

He grinned lopsidedly. "Darling, for you I'll even join the Brownies!"

Chapter Twenty-nine

Tuesday

As Luke was not needed on set until the afternoon, Shelby bought a large bouquet of roses (on her credit card) and caught the bus to the hospital to visit Ross. But as she walked across the car park, a chauffeur-driven BMW pulled away from the entrance, with a grey-faced Ross in the back seat, accompanied by a scowling Paige. So Shelby dropped the roses into the nearest bin and jumped on the next bus back to the hotel.

She found Luke in his room, half-heartedly packing.

"Tired of me already?" she joked, although her heart wasn't in it, and she stumbled across to sit on the window seat, gazing out onto the garden so that she wouldn't have to look him in the eye. Although Ross's libertine behaviour had effectively killed her love a long time ago, she could not help feeling disappointed.

When he had poured out his heart to her, revealing the horrors of his childhood and admitting to his complete inability to form any meaningful relationship, she really thought he had reached his own personal turning-point. But then he had effectively fired Irving for no particular reason, lied to her about it, and was still keeping Paige on ice.

Some people never change.

"I thought I'd start getting my stuff ready for Friday," said Luke, as though he could bear the silence no longer. "I'm leaving straight after the Wrap Party."

"Wrap Party?" said Shelby, thinking vaguely of pass-the-parcel. "What's a Wrap Party?"

"It's where all the cast and crew get absolutely plastered, spend a fortune on buying each other farewell 'trinkets' and cards, and become extremely maudlin about parting – secretly delighted they are never going to see each other again."

"Oh, we have those in the police. We call it retirement. Goodbye, Bath," she sighed, pressing her nose against the glass. "It doesn't seem more than a couple of days since I arrived but at least I visited the Roman Baths."

"More than I ever did." Luke, after rolling his underpants into little balls, began stuffing them into his shoes – jammed into the corners of the suitcase. "So when did you have time to visit the Roman Baths?"

"The weekend you returned to London." Realising she had just incriminated herself, she added, "Courteney insisted on a culture trip. Don't you remember? You were there when she asked me to go."

He looked grim. "Courteney, eh?"

Shelby refused to bite. She watched Luke's reflection

in the old warped glass. Now he was tearing off sheets of tissue paper to lay between his clothes. Sometimes he could be too perfect. If only Luke hadn't antagonised her from the first moment they met, maybe she would have fallen in love with him instead of Ross. He was kind, loyal, sexy, funny and supposedly crazy about her to boot. But now it was too late.

Luke carefully folded in another layer of clothes. Perhaps if she asked him nicely he would pack for her too.

"I went to see Ross in hospital today," she said.

Luke barely glanced up. "I thought he had discharged himself?"

"He has." She paused but was unable to stop the words coming out, sounding for all the world like she was spitting tin-tacks. "Paige was there to collect him."

"How sweet." Perhaps because Shelby didn't throw back her usual retort he said slowly, "You're still stuck on him?"

"No."

It was plain he didn't believe her. "Never mind, you have forty-eight hours to get over him. He's gone home to convalesce."

"Gone home?" she repeated faintly. So that was it. She would never see Ross again. Her steely resolve was no longer needed. The irony of it all. Fate didn't even trust her with her own destiny.

"Yes." Luke suddenly started shoving his belongings into his case any old how. "But unfortunately the bastard's coming back."

* * *

Friday

Filming with Irving was a very relaxed affair and Firestorm Productions finally finished *A Midsummer Kiss* on their deadline, although a good six-figure sum over budget. There was an end-of-term atmosphere about the set and, as the last scene was shot, Luke broke open the first of several bottles of champagne, pouring it over Irving's head to loud cheering.

The party was in the grounds of the hotel. The set designer had tried very hard, running amuck with left-over props and fake shrubs, and miraculously transformed a small lawned area with an insignificant ornamental pond into Vauxhall, the legendary pleasure gardens of 18th century London.

Courteney had borrowed her pale pink ballgown from wardrobe and bullied Kit into threading one of his wigs with seed pearls, ribbons and flowers. She had offered to borrow a gown for Shelby too, as some of the other actresses were wearing their costumes but Shelby, having no wish for her own inadequate bosom to be jacked up and exposed to the world at large, had politely declined. Instead she had taken her overdraft into one of Bath's boutiques and come out with another English Eccentrics gown. It was an exquisite silver-blue, delicately embroidered, cut straight across the bodice and held in place by the most fragile silver chains. On her feet she wore transparent, high-heeled mules.

"Wow," said Courteney, when she saw her. "You look like a fairy princess."

"Now all I need is a fairy prince," sighed Shelby, wirling in front of Courteney's full-length mirror.

"Wrong on two counts," said Courteney. "Firstly, gays might be more fun but they make lousy husband material, and secondly, princes have an awful habit of turning into frogs. Trust me on this."

Emboldened by her friend's happy-go-lucky mood, Shelby said, "Courteney, may I ask you a personal question?"

Courteney had begun to carefully paint her lips the palest pink, using a long thin brush. Her eyes twinkled mischievously. "Are my intentions towards your brother honourable? Not in the slightest."

Shelby grimaced. Hell, this was going to be worse than she had thought. Not for the first time, she wondered why she couldn't leave the matter alone but the question she longed to ask kept springing into her mind so often she worried she might blurt it out by accident – perhaps when Irving was around.

As Shelby had remained silent, Courteney quizzically flicked her eyes towards her. "Are you OK? You don't mind me dating Irving, do you?"

She took a deep breath. It was now or never. "Did you send the scan photograph to yourself?"

Courteney froze. The lip liner began to tremble. Slowly she set it down on the dressing-table. "No," she said, her voice oddly flat. "I didn't. Who told you about it?"

Shelby met her challenging gaze head on. Confession time. But why did it have to be so gut-swirlingly awful?

411

"I was in Ross's suite when you came to tell him you'd got it," she replied wretchedly. Then, when the actress merely continued to gaze blankly back, added, "I overheard everything."

"Everything, huh?" Courteney gave a twisted smile, her aquamarine eyes suddenly dull. "No wonder you don't want me to date your brother." She began to carefully line up the bottles of make-up on the dressing-table. "What do you want me to do? I was going to tell him eventually but I thought I'd wait to see how our relationship went. You never know how a guy is going to react. I wanted the moment to be right."

Shelby closed her eyes. It just got worse. "So Irving doesn't know about the abortion?"

"No. You saw how he reacted when I told him I'd dated Ross. How's he gonna feel when he finds out I aborted the man's baby?" Courteney's voice quivered. "I keep telling myself that if I don't think about it, it never happened." She laughed harshly. "I'm your regular, born-again virgin."

Mortified, Shelby put her arm around her shoulder. "Please don't be upset. Forget I ever brought the subject up. If you and Irving love each other that's fine by me. I couldn't be happier. It's just . . . aren't you worried about who sent the picture to you? It obviously wasn't Bruno."

Courteney grabbed a handful of multi-coloured tissues from the complimentary box on the dressing-table and blew her nose. "Oh, I know who sent it. You see, there were only two photographs taken. Mine, which I eventually destroyed, because I couldn't bear to think what might have been, and the one I sent to Ross – to try to get him to change his mind." She laughed hollowly. "As if!"

Shelby felt as though something died inside her. "You think *Ross* sent the photo to you? As some kind of warning not to get involved with Irving?"

"Not his style." Courteney tugged another stream of tissues from the box, like some manic magician, and buried her face in them. "He's not that underhand. No, I reckon it was Paige."

"That doesn't make sense. If you and Ross were no longer seeing each other what has she got to be jealous about?"

"I think it's just a power thing," Courteney caught a glimpse of her reflection, blue mascara streaming down her face, like a seventies Pierrot poster, and winced. "She was just letting me know that she knew all about the baby and it didn't faze her one little bit."

"Interfering bitch," muttered Shelby. "That girl has got a serious problem. You know, I really think she and Ross deserve each other."

Courteney shrugged and dropped a sodden ball of tissues into the bin. "She's just an inadequate, but what really disturbs me is why Ross retained the photograph." Carefully she began to reapply her make-up, although her hand still trembled. "It happened nearly a year ago and he was the one who wanted the termination. *He* was the one who pressurised me, calling night and day to go through with it. Why would he want to keep the damn photo – be reminded of it forever?"

Louise Marley

Shame? wondered Shelby. Remorse? Ross was such an enigma it was impossible to get inside his head, make assumptions about the way he would react, the way he would behave. There was only one person who knew the man behind the carefully constructed facade – and that was Ross himself.

They jumped guiltily as there was a knock at the door. As Courteney showed no sign of moving, Shelby answered it and found Irving on the other side, self-conscious in frock coat and pale yellow breeches, accompanied by Luke wearing crumpled T-shirt, jeans and co-ordinating scowl.

"Come on, Courteney," Luke grumbled, tapping his fingers irritably against the door frame. "We're wasting valuable drinking time. Even I don't take so long to get ready."

"I'm not surprised." Courteney eyed his faded and distinctly ragged jeans disapprovingly. He looked as though he'd just changed the oil-filter on a Mini Cooper. "As you Brits would say, you're letting the side down, Luke."

"Listen, I'm the one that's had to wear the blasted ball-crushers for three months. I deserve time out." He grinned wickedly. "Actually, if you want the truth, I've just set fire to the fucking things. A couple of matches and they went up like Guy Fawkes Night. And when I remember dancing beneath all those spluttering candles at the Assembly Rooms, well, it brings tears to my eyes just thinking about it! It's all right," he added, seeing their staggered expressions. "I had the barbecue

414

on the balcony so I wouldn't set off the sprinkler system."

There wasn't much anyone could add to that. Except Irving, who had gone slightly pale.

"I think Ross was going to flog the costumes to the BBC," he muttered. "But hell, what do I care?" He kissed Courteney's hand. "May I escort you to the ball, Miss O'Connor?"

Courteney dimpled at him. "Oh Irving, you're so romantic . . ."

Luke winked at Shelby and pretended to put his finger down his throat.

Shelby moved in front of him, effectively blocking Irving's view. This new relationship meant a lot to her brother and he could be very sensitive sometimes. Well, *all* the time really.

As she watched Courteney and Irving float off down the corridor, hand in hand, happily in love and blithely oblivious to anyone else, she turned to reprimand Luke for his lack of tact and found he was looking at her very oddly indeed.

He caught hold of her wrist and slammed the door with his free hand. "Gotcha," he smirked, like a schoolboy who had just won at kiss-chase.

She glanced down at his hand, enveloping her wrist, and back to his eyes, alight with triumph and mischief, and felt totally non-threatened. This wasn't a problem, she assured herself. This was just a teensy misunderstanding. All she had to do was explain that, while she found him deeply attractive, and was flattered by his attentions, she couldn't possibly reciprocate them. What could be simpler than that?

"Now, listen, Luke . . . "

"I'm listening." Slowly, teasingly and ultimately relentlessly he pulled her towards him, until her free hand was splayed against his white cotton T-shirt as she tried to gently push him away, without resorting to physical violence.

She could feel the warmth against her palm, his heart beating against her skin. He really ought to do something about that rapid heartbeat, she thought abstractedly, hypnotised by the intense way he was staring at her, his violet-blue eyes almost black with desire.

Of course, I could throw him over my shoulder, she reasoned, thoroughly unsettled by the emotions stirring up inside her. Straight through the open bathroom door. But he would probably end up in the Jacuzzi, or worse, the empty bath, and that would be undignified. Besides, it wasn't as though she didn't like him. Why was she stalling?

His face was several inches closer than it had been and was starting to tilt to one side. It was a while before she realised this was so his nose avoided bumping her nose and he could kiss her more thoroughly. She was now free to escape. Strange thing was, she found she didn't want to. Instead, she kissed him back and everything got rather passionate.

They paused, breathing heavily, staring at each other in shock, then he gathered her up into his arms, strode manfully across the sitting-room and kicked open the bedroom door.

Shelby lent back against his shoulder and savoured the moment. After all, this sort of thing didn't happen to her very often. This sort of thing didn't happen to her at all.

She was dropped gently onto the bed, before his elbows came to rest on either side of her, his eyes looking directly into hers, desperately serious.

"I love you . . ." he said, looking unsure of himself, or perhaps, her . . .

She felt an unfamiliar warmth spread throughout her body. She had been miserable for so long, it took a while for her to identify it as happiness.

"Why are you laughing?" he asked, his handsome face suddenly etched with worry.

She kissed his nose; he looked so sweet. "Because I'm happy."

"Good," he said, suddenly smiling. "I'm happy too."

* * *

He emerged from the bathroom in a cloud of steam, incongruously sexy with a tiny pink hand-towel wrapped inadequately around his waist. "Where's all the towels?" he grumbled. "It was this or a face flannel."

"Maybe Courteney used them all up – it is her bathroom." Shelby lay back and watched him pull on his jeans. "Where are you going?"

"As much as I would like to stay here all night, I think we'd better get to the party before Ross sends someone to look for us."

"Party?" Shelby gave a huge yawn. "What party?"

* * *

As they walked hand-in-hand through the restaurant, and out onto the terrace, they could hear someone playing the piano, loudly but eloquently.

"That doesn't sound like 19th century music," hissed Shelby, as they stepped through the French windows and into the moonlight. "In fact, it sounds very much like 'Jailhouse Rock'."

Luke grinned. "Let me introduce you to our pianist for the evening."

But Shelby was ahead of him. "Floyd!" she squealed, running across the terrace to where the piano was set up in the corner, and flinging her arms around him. "I thought you were in hospital!"

"I dug a tunnel and escaped." He beamed at her, obviously gratified that she was so pleased to see him. "I had to bring a couple of warders along though." He indicated two pretty nurses leaning on the balustrade behind him, agog at the sight of Luke. "But it's no punishment. You know how I adore being surrounded by beautiful women."

As one of the nurses shyly asked Luke for his autograph, which he wrote in eyeliner on her bare arm, Floyd lowered his voice and added, "Darling, you don't happen to have a bottle of Glenfiddich about your person?"

"In this dress?" laughed Shelby.

"*C'est la vie!*" He began to toy with a melody.

She leant against the piano, marvelling at the wonderful music that seemed to spontaneously burst from his fingertips. "It's lovely to see you, Floyd, but shouldn't you be taking it easy? You've only just come out of hospital."

"This *is* taking it easy," said Floyd. "I'm sitting down, aren't I?"

"Yes but –"

Floyd glanced over her shoulder at the grips and the sparks, for some reason dressed as pirates with bandannas around their head like David Beckham, who had started a slow handclap.

"The natives are getting restless, my dear," he said, "and I'm growing tired of Elvis Presley. Do you have any requests?"

"I don't know . . . you don't like Oasis, do you?"

Floyd shrugged and began to bang out 'A Hard Day's Night'."

"That's the Beatles."

He grinned mischievously. "Same thing." He played another chorus then whispered, "Save Luke, will you? I think he needs rescuing."

Shelby glanced across to where Luke was arm-in-arm with the two pretty nurses and did not look remotely as though he needed rescuing but, after kissing Floyd goodbye, she wandered over, slightly embarrassed that she should break up someone else's private party.

Luke untangled himself. "This is my bodyguard," he said proudly, patting her heartily on the back, as though she was one of his drinking chums. "She's a black belt in judo and karate."

The two nurses looked her up and down, particularly taking in the silver-blue dress, but smiled politely and shook her hand all the same.

"Do you do kick-boxing?" enquired one, without a whiff of sarcasm.

"Only for fun. Erm, Luke," she added, "sorry to interrupt. Would you like to dance?"

"Dance?"

Vaguely she realised Floyd had started on 'She Loves You', the mean, rotten ratfink. Talk about your stitcher-upper. "You don't have to if you don't want to. I know you're not very keen on it."

"I'd love to dance," said Luke firmly. "'Scuse us, ladies," he added to the nurses, taking her firmly by the arm and leading her away to the dance floor. "And I promise not to tread on your feet." As Floyd slowed the tempo to a romantic number that Shelby didn't recognise, Luke rested his head on the top of her hair and surreptitiously gave Floyd the thumbs up. "Just remind me again, which is my left foot?"

Floyd's next visitor was Ross, who growled, "I hope you're not wearing yourself out?"

He sat on the balustrade, watching Shelby and Luke moving slowly around the dance floor. Shelby had her hands stuck in the back pockets of Luke's jeans. Ross's face began to resemble the aftermath of Hurricane Andrew.

With his left hand, Floyd pinched a sherry from a

passing waiter without Ross noticing. He managed to drink it too. Ross's eyes never left the couple dancing. "If you've got it that bad," said Floyd airily, the alcohol perking him up, "you should have asked the girl to dance yourself."

Ross shot him a withering look. "May I remind you, I have only just been discharged from hospital."

"It was only a small puncture wound." Floyd helped himself to another glass as another waiter squeezed past. "It's not as though your insides are going to fall out."

"Thank you for that thought." Ross turned his head just in time to see Floyd place an empty glass on top of the piano. His father's cheeks were already glowing pink in the light from the fairy lamps. Ross frowned. "I thought you promised the doctor you would give up drinking?"

"I promised that I would give up Glenfiddich," agreed Floyd blithely. "But you see, this is Harvey's Bristol Cream."

"Sherry?"

"I'm turning into quite the Dowager. I also promised to give up smoking cigars."

"You don't smoke cigars! Just cigarettes in those silly little holders."

"Which is why giving them up was such a doddle!" Floyd was able to gulp down his sherry with his left hand without losing the melody played with his right.

"There's a surprise." Ross eased himself down from the balustrade, almost managing to keep his breathing steady and not wince at the familiar sharp pain as the skin tightened across his stitches. "I'm going to get myself a drink. Can I get *you* anything? Orange juice? Cola? A mug of Horlicks?"

Floyd ignored the sarcasm. "I'm fine, thank you." He watched Ross limp off across the terrace – but not towards the bar. Instead he walked over to a beautiful redhead in an ethereal silver-blue dress, gazing up at the stars, as she waited for her partner to return.

"Fool," muttered Floyd and helped himself to another glass of sherry.

Chapter Thirty

Shelby leant against the stone balustrade surrounding the terrace and thought how beautiful everything was. The shower of stars across the blue velvet sky, the multi-coloured glass fairy lanterns hanging in the trees; after a couple of glasses of champagne she was beginning to feel like her old self and, as Floyd began to play a jazzed-up version of 'Love Hurts', she even did a few dance steps. It was a lovely warm evening and, if she stared long enough at the stars, they appeared to change colour, to echo the fairy lights; red, blue and green.

Hearing footsteps behind her she said, "Darling, isn't this perfect?"

"Some enchanted evening," agreed a deep voice but it wasn't Luke's.

Shelby spun round and found herself staring up at Ross's pale face, thinking how dreadful he looked. "Hi," she said nervously, hoping he wasn't going to make a scene. "Are you feeling better now?"

"I'm fine." Ross obviously had no wish to discuss his health. "Are you enjoying the party?"

At least it gave them something neutral to talk about. "Your set designer did a terrific job with the garden," she replied, looking back across the balustrade, so that she wouldn't have to look at him. "I think it's lovely idea – a party to thank the cast and crew for their contributions."

"And generate publicity for the film," added Ross dryly, almost as though he wanted to deliberately antagonise her. "Didn't you see the film stills pasted up in reception? The TV cameras, the show-biz journalists, the photographers?"

Oh God, was she going to end up on Page 3 again, all carroty hair and teeth? No wonder there were so many people milling about that she did not recognise. "From the tabloids?" she asked, her voice terse.

Ross shrugged. "The results will appear in the gossip columns and trade press. I realise you think I'm a hypocrite but we need all the publicity we can get. Promotion gets the public into the cinema; word of mouth does the rest."

It was his complacency that infuriated her. *He* had not been the one to have his private life – and old school photos – paraded through the press for everyone to snigger at. "And if that means some two-bit story about a non-existent love affair between me and Luke, so be it?"

Ross ran his hand through his thick chestnut hair and looked not unlike a cornered fox. "That wasn't what I meant," he said wearily. "You know I'd never do anything to hurt you."

Ha! Glib words from a slick operator. Did he actually believe what he was saying? He had done nothing but hurt her since the day they met and all because of his precious film. Not for the first time did it occur to her that any woman, no matter how much he professed to love her, would always come second to Ross's love of film-making. He had admitted as much himself.

As though realising he had just made a gaffe, Ross took a deep breath. "Where's Luke? Fiona's lined him up with a couple of interviews."

Didn't the poor guy ever get the chance to relax? "He went to fetch me a drink," she said in Luke's defence. "Floyd's music is so addictive we've not missed a dance." As soon as she spoke she realised her mistake, as Ross's eyes darkened, his heavy brows drawing together in a scowl.

"I know," he said. "I saw you."

Surely he wasn't jealous? Although it would certainly do him good to suffer – considering the casual way in which he had treated her. Shelby glanced over his shoulder to see if Luke was on his way back, wishing Ross would go away. But she didn't need Luke to fight her battles, she reminded herself. All she had to do, was remain calm, reasoned, adult . . .

"Did you?" she murmured indifferently, turning back to gaze at the stars. "By the way, if you're looking for Paige, I think she's dancing with Dean." Oops, so much for her resolution. Snide remarks certainly weren't the hallmark of adult behaviour.

"I'm not interested in Paige. I'm only interested in you."

Her mouth tightened. And where had she heard *that* before? And how many times? The man was beginning to repeat himself.

Ross, however, seemed to be misreading her emotions. His hands slid over her waist, slowly turning her round. "Don't let's fight, Shelby. This could be the last time we're together. Tomorrow I fly to the States. Come with me."

"To America!" Shelby was stunned. The irony! If only he had asked her a fortnight ago – she'd have swum the Atlantic herself just to be with him. "I couldn't just drop everything . . ." she lied, unwilling to admit to her relationship with Luke.

There was a slightly desperate look about him. "If money's a problem, I'd pay you a retainer."

"A retainer!" Shelby bristled, deeply offended. "Like you would some tart!"

"God, Shelby, you know that's not what I meant! I just want to be with you."

"Like you wanted to be with Courteney, and Paige, and Dulcie? And how about the way you dumped poor Courteney when she became pregnant?"

"That was in the past! Besides, you know what an unhappy childhood I had. I could never inflict that kind of pain on any kid of mine."

"So you had it terminated instead," muttered Shelby,

feeling sick. "Have you never heard of condoms? And besides, if you hadn't slept with Courteney, so that she'd agree to do your movie, she would never have become pregnant. And what was your excuse for fucking Paige?" Her voice took on a mocking tone. "Oh yes, to give her the confidence to film sex scenes. And what about Dulcie? And me? What were we? The commercial break – sorry, *interval* – choc-ice and fucking popcorn?"

His face was suddenly grim, the good-humour suddenly swept away. "You know that's not true."

"But what about you *is* true?" she countered. "All those lies. How do you remember them? Are you working to some script gathering dust in your attic?"

"I think you're getting muddled with Dorian Gray –"

"Don't patronise me!"

"You know I would never do that. Shelby, there's something I've got to say, please hear me out. It's about us –"

"There is no us," she said dully. "When will you get it into your head? We never had a proper relationship, we didn't fall in love, we didn't meet each other's parents – we certainly didn't pick out curtains. We fucked a couple of times and that was it."

"Shelby, I love you."

He meant it too. She stared at him, shocked into silence.

"Shelby?" he repeated, his voice uncertain.

"Good," she said slowly. "Because now you know how it feels."

The steely demeanour that was Ross Whitney

suddenly disintegrated in front of her. The layers of fabrication fell away and she had a glimpse of the real Ross, behind the Oscar-winning performance, his face contorted in misery as he reached out to take her into his arms, perhaps unable to believe she could possibly be rejecting him.

Later, Shelby could not work out how it occurred. Everything transpired so quickly. One minute she was shrinking back to avoid Ross's embrace and the next he seemed to rise up into the air and topple headfirst over the balustrade.

Shelby, forgetting they were only a foot or two above the level of the garden, screamed and peered desperately over the balustrade, expecting to see him splattered all over the path. "Ross? Are you all right?"

Ross had landed in the herbaceous border below and was sitting up, gingerly feeling the back of his head. "I think so," he said, extracting a twig from his hair, "but the azaleas are going to need Valium and several weeks of counselling."

The mask was securely back in place. He would never let his defences down like that again.

"I am so sorry," she murmured. "I don't know what came over me." Feeling dreadful, she watched him struggle silently out of the flowerbed. "You're taking this awfully well . . ."

Ross swung himself back over the balustrade. He landed lightly beside her, his face as inscrutable as ever. "I suppose deep down I know I deserve it. You know," he added, his voice hardly showing the strain of his words, "if you didn't want me any more, you only had to say."

There were a million more things she *wanted* to say but she knew they would just come out wrong and then he would feel more hurt than ever. And she knew exactly how *that* felt. Besides, she wasn't angry any more, merely sad that it had to end like this.

So all she could manage was to stammer inadequately again, "I know. I'm terribly sorry."

Ross turned on his heel and strode across the terrace, ducking through the French windows into the hotel. Shelby watched until his long dark shadow merged with others and he was gone. She would never see him again. Curiously, she didn't feel particularly sorry.

"*Ill met by moonlight, proud Titania,*" said Luke's deep voice beside her. "I was about to steal a kiss but think I've just changed my mind." He thrust a large glass at her, smeared in pink crystals and over-flowing with umbrellas and brutally kebabbed fruit. "Strawberry daiquiri," he said. "Kit thinks they're wonderful."

Shelby regarded the cocktail with trepidation, remembering the dreadful hangover she had experienced the night after Luke's birthday party. It was sweet of him to go to so much trouble, but still! "A beer would have been fine, even a cola."

"A cola? On a romantic evening like this?" Luke leant over the balustrade to gaze at the party below, waving as Courteney and Irving swept past in an out-of-time waltz. "Sometimes you can be such a philistine, Shelby Roberts."

As his arm slipped easily around her waist, Shelby sipped her drink thoughtfully. An attractive reboundee, she found herself thinking. Luke was certainly that. And sexy, funny, kind – yet what kind of girl fell out of love with one man, only to leap straight back into it with another? A fool.

Luke turned his head suddenly and, catching her staring at him, misread her expression. "I think you can relax. I don't think anyone is going to want to assassinate me now – not unless it's in two-inch-wide columns of newsprint."

She forced herself to concentrate on the banalities of polite conversation. "I thought you had good reviews for *All That She Wants*?"

"I did – well, they insinuated that as I more or less played myself I couldn't fail. Paige got a terrific write-up though. According to Paige she's got every top producer in Hollywood falling over themselves to sign her up. Good luck to her, I say."

If there was one person she did not want to talk about it was his, and seemingly everyone else's, ex-fiancée. Shelby took another sip of her drink. It was like drinking an alcoholic Slush Puppy. Interesting – and certainly refreshing but not really very sophisticated.

"How about you?" came Luke's deep voice. "What are your plans now this film's finished?"

"Baby-sitting some American author on a publicity tour of the UK – he's had death threats from an extremist right-wing group – or a stint at the Cannes Film Festival." She grinned. "I know which one I'm going to choose."

"Why don't you come and work for me?"

She stiffened. "You don't need a bodyguard."

"So come as my girlfriend." Luke slowly turned his head to look at her. "You do love me, don't you? What happened earlier, it did mean something to you?"

His eyes certainly seemed sincere. But he was an actor. Perhaps it was all a game to him. Perhaps he saw her as another conquest – like Ross had done.

His head moved closer, blotting out the stars. "What do you think, Shelby? Say something, for Christ's sake!"

His eyes seemed to blend with the midnight sky, she felt his breath on her cheek, her treacherous heart beat a fateful tattoo, as though it too realised there was no hope – given a half-way decent man and she was likely to fall in love all over again. Hadn't she learnt *anything*?

She saw his eyes close as his lips met hers and he kissed her gently, the sweetest kiss, and she had to push her drink onto the balustrade before she dropped it. She no longer had any control, all she could think of was him, and if anything was going over the balustrade this time it was the cold voice of reason.

Be careful what you wish for, a little voice was saying inside her head. *It might come true.* She had wished for Ross, and had got him, albeit on a part-time basis. And look what a catastrophe that that turned out to be.

With a supreme effort she pushed Luke away.

He stared at her, eyes wide with concern. "What is it? What's the matter? What did I do?"

"N – nothing."

"I don't understand. I thought you loved me, like I love you. We were getting along so well." He paused. "Why are you looking at me like that?"

"Like what?" she replied automatically.

"Like I've just turned into a frog or something."

God, he could read her mind . . .

"Do you feel ill? Take some deep breaths. It must have been that blasted daiquiri. Here, let me go and get you something else. What would you really like?"

A Relate Counsellor and a packet of Prozac. "Another daiquiri would be fine," she whispered, clutching at her head. She had to get her act together. She was going out of her mind . . .

She watched him weave his way through the dancers, back across the terrace towards the bar.

Halfway across he bumped into Kit, who heartily slapped him on the back and breathed banana daiquiri fumes all over him.

"I've just won £200 from Jeremy," said Kit triumphantly, swaying slightly. "Played some ancient card game called Hazard. Here, you'd better have it."

Luke stared at the crumpled bank notes in his hand. "What for?"

"You remember, the bet?"

Luke sighed. "Was that the diving-off-Pulteney-Bridge-with-a-rose-between-my-teeth bet or the walking-naked-down-Stall-Street-at-two-in-the-morning bet?"

Shelby was totally baffled. What the hell was Kit talking about? He must be drunk.

"The getting-Shelby-the-Shadow-into-bed-before-the-end-of-filming bet," said Kit. "Don't tell me you've forgotten?"

"Well, actually I *had* forgotten." Luke glanced again at the pile of ten and twenty pound notes in his hand and then back to Kit. "How did –"

"The way you two are floating about with silly smirks on your faces, I should think the whole crew knows." Kit suddenly grinned. "Besides, Shelby's dress is inside out. So you'd better take the money while I've still got it. Jeremy's searching the garden for me at this very moment, determined to have a re-match."

Kit had bet Luke that he wouldn't be able to get her into bed before the end of filming. Shelby had to clutch hold of the balustrade to steady herself and in doing so knocked her empty daiquiri glass onto the flagstones where it shattered, the long thin shards biting into her bare legs, scratching pinpricks of blood across her skin. But Shelby didn't notice. All she could do was stare at Luke in horror.

She had been set up! She had exchanged one professional Romeo for another. She should have trusted her instincts. Yet, cruellest of all, the bet probably didn't mean a thing to Luke. The challenge was wooing her away from Ross. All his talk about love. How could she have been so *stupid*?

Conversation died as the sound of the smashing glass reverberated around the terrace. Luke, seeing an expression of consternation flit across Kit's face, turned slowly and caught a glimpse of Shelby just as she turned and ran down the terrace steps into the garden.

"She heard me," whispered Kit. "Oh my God, Luke, I'm sorry . . ."

But he was talking to air. Luke had jumped down the terrace steps, taking them all in a single bound and was racing across the lawn after Shelby.

As Shelby jumped into a taxi, waiting on the off-chance outside the hotel entrance, she heard Luke's footsteps sprinting over the tarmac drive.

"Shelby! Wait a minute! Let me explain!"

The taxi driver solemnly regarded her reflection in the rear-view mirror. "Do we wait for lover-boy or are we making a grand exit in a cloud of swirling dust?"

A taxi driver with a sense of humour! "Just drive!"

"Lady, it's what I do."

"Stop!" cried Luke, banging on the roof. "Where are you going? Don't leave me like this! Shelby!"

But the taxi driver put his foot down, shooting off down the drive, leaving Luke running ineffectively behind.

"OK, Cinderella," drawled the taxi driver. "Where to?"

Cinderella! Shelby dragged her eyes away from Luke, growing forever smaller behind them, and glanced at her feet. Glinting in the passing streetlamps were her transparent mules – crystal slippers. Both of them, thank goodness.

Shelby felt she'd just about had enough of fairy tales. And if this taxi showed any sign of turning into a pumpkin, she'd flipping well eat it.

Chapter Thirty-one

Two weeks later – Côte d'Azur International Airport, France
So, thought Shelby despondently, Luke hasn't rung, he hasn't called, he hasn't even sent flowers. Am I surprised? Do I care? Of course I don't. Luke means nothing to me – it was Ross who broke my heart.

Strange then, whispered her conscience, *that you haven't given Ross a thought in days* . . .

"*Excusez-moi, mademoiselle.*"

Realising she was blocking the way of some dapper little Frenchman in a navy pinstriped suit, Shelby obediently shuffled to one side and he made straight for John Ivar, gabbling away in French, waving his hands in true continental fashion.

"Good news," said John, translating. "Cherish's plane has landed so she should be through Customs shortly."

All those words for so little information, marvelled Shelby. "Provided her luggage hasn't been re-routed to Milan," she said out loud.

"Relax," murmured John, mistaking her sarcasm for nervousness. He knew how much she hated crowd scenes. "There's no need to panic. We're just here to ensure Cherish doesn't get pushed and shoved, or hassled by the press. Provided everything goes according to plan, we don't really have a job to do."

And just how often does everything go according to plan? thought Shelby glumly. Some kamikaze fan will throw himself in front of the car, or some Neanderthal minder will get into a punch-up, and I'll end up in some French hell-hole of a gaol, with a room-mate called Big Bertha, where the only loo is a hole in the ground.

The Frenchman's radio squawked. "She is on 'er way," he said nervously. *"Bonne chance!"*

"I wish I could get through baggage control so quickly," grumbled Shelby, looking at her watch. "It took me two hours while they searched my entire luggage. I ask you, do I look like an international drugs courier?"

John regarded her with irritation, tired of the little black cloud hovering permanently above her head. "Do you have PMT?"

"Crossed in love," muttered Shark. After four hours stuck in an airport lounge with a gregarious Yorkshireman and a cantankerous redhead for company, his laid-back demeanour was starting to crack too.

Shelby glared at them just as a tiny, blonde thirty-something, swathed in a black fur coat and huge sunglasses, swept past, accompanied by a mini tidal wave of PR men, stylists, personal assistants and general sycophants.

"What a woman," murmured Shark.

Shelby shot him a scathing look. "Is it snowing in New York? That had better be a fake fur."

"There's nothing fake about Cherish," reproved a PR man, offering them glossy press handouts. Shelby dropped hers into the nearest bin. "She's all woman."

"Amen," breathed Shark.

Apart from her boobs, her teeth, her hair, her name . . . thought Shelby sourly. The woman's got more plastic than Tupperware.

As they joined the entourage and moved into the public area, they were suddenly encircled by the press, firing off the most banal questions in rapid succession. Cherish's league of fans, mostly young and male, were sectioned behind crash barriers, all wildly shrieking her name and waving pieces of paper for her to sign – which she ignored – or throwing pink rosebuds (her trademark) – which were just crushed by her pink, high-heeled, snakeskin boots – certainly not made for walking.

Luke would have stopped to talk, thought Shelby sadly. He would have signed their tatty scraps of paper, cracked a few jokes, flirted with some of the prettier girls – not stalked past with his nose in the air. She felt the familiar pang in her heart. *God, this was horrible.* What the hell was she doing here? Why didn't she admit to her mistake, go back to England, phone him, do *something*.

She forced herself to concentrate on Cherish, who had not only brought along at least three of her own bodyguards, but was also accompanied by airport security men, plus two French police officers. It was chilling to realise the police carried guns. The whole scenario was totally over the top.

Shelby remembered DS Meyer's cynical words about celebrities causing their own problems. Would anyone have noticed Cherish if she had sneaked through as an ordinary passenger, in jeans and T-shirt, minus the guns, the journalists, the security, the hangers-on? But then, that was probably not the point.

Suddenly they were outside in the brilliant sunshine and Cherish was bundled into a waiting limousine, which began to move away almost before Shelby had time to duck inside. She was rather disconcerted to find herself squashed up between Shark and some nameless gorilla, opposite the great diva herself.

She smiled nervously, tried to be polite. After all, the woman had spent her whole life as a rock star, detached from normality; she wouldn't recognise reality even if she snorted it through a fifty-dollar bill.

"Hi," said Shelby. "Um . . . good flight?"

But Cherish was regarding her over the top of her huge sunglasses with the sort of look she might have used had she seen a cockroach sitting there wearing an Armani suit and shades. "You're a woman!"

"Er, yes . . ." replied Shelby. Hell, was she so flat-chested it was that hard to tell? She leant forward and politely held out her hand. "Pleased to meet you Miss – Ms – er, Cherish. I'm Shelby Rob –"

But Cherish had replaced her sunglasses and was

already jabbing at the keys of a mobile phone with curling red talons. Shelby sat back in her seat, feeling her face colour and stared determinedly out of the window to avoid the sympathetic glances of the other minders.

It was only fifteen miles to Cannes along the Estérel motorway and, after a very short time, Shelby could see the sparkling sapphire blue of the Mediterranean, tantalisingly glimpsed between terracotta rooftops as the limousine deftly negotiated the one-way system. Finally she saw the exquisite sandy beach edged by the tarmac road and a fringe of towering palms, like an army of skinny Rastafarians.

Shelby caught her breath. It was beautiful. As the car slowly pulled up outside a great white wedding-cake of a hotel, a couple of mounted policeman sauntered past, raising their hats when they saw Cherish slide elegantly from the car. What a brilliant job they had, envied Shelby. Sun, sea, sand and *horses*!

Shelby had hardly stepped into the reception when she was assaulted by a whirlwind wearing a pink crocheted dress and silver trainers. "Shelby!" it squealed, kissing both cheeks, oblivious to any commotion caused. "How are you?"

Shelby tried to untangled herself without giving offence, conscious that Cherish was, for the second time that day, peering over the top of her Jackie 'O' sunglasses in utter amazement.

"Hi, Courteney," grinned Shelby. At least someone was pleased to see her. "Is Irving with you?"

"Oh yes, he's taken my shopping back to our room.

He insisted paying for it all himself – although I don't think he guessed how much it was gonna cost." Courteney laughed. "Have you been in any of the boutiques? Heaven on earth. You must see Rue d'Antibes, or La Croisette. There's Chanel, Gucci, Cartier, every name you can think of!"

"Quality Seconds?" teased Shelby.

Courteney regarded her reprovingly. "This is Cannes, France!"

Cherish, evidently affronted at being upstaged, teetered across reception and kissed the air in the vague vicinity of Courteney's tanned cheeks. "Hi honey, loved you in *All That She Wants*. See you at the Cartier party tonight?"

Courteney pulled a face. "Six hundred and fifty people squashed into a hot, stuffy tent? Besides, it's seafood and that brings me out in a rash."

"Too bad." Cherish shrugged her thin, bird-like shoulders. "I must vamoose. Ciao."

"Vamoose?" echoed Courteney blankly. "Is she going to, like, hoover the rug?" She watched Cherish weave off through the potted palms. "Is that fur for real?"

"Put it this way," grinned Shelby. "It tried to mount a stray dog outside the airport. Listen, I've got to go – could we meet up later? Are you in Cannes for long?"

"Yeah, Ross has got us publicising *Midsummer Kiss* and it's only been finished a fortnight. Well, actually it'll be edited for months yet but they've rushed out some trailers for press showings – you know how the guy is about publicity!"

Did she ever! "He's . . . he's not here, is he?"

"Yeah, ensconced in the Hotel du Cap with Paige, instead of 'slumming it' in town with the rest of us. Don't worry, you won't meet him. He'll be watching every movie screening he can get into, if only to get away from that bitch's nagging."

"And . . . er . . . Luke?"

Courteney smiled. "Suffering withdrawal symptoms already? If it's any consolation, he's missing you dreadfully. I thought you guys made an excellent couple. Did you fight? Why rush away from the Wrap Party like that?"

"I had to get back to London for another job," Shelby lied easily. She was getting used to it. "How do you know Luke missed me?"

"Why don't you come along to my party tonight and ask him yourself? It's on Daddy's yacht, *The Savannah*, moored in the Old Harbour. Please come – Irving and I will be announcing our engagement. You've gotta be there. You're family."

"OK," said Shelby. "I'll be there." She glanced across at Cherish, being fawned upon by manager and reception staff alike. "Provided I can shake off Cruella de Vil . . ."

* * *

Cannes. The Riviera. The South of France. Even the names conjured up wealth, glamour, success. Shelby was living the high life again – and again through somebody else. It was a pity that she felt like jumping out of this window. Yet down in the depths of her depression there was a tiny spark of hope. Courteney had said Luke missed her. *Like a cat would miss a canary when bereft of someone to torment?*

Shelby pressed her nose against the glass, wondering if she would be able to see Courteney's father's yacht but the massive Palais des Festivals completely blocked the view of the Harbour. So she looked out across the Mediterranean, as blue as Luke's eyes, at the two islands just beyond the coast; the pretty wooded Iles des Lérins, and Ste Marguerite where legend had it that the Man in the Iron Mask had been imprisoned. It was far too lovely to be a prison, thought Shelby, although she was beginning to think of a few people who might benefit from being locked behind an iron mask for a few hours . . .

It was dark before Cherish finally emerged from her bedroom, accompanied by a flushed stylist and visibly wilting make-up artist. The length of time she had taken to get ready was inconsistent with the amount of clothing she had on – amounting to little more than an emerald and sapphire bejewelled bikini top, a miniskirt of peacock feathers and her inevitable snakeskin boots, this time in electric blue.

"That will out-Hurley Hurley," beamed the stylist, smoothing down the feathers.

"A bird that's ripe for plucking," sighed Shark.

John was unimpressed. "Let's hope she doesn't moult before we get her to the party."

Shelby patted his shoulder. "If I had said that, you'd have told me off for bitching."

John shot her a sideways glance. "I'm beginning to think that taking this job on was a dreadful mistake. Can you hear that roaring sound?"

"The sea?"

"No, check the window. Look right down onto the pavement."

Shelby pressed her nose against the glass. She couldn't see directly below but streaming out onto the road were hundreds of people all screaming '*Cherish!*', as a group of mounted policemen ineffectually attempted to control them.

Shelby felt that familiar knot of fear. "How the hell are we going to reach the car? Parachute?"

"I wouldn't mind but it's entirely self-inflicted," grumbled John. "The PR people telephone everyone they know to say she's here then, when Cherish appears, they turn nasty and say 'No photographs'! No wonder the fans and journalists get fed up."

"Perhaps we could creep out the back way and try not to look conspicuous?"

"Sure," agreed John caustically, "a half-naked rock star surrounded by a dozen bodyguards – nothing conspicuous about us . . ."

* * *

In the end they had to literally force a path through the bodies outside. Shelby was aware of hundreds of hands all reaching out, trying to touch Cherish, grab a tiny piece of her, endlessly screaming her name, before Shark bundled them into the limousine and the door slammed shut. It was terrifying, yet peculiarly Cherish appeared to get off on all the adulation.

"Wait," cried Shelby, as the chauffeur began to pull away from the kerb. "You've left Shark on the pavement."

But the chauffeur was staring anxiously at the fans crawling across the bonnet of his car. "I do not think we are going anywhere, mademoiselle. All these people! I cannot drive over them!"

"Sure you can," said Cherish, lighting a cigarette and breathing smoke into Shelby's face. "They're not important."

The chauffeur pushed his cap back on his head and regarded Cherish with a troubled expression. "But, madame, there are people in the way. They are standing in the road!"

"Just put your foot on the gas-pedal, honey. It's what you're paid for."

"Wait!" Shelby rested her hand on the chauffeur's shoulder. "Someone might get hurt!"

"It's not my problem if they're crazy enough to stand in the road." Cherish tapped her scarlet nails against her bare thigh. "Either you drive on, or I'll get one of these guys to do it. *Comprenez-vous*?"

"*Oui, madame*," muttered the chauffeur sullenly and, releasing the brake, began to lurch forward. There was a dull thud. The chauffeur crossed himself and began to hysterically pray in French.

"Oh my God, you've hit someone!" Shelby threw open the door. "I think it was a journalist. He had a camera – at least, he used to have a camera. It's in pieces all over the road . . ."

"Oh, a *journalist*," drawled Cherish, winking at her PR man. "Honey, journalists don't count."

"But he could be injured!"

The PR man squinted through the tinted windows. "He can't be that badly hurt. He's running off down the road. At least he's not gonna sue us."

Cherish took a drag on her cigarette. "OK guys, panic over. Get back in the car, Shannon."

Shelby hesitated, then directed her comments towards John. "Do you know, I think I'd rather walk."

"*Walk*?" Cherish nearly choked on her cigarette.

"Yes, it's such a nice evening. I think I'll take a stroll along the beach."

John smiled ruefully. "When you get back to Blighty, phone me."

Cherish took the news less calmly. "Honey, I know you English are supposed to be eccentric but if you don't get back into the car you can consider yourself fired."

"Cherish the thought!" retorted Shelby and slammed the door shut in the silly cow's face.

* * *

Shelby walked along the beach to clear her thoughts. Rolling up her trousers and trailing her sensible shoes by their laces, she played chicken with the surf. Because of the marquees pitched on the sand, there was only a narrow strip beside the water to walk on. As she passed each tent, music pounding, laser shows lighting up the sky, the rebel inside her felt like crashing one.

As she stood outside the largest, a gang of drunken revellers fell out of the door, totally over-excited, spraying champagne over each other and releasing great armfuls of helium-filled balloons towards the stars. The men were in dinner jackets, their girlfriends in jewel-coloured ballgowns, sparkling with diamonds. Shelby recognised Dean, the pop star Luke had been filming with last month, although he totally ignored her. The girls were English soap stars.

For a moment Shelby felt bitterly jealous; they seemed to be having such fun, and it hadn't been so long ago that she had been part of this in-crowd. Then one of the girls clutched at the bouncer guarding the entrance, threw up over his shiny black shoes and collapsed in hysterical laughter on the sand, her vomit still staining the front of her designer gown. The bouncer's face remained impassive but her friends seemed to think this funnier still, throwing the empty champagne bottle at him before staggering off to the next party.

Shelby turned away in disgust. That little scene just summed it all up really. Minding celebrities was not for her. High society had given her nothing but trouble. She was going to rejoin the police, watch over the people who really deserved her protection – Joe Public.

As Shelby left the beach she passed the pink Palais des Festivals and could see the crimson carpet still trailed up the steps to the entrance, over which was hung a large cardboard Palme d'Or. She stopped to examine the chunk of pavement bearing the palm prints of Catherine Deneuve and other film stars – mostly French – whom she had never heard of.

The Old Harbour was crammed with identical luxurious white yachts, mingling with the more primitive, brightly painted, fishing dinghies. It reminded her so poignantly of Calahurst that she felt her eyes begin to water and she blinked furiously.

Randomly picking the biggest yacht she could see, just one notch down from the *Oriana*, Shelby walked lightly along the boardwalk towards it. Across the stern was written *Savannah*. Bingo! Nervously she stepped aboard. Finding the aft deck deserted, she walked around to the forward deck, her feet leaving sandy footprints across the narrow boards.

This was more like it! The deck had been decorated with fairy lights, a table had been set with a buffet, beautifully arranged amongst exotic leaves and flowers, a bottle of Chardonnay was cooling in an ice bucket and from below deck she could hear soft classical music, the sound rising over the gently lapping waves. Strange though, how there were only two glasses . . .

"Hi, Shelby," said a deep male voice. "You're late again. Typical woman! I was just about to start without you."

A party for two, a bottle of Chardonnay, leg-over music? Some detective she was!

"Hello, Luke," she said, trying not to look so pleased to see him. He wasn't the only actor around here. "Where's Courteney?"

"Celebrating her engagement with Irving and her family at the Palme d'Or Restaurant."

"Double-cross," she muttered beneath her breath. Bloody Courteney, she ought to wring her neck.

So, if there wasn't a party, and he hadn't been expecting her – he must be expecting someone else.

Her heart crashed onto the deck and lay there bleeding. "I'm sorry for barging in on your romantic tête à tête," she said. At least, that was what she intended to say. In between gulping back tears it came out a bit garbled.

He frowned. "What did you say?"

Shelby turned and fled, unable to hold back her emotion any longer. But, horror of horrors! There was no gangplank and, worse still, an ever-increasing stretch of inky-black water between her and the mooring.

"Oh no," she wailed, clutching at the white railings, "we're adrift!"

Luke, having followed at a more leisurely pace, seemed strangely unmoved. "Oh dear, so we are."

"But what about your date?"

"She's here already."

"Oh my God, how embarrassing! Perhaps you can explain me as some mad fan – or better still, have you got any lifeboats? I'll row back to shore. I'm sure it can't be that difficult."

"Lifeboats?" Luke shook his head. "Shelby Roberts, has anyone ever told you that you're totally mad?"

"Not as mad as your date is going to be when she finds me here!" retorted Shelby. "There'll be flying food and smashed crockery – it won't be pretty, I assure you."

"Not my girl. She's not like that."

Shelby regarded him pityingly. "You don't know women. Particularly women scorned."

"I know my woman." Then he laughed. "Shelby, you silly fool – *you're* my date! The dinner for two – it's for us!"

"But . . . I don't . . . how did you . . . ?" Then she realised she could feel the throb of the boat's engines, vibrating against the wooden deck beneath her bare feet. They weren't adrift – *they were sailing off into the sunset!* "You planned this!"

"No – but I'm willing to take all the credit." He grinned widely. "Would you like me to walk the plank?"

Shelby tried to think rationally. The idiot must have been at the Chardonnay again. "But why go through this elaborate charade? Why not just call me up, arrange a date, like normal people do?"

"I thought you would hang up on me," he admitted. "I couldn't be sure you'd even turn up. This was the only way to get you alone, to make you stay, listen to what I have to say without running out on me again." The smile faded from his face. "I think we need to talk. There seems to have been a misunderstanding."

"Talk?" Shelby heard her voice going up an octave. "Why does everyone want to talk?"

"Perhaps because it's considered an excellent method of communication." He took two steps towards her, his hand reaching to smooth one of her curls back into place. "Shelby –"

Shelby quickly took two steps back, her heart thudding.

"Look, you won your bet, you don't have to pretend any more –"

"Listen, Shelby, Kit knew I was crazy about you and he thought it hilarious that you were not at all enamoured by me. So he goaded me into making the bet. He didn't mean any harm by it. In fact, he's feeling pretty devastated now. This is the second relationship of mine he's buggered up."

Shelby stared miserably at the harbour lights. "Perhaps you should take it as a sign."

"You don't understand. Kit likes you. He thinks you're great. He's really upset that you found out about the bet when it didn't matter any more." He paused. "For heaven's sake, Shelby, do I have to write it out one hundred times? I'm trying to tell you I love you!"

She turned away so he could not see her tears. Words – they came so easily to an actor. "Don't be ridiculous. We've only known each other a few weeks."

His hands dropped to his side. "You only knew Ross a few days before you decided you loved him."

"And look what an appalling mistake that was. I didn't know anything about him – and you don't know anything about me."

"I know you want to make love out of doors," she heard a hint of amusement in his voice. "I know you hate your freckles –"

"The whole world knows I hate my freckles."

"I know you joined the police because you didn't want a dead-end job. That you wanted high spirits and adventure."

"You've been talking to Irving. That's cheating."

"He told me how you've always wanted to travel the world and yet now you're actually here in Cannes, it seems all you want is to go back home – and you can't understand why. But there is something I admit I don't know," he added softly. "Why haven't you thrown me overboard yet?"

"That can be arranged."

"Shelby . . ." He rested his hands on her shoulders, drawing her back against his body. "Don't you care for me at all?"

Shelby looked up at the stars, trying to ignore the electric thrill which ran through her. And he's only got to touch me, she thought bitterly. If he kisses me I'll just melt into a pool of gunk. How pathetic. *Yet was that really so bad?*

She felt Luke rest his cheek on the top of her head and was unable to stop the sigh of contentment that breathed through her lips. She closed her eyes, unsure whether the fireworks were across on the beach or sparking inside her. This is Luke, she reminded herself, breathing his scent – no flashy, expensive aftershave, just him – womaniser, philanderer, practical joker. If she thought a lifetime of women throwing themselves at Ross was bad enough, how would she cope with the positive legion of Luke's fans?

I want to see the sunshine after the rain. The music was pounding from the beach bars. *Where is the silver lining, shining at the rainbow's end?*

But perhaps real love wasn't moonlight and roses.

Perhaps the fireworks and bolts of lighting were just a distracting sideshow and that true love crept up unexpectedly, silent and deadly – like a comfortable pair of Marks & Sparks slippers.

Did she *truly* love Luke? Or was it just another wild passion which would eventually burn itself out, like her obsession for Ross?

Luke slowly turned her around, cupping her face in his hands, gazing down into her very soul with eyes more black than blue. There was no misreading the message there, she thought, as he bent towards her. But what about his kiss? As the song said, if he truly loved her, it would be in his kiss. She closed her eyes. His lips moved against hers, cool, tasting faintly of salt water, as she waited for the magic to detonate . . .

Luke paused. "It helps if you kiss back."

Shelby chuckled.

"Does this mean I'm forgiven?" he asked.

She wrapped her arms around his neck. Why didn't she stop analysing every single emotion she felt and get on with the rest of her life? "Completely," she said and kissed him, knocking him off balance. They hit the deck, laughing uproariously.

Luke raised himself up on an elbow and, dropping a kiss on her forehead, began to undo the buttons of her Armani dinner jacket. "Well, I can't do anything about your freckles but does the deck of a millionaire's yacht count as 'Out Of Doors'?"

Lying back in his arms she smiled impishly. "Oh, I should think so . . ."

Maybe this wasn't a love that would last forever, was Shelby's last coherent thought. But she very much hoped it was. And besides, they were going to have one hell of a time finding out . . .

THE END